Heidi Swain lives in Norfolk with her husband, two allegedly grown up children and a mischievous black cat called Storm. She is passionate about gardening, the countryside and collects vintage paraphernalia. *Sleigh Rides and Silver Bells at the Christmas Fair* is her fifth novel.

You can follow Heidi on twitter @Heidi_Swain or visit her website: heidiswain.co.uk

Heidi Swain

Sleigh Rides and Silver Bells at The Christmas Fair

**SIMON &
SCHUSTER**

London · New York · Sydney · Toronto · New Delhi

A CBS COMPANY

First published in Great Britain by Simon & Schuster UK Ltd, 2017
A CBS COMPANY

Copyright © Heidi-Jo Swain, 2017

is available from the British Library

Paperback ISBN: 978-1-4711-6485-9
eBook ISBN: 978-1-4711-6486-6

This book is a work of fiction. Names, characters, places and
incidents are either a product of the author's imagination or are
used fictitiously. Any resemblance to actual people living or
dead, events or locales is entirely coincidental.

Typeset in the UK by M Rules
Printed and bound by CPI Group (UK) Ltd, Croydon, CR0 4YY

Simon & Schuster UK Ltd are committed to sourcing paper that is made
from wood grown in sustainable forests and support the Forest Stewardship
Council, the leading international forest certification organisation. Our
books displaying the FSC logo are printed on FSC certified paper.

To Oliver
One for you at last
Merry Christmas

Chapter 1

Most people, at some point during their adult lives, struggle to come up with what to put on their Christmas list, but not me. Asking for the same present every year since I turned eighteen has ensured that I've never encountered that particular problem and now, almost twenty years later, it's still my first choice.

My longed-for gift of working every day of December, including right through the Christmas holidays, might not be everyone's cup of tea, but for the last two decades it's proved an absolute sanity saver for me. However, this is one present that I have to sort for myself and it simply has to be wrapped up well in advance of the Big Day. So, to give myself the best possible chance of securing the right post, I begin the search when the first leaves fall in autumn, and this year was no exception. By the middle of November I had the choice of two situations, but it was the isolated location of one of them which left me powerless to resist.

'And just how remotely situated would you say Wynthorpe Hall actually is?' I asked, during the brief telephone interview with Angus Connelly, the hall owner, who was keen for me to take the temporary job he had to offer.

'Very,' he cautiously replied. 'And is that going to be a problem do you think, Anna? Because this really isn't the sort of place where you can just pop round the corner for a bag of sugar, I'm afraid. It's more like a forty-minute round trip into town and there are no other houses nearby.'

Little did he know it of course, but his words were music to my ears. The other job I had been offered was back in central London and although the pay and perks were vastly different, so was the atmosphere at this time of year. The city would already be awash with lights, cheesy tunes and festive cheer and as far as I was concerned that was far too hefty a price to pay for an extra zero on the salary. Hunkering down in the barren and frosty Fenland landscape, without so much as a carol singer in sight, would be a much appreciated soothing balm to my troubled soul and I mulled it over with relish.

'Of course I appreciate that compared to some, we don't have much to offer in terms of inducements,' Mr Connelly continued, no doubt taking my hesitation for a refusal, 'but the work is light and it will be quiet here for most of the time. My wife, Catherine, is recovering well from her surgery now so—'

'And that's what I don't really understand,' I interrupted. 'According to your email your wife had knee surgery some weeks ago. Surely if she's up and about she doesn't need someone to look after her now, especially as you just said yourself you have no grand plans for Christmas this year.'

I know I sounded blunt, but I needed to secure a position that would keep me busy and occupied. I couldn't abide wasting time during any month of the year, but especially during December. Twiddling my thumbs would lead to thinking, and thinking when the decorations were out of the loft was the one thing I never allowed myself to do.

This telephone call was my one opportunity to ascertain that I wouldn't be besieged by free time, or conversely that I wouldn't be roped into helping to prepare some grand country-house Christmas either, and therefore I was determined to have everything settled in my mind, every wrinkle smoothed out, before I made my final decision.

'Well, you see the thing is, I can't help thinking she's started to overdo things a bit,' Mr Connelly elaborated, lowering his voice a little. 'She won't have it of course, but I think she's taking on too much. She insists she's just pottering about, but I'm afraid she's going to suffer in the long run and she's come so far. I'd hate to see her slipping back to square one.'

His voice trailed off, but the tenderness in his tone had penetrated my heart and unexpectedly made my eyes mist up a little.

'If she had someone here she could delegate to,' he continued with a sigh. 'Someone discreet and unimposing with whom she could do things, someone who could keep a subtle eye on her . . .'

'Well, I am discreet,' I acknowledged.

'So you'll come?' he quickly cut in. 'She doesn't want to let me or the rest of the staff do much for her at all so she may take some talking round to begin with, but you'll take the job, won't you?'

I thought back over the last three contracts I had worked, caring for a succession of rather spoilt under-eights in various cities dotted around the country and the idyll of a child-free, low-key Christmas in the sticks looked and sounded more appealing than ever.

As an experienced 'Girl Friday' I could turn my hand to a variety of jobs including nanny, housekeeper, secretary, companion and carer. I loved all of my chosen roles, most of the time, and this position, according to the advertisement in the recruitment pages of *The Lady* magazine, looked as if it combined practically all of them, along with the added benefit of avoiding anything to do with a commercial city Christmas of course.

Even if my charge was initially going to need careful

handling, this was exactly the sort of brief and straightforward arrangement I was looking for to tide me over until January when I would be ready to jump back on the treadmill as soon as Twelfth Night was ticked off the calendar.

'All right,' I said decisively, 'I'll take the job. I'll see you next Friday afternoon, Mr Connelly.'

'Oh that's marvellous!' he exclaimed. 'And please, call me Angus.'

'Angus,'

'And you're quite sure you don't want to come and have a look at the place first, just to make absolutely sure you'll be happy here?'

I had already had a brief glimpse at Google Maps to confirm the hall really was the perfect spot to see out the silly season for a 'bah humbug' like me, and with regards to my happiness, I didn't think a few weeks was anywhere near long enough to warrant taking it into consideration.

'No,' I reassured him. 'But thank you. That really won't be necessary.'

'Well in that case,' he sighed, sounding well pleased, 'we'll see you next week.'

The weather had turned foggy and frosty by the following Friday and the driving conditions from my last post in Winchester to my new one bordering the furthest reaches of Wynbridge couldn't have been worse. I hadn't planned

5

to stop en route at all, but as the three-hour journey turned into four I began to flag, and knew that if I wanted to present myself in the best possible light at the door of Wynthorpe Hall, I was going to need to freshen up first.

My heart thumped hard in my chest as I crossed the bridge into the little market town and my eyes fell upon huddles of locals rushing about with clipboards, strings of lights and boxes of enormous baubles. The hall might have been planning a simple festive celebration, but here in town it looked suspiciously like the preparations for Christmas were already in full swing.

'What can I get you?' asked a waitress wearing a cupcake-patterned apron as I bagged myself a tucked-away table in a place called The Cherry Tree Café. 'We're just about to start serving lunch if you fancy something hot.'

The delicious aroma wafting from the kitchen was enough to set my stomach growling and although I didn't normally eat a hot meal at lunchtime I thought the chill in my bones justified the extra calories on this occasion. I had only walked a short distance from the car to the café, but my winter go-to 'first impression outfit', comprising of a grey pencil skirt and soft cream cashmere jumper, did little to stave off the chill, even though I was still wearing my Burberry quilted jacket.

'We're launching our special Winter Warmer menu today,' the woman continued, sensing I was about to crumble. 'The soup is butternut squash, served with pumpkin bread, and the roasted vegetable quiche comes with a twice baked cheesy jacket potato and winter salad.'

'In that case, I'll have the quiche please,' I surprised myself by saying, 'and a coffee.'

'I'll have your coffee sent straight over,' she smiled, watching as I rubbed my hands together and blew on my fingers. 'It'll warm you up.'

It didn't take long to thaw out inside the cosy café and as I hungrily devoured the delicious quiche I watched with interest as customers bustled in and out, most of them taking with them a slice of something sweet packed inside a cherry-patterned box, doubtless destined for afternoon tea at home.

'Are you always this busy?' I asked the curly-haired waitress who came to clear away my dishes.

'Always,' she grinned, 'but especially on days like this. It's the grand switch-on tomorrow night, so the market is heaving. Are you going to be in town for the party?'

'Oh no,' I said, perhaps a little too quickly. 'I'm just passing through.'

'That's a shame,' she tutted. 'It's going to be quite a celebration.'

'I can imagine,' I said, looking out of the window as two enormous trees were being hoisted into place at either end of the market. I quickly averted my gaze, pretending to be engrossed in something on my phone.

'Would you like another coffee?'

'No thank you, but the lunch was delicious.' I replied, suddenly noticing the time on the screen. 'I really should be getting on. I'm expected at Wynthorpe Hall this afternoon.'

'Not passing through far then,' she grinned. 'You aren't Anna by any chance, are you?'

'Yes,' I frowned, taken aback. 'Yes, I am.'

'Angus is so pleased you've agreed to take the job,' she continued, plenty loud enough for everyone to hear and as if we were picking up the thread of a former conversation.

So much for being discreet.

'He's been really worried about Catherine rushing her recovery.'

'Which is ironic really, isn't it, Lizzie?' added the other waitress, who had tuned into the conversation, 'because usually she's the one fretting over him.'

'He's known around here as Mr Toad, isn't he, Jemma?' Lizzie expanded. 'Because he's always up to mischief with some crazy scheme or another.'

'But he's an absolute sweetheart,' Jemma beamed.

'Completely eccentric of course,' Lizzie laughed, 'but thoroughly lovely.'

I didn't know what to say. I'd literally just arrived in the county and already my presence was common knowledge and my employer was being described as a comical, if some-what exasperating, fictional character. It was an unusual situation to say the least. I was used to the anonymity of city living and working in places where my employers' idiosyncrasies weren't commented on.

'Did I hear that right?' boomed a man's voice from the other side of the café. 'Are you the lass who has taken the job up at the hall?'

'Yes, Chris, she is,' confirmed Jemma, before I had a chance to even open my mouth.

'Then would you do me a favour and take their fruit and veg order with you when you go? I'm rushed off my feet today, what with the deliveries taking twice as long in this fog, and the tree-decorating to oversee ahead of tomorrow night.'

'All right,' I agreed, too shocked to refuse as I fumbled in my bag for my purse.

I thanked and paid the Cherry Tree ladies for my lovely lunch, then led Chris Dempster, who declared himself the very best fruit and veg trader in the local area, over to my car where he proceeded to dump my suitcase on the passenger seat and stock the diminutive boot with enough produce to feed a small army.

'I won't ask you to help,' he said, taking in my outfit. 'Not in that gear.'

I picked up a large bag of potatoes and hauled it onto the back seat, keen to show that despite what he may have assumed about me, I was certainly no princess. He chuckled and raised an eyebrow, but didn't comment.

'Are you sure this is their order?' I asked, taking in the bulging bags of carrots and sack stuffed with sprouts when I had got my breath back. 'There seems to be an awful lot here for so few people.'

'They're no doubt stocking up ahead of Christmas,' he said, tapping the side of his nose and making my heart hammer in my chest again.

'But that's weeks away,' I said with a squeak, my cool facade slipping a little in my panic. 'And Mr Connelly told me they're planning a rather low-key Christmas this year.'

'Well, I shouldn't worry,' Chris grinned, before adding with a throaty chuckle, 'this lot won't last five minutes at the hall. That cook of theirs likes to keep the troops well fed. By this time next week you'll no doubt be heading back for more of the same.'

Chapter 2

Thanks to Mr Dempster's in-depth knowledge of the local lanes I didn't approach the hall via what he called the 'treacherous river road', but instead drove down a meandering track which, although it took longer than the route suggested by my satnav, was apparently far safer given the increasingly icy conditions.

It was barely two o'clock when I pulled through the ornate black iron gates and onto the narrow strip of drive, but because of the thick cloud cover it was already getting dark. I slowed down to negotiate a tight right-hand bend and the drive narrowed again, the towering shrubs crowding in to hide the wider landscape and making the approach feel more like an overgrown woodland trail than a journey to somewhere spectacular.

In the interests of preserving my little Fiat 500's suspension I slowed to a snail's pace to negotiate the final bumps and dips and gazed open-mouthed as the darkness thinned and the shrubs were replaced by pillars of towering trees which seemed to take a step back before revealing the secret at their heart.

'Wow.'

My Internet search had presented me with a plethora of photographs and descriptions, all announcing the hall as an historically important Grade One listed Elizabethan manor house, complete with majestic vistas, landscaped grounds and the obligatory lake, but in reality Wynthorpe Hall instantly appeared to be so much more than what its high-spec online credentials had suggested.

I let out a long breath and shuddered as something deep within me seemed to stir and shift, and I couldn't help thinking that for somewhere so grand the hall looked disarmingly comforting and homely. I gazed up at the ornate hexagonal chimney stacks, stone mullion windows and decorative terracotta-coloured brickwork and realised that what had appeared imposing online was comfortably informal close-to, and reassuringly worn around the edges. This hall was clearly a 'real home' as opposed to a 'show home', and I congratulated myself on making what I already knew would turn out to be the right choice.

I followed the drive around the side and through a small gate which led to a high-walled stable block. The place didn't look as if it had seen anything even remotely equine in years, but there were a variety of haphazardly parked vehicles along with various piles of machinery, an ancient cherry picker, some garden furniture and, unnervingly, a set of wooden stocks. The motley collection suggested the area was still in use, but as what I wasn't quite sure. Perhaps it was some kind of upper-class junkyard, or possibly it was the place where the things that had formed the basis of Mr Connelly's toad-like schemes went to die.

A sharp tap on the passenger window brought me quickly back to my senses.

'You can park where you like,' shouted a man's voice, 'as long as it's not behind the Land Rover.'

I tucked my little car as far out of the way as I could, swapped my driving pumps for my Manolos and smoothed down my dark hair, ready to meet my new employer.

'Hello,' I said, smiling up at the man who, judging by his threadbare boiler suit and wellies, clearly wasn't Angus Connelly after all. Or was he? Given what the ladies at The Cherry Tree Café had said, I wasn't so sure now. My assumptions about who to expect had taken a bit of a knock. 'I'm Anna.'

'I know,' said the man, whipping the bobble hat from his head, 'and I'm Mick. I'm the handyman here.'

Not the boss then, but a friendly-looking face nonetheless.

'I'm pleased to meet you, Mick.'

'I'm also the gardener,' he added.

'Right,'

'And the builder.'

13

'OK,'

'And I have been known to unblock the occasional drain and build the odd wall.'

'I see.'

'The job descriptions here are a bit sketchy,' he laughed, rubbing his stubbly chin before shoving his hat back on his head. 'You have to be prepared to take on whatever the place throws at you really.'

'Well, that's fine by me,' I smiled. I was always happy to adapt to whatever the job required. 'But thanks for the heads-up.'

I guessed Mick was in his mid-sixties, but judging from the list of roles he had just reeled off he wasn't quite ready to retire just yet.

'You'll no doubt find the set-up here all a bit strange to begin with,' he carried on, stepping forward and fiddling with the boot catch on my car, 'but give it six months and you'll think nothing of it.'

'I'm only going to be here a few weeks,' I told him, as he began to quickly unload the fruit and veg that had been packed back in town. 'How did you know I was bringing this lot with me?'

'A few weeks, eh?' he cut in with a wink.

'Yes,' I said.

'Chris phoned ahead,' he explained, returning his attention to the boxes and bags. 'He told Dorothy, the cook here, that you were on your way. He said he'd sent you the long way round. What were the roads like?'

'Not too bad,' I said, thinking that what with the grocery delivery and the town-to-country network announcing my arrival, this really was the strangest introduction to a place I'd ever had. 'A bit icy in places.'

'Would have been far worse if you'd come by the river,' he said darkly. 'Come on, let's get you inside.'

The entrance to the sprawling kitchen was via a little courtyard and a welcoming porch that housed a muddle of wellington boots, abandoned coats and umbrellas.

'Hello, hello!' called another voice, the second Mick and I had crossed the threshold. 'Come on in and get warm.'

Struggling a little with my bags and tripping over an excited black and grey bundle, which turned out to be a fluffy little cocker spaniel called Floss, I weaved my way through a part of the kitchen that housed sinks, cupboards and various antiquarian gadgets and into another.

'Here you are at last, my dear,' laughed a man who could only be Angus.

As wide as he was tall, with an unruly head of wispy grey hair and a pair of broad red braces, he rushed to set aside my bags and steered me towards the seat closest to the Aga.

'I can't tell you how lovely it is to finally meet you,' he beamed, his eyes sparkling and his cheeks aglow. 'We're all so delighted you agreed to come.'

Had I not known better I would have thought he was Father Christmas rather than Mr Toad, and the arrival of a petite white-haired, elderly Mrs Claus, wearing a flour-marked apron, only compounded the illusion.

'You look frozen solid,' she tutted, rushing to fill the kettle. 'Let me make you some tea – or would you prefer coffee, my dear?'

'I'm Angus,' confirmed the man, before I had time to answer her, 'and this is Dorothy, she's our trusty—'

'Cook,' I interjected with a knowing smile towards Mick.

Angus, Mick and Dorothy all began to laugh and I couldn't help but join in.

'She's got the measure of us already,' Dorothy giggled, setting down a cup and saucer and a plate of chocolate digestive biscuits. 'I daresay you wouldn't normally,' she added, with a nod towards the plate after she had looked me up and down, 'but just this once won't hurt.'

Obviously she had got the measure of me as well. Always careful about my calorie intake I knew the lunch and biscuits combined would put me well over my daily allowance, but I forbore to comment. Dorothy didn't look like the kind who worried about keeping count when it came to food and nor did either of the men for that matter.

'I hope you've saved me at least one of the custard creams, Mick Weaver,' pouted a young woman who noisily marched in through a door at the other end of the kitchen. She was

16

carrying a vacuum cleaner, which she managed to bump on either side of the frame, and was poured into the tightest pair of jeans I had ever seen.

'I haven't had a chance to eat anything yet,' tutted Mick, as he put his hands above his head in a gesture of surrender. 'Let alone the custard creams you covet so ruthlessly. Come and say hello to Anna.'

'Pleased to meet you, Anna,' she said, her over-made-up eyes swivelling in my direction as she smiled broadly and clattered the vacuum cleaner on the stone-flagged floor. 'I'm Hayley. The Wynthorpe Hall dogsbody and—'

'A bloody nuisance,' teased Mick.

'I throw the Hoover around most days,' she explained, pointedly ignoring Mick. 'And sometimes I flick a duster about, but only if I feel like it. I don't live here though.'

'Although we do keep a room ready for her, should she want it,' said another voice.

'Catherine,' said Angus, rushing to his wife's side. 'This is Anna, my dear.'

Taller than both Dorothy and Hayley, and slender, with an abundance of silvery grey hair escaping a loose bun, Catherine had slipped unseen into the kitchen through the door that had announced her youngest employee's considerably noisier entrance.

I noticed she didn't carry a stick and that she moved elegantly, without so much as a hint of discomfort or unease.

17

She didn't look to me as if she needed any assistance at all, but she did look surprisingly pleased to see me. After all, Angus had suggested on the telephone that she was somewhat reticent about the idea of having some help and I had expected a far chillier welcome, from her at least.

Self-consciously I stood up, walked around the table and held out my hand.

'I'm so pleased to meet you, Mrs Connelly,' I smiled. 'As I'm sure you are aware, Angus has asked me to come and stay for a few weeks, until you are completely recovered from your surgery.'

She took my hand and shook it warmly, her grey eyes never leaving my face. I couldn't make out what she was thinking, but tried my best not to look away as she scrutinised my appearance.

'Of course,' she nodded, eventually looking over at Angus and smiling.

I couldn't fathom the look that passed between the pair, but something very definite was communicated between the two in that moment.

'My husband is very naughty to assume that I needed some help but, having spoken to him about the details of your application, I can understand why he picked you, and of course you are most welcome, my dear, even if you are going to be here for such a short time.'

There was a hint of amusement in her tone, as if the

suggestion that I would be leaving so soon was laughable, but I didn't have time to reiterate that I would be leaving for another job in January because Hayley was off and running again.

'Staying for just a few weeks,' she snorted, rolling her eyes as Dorothy ushered her mistress into a comfortable chair. 'Now where have I heard that one before?'

'And please call me Catherine,' Mrs Connelly insisted. 'We don't stand on ceremony here.'

'That's true enough,' agreed Mick, passing Hayley two custard creams and pouring everyone tea.

I looked around the vast high-ceilinged kitchen, where every surface seemed to be stuffed to the gunnels with paperwork, postcards, magazines, plants and curios, and then at the smiling staff who were clearly as welcome as family around the massive table, and wondered whatever kind of non-Christmas I had let myself in for.

'Come on then,' said Hayley as soon as we had finished our tea. 'I'll take you up to your room if you like.'

I followed her through what seemed to be a never-ending maze of rooms and corridors. More than once I stopped to admire an interesting portrait or particular piece of furniture and almost got left behind.

'Don't stress about getting lost,' she grinned over her shoulder as I caught her up and we negotiated a flight of spiral stairs and yet another winding corridor. 'Everyone takes a while to get their bearings, but you'll manage it in the end,' she added, before stopping to appraise me, 'though I daresay you're used to finding your way around fancy places like this, aren't you?'

'Sort of,' I admitted, 'but I don't think I've ever been employed by anyone like Catherine and Angus before.'

Hayley grinned and hoisted up her jeans.

'You won't have been,' she said. 'They're the best. I wouldn't work anywhere else, not even for double the money.'

'So how come you don't live here?' I asked. 'From what Catherine said earlier, I'm guessing you'd be more than welcome.'

I couldn't help thinking that the hall staff were the most eclectic mix of characters and ages I had ever come across. First there was Mick, then Dorothy, who wouldn't see seventy again and, if her apron was anything to go by, was a Baking Queen, then Hayley, only just out of her teens and a bundle of energy, responsible for keeping the hall spotless – apart from the muddle in the kitchen that is. And now here I was, wondering where I would slot into this strange but fascinating household.

'It's a long story,' she said, coming to an abrupt stop outside a massive oak door. 'This is you,' she announced, throwing it open.

'Bloody hell!'

The words were out before I could check them and Hayley grinned. I was annoyed to have let my circumspect demeanour slip, but given the room I had been allotted, the faux pas was hardly a surprise. However, I was still relieved that it was Hayley rather than Catherine or Angus who had shown me upstairs. Swearing in front of the boss was not something I would ever want to do and especially not on my first day.

'I know,' she beamed.

My bags were already on the bed, the massive four-poster bed, that is. The one hung with old-fashioned tea-rose-patterned drapes that matched the curtains and the cushions on the little sofa positioned in front of a roaring log fire.

'Angus said to put you in here,' said Hayley. 'It's called the Rose Room. Obviously. He seemed to think you might like it.'

Sudden tears sprang into my eyes and I furiously blinked them back. The pattern had instantly dragged me back to another bedroom, nowhere near as grand, but achingly familiar nonetheless. I gave myself a little shake, thinking that if I had been prone to superstition I would have said there was some sort of magic playing out within the walls of Wynthorpe Hall.

'No need to get all teary,' nudged Hayley.

I shook my head, telling myself it was just a coincidence, nothing more.

'Well, not until you've seen through here anyway,' she added.

She pulled me into the en suite, which was almost as big as the bedroom and as warm as toast. The tub was huge and there were stacks of soft towels and beautifully packaged, exquisitely rose-scented Jo Malone soaps.

'Are you sure this is the right room?'

This was all far more boutique hotel chic than employee accommodation. Most of the historic homes that I'd worked in were draughty and dilapidated, not cosy and cosseting, and you were more likely to wake with frost inside the windows than a glowing fire in the grate.

'Yeah,' said Hayley, plonking herself on the bed and curling her feet under her as Floss nestled close. 'In case you haven't worked it out, everyone gets treated the same here. Family, pets, friends and staff, we all get looked after. Some parts of the building might be getting a bit rough around the edges, but when it comes to hospitality, there's always a warm welcome at Wynthorpe Hall.'

I ran my hands over the rose-patterned drapes and nodded, struggling to push down the rush of emotion I thought I had become so adept at keeping a lid on.

'So what are the plans for tomorrow night?' asked Angus at dinner that evening.

I sat agog as he piled plates high with hearty stew and

dumplings before handing them to Dorothy, who then added as many vegetables as the plate could hold. Chris Dempster had been right about her keeping the troops well fed, and it was more than obvious that these friendly folk had no comprehension of portion control.

'Are we going to take the car and the Land Rover, or just the car and make two trips?'

I'd eaten such a massive lunch in town, and then two biscuits with my afternoon tea, that I didn't think I could manage Dorothy's stew as well, but I took the plate she offered so as not to appear ungrateful.

'Help yourself to more gravy,' she said, pointing at the boat, which was steaming and full to the brim.

'Thank you.'

'I think it would make more sense to take both,' said Mick. 'That way we can take Hayley along with us and travel back separately if we don't all want to come back at the same time.'

Mick had already driven Hayley back to Wynbridge for the night. Ordinarily, she had explained as she keenly helped me unpack my bags and surreptitiously tried on my precious shoes, she would cycle to and from the hall, but with the roads currently so treacherous, Mick and Angus were taking it in turns to ferry her about. It was my intention, in line with what Mick had said about the blurred job descriptions, to make myself available to take her as well, should I be needed.

'Well, that sounds like an excellent idea,' Angus agreed. 'I can't tell you how much I'm looking forward to it, especially now Ruby and Steve are back in town.'

'What are they talking about?' I whispered to Dorothy as I tentatively tasted the first mouthful of succulent steak, which melted on my tongue and tempted me to take another bite.

'The Christmas switch-on,' said Angus, his eyes alight with childlike excitement. 'It's happening in Wynbridge tomorrow night and the young couple kicking the festivities off were responsible for regenerating the market a couple of years back.'

'Well, turning around the fortune of the market was mostly down to Ruby really,' Dorothy put in.

'Well, yes, I suppose it was,' mused Angus. 'Anyway, Ruby and her other half Steve—'

'Who happens to be Chris Dempster's son,' said Dorothy, filling in another blank.

'Have been off travelling the world.'

'Not unlike our Jamie,' came Dorothy again.

'But they've made it back just in time to kick off Christmas in Wynbridge.'

'Unlike our Jamie,' Catherine sighed.

'And everyone's so excited to see them again.'

'Who's Jamie?' I asked, trying to process the names and information I had just been bombarded with.

'Our youngest,' elaborated Angus. 'He's been away from home for a few months now.'

'It's actually been nearer a year,' corrected Catherine.

I got the impression that she was missing her son and although keen to hear more about him, I felt it wasn't my place to ask, especially as I'd literally only just arrived.

'So,' said Mick, thankfully pulling everyone's focus back to the matter in hand, 'we'll all head off together then.'

I suddenly realised that I was being included in this festive outing to town.

'It's all anyone's been able to talk about for weeks,' said Catherine, her enthusiasm for the event gaining momentum as talk moved on from her currently empty nest.

'And it's going to be an even bigger celebration than usual,' agreed Mick, looking over at Angus and winking. 'Because rumour has it that Santa's going to put in an early appearance.'

I swallowed hard and stared at my plate as my plans to see out a quiet Christmas in the sticks slipped further from my grasp. From what I'd already seen for myself back in town, if I didn't put the brakes on now, by this time tomorrow I was going to be up to my neck in festive frosting. I shuddered at the thought.

'Would you all mind if I didn't come with you?' I blurted out, thinking it was best to nip the assumption that I would be tagging along in the bud.

The four of them fell silent and looked at me in amazement.

'Not come?' gasped Mick incredulously.

'Only I'm not all that keen on crowds,' I added creatively. 'And if I didn't come then you could all squeeze in the car and not have to take the Land Rover at all.'

'But we might not all want to come back together,' Mick reminded me.

'And if you don't go,' said Dorothy, looking crestfallen, 'then Catherine can't go.'

I looked from her to Catherine.

'It's fine,' said Catherine, shaking her head.

Her expression suggested that she was somehow aware of my reluctance, even though she had no inkling as to the reason behind it, and I was grateful for her kindness and consideration. For about thirty seconds.

'It would probably be too much for me anyway,' she added, trying to justify her reason for missing out. 'After all, I've only pottered around here since coming home from hospital and Anna's right, it will be crowded.'

'I could chaperone you,' said Mick.

'But you're going to be serving the hog roast,' Catherine reminded him, 'and Dorothy,' she continued before the lady had a chance to speak up, 'you'll be rushed off your feet with the WI.'

This was terrible. I felt awful knowing I was setting myself up to be the reason she was going to miss out on all the fun, and it was hardly the way to make the good first impression I was always so keen to secure.

'But what about you, Angus?' I suggested, hoping he could step into the breach.

'Ho ho ho,' he said, shrugging his shoulders and pointing at his belly.

Clearly he had important duties of his own to see to.

'Oh well, all right then,' I swallowed, painting on a smile and knowing I really didn't have any choice. 'In that case . . .'

Chapter 3

Even after the hour-long soak in the massive bubble-filled tub I still couldn't sleep that night. There was nothing unusual in my inability to nod off during my first night in a new bed, but that particular night I had an awful lot more to think about than the firmness of the mattress and the somewhat disconcerting familiarity of the rose-patterned fabrics.

The whole set-up at Wynthorpe Hall was a completely new experience for me. I'd never worked anywhere so grand, where the family and staff lived cheek by jowl like one big, happy clan. In my capacity as nanny I had occasionally eaten meals with my employers, but more often than not that was because I was expected to keep control of the unruly children I was in charge of, not share news over a glass of wine at the end of a long day.

I had no idea how to behave in front of these people or which persona to adopt. My head was telling me to keep it professional, but my heart suggested a more personal touch was going to be required and, truth be told, I wasn't sure I could remember how to be 'personal'. Surely that would mean being 'me', wouldn't it?

And, on top of trying to come to terms with the potentially claustrophobic family feeling I was so unused to, there was now the grand Wynbridge Christmas switch-on to get my head around as well. *So much for a quiet few weeks in the countryside*, I thought as I thumped my pillows into what I hoped would be a more sleep-inducing shape.

Early the next morning I skimmed through the contents of my wardrobe and decided, having taken on board what everyone else had been wearing the day before, that I should swap my slightly impractical skirt for a pair of smart trousers, boots and a warm jumper and scarf. I was still unsure as to exactly what my duties were going to be, but I was pleased I had opted to arrive wearing a formal outfit as, over the years, I had learned it was far easier to 'dumb down' in the clothing department than 'dress up' when settling into a new role.

There was yet more food on offer when I went down to breakfast and I was amazed to find myself drawn towards the sizzling bacon rather than the blueberries, but I resisted temptation and reached for the granola.

'Will you want one boiled egg to go with your cereal, or two?' asked Dorothy from her station in front of the Aga.

'No eggs for me, Dorothy,' I insisted, 'but thank you.'

'Perhaps a couple of slices of toast and honey, then?' she suggested, whipping a loaf out of the old-fashioned bread bin. 'It's granary, homemade.'

'All right,' I caved, 'but please, I can get it myself.'

Dorothy shook her head.

'I cook and serve the breakfasts,' she explained. 'You lot deal with the dishes while I take Floss for a walk around the garden.'

That sounded fair enough.

'Do you think Catherine and Angus would mind if I went for a run around the grounds in the mornings?' I asked.

'A run?'

'Yes, I like to get a few kilometres behind me before the day starts,' I explained. 'That way keeping in shape doesn't interfere with my duties. Do you think they'd mind?'

'I wouldn't have thought so,' she shrugged, eyeing me shrewdly. 'I've been wondering how you keep so trim.'

'Well, now you know,' I smiled.

'Oh look out,' she tutted, cocking her head to listen as the back door opened and was then slammed shut. 'Here we go. Brace yourself, my dear, here comes the north wind.'

'Morning,' said Hayley, breezing in and bringing with her a blast of what felt like Arctic air. 'Anna, you look like—'

'Careful,' warned Mick, who had traipsed in behind her.

'Well,' she said, considering the dark circles under my eyes before speaking again. 'You look knackered. Did you not sleep? And what's all this about you not wanting to come to the switch-on tonight?'

For someone who had known me for less than a day, she certainly didn't hold back. Tact, I guessed, was an unknown concept to someone as straightforward as Hayley.

Dorothy shot Mick a look behind her back and he shrugged and mouthed 'sorry' to me.

'Good morning, Hayley,' I said. 'No, I didn't sleep particularly well, but I rarely do in a new bed and I am coming to the switch-on.'

'Well now,' she said, reaching across the table and grabbing the two rounds of toast that I had just lightly buttered, 'that's all right then. So what was all the fuss about, Mick?'

'There was no fuss,' he said exasperatedly. 'I told her there was no fuss, Anna. I just said that for some reason, to begin with, you didn't fancy coming to town.'

'Don't worry,' I said, guessing that Hayley liked to make a drama about anything she could. 'It's fine and I'm definitely coming tonight, so that's that.'

I realised I was going to have to watch my step as far as Hayley was concerned. I got the distinct impression that she could winkle out secrets in a heartbeat and I had absolutely no intention of letting anyone know why I was planning to work my way through Christmas for the umpteenth year on the trot.

After preparing a breakfast tray for me to take to Catherine, Dorothy took Floss for her walk and Hayley, having pointed me in the direction of the room referred to as the morning room, charged off to finish the dishes and begin her mammoth vacuuming session. There was no sign of Angus anywhere.

I knocked quietly on the door and reversed inside to avoid bumping the tray. Catherine was sitting at a desk in the window staring intently at a large photograph in a silver frame.

'Oh my goodness,' she gasped, when she saw what I was carrying. 'Now this is a treat; normally we all eat breakfast together in the kitchen, but I seem to have lost track of the time this morning. This all looks lovely,' she added, taking a peek at the carefully laid-out tray. 'Very Downton Abbey.'

'It was Dorothy's idea,' I told her. 'Shall I pour your tea?'

'Yes please,' she said, 'but two cups. You will join me, Anna, won't you?'

Her suggestion was yet another nod to the unusual nature of the Connelly household. The breakfast tray might have been Downton Abbey, but the relaxed attitude was definitely Wynthorpe Hall.

'All right,' I agreed. 'Thank you. Then perhaps we can talk through what it is you would like me to help you with while I am here.'

'Oh there's no rush,' she said, waving the idea away. 'I'm sure we'll come up with something for you to do at some point.'

I was beginning to wonder if I was actually going to have to work for my living at the hall at all.

Once Catherine was comfortably settled, and I had poured us both tea, I sat on the edge of the sofa opposite with my cup and saucer.

'So, what do you make of our three boys?' she asked, nodding towards the photograph that had held her attention when I came in. 'They're a handsome trio, don't you think? Or is that just a doting mother's bias talking?'

I put down my tea and went over to the desk. Three Connelly brothers laughed up at me. They were all certainly handsome, the perfect combination of Angus's mischievous personality and Catherine's stately features, but hardly boys. These guys were all somewhere in their thirties, possibly even forties.

'That's Christopher on the right,' Catherine explained. 'He's our eldest and by far the most sensible, now married with two sons of his own. He celebrated his fortieth this summer. Jamie is on the left,'

'It's Jamie who's travelling, isn't it?' I asked, taking in the abundant freckles and foppish hair. He was very handsome and, looking at his eyes, I couldn't help wishing the photograph was in colour rather than black and white.

'That's right,' said Catherine, an edge of melancholy creeping into her tone. 'I was rather hoping he would have come home by now, but . . .'

Her voice trailed off and I stole a quick glance in her direction. Just like the evening before, when we had been eating in the kitchen and talk had turned to her absent son, she looked incredibly sad.

'And that's Archie,' she said, with a nod back to the photo. 'He's the middle son, currently living, and allegedly working, in London.'

She sighed, but didn't add anything else, and I was left with the distinct impression that there was definitely more to the relationship between these three brothers than the photograph let on. From the little I knew for myself of family life, it didn't seem to me to matter where you lived or what your social standing happened to be, it was usually complicated, occasionally excruciating, and personally, in that moment, I felt blessed not to be troubled by it.

We sat quietly for a while, each lost in our own thoughts as Catherine finished her breakfast.

'Do you know what I would really like to do this morning?' she asked when I had taken the tray back to the kitchen.

I had always been proud of the fact that I could second-guess the wants and needs of those I worked for, but this was going to prove a tricky question to answer, given that this time yesterday I hadn't even met Catherine. I played for time, straightening the cushions, and thought back over the conversation from the night before.

'My guess is that you'd like to get outside and perhaps have a look at the garden,' I eventually began. I was instantly encouraged by the smile that lit up her face and continued, 'because you said yourself last night that you've hardly been out since you came home from the hospital and you probably want to see if your knee will stand up to walking about on uneven terrain before we go into town this evening.'

'Well I never,' she laughed, clapping her hands. 'Bravo, Anna, bravo!'

We took a leisurely stroll around a small part of the gardens, stopping to admire the fiery skeletons of the dogwoods in all their winter glory and watch the blackbirds squabbling over the remains of the glossy red pyracantha berries. The fog had finally begun to thin and it was just about possible to make out the watery outline of the sun, but it was still bitterly cold.

'Let's go and sit in the summerhouse in the fern garden,' suggested Catherine, who appeared much invigorated by the bracing air and birdsong. 'We can see how the hellebores are coming along.'

Sitting in the little house at the furthest end of the currently dormant fern garden, Catherine was grateful for the blanket and flask I had brought out with us.

'Now,' she began, sounding concerned. 'About this trip to town tonight, Anna, if you really don't want to go, I won't mind.'

'No,' I fibbed, 'it's fine, honestly. I don't mind at all. Last night I was just tired from the journey and didn't think I'd be up to it, but I'm feeling much better today.'

'But you said you didn't want to go because you don't like crowds,' Catherine frowned. 'And I wouldn't want to put you in a position where you felt uncomfortable.'

My mum had been right – you should never tell lies. Now, not only was I feeling guilty for lying, I had also made someone else feel responsible for putting me in an awkward position, which they weren't. My problem was dealing with Christmas. Christmas trees were a nightmare, Christmas carols sounded like hell on earth and Christmas lights were annoyingly upbeat, but coping with crowds I could manage no problem.

'I'll be fine,' I insisted, but truth be told I was a little aggrieved that my overwhelming desire to distance myself from all things festive had already landed me in a tight spot in a job where I hadn't for one second imagined it was ever going to be an issue.

'Well, as long as you're really sure?' Catherine quizzed.

'I promise,' I told her, my fingers crossed in my jacket pocket, 'but how about we take my car along with the Land Rover instead of Angus's? That way,' I proposed, 'if you get too tired or I start to flag again, we can come back together, under our own steam, without having to trouble everyone else.'

'That sounds like a wonderful idea,' she agreed. 'And that way, everyone will be happy.'

Not quite, I thought, but I was going to do my utmost to make it look that way.

Walking around the bustling little market town of Wynbridge arm in arm with Catherine that evening, I felt it was a shame that every blow life had dealt me had struck when the Advent calendar was putting in an appearance, because the switch-on would have been the perfect event to stock up on Christmas spirit.

The place was awash with smiling families, excited children, exquisite handmade gifts (many of which, I discovered, were made by Lizzie from The Cherry Tree Café), and enticing aromas. The carollers were perfectly in tune, the gingerbread families were fabulously frosted, and even the clouds had cleared to give the firework display a celestial backdrop.

It was quite a blow to acknowledge that my pain and bitterness towards the season was for the first time ever tinged with sadness because I was unable to properly join in. I didn't know how to. I had spent so long avoiding such gatherings that I had forgotten how they worked. I had forgotten how it felt to be looking forward to something so wholeheartedly, and that wasn't just me being over-the-top, Hayley-style melodramatic. My Christmas cheer really was beyond reach and, given the fluttery feeling in my chest, my heart rate was heading a little out of control.

'Are you all right?' asked Catherine, as I let out a long breath to try and calm my nerves.

I pulled myself out of my reverie, knowing it was my job, quite literally, to be asking her that question.

'Yes,' I said, pulling the cheery smile back into place. 'I'm fine. Just still a bit shell-shocked from seeing Angus take that lap around the square in his sleigh at such speed.'

Angus had thoroughly enjoyed playing the role of a very jolly Santa Claus, and the children he had handed out the presents to were completely convinced of his authenticity.

'He was rather good, wasn't he?' laughed Catherine. 'Even better I think than the last time he did it.'

'So this wasn't his first appearance then?'

'No,' she explained, 'and it won't be his last either. There was a problem one year when it was discovered the former Santa preferred rum to reindeers. Steve stepped into the breach on that occasion but now the role belongs to Angus and I wouldn't be at all surprised if he doesn't commandeer that sleigh for the hall.'

She sounded really rather concerned but I couldn't help thinking it was more likely to end up in the stable yard, along with all the other bits and pieces that had briefly held his attention over the years, rather than being pulled around the gardens.

'Oh look,' she said, banishing the thought, 'there's Ruby. Ruby!' she called.

'Hello!' shouted back a pretty dark-haired girl, dragging a man who I guessed was her other half and one time Santa, Steve, behind her.

'It's so lovely to see you,' beamed Catherine, pulling her into a hug. 'And you, Steve. What an honour to be asked to turn the lights on this year! Gosh, you both look amazing.'

'Well thank you,' said the pair, grinning at each other with unadulterated adoration.

'So tell me,' asked Catherine, 'how was the world?'

'Exhilarating,' laughed Ruby.

'Enchanting,' added Steve.

'But surely Jamie has told you all that?' said Ruby, looking over her shoulder as if she expected the man himself to appear.

'No,' Catherine sighed, her smile suddenly faltering. 'He hasn't come home yet.'

'Oh,' said Ruby, looking surprised. 'When I spoke to Mum about him a couple of months ago I got the impression that he was going to be back at Wynthorpe well before winter.'

'Well, that's what we thought too for a while,' said

Catherine sadly. 'Anyway,' she added, turning to me. 'Anna, please forgive my shocking manners. Ruby and Steve, I would like to introduce you to the newest member of the Wynthorpe team. This is Anna. She only arrived yesterday, but she's already part of the family.'

I felt very flattered to be referred to as family and my curiosity regarding the reason behind Jamie's prolonged absence from home was now well and truly piqued.

'Hello, Anna,' said the pair in perfect unison.

'Hello,' I smiled back.

'So,' said Steve, 'how long are you planning to stay at the hall?'

'Literally just a few weeks,' I explained. 'I'll be long gone by mid-January.'

'That's what they all say, isn't it?' he laughed, reminding me of the comments Mick and Hayley had made the day before.

Catherine nodded, but didn't contradict him.

'I don't know about you,' she said instead, 'but I think it's getting far too cold to stand about out here. I think we should all go and find a cosy spot in The Mermaid.'

'Sounds good to us,' chorused the happy couple.

The pub was warm, busy and, for me at least, a welcoming refuge from the carols and chaos in the market square. The delicious cider, mulled and infused with an extra hit of cinnamon, soon chased away the chill and within a few minutes the entire Wynthorpe clan, along with Ruby and Steve, were gathered around the fire, fussing over Catherine and comparing purchases from the market.

'I found these on the Cherry Tree stall,' said Dorothy, holding up two strings of pretty bunting made from scraps of festive fabric. 'I thought they would look lovely in the kitchen, above the Aga perhaps?'

'And these,' butted in Hayley, producing a pair of slightly overstuffed felt robins and some cellophane-wrapped bags of fudge, 'were from the primary school stall. Not that I expect the fudge will make it until the first of December, let alone Christmas Day!'

When everyone had finished emptying out their bags, all eyes turned to me.

'Didn't you buy anything?' frowned Hayley, checking out the empty space around my feet.

'No,' I said, my voice catching in my throat and inconvenient tears springing up out of nowhere. 'Not tonight.'

I tried to look relaxed and was determined to play down the fact that I wasn't at all comfortable to have been singled out as a purchase-free zone.

'Wynbridge is the perfect place to buy locally made presents,' Dorothy rushed on. 'We have so many talented craftspeople here in town, you know.'

'Not even one thing?' Hayley persisted doggedly.

'No,' I said again, sinking further back into the sofa

cushions in the hope that they would swallow me up. 'I didn't need anything.'

'Don't you have anyone to buy for?' Hayley pounced.

I sat back up again.

'I hardly think that's any of your business, do you?' I snapped.

I shook my head, hating myself for losing my temper. It was so unlike me, and poor Hayley looked mortified. I think she was as shocked by my outburst as I was.

'I'm so sorry,' I quickly apologised as she and Dorothy exchanged glances. 'I didn't mean to bite your head off.'

Catherine sat up a little straighter and levelled her gaze at her youngest employee.

'I'm quite sure that Anna is perfectly organised, thank you, Hayley,' she said, sounding almost stern. 'She's no doubt finished her Christmas shopping already. Isn't that right, dear?'

Her suggestion couldn't have been any further from the truth of course, but I wasn't about to admit it, especially not with Hayley hanging on my every word, although I did feel bad for getting her in trouble.

'Yes,' I lied. 'I'm all set.'

'Well, that's all right then,' Hayley shrugged, her cheeks glowing as she eyed me curiously. 'For a second there I thought I'd put my foot in it. I had you down as a right old Billy-no-mates. Now, who wants another cider?'

Chapter 4

It was really rather fortunate that Mick had decided not to join the rest of us drinking cider that evening as the brew turned out to be far headier than I first realised. When it was time to head off I was surprised to find that even though I had supped very little compared to some, my legs were a bit wobbly and there was no way I was going to drive myself back to the hall. Legally I was undoubtedly under the limit but I certainly wouldn't have felt comfortable climbing back behind the wheel.

'Don't you worry about it, Anna,' Mick reassured me as he, Hayley and I wandered over to the market square after The Mermaid had closed. 'You can come back with me now and we'll pick your car up later tomorrow.'

He had already driven Catherine, Angus and Dorothy back earlier in the Land Rover, but I had stayed on with Hayley after my generous employers had insisted that I should enjoy the rest of the evening, especially as the next day was Sunday and everyone would be having the day off anyway. I had spent most of the time apologising for biting Hayley's head off, but she didn't seem worried by my out-of-character reaction at all. Probably because she hadn't known me long enough to know how out of character it was.

'You know what,' I said to her, as we set off to take her home.

'What?' she said, looking soberly across at me as I marvelled at the fact that she had drunk three times as much as I had, but didn't seem even remotely squiffy.

'You were right really.'

'About what?'

'About me being a Billy-no-mates,' I said, my usual reticence to talk about myself rather reduced by the impact of the delicious two halves of Skylark Scrumpy.

'Well, of course you're a Billy-no-mates,' she tutted, before bursting out laughing.

I stared at her open-mouthed and feeling really rather appalled that she found my brave announcement, and indeed my alcohol-induced despair, so amusing.

'That's why you've ended up at Wynthorpe Hall, love,' Mick said quietly.

I had no idea what he meant.

'What?'

'When Angus was sorting through the applications for the job—' Hayley began.

'Hayley,' warned Mick, but she carried on anyway.

'Yours was the only one that didn't specify that you wouldn't be able to work Christmas Day. All the others said they wouldn't be available on the twenty-fifth because they would be spending the day with their families, but yours didn't.'

'Not that he discussed anyone's application in any real detail with us,' said Mick defensively.

'Well, no,' Hayley relented, turning slightly pink as she finally realised just what she was suggesting, 'more mentioned them in passing, is what he did, but yours stuck out like a sore thumb apparently,' she added, thrusting her thumb under my nose to hammer home the point. 'And he knew.'

'Knew what?' I sniffed.

'That he'd found the right person for the job.'

'What, because I came across as so lonely, unloved and unwanted?'

Even in my relaxed state I didn't feel particularly comfortable with the idea that it was my solitary, sad, home-alone status that had secured me the job, rather than my wealth of experience and glowing references.

'Exactly,' said Hayley, leaning across to pat my knee as she undid her seat belt. 'He felt that you and your solo microwave-meal-for-one existence were the missing link in

45

the Wynthorpe chain and I think he was right. I'll see you Monday, Mick,' she shouted as she jumped out, 'and cheer up, Anna. There are worse places you could have ended up.'

I didn't have even a hint of a hangover and was out of bed before my alarm on Sunday morning. In the kitchen I pulled on my trainers, fired up my Fitbit and cajoled Floss into joining me for a run around the grounds before the rest of the world was awake.

I thought back over snippets of the conversation from the night before as I limbered up, then set off, my feet pounding the frosty paths with Floss panting before we'd even reached the garden. Thanks to the calming impact of the cider I'd slept well, but I still felt uncomfortable that I'd mentioned my one-is-fun, non-celebration Christmases.

It was just starting to get light when I arrived back at the porch door some forty minutes later and I was amused to see the little dog, who had been trailing behind and complaining practically the whole time, have a final burst of energy as she caught the salty scent of bacon as it drifted through an open window and out into the ether.

'Good Lord!' squawked Dorothy as I shut the back door with perhaps a little more force than was entirely necessary. 'Where on earth have you sprung from?'

'I've been for a run,' I panted, pulling my trainers off again and filling Floss's water bowl.

'You scared me half to death,' she tutted. 'What on earth do you want to be running about in this weather for? There's nothing of you to run off as it is.'

'Like I told you, it's my way of keeping in shape,' I shrugged. 'And it's not that cold.'

'What's the point in me going out of my way to feed you up,' she complained, shoving a plate of scrambled eggs and yet more crispy bacon into my hands, 'when you keep tearing about and burning the calories off? You need some meat on your bones if you're going to survive a Wynbridge winter, young lady.'

'But I'm not going to need to survive a Wynbridge winter, am I?' I said, sliding the plate onto the table and heading for the door. 'I'll be long gone before winter really digs its heels in.'

I might have managed to avoid the belly-busting breakfast, but there was no escaping the Sunday roast.

'Although we all get a day off on Sunday,' explained Dorothy, who was still very much in charge of the kitchen, 'we all like to eat together if we haven't got anywhere else to be and that way we can discuss any plans for the following week.'

That sounded like a lovely idea to me, and the accompaniment of roast beef with – my number one guilty pleasure – ginormous slabs of Yorkshire pudding, made it all the more appealing. If Dorothy really was going out of her way to feed me up then she was doing an excellent job, because I could have sworn my waistbands were already feeling the strain. So far I had been trying to resist all temptation but after just a couple of food-filled days in the Fens I was beginning to crumble. I was also beginning to settle in far more quickly than I would have ever thought possible. Wynthorpe Hall had a magical way of making you feel at home, right from the very first moment you crossed the threshold.

'And once the dishes are done,' said Mick, reaching for the horseradish, 'we'll go and collect your car, Anna.'

'Thank you, Mick,' I said, before turning my attention to Catherine. 'And how are you feeling today, Catherine?' I asked.

To my mind she looked in perfect health. Her cheeks had a definite glow and there was a sparkle in her eye that could almost rival Angus.

'I feel wonderful,' she said, confirming what we could all see for ourselves. 'It was such a pleasure to get out of the house and especially for such an exciting evening.'

Everyone murmured in agreement and I was pleased my outburst in the pub wasn't mentioned. The last thing I wanted was to have anyone making a fuss, no matter how well intentioned.

'I did wonder if I would be a little stiff after all the extra walking about, but there's no pain in my knee at all.'

'You certainly sound well on the road to recovery to me,' I nodded, 'although perhaps I shouldn't say that. At this rate, you'll be sending me away by the end of the week, Angus.'

I still hadn't really got my head around why he wanted an extra pair of hands at the hall at all. From what I'd already seen Catherine was more than capable of pacing herself, even though her husband thought otherwise, and the household itself, thanks to the competent ministrations of Mick, Hayley and Dorothy, ran like a well-oiled machine.

'I certainly will not,' he said, his head snapping up from the sheet of paper he was reading. 'In fact,' he said, his cheeks flushing scarlet, 'it's looking highly likely that we're going to need you more than ever now, my dear.'

'What are you up to, Angus Connelly?' Catherine frowned. 'I don't think I like the sound of that at all. Surely you had enough excitement whizzing around the market square in that sleigh last night to last you a lifetime?'

Dorothy and Mick shook their heads.

'This is the same Angus Connelly we're talking about, is it, Catherine?' said Mick. 'The person who we all know never has just the one trick tucked up his sleeve?'

'All right,' Catherine conceded, 'I take your point, but I hope this isn't one of your crazy schemes, Angus, because even if I am feeling better, I'm certainly not up to dealing with any of your mischief. That sleigh can stay where it is in town as far as I'm concerned.'

Angus carefully folded the sheet of paper, slipped it in his pocket and came round the table to stand next to his wife.

'I solemnly swear—' he said, placing a hand on her shoulder and planting a tender kiss on her cheek.

'That you are up to mischief?' Catherine mused, taking hold of his hand.

Angus shook his head.

'On the contrary,' he said. 'I solemnly swear,' he began again, 'that by this time next week, you'll be the happiest woman in the world.'

'So are you going to tell me then?' I asked as we stood side by side at the sink, me washing the dishes and Angus drying. 'Are you going to tell me what it is that's going to make Catherine so happy?'

'Absolutely not,' he said, brandishing the tea towel and sending suds flying.

'But don't forget that I'm actually here for Catherine,' I said, trying another tack. 'I'm here to aid her recovery, so perhaps it would be best if I could prepare her for whatever it is . . .'

'What,' said Angus, pretending to be outraged, 'and ruin the surprise? I don't think so.'

'All right,' I said, 'keep your secret, but on your head be it if she isn't pleased and you haven't given me the opportunity to soften her up first.'

Angus was having none of it. He was clearly well practised in the art of fending off all enquiries that were likely to stop him in his impish tracks.

'She's going to be delighted,' he said, 'trust me, and I have to say it's a relief seeing you get stuck into those pots and pans.'

'Oh,' I said, trying not to think about the state of my recently manicured nails, 'and why's that?'

'Because,' Angus whispered, 'during the next few weeks you're going to find yourself getting stuck into a lot of little chores that weren't listed on that job description of yours.'

I felt my heart thump a little harder, but as long as he hadn't changed his mind about the low-key Christmas he had promised I knew everything would be fine. I was more than capable of playing the role of the adaptable employee and of course, the busier I was at this time of year, the happier I was.

'Is that right?' I said, willingly playing along and suddenly realising that the professional persona I had been so sure would be so difficult to throw off had already started to ebb away.

'It is,' he said, reaching for a fresh tea towel. 'I'm calling a family breakfast meeting at seven tomorrow morning, so don't be late or you'll miss all the fun.'

I was never late, never. Being on time, early even, was one of my top priorities, so the fact that my alarm didn't go off, that I missed my run and arrived at the table in a less than pristine state at two minutes after the allotted time the next morning, was mortifying to say the least. Three days I'd been in the employ of Wynthorpe Hall, just three days, and in that time I'd been tipsy, late *and* sloppy. I really needed to get a grip.

'I'm so pleased you've finally settled into your room,' smiled Catherine as I slipped into an empty seat. 'The first proper night's sleep somewhere new is always a relief, isn't it?'

'It is,' I agreed. 'Thank you, Catherine.'

Honestly, the woman was a saint.

'Here,' said Hayley, passing along a mug of coffee with considerably less discretion. 'This'll wake you up. Now come on, Angus, don't leave us in suspenders.'

Angus, at the head of the table, was looking every inch like the cat that got the cream, the delectable Cornish clotted cream in fact.

'I'm just waiting,' he said, tapping away on the screen of his phone, his glasses perched unhelpfully on top of his head, 'for one more message to come in, and I'll be right with you.'

The tension and excitement around the table was palpable and I didn't think I needed the extra shot Hayley had laced my coffee with to wake me up.

'There,' said Angus gleefully as his phone pinged in his hand. 'That's that then.'

'That's what?' demanded Catherine. She sounded almost

annoyed, certainly exasperated. 'Angus, you've been on that blasted phone half the night. What exactly is it that you are up to?'

'Could someone please just remind me,' he said, ignoring Catherine's plea to put us all out of our misery, 'what the date is today?'

'November the twenty-seventh,' I shot back.

Every single day between now and Twelfth Night was etched on my mind.

'So that will definitely make Friday, December the first?' he asked, looking at me over the top of the glasses he had finally pulled into place.

'Yes,' I nodded, 'Friday's the first.'

'So?' said Hayley. 'Come on, Angus. I've the second-floor windows to clean today. This place doesn't scrub itself, you know.'

'I do know,' he said, 'we all know, my dear. Which is just as well really, because it's going to be all hands on deck to help get everything ready.'

'Ready for what?'

Everyone held their breath.

'Jamie's homecoming,' he announced.

'Be serious,' Hayley spluttered, choking on her coffee.

'I am being serious,' said Angus, looking nowhere other than at his suddenly very pale wife. 'Jamie's coming home.'

'Really?' questioned Dorothy. She sounded astonished.

'Do you really think he'd joke about that, of all things?' Mick quickly cut in.

'When?' whispered Catherine.

'Friday,' Angus smiled, walking around the table and bending down to kiss her. 'Friday evening.'

'And is he—?'

'Yes,' he nodded, his eyes full of tears. 'He's coming back for good.'

'So he's agreed?' asked Mick. Now it was his turn to sound disbelieving. 'He's actually going to do it?'

'Yes,' confirmed Angus. 'He's actually going to do it.'

'Well I never,' muttered Hayley. For once even she sounded almost subdued.

I was desperate to ask what 'it' was that this much-missed son had decided he was going to do, but just one quick glance at the expressions on the faces gathered around the table told me that now was not the time. In their dream-like state not one of them looked capable of telling me anything.

'But when,' asked Catherine, 'how?'

'I've been talking to him for a couple of weeks,' admitted Angus a little sheepishly as he turned a shade redder. 'But I didn't say anything because I didn't want to get your hopes up.'

'I can't believe it,' laughed Catherine, through what to me looked like very happy tears.

'Me neither,' snivelled Hayley as Dorothy delicately sniffed and wiped her eyes with a pristine lace handkerchief she had produced from her apron pocket. 'This was one Wynthorpe mess I never thought I'd see sorted.'

'Well, it is now,' said Angus with a contented sigh.

I was delighted for Catherine and indeed for everyone. It was obvious that Jamie's prolonged absence from home had been keenly felt and that he was loved by all. Having seen the photograph in Catherine's study I was rather keen to meet him myself. Not that I ever mixed business with pleasure of course, but sometimes it was nice to have the view and working conditions enhanced by a handsome face.

'And he's going to be home in time for Christmas!' exclaimed Catherine, making everyone jump. 'Oh I only just realised,' she cried, 'how wonderful. It's going to feel just like old times.'

As thrilled as I was to see her so happy, I have to admit my heart sank at the mention of the dreaded 'C' word. I'd got through the Christmas switch-on by the skin of my teeth and was hoping I'd seen the last of that intense level of festive fun, but Angus's dreamy expression suggested I was potentially in for more of the same.

'It's going to feel more like old times than you could possibly imagine, my dear,' he laughed, while clapping his hands together and jiggling up and down on the spot.

He had puffed out his chest so far that I thought his braces were going to burst.

'Why?' asked Mick. 'What have you done?'

'Well,' said Angus, his exhilaration barely contained as he took another deep breath, 'in view of the fact that Jamie's coming home—'

'Yes,' said Hayley, urging him on.

'And bearing in mind that we have an extra pair of very competent hands to help out,' he added, looking pointedly at me.

'Uh-huh,' again, this from Hayley.

'And not forgetting that we haven't had a houseful for absolutely ages—'

'Go on.'

'I've decided to ask everyone here for Christmas this year!'

'You haven't?' spluttered Catherine, wide eyed.

'I have,' he laughed. 'In fact, I've already done it and they've all said they'll come.'

'Oh Angus,' Catherine gasped, properly sobbing now.

'Everyone?' questioned Dorothy.

'Everyone,' he confirmed. 'Christopher and the family will be travelling up as soon as the boys break up from school and Archie and Elise will follow on as soon as they finish work sometime before Christmas Eve, and Jamie of course, will be here already.'

Hayley began to squeal with excitement and Dorothy and Mick hugged and cheered with something bordering on a childlike excitement, the like of which I had never witnessed in adults. Evidently, a Wynthorpe Hall Christmas was something to behold, but I already knew I wouldn't be sticking around long enough to see it. The room was already beginning to spin and that was just at the mere mention of it.

'So you see, Anna,' said Angus, turning his attention squarely to me, 'this is why I was so pleased to discover that you really are one of us.'

'One of you?' I queried, shaking my head.

'Yes,' he explained. 'You proved yesterday you're someone who gets stuck in and we're really going to need you and your can-do approach more than ever now, aren't we?'

'Indeed we are,' agreed Catherine.

Hayley grabbed my hand and pulled me into a tight hug.

'There,' she whispered, 'what did I tell you? It really is a blessing that you're a Billy-no-mates who has nowhere to go this Christmas, because we all need you right here.'

I nodded and tried to smile, but an all-consuming sense of dread had descended, my vision was blurred and my insides were in turmoil.

'That is all right, isn't it, Anna?' asked Angus.

He was looking at me curiously, evidently unsure about my subdued reaction to his grand announcement.

'Of course,' I lied, somehow managing to conjure another painted-on smile. 'Absolutely.'

Suddenly I was desperate to get out of the kitchen and hide away for an hour or so. If I could just distance myself from Hayley's squealing and Catherine and Dorothy's chatter about lists, plans and countdown schedules, perhaps I would be able to come up with a dastardly excuse to leave that wouldn't give away any hint as to the real reason why I was going.

Perhaps I could suddenly magic up an elderly invalid aunt who needed her helpful niece around the house or perhaps there was still time to win a fictional competition where first prize was a winter sun tour of Tenerife.

'Because I do realise that this isn't exactly what you signed up for,' Angus continued meaningfully.

It was obvious that he was referring to my dogged determination during my initial enquiry about the job and in the subsequent interview to ascertain that an over-the-top Christmas wasn't planned for Wynthorpe Hall this year.

'But I really do think you'll enjoy it,' he went on.

'Of course she will,' said Hayley, slapping me none too lightly on the back.

The look she gave me suggested that I should have been feeling grateful for landing this job at this particular time of year and that I was in for the time of my life living amongst this extraordinary family for the next few weeks. And had I been anyone else she would have been right. Most people in my position would have been relishing the thought of enjoying a country-house Christmas, but I wasn't most people.

Just the thought of Christmas was enough to set my pulse

racing and not in a good way. One whiff of Christmas pudding, one chorus of *Deck the Halls*, made me nauseous and terrified and turned me back into the traumatised child who had lived through more things on December the twenty-fifth than any one person should have to experience in a lifetime.

I didn't want to spend the holidays trapped watching a family being reunited, seeing the love and unity that I would never experience for myself being rolled out in front of me, even though I knew no one here would do that maliciously of course. It wasn't Angus's fault, or kind Catherine's, but my first instinct when Angus explained what he was planning was, I was sure, the right one. I had to leave and the sooner the better.

Chapter 5

The very first opportunity I had, I slipped out of the kitchen and up the stairs to the sanctuary of my rose-filled room. I sat on the edge of the bed mulling over, and trying to make sense of, what had happened to me and my so-called professional persona during the last few days.

I reminded myself that I was an independent woman who lived my life on my terms. End of. I had no ties, no family and no pets, not even a permanent address to call my own, and I liked it like that. Or I did until I had turned the final corner in the drive and Wynthorpe Hall had emerged from the fog and filled my horizon.

Until that moment, when I had become unwittingly ensnared by the homely facade, I had thrived on the freedom and control that living a slightly detached existence awarded me. I know some people might have considered my attitude a little superficial, selfish even, but I had my reasons and they all justified my choices. My lifestyle was formed as the result of everything I had lived through and I knew from bitter experience that the fewer people you had to care about, the less opportunity you had to get hurt, and I was very much in favour of avoiding further pain.

But that, I realised with a jolt, was what I was feeling right now. The thought of packing my bags and making my apologies was causing me real physical pain as well as mental anguish; my brain ached, my mind was muddled and my stomach was in knots. I had always made a conscious effort not to get involved with or form attachments to the people I worked for, but of course, I reminded myself, the eclectic mix of staff here didn't work 'for' the Connelly family, they worked 'with' them and just three short days of living at Wynthorpe Hall, amongst this very unusual group, had turned my ethos on its head. Somehow, I had hastily and inadvertently formed affections for the people living here. I had got sucked into the minutiae of their lives and now, if I decided not to head for the hills, I was walking blind into uncharted territory.

I was still thinking through what I was going to do when there was a light knock on the door.

'Why is it,' asked Catherine, when I opened it just an inch and Floss had nosed her way inside, 'that I get the distinct impression that you are getting ready to run, Anna Woodruff?'

'Run?'

'Yes,' she said, 'run, and you know I'm not talking about taking yourself off for another lap around the grounds.'

I didn't know what to say. It might not have been the first time I'd felt like moving on from a job before I'd reached the end of the contract, but it was certainly the first time an employer had noticed.

'Do you think I could come in for a minute?' she asked.

'Of course.'

Catherine settled herself on the sofa and looked around the room. I thanked my lucky stars that she hadn't caught me in the act of packing.

'I had absolutely no intention of mentioning any of this,' she began, 'but in view of Angus's now very altered plans for Christmas, I simply can't not say anything at all.'

'What do you mean?' I asked, feigning ignorance.

'Your job application,' she said softly. 'When Angus finally got around to telling me that he had placed an advertisement for some help and that he had picked you to join us we sat together and looked through your paperwork, and talked through what had been said during your telephone interview.'

'Oh,' I swallowed, knowing the game was up. 'I see.'

I sat heavily on the other end of the sofa.

'And it really isn't any of our business of course,' she continued, 'but we couldn't help but notice that you made absolutely no mention of your plans for December the twenty-fifth either on the forms or during the call.'

I nodded.

'You didn't request any time off, or state that you wouldn't be available, and I can't help worrying that, in view of our now drastic change of plans, you are now going to find yourself in an awkward position.'

'Because you won't want me here, you mean?' I asked. 'Because you and Angus would rather be alone to celebrate with your family on the twenty-fifth?'

Catherine looked aghast.

'My dear girl, no,' she insisted, 'absolutely not. That isn't what I meant at all. You, along with everyone else, will be more than welcome to spend Christmas with us. In fact, we're counting on us all being together.'

'Then I don't understand.'

'I mean,' she said in a rush, reaching across for my hand, 'that taking into account how reluctant you were to attend the switch-on, and how horrified you looked when Angus made his announcement just now, that it doesn't take a genius to work out that you and Christmas are hardly happy bedfellows. I can only imagine that what is going to be happening here now has put you in a rather difficult position, and cast a very different light on your decision to work here for the next few weeks.'

I didn't say anything.

'It has, hasn't it?'

'Yes,' I eventually whispered, knowing I had to say something. 'I'm afraid it has.'

'I thought so,' she tutted, biting her lip. 'When we talked it all through, Angus had stressed how keen you were for him to confirm that there would be no big hurrah here this year before you accepted the post.'

I was disappointed that I had been so transparent, but couldn't deny that the hall's isolation and the promise of a tinsel-free few weeks had been the sole motivation behind my decision to work here.

'And now everything's changed and you've found yourself slap bang in the middle of his silver bells and sleigh rides extravaganza and potentially the biggest Christmas the hall has ever seen,' she continued, sounding mortified.

'But the plans have all changed with good reason,' I reminded her. 'Jamie's homecoming is clearly a cause for celebration and it couldn't be happening at a better time.'

'That's true,' she frowned, 'in part.'

'And I'm sure if you advertised the post again you would have plenty of applicants,' I went on, warming to the theme. 'Most people would jump at the chance of spending the holidays here, helping to create the perfect country-house Christmas.'

'But not Anna Woodruff,' she said sadly.

'No,' I said, matching her despondent tone, 'not Anna

Woodruff. I'm sorry, Catherine, but there are plenty more Annas out there looking for work. By this time next week, you'll have forgotten all about me. I mean, I've hardly been here long enough to unpack.'

Catherine shook her head.

'That isn't how it works here,' she said simply.

'What do you mean?'

'It's difficult to explain,' she said, shaking her head, 'especially as you've been here such a short time.'

'Then perhaps you shouldn't even try,' I said, 'perhaps we should all just erase the last few days from our memories.'

I for one was quite happy to give that a try, because being here was making me 'feel things', things I didn't want to feel. Ever since the switch-on party in Wynbridge I'd felt as if someone had taken a big stick and stirred up my memories and emotions. The secret chest where I had kept my feelings locked away for so long had been plundered and whereas before I would have tried to power through regardless, now I found myself experiencing a pang of unexpected regret that I didn't know how to join in with the fun I had witnessed.

'No,' she said, sitting up straighter. 'That's not possible.'

'Why not?'

'Because we just can't do that. You were meant to come here, Anna,' she said simply but forcefully, 'and I know, we all know, that you are meant to stay, even though it is going to be difficult and uncomfortable for you now. Do you believe in fate, my dear?'

'I don't know,' I said, because I didn't know.

'Well, what would you say if I told you that there's every possibility that you chose to accept this job for reasons other than the fact that you thought you were going to get away with avoiding Christmas?'

'I'd think you were—' I stopped myself before I said something rude.

'Mad,' Catherine suggested with a little smile, 'bonkers, off my rocker?'

I was relieved she didn't force me to answer because that was exactly what I was beginning to think.

'One day,' she said, 'we'll tell you the stories behind how Mick, Dorothy and Hayley all came to be here and then you'll understand.'

'Why don't you tell me now?' I asked, seeing as she was so determined to see me stay.

'No,' she said, 'now is not the right time and they aren't my stories to tell.'

'But what if I'm long gone before anyone thinks it is the right time?'

She ran a hand over her hair and tucked a long, silvery strand behind her ear.

'Look,' she said, turning to face me. 'I can't force you to stay, but I can ask you not to go, at least not yet. Christmas is still such a long way off and there's so much to do and get through first.'

'But I can't bear it,' I said, thinking of the preparations and planning that I would get dragged into and that would cause me even more pain than I was experiencing now. 'I don't want to be making mince pies and humming carols.'

I stopped and checked myself, desperate as always not to get carried away and reveal too much.

'Then don't make mince pies and hum carols,' she said, 'but please stay, for me,' she added, her tone pleading me to see the job through, for a while at least.

I could feel my resolve weakening in spite of my efforts to harden my heart. She sounded so sincere and I can't deny it felt nice to have someone fighting for me. Had this been happening anywhere other than Wynthorpe I would probably have been handed my P45 and told in no uncertain terms what an inconvenience my desertion was.

'Stay and help me keep an eye on Angus, and help smooth the way when Jamie comes home next week,' Catherine continued.

'But I thought Jamie's homecoming was a good thing?'

'Oh it is,' she insisted, 'it's the best possible thing, but it's all still a little complicated.'

That much I had guessed from the 'muddle' Hayley had referred to earlier in the kitchen.

'It may take a while for him to settle back into life at home and there are some formalities to iron out in connection to the future of the hall.'

'Then surely having me here isn't going to help,' I said reasonably. 'Surely what you, Angus and Jamie need is some privacy and the opportunity to be together without the pressure of having a stranger under your feet?'

'That really isn't how things work here,' she said yet again. 'The more the merrier is our philosophy.'

Perhaps if I did decide to stay I would have that phrase printed on a T-shirt, because everyone around here seemed to say it, or something very similar.

'You might have only been here three days, Anna, but already you're—'

'Family,' I cut in. 'I know.'

I couldn't help but notice how hurt she looked by my blasé use of the word, which clearly meant so much to everyone who lived here. However, had she had to live by my definition of 'family', she would have understood why it wasn't anywhere near as important to me as it was to her.

'Look,' she said, 'I know you're itching to leave, and I daresay you've plenty of reasons to justify why, but Jamie isn't due back until the end of the week and I need a chaperone to my hospital appointment tomorrow at least, so how about we come to some sort of compromise?'

'What are you suggesting?'

'That you stay for this week and help out where you can, and that we'll talk about you moving on next weekend.'

'I don't know,' I said, standing up.

'At least that would give you time to look for another post,' she carried on, 'and the chance to make a proper plan to see you through to the New Year. Perhaps I could even help you?'

'You don't have to do that, Catherine. You aren't obliged.'

'Of course I am,' she said firmly. 'Because had my muddle-headed husband not moved the goalposts we wouldn't even be having this conversation, would we?'

'I suppose not,' I conceded.

Everything had been pretty perfect up until Angus announced he'd got Christmas all sewn up.

'So, that's agreed then,' she smiled, standing up and heading for the door. 'For the time being, we'll carry on as originally planned.'

I watched as Floss plodded after her and couldn't shake off the feeling that she wasn't really expecting me to go anywhere when the week was up.

Fortunately the fog didn't make a comeback and Catherine and I set off to Norwich early the next afternoon amid clear blue skies and accompanied by the sun which was so low over the horizon that I spent the entire journey wearing sunglasses and squinting out from under the visor.

Catherine was most taken with my little Fiat and its

colourful, cosy interior and chatted away about her impending appointment and a little treat she had lined up for afterwards. She had made no mention of the 'C' word or Jamie, and neither had anyone else that morning. I got the distinct impression that they had all been primed and were going to go out of their way to keep schtum whenever I was in the vicinity. There might have been no real, live elephant roaming the hall, but in my mind's eye the corner of the kitchen was now occupied by the biggest, twinkliest Norwegian spruce outside of Trafalgar Square.

We arrived at the hospital in plenty of time, which was just as well given how difficult it was to secure a parking space, and then there was a short wait until a nurse came to take Catherine to see her consultant. I sat in the corridor flicking through a variety of out-of-date magazines and managing to avoid anything with a glittery cover which listed 'the top ten festive gadgets for Dad' or how to 'time the turkey to perfection'.

I didn't have long to wait before Catherine reappeared and was escorted back to where I was sitting by a tall, slim gentleman who introduced himself as Mr Singh.

'So,' he said, looking me up and down and nodding in approval. 'You must be Anna. The latest Christmas recruit, yes?'

Clearly much more had been discussed during her brief appointment than Catherine's recovery and I wondered fleetingly if all the Wynthorpe staff had been 'Christmas recruits'.

'I trust I can rely on you to keep Mrs Connelly here in check, my dear?'

'Of course,' I smiled, standing up and offering Catherine my arm.

'Because I'm afraid,' he said, looking sternly at my employer, 'like most people I see, she's in too much of a rush to get back to normal, now she thinks she's all better.'

'Is that right?' I said. 'I was under the impression that she was doing just fine.'

When I first met Catherine I had assumed that the fears Angus had spoken of during my interview were unfounded and that his worries were merely an over-protective concern for his wife, but perhaps I had misjudged the situation. After all, I wasn't an expert in knee surgery recuperation. Perhaps I needed to spend my online time during the coming days Googling post-op exercises, rather than looking for another job. That way I might actually prove to be of some use to Catherine before we parted company.

'She's doing OK,' said Mr Singh, 'but with everything happening at the hall over the next few weeks I think there's every possibility that she'll take too much on and consequently hamper the progress that she has made so far.'

I couldn't help wondering if Catherine had told him about the latest Wynthorpe news with an ulterior motive. Had she perhaps hinted that I was the one who would be making sure she behaved herself? Perhaps she thought cranking up the guilt would stop me deserting my post. If that was the case, she was a very clever woman.

'I'll make sure everyone at the hall is aware of the situation,' I told Mr Singh seriously. 'And I'm sure Angus and Dorothy will have plans in place to make sure that doesn't happen.'

'Thank you, Mr Singh,' said Catherine who gave no flicker as to whether or not I'd jumped to the right conclusion. 'I'll see you in the New Year.'

As I negotiated my way around the busy ring road system and into the centre of Norwich, Catherine became subdued and quiet and not at all like the chatty passenger who had travelled with me earlier.

'Are you all right?' I asked when I eventually parked. 'Are you sure you're up to this? We can drive straight home, if you'd rather.'

'No, no,' she insisted, 'absolutely not. I've been looking forward to this ever since I booked the table. I'm sorry if I'm suddenly not the most loquacious companion, Anna, but I have so much on my mind. I keep forgetting about it all for a little while and then it all comes back and I find myself almost wishing Angus hadn't gone to all this trouble over—'

She had stopped just short of saying the word.

'It's all right,' I said, 'you can say it.'

'But it isn't just Christmas,' she tutted, unfastening her seat belt. 'There's much more to it than that. Jamie's decision to come home is wonderful of course and I'm delighted, but I can't help worrying about *why* he's decided to come back now. I hope Angus hasn't been pressurising him, because that's no way to go about it.'

'Go about what?'

'Do you know,' she said, ignoring my question and following her own train of thought, as I helped her out of her seat, 'Wynthorpe Hall has been in my family for four generations now and securing its future is more important to me than anything. Well, almost anything. It's a magical place and I adore owning it, but its upkeep and its future are such a massive responsibility.'

I hadn't realised that the hall had been passed down through Catherine's side of the family and I couldn't really see what the future of the hall had to do with Jamie either. Surely it would be left to Christopher, the eldest son, assuming Catherine and Angus were following tradition of course. Although, given what I now knew of the place, that probably wasn't the case at all.

'Anyway,' she said, 'I don't suppose fretting over it all before he's back in the country will make any difference, will it? Let's go and enjoy our tea.'

The gilded Georgian Assembly Rooms in Norwich were a sight to behold, as was the dainty, delicious afternoon tea Catherine ordered. Regimented smoked salmon and ham and Colman's mustard sandwiches, warm savoury and sweet scones and a variety of miniature cakes and macarons arrived shortly after the pots of delicately fragranced, loose-leaf tea.

Catherine had been greeted like an old friend by the waitressing staff and told me that she had been a regular at the rooms since she was in her teens and that her mother had insisted it was the only place to take refreshment during a trip to the city. It was all a far cry from the burger, fries and soda I had occasionally tasted courtesy of the golden arches when I was growing up.

I wasn't familiar with the city at all, but had caught a glimpse of the famous striped market canopies and the Forum and Millennium Library as we walked around from the car park, and promised myself that I would come back and explore before I moved to some other far-flung part of the country.

'And what about you, Anna?' Catherine asked, cocking her head to one side as she carefully cut one of the sandwiches into even tinier, neat squares. 'Do you get to spend much time with your family?'

I felt the heat rise in my cheeks and took a sip of tea while thinking how best to phrase my answer. I had no desire to lie, but blurting out the plain, hard truth wasn't something I relished under any circumstances, and certainly not when enjoying myself in such lavish surroundings.

Tea and tears would not be a good way to end the day, but I couldn't trust myself to say much without becoming either upset or aggressive. My default setting when talking about my family seemed to maraud from one extreme of the emotional scale to the other and it wasn't something I wished to put on public display among the well-heeled Norfolk diners.

'No,' I said simply, quickly opting to bring down the wall and drag my professional persona back out of the wings.

If I played it straight down the line I would hopefully put a stop to further uncomfortable questioning and would be able to enjoy my miniature carrot cake in perfect safety.

'I'm afraid I don't have any family.'

'None at all?' Catherine gasped, looking shocked.

'No,' I said lightly. 'None at all.'

Given my aversion to the upcoming season I had assumed that she, and everyone else at the hall, would have put two and two together and reached the only possible conclusion for themselves. After all, the maths was pretty simple – I hated any mention of Christmas, plus I had nowhere to go on the Big Day, equalled no family. It was hardly rocket science.

'But never mind that,' I said as if it didn't matter at all and picking up the teapot before flashing a winning smile so she wouldn't think me rude. 'Would you like more tea?'

Catherine pushed her cup across the table and briefly rested her hand over the top of mine.

'You do have family, my dear,' she said tenderly and not taking the hint that I was doing my utmost to shut the conversation down. 'Like I keep telling you, you have mine.'

Chapter 6

Whether it was pure coincidence or part of some far wilier plan that Catherine had cooked up during the meandering journey home from Norwich I couldn't be sure, but the next few days leading up to December first flashed by in a heartbeat. The evenings were just as busy as the days and I didn't even have time to think about looking for another job, let alone setting about making an online search to secure one.

Christmas was never actually mentioned when I was in the vicinity, but it was obvious that everything we were doing was with an eye, an ear and a nod to that much anticipated celebration. I thought it was a little early to be making a start, but according to everyone else there would be barely enough time now to get everything done. There was a plethora of rooms, bedrooms mostly, to reorganise, clean and then air ahead of the arrival of the rest of the family, and I was assigned as understudy to Hayley in that particular department.

I have to admit I found myself somewhat surprised by both her knowledge and her skill but when it came to cleaning and conservation she really knew her stuff.

'Dorothy taught me quite a lot,' she explained, as together we set about wrapping and moving some of the more delicate ornaments from what was to be the grandsons' bedroom and into another assigned to storage until the New Year. 'She used to do everything here, until I came along.'

I was curious to ask how long both she and Dorothy had been a part of life at the hall, but I didn't because getting to know just the hall was proving dangerous enough. Every corridor revealed yet another room, more fascinating history and another treasure, and as the days slipped by I was feeling more and more attached to the bricks, mortar and wattle and daub. I simply couldn't allow myself to form that level of connection and sentimentality towards the folk who populated it as well or I would never be able to move on, Christmas or no Christmas.

'And I've been on a couple of courses as well,' Hayley continued.

'Courses?'

'Yes,' she said, stopping to carefully run her massive feather duster lightly over some intricate fretwork on the stairs. 'They were run by some big historical conservation organisation – English Heritage or the National Trust, I can't remember now – but they specialised in how to properly look after furniture and fabrics. That sort of thing.'

'Oh,' I said, looking at my young and usually brash colleague with fresh eyes. 'Right.'

'I know I said "I fling the Hoover about a bit" the day we met,' she blushed, 'but there's actually more to it than that. Some of the pieces here are older than Angus and need careful handling.'

She was trying to make light of it, but I could tell how much her job really meant to her now, along with how much she cared.

'And have you ever thought of looking for a position with the National Trust or English Heritage?' I asked. 'Would you consider moving to somewhere beyond the confines of the Fens, perhaps?'

'No way,' she guffawed. 'They wouldn't be interested in taking on the likes of me, especially with my background.'

I didn't ask what difference she thought her background would make to her employability.

'And besides,' she said wistfully, 'I have everything I want right here. I consider myself very lucky to be in the employ of Catherine and Angus.'

'Of course,'

'And so should you,' she added meaningfully.

When I wasn't reassigning rooms or polishing the silver, there were freezers to begin filling, and plenty of them.

'I still can't believe you're starting to do this now,' I

told Dorothy, who was carefully counting and cutting out another batch of pastry to make yet more sausage rolls. 'It isn't even December yet.'

'That's as maybe,' she said sagely, 'but before we know it there'll be over a dozen mouths to feed under this roof.'

I counted up on my fingers just to check she was right and tried not to look at the jars of homemade mincemeat she had lined up to make the first batch of mince pies. I had been adamant when I spoke to Catherine about staying for the week that I wouldn't be getting roped into baking anything festive, but my resolve seemed to have been magically worn down a little when I was looking the other way.

At least the radio hadn't been re-tuned to Smooth Christmas or Classic FM just yet, I told myself. That really would be too much. However, I couldn't help wondering how my brain was going to react when it caught the once familiar and adored scent of the spices battling to escape from the mincemeat jars.

'I see.'

'And if everyone sits down for a snack in the middle of the afternoon, on just one day,' she said, pointing a floury finger at her handiwork, 'then that's potentially an entire batch of sausage rolls gone.'

I could see her point.

'And that's even before Angus has come back for seconds and thirds,' I smiled.

'Exactly,' she said, clearly pleased that I was finally getting to grips with the amount of work involved.

Not that she looked or sounded like she resented it, of course. None of them did. Staff and family alike, or the entire family I should say, were looking in the rudest of health, all bustling about and thoroughly enjoying the extra work and logistical untangling.

'So,' said Dorothy, tossing an apron in my direction, 'I reckon a couple of hundred sausage rolls will be enough to be going on with this afternoon.'

Oh well, in for a penny and all that and, I reminded myself, sausage rolls weren't necessarily confined to the ranks of festive baking.

'And if you're interested,' I said lightly, while tying the apron in place, 'I happen to know a great recipe for Stilton straws that freeze beautifully.'

The first batch of rolls and straws was barely out of the Aga before the hordes descended and Dorothy and I were fending off advances from every corner.

'See,' she tutted, 'this is exactly what I mean.'

'Is this sausage meat from Skylark Farm?' asked Angus, who had seemingly appeared from thin air the second the trays were lined up on the table.

I hadn't seen very much of him during the last couple of days, but I had noticed his clothes were getting grubbier and grubbier and I began to wonder if he was up to something specific that required my closer attention. Catherine had asked me to keep an eye on him and, taking in his mucky knees and oily cuffs, I felt she had been right to be concerned. I made a mental note to go and investigate as soon as I could.

'Oh, Angus,' scolded Dorothy, also spotting the state he was in, 'please don't tell me that is one of your new tailored shirts.'

Angus snatched his hand away from the tray of Stilton straws he had been aiming for and rolled up his sleeves.

'Because I'll never be able to get the grime out of those cuffs,' she continued, sounding stern and frankly a little scary. 'You know full well they were supposed to be for best.'

'I couldn't find any others,' he protested half-heartedly.

'Well, you can't have looked very far,' Dorothy shot back. 'Your bottom drawer is full of work shirts and besides, why can't you wear a boiler suit like Mick? That way I can shove the whole lot in on a boil wash.'

'I know for a fact that he has overalls,' said Hayley, dobbing her boss in. 'Brand-new ones with extra pockets, because I gave him a pair for his birthday.'

It made me smile to hear them talking about him like some naughty schoolboy, rather than the man who paid their wages.

'I don't know what you're smiling at, Anna,' he said, pretending to sulk. 'Mick wants you outside to help with the log pile this afternoon and you're going to get filthy as well.'

'Well, in that case,' I told him, 'perhaps I'll just ask Hayley to find me the overalls she gave you for your birthday.'

'That sounds like a very good idea,' said Dorothy, rewarding me with one of the biggest sausage rolls on the tray, 'and yes, Angus, this is Skylark sausage meat.'

I took a bite through the still warm, flaky pastry and into the succulent filling.

'Oh wow,' I mumbled, trying not to spray everyone with crumbs before wondering how many calories stacking a log pile was going to help to burn off.

As it turned out it wasn't just moving a few bits of sawn timber from one spot to another that Mick needed help with and I soon burnt off the sausage roll and Stilton straw calories as well as any that had been left over from the afternoon tea with Catherine in Norwich.

'I hope you're up for this,' Mick said when I joined him in the stable yard. 'There's not much of the day left, so we better get on.'

I hadn't seen the quad bike and trailer before, or taken on board the extent of the woods that surrounded the hall, but we were soon weaving amongst the trees, Mick expertly steering and me hanging on to the trailer for dear life. Eventually he came to a clearing in what looked like an almost perfect circle of beech trees and turned off the engine.

'Crikey,' I said, jumping out as my ears tuned into the cawing crows and the breeze among the creaking branches. 'Does all this belong to the hall?'

There were trees as far as the eye could see, and although perhaps not the most spectacular time of year to be taking in the scene, their unashamed nakedness did give me the opportunity to take in their girth. This place was old and, truth be told, a little spooky in the fading light of a winter's afternoon. I pulled my coat, Angus's work coat actually, a little tighter around me.

'It does,' said Mick, sounding like a proud father. 'It's hardly ancient woodland, but it's pretty old. You won't find anywhere else like it round here for a few miles. Now come on, let's get to work before it's dark.'

It seemed to take as long for Mick to give me the health and safety lowdown as it did to gather the logs, but as he kept reminding me, 'Where chainsaws are involved you don't get a second chance.' I didn't think it wise to remind him that I wasn't going to be using the chainsaw, nor to ask if we could just get on with it.

Wearing all the appropriate clothing, boots and headgear, he soon carved up the trunk of a tree that had fallen victim to the autumn gales the year before and I, also sporting a hard hat and goggles, collected the more manageable pieces and stacked them in the trailer.

It was hard work and I was grateful that it was cold,

because it wasn't long before I was working up a sweat, and a thirst to go with it.

'Let's take a break,' said Mick, a short while later. 'We'll have a drink and then load up these last few bigger pieces together.'

I was more than happy to agree. My back ached and in spite of the thick gloves my hands felt sore.

'A tot of whisky to go with this wouldn't have gone amiss,' I joked as he handed me a mug of steaming tea and a wedge of Dorothy's moist fruitcake.

'Not for me,' said Mick with a sniff. 'I don't drink.'

'What, never?' I asked, only just remembering that he was the only one who had resisted the charms of the Skylark Scrumpy at the switch-on.

'Never,' he said firmly. 'I used to, too much, and it was almost the ruin of me.'

I didn't know what to say. I hadn't meant to pry. I had enough knowledge about the demon drink to know that talking about the damage it could inflict didn't come easy.

'In fact,' he continued after a second or two spent thought-fully chewing his lip, 'had I not crashed my car into the hall gates I probably would have drunk myself into an early grave.'

'Did you do much damage?' It was a stupid question, far too flippant for the admission he had just made, but I didn't know what else to say.

'The car was a wreck,' he said with a smile, 'but the crash saved my life.'

'What do you mean?'

'Well it was the Connellys' wall I hit too, wasn't it? Angus made me rebuild it and Catherine insisted I stayed at the hall until the job was done. By the time the last piece was in place I'd all but given up drinking and found a reason to live, along with a new home and job.'

'You didn't have a reason to live before?' I asked, staring straight ahead.

'I thought I had,' he said sadly. 'All the time I was on my final tour in the Army I thought of nothing but coming home to my wife and starting a family. I didn't expect to arrive back early and find she was having a fling with my so-called best mate.'

'Crikey, Mick,' I swallowed. 'I'm so sorry.'

'Anyway,' he shrugged, closing the conversation down, 'that's enough about me. How are you enjoying the week so far?'

I leant back against the edge of the trailer and warmed my hands around the mug.

'It's been wonderful,' I said, because it had been. 'To be honest, I can't remember the last time I enjoyed my work so much, but given everything you've just said I'm guessing you can understand that.'

Working at Wynthorpe Hall didn't feel like 'work'. There was more of a commune vibe about the place, and even though Catherine and Angus were the wealthy landowners there had never been so much as a hint of the 'them' and 'us' moment that I had experienced in every other similar property I had worked in.

The hall, Dorothy had told me one afternoon while she was making dinner, had once been made available to everyone, like a rather upmarket local resource, and the local community had appreciated that and made full use of it. The WI used to hold special talks and events there and there were story-time sessions for the younger members of the local library as well as brief tea and refreshment stops for the local rambling group. When I asked why those things weren't currently happening she became evasive and changed the subject and I hadn't yet had the opportunity to bring it up again.

'Almost a shame to leave then,' said Mick with a sniff.

'Almost,' I agreed.

Neither Hayley nor Dorothy had asked about my aversion to Christmas or been so forthright about my determination to move on. Not that my behaviour had suggested I was particularly determined, since my decision had become common knowledge. I opened my mouth to make some kind of explanation to Mick, but a movement in the trees to my left stopped me in my tracks. I stayed quiet, initially thinking it was perhaps a deer or a fox, but it was neither.

'What the hell,' I whispered, plucking at Mick's sleeve. 'Mick, are you seeing this?' I pointed into the middle distance with a shaking hand and wondered if I was hallucinating.

'I am,' he said, sounding almost amused. 'Don't look so worried.'

'But,' I spluttered, trying to keep as quiet as possible, 'that's a witch. Isn't it?'

To my mind, the sweeping cloak and black hat were incontrovertible evidence, but if I really was hallucinating then perhaps Mick was seeing something completely different. I risked a glance over at him, just to make sure we were on the same wavelength, and when I looked back the figure had disappeared.

'Come on,' he chuckled, tapping me on the shoulder and making me shriek in shock, spilling the remains of my tea. 'We'd best get on before it's dark.'

He wasn't wrong. I leapt to my feet, packed away the flask and began piling the wood in the trailer as if my life depended on it.

I didn't have much of an appetite that evening. A fact that didn't go unnoticed by Dorothy, who watched like a hawk as I pushed her homemade chicken and vegetable pie around my plate.

'Are you sure you're all right?' she asked, peering from the plate to me and back again. 'You look a bit peaky to me. Is it the pie?'

Mick didn't give me the opportunity to say that it was absolutely nothing to do with her impeccable pie.

'I reckon,' he sniggered, 'she looks as though she's seen a ghost.'

'Well, now,' smiled Catherine with pride. 'Have you seen our grey lady?'

She didn't wait for me to answer either.

'Lucky you, Anna,' she went on. 'She doesn't show herself to everyone, you know. '

'You should feel honoured,' sniffed Dorothy, clearly a little put out. 'I've never seen her. Not once in all the time I've lived here.'

Now this was a brilliant development. Not only were the surrounding woods overrun with witches, the hall was haunted as well. The sooner I found another post the better. I tried to count up on my fingers how many days I had left to secure another job. Amazingly the week I had agreed to stay on for was almost up. I was beginning to think there really was magic within the walls of Wynthorpe Hall after all, because it was certainly capable of making time disappear, if nothing else.

'No,' I croaked. 'No ghost, no grey lady.'

'Oh, that's a shame,' said Angus, mopping up his gravy with a thick slice of Dorothy's homemade granary.

It really wasn't, but I didn't say as much.

'But she has seen a witch,' winked Mick.

'Oh you've seen Molly, have you?' beamed Angus, gravy dribbling down his chin.

'Who?'

'Molly,' said Catherine again. 'Although I'm not sure that she really is a witch.'

'Well, whoever she is, she looked like a witch to me,' I said. 'Wandering about in a cloak and pointy hat, I don't really think she could have been anything else. It's not as if it's even close to Halloween now. Is she a local?'

'Yes,' said Angus, 'she lives in the old woodsman's cottage at the edge of the woods.'

I gave a little shudder. This was sounding more and more like one of the Grimms' fairy tales to me and I was pleased I hadn't been close enough to see if she had left a trail of breadcrumbs or had a warty nose.

'I expect she was visiting the Wishing Tree,' Angus went on.

'What's the Wishing Tree?'

'We have a hawthorn in the woods,' Catherine explained. 'No one really knows how old it is, but judging by its gnarly old trunk we think it's reasonably ancient.'

'And it's where people go to make a wish for something they would like, or give thanks for something they've received,' joined in Angus. 'They say a few words and then tie something to the branches as an offering or little thank-you.'

'What sort of things?'

'Slips of paper, lengths of ribbon, all sorts of things.'

'I've even seen a child's pacifier,' said Dorothy. 'And a train ticket.'

I noticed she had gone a little red as she said it and wondered if she had ever tied anything to the branches.

'And who exactly are the people thanking or asking?' I frowned.

This was all completely new to me. I'd never seen a real live witch before or heard of a Wishing Tree. It all sounded a little strange, but in the context of the hall, I had to admit, it didn't seem quite so fanciful.

'The universe,' sighed Catherine wistfully, 'perhaps.'

'The universe,' I repeated.

'Have you got something you would like to ask for, Anna?' asked Catherine. 'Any unfinished business in your life you wish to have resolved, or perhaps some wish you'd like to see come true?'

'Not that I can think of,' I said, my face flushing.

Fortunately Angus piped up again before Catherine had the opportunity to arrange an excursion under the light of the full moon that required chanting and incense.

'You know,' he said, pointing his fork at Mick and me, 'I think you two seeing Molly might be a sign.'

'A sign?' questioned Mick.

'Mm,' nodded Angus. 'I've been thinking about reinstating our old Solstice celebration.'

'Now that's a wonderful idea,' said Catherine, thankfully

diverted from my wishes and dreams, for the moment at least.

'Yes,' he said. 'That's what I thought. It always used to be so popular, didn't it?'

'And what is the Solstice celebration?' I asked.

'Well, the December Solstice is the shortest day,' Angus explained, 'and people used to come to the woods to search for their Yule log. As the sun set, assuming it had put in an appearance of course, we would sit around a fire and listen to the story of the passing of the crown from the Holly King to the Oak King.'

'Then everyone would come back to the hall for mulled cider and dancing,' added Dorothy.

'It sounds like quite a party,' I smiled.

I had no idea who the Holly King or the Oak King were, but my professional persona had kicked in and my business brain was telling me that Angus and Catherine would need to check their public liability insurance if they were going to have locals stumbling about in the woods, in the dark, especially after a flagon of cider or two.

'It was,' smiled Catherine. 'And I think starting it again is a wonderful idea, Angus.'

'I thought you might,' he winked at his wife and then turned to me. 'And as it's your birthday on the twenty-first, Anna, you can be the one to pick out our Yule log this year.'

Chapter 7

I didn't waste my breath reminding Angus or the others that I would be long gone before my birthday dawned, because along with everyone else, at that precise moment, I couldn't imagine how my departure was going to happen. I still didn't want to be at the hall when Christmas was in full swing, but for the time being at least, I couldn't find it in me to look for another job either. Perhaps I would feel differently when the family descended and the tree went up, but for now, I was content to get on with the work I was doing, which so little resembled the job description in my 'saved' email folder.

That evening I did fire up my laptop, but only to help Catherine set up a public liability insurance policy. Angus had been rather amused when I asked who they were insured with and insisted that no one in the past had ever come to any harm, and even if they did in the future, he was certain that they wouldn't hold him or Catherine accountable. Catherine had been considerably quieter however and had taken my comments on board, especially when I reminded her that the Solstice celebration would include quaffing gallons of cider, in the dark, next to a roaring fire.

'Let's just go ahead and set something up,' she said to me in hushed tones after dinner. 'We won't say anything to Angus because he'll only make a fuss.'

'All right,' I agreed.

I got the impression this may have been territory she was revisiting.

'You must think us incredibly naïve about this sort of thing,' she had added.

'Not at all,' I told her, not completely untruthfully. 'You and Angus simply see the good in people and consequently I can imagine there may be a time in the future when you decide to open the hall to the public again, in much the same way as Dorothy said you had before. Both you and Angus are incredibly generous and kind, but I don't think there would be any harm in protecting yourselves as well as those who come to enjoy your kindness.'

I was fairly certain that it was probably some sort of legal requirement, as well as good old-fashioned common sense, but couldn't imagine for one second that either Angus or Catherine had ever been much hampered by worrying about that sort of thing.

Once the policy was in place and Catherine had gone

to bed I researched what I could about the deeper meanings of Wishing Trees and the Holly and the Oak King. I wasn't usually into that sort of thing, but I found it all rather intriguing and vowed to make a trip back into the woods before I left, to seek out the tree and perhaps even make my own wish and leave a little gift behind to mark my time at the hall.

Friday the first of December, the day of Jamie's homecoming, dawned bright and clear and there was much excitement when I went down to the kitchen that morning and not only because the prodigal was due to put in an appearance.

'Oh, Angus!' I heard Catherine laugh as I pushed open the door. 'Where on earth did you get it?'

'And where on earth have you been hiding it?' gasped Hayley.

I braced myself, wondering what on earth it could be that Angus had revealed, and whether this mysterious thing was responsible for his recent disappearances and grubby returns.

'My goodness,' I gulped, as my eyes alighted on what it was that held everyone's attention. 'Angus, that's amazing.'

'It's American,' he declared, looking immensely proud. 'Which accounts for its size, I suppose. I tracked it down online and had it shipped over. I know it's a little over the top . . .'

'A little,' snorted Hayley.

'But I think the wall should be able to bear its weight,' he continued. 'We've used some pretty hefty fixings to secure it, haven't we, Mick?'

'Yes,' said Mick. 'I don't think it's going to be moving anywhere.'

I stood and gazed open-mouthed at the ginormous, brightly painted wooden Advent calendar which was now adorning the wall above Floss's bed. Even the little dog was looking up at it, but whether in bewildered awe or more in concern that it might fall on her head, I couldn't be sure.

The calendar, which was decorated with various traditional Christmas-associated themes such as wreaths, nutcrackers and trees, had twenty-four drawers, each, I guessed, hiding a considerably larger treat than a chunk of chocolate. Along with every other marketing ploy connected to the season, I didn't hold any truck with Advent calendars, but this magnificent creation couldn't fail to raise an eyebrow and draw attention.

'There are treats for everyone,' Angus confirmed, 'and in some cases two. It's taken me a while to track some things down, but I think everyone will like what I've found.'

'So, is this what you've been up to all week?' asked Catherine. I could tell she was feeling relieved.

'It is,' he beamed, 'I've been looking for just the right present for each person, but there's to be absolutely no peeking.'

We all laughed, wondering who was going to be first in line to open a drawer, but I wasn't convinced that this was all Angus had been up to. Searching out presents for an Advent calendar, irrespective of its size, wouldn't usually involve oil and soil-stained shirts. His wife might have been happy with his explanation, but I still had my sights firmly set on Angus and his antics.

'And in view of the very sad fact that you might not be with us all that much longer, my dear,' he said, turning to me and making me blush to my roots, 'I thought it was only right that you should open the first drawer.'

I didn't know what to say, especially as I still hadn't made any effort to look for another post. Even though I had used the computer to set up the insurance policy and look up various Pagan rites and rituals, I hadn't bothered to take even just a minute to look for a new job, but I knew I couldn't put it off much longer. After all, Jamie was due home in just a few hours and the festive preparations would begin in earnest as soon as he was settled and I certainly didn't want to be around then.

'Go on,' said Hayley, giving me a little shove of encouragement when I didn't move. 'We're all dying to see what's inside.'

I took a tentative step towards the calendar and ran my hands over the drawer marked '1'. It was decorated with a pair of plump robins and, much to my consternation, a painted red ribbon of silver bells.

'The illustration might be a clue as to what's inside,' Angus said eagerly.

'Don't ruin it,' joked Mick. 'I thought the presents were supposed to be a surprise.'

Carefully I pulled open the drawer, which was deeper than I expected, and lifted out a gift-wrapped box, complete with a handwritten label.

'For Anna,' I read aloud, in a slightly shaky voice.

'So open it then,' Hayley urged.

Gingerly I tore through the paper and carefully opened the little cardboard box inside.

'What is it?' she said, rushing forward to peer over my shoulder.

'It's a music box,' said Angus, when I didn't answer her. 'Turn the handle, Anna.'

I looked at the little silver hand crank and licked my lips, which were suddenly as dry as my throat.

'What's the tune?' I croaked.

'Just turn the handle and see,' he encouraged again. 'I think you'll like it.'

The hall was suddenly so silent you could have heard a pin drop. Tentatively I turned the handle and the first few tinny bars of the song rang out, the song I was fully expecting to hear.

'I think I know that tune,' said Dorothy, her head inclined towards the sound. 'Oh, whatever is it?'

'Silver Bells,' I said, tears springing to my eyes as the words caught in my throat. 'It's Silver Bells.'

'Of course,' she said.

I played it through for a second time and she and Catherine began to sing while Hayley beamed and Mick shrugged and shook his head, suggesting he didn't recognise it.

I took little notice. My body was standing in the Wynthorpe kitchen, turning the handle, but my mind was far, far away. Decades away, watching my mother as she bustled about the kitchen, her hands covered in flour and the comforting scent of pine from the Christmas tree mingling with cinnamon, ginger and cloves as the fire crackled in the dining-room grate. How she had loved Christmas. Her voice reached me as clearly as if she was standing by my side and as she turned to bathe me in the warmth of her smile I stopped turning the handle and without a word packed the music box back into its little box.

Why that tune, I wondered, turning my gaze to Angus, and why that particular rose-patterned bedroom? Practically everything that had happened since I arrived at Wynthorpe Hall had thrown my past across the path of my present. Was it just a coincidence, or was there really some kind of magic afoot?

'Don't you like it?' asked Hayley, her brows knitted together.

'Yes,' I said, still looking at Angus. 'I always have.'

*

I excused myself from breakfast the second I felt I could get away without raising suspicion and took myself back to my room. I couldn't linger long because there was still so much to do ahead of Jamie's arrival, but I just needed a private moment in which to order my thoughts and at least try to make some sense of what was happening – what had been happening since the moment I flicked through the recruitment pages of *The Lady* magazine and my eyes fell upon the Wynthorpe Hall advertisement.

I lay on my bed with the music box, still in its wrappings, by my side and inhaled deeply, trying to think things through and formulate a revised plan for December. I didn't intend to but I must have fallen asleep, or at least almost asleep, because how else could I explain the hazy outline of a woman sitting at the foot of my bed if she hadn't come to me in a dream? She was very definitely not the grey lady, but bore a striking resemblance to the woman my heart still ached to see. Not the last, cancer-ravaged image of her, but the happy, healthy, Christmas-loving version who had been so cruelly taken from me when I was too young to make any sense of the whys and wherefores. It was those very whys and wherefores, I finally realised, that I had been denying ever since, but as her last few coherent words drifted back to me I sat up, knowing that this was a very special moment and exactly what I had to do with it.

Mum had warned me, before the disease really took hold,

that she would be gone by Christmas or just after it, and that in losing her I would most probably lose my love for the season, but I would come back to it one year, when I least expected it. She had told me that she would never leave me, that when I needed her most, and when the time was right and I was in the right place, there would be signs to let me know.

She was insistent that she would find a way of telling me it was time to move on and that I should let go and embrace Christmas again. Of course she had no way of knowing what other horrors would play out during the Decembers after she had gone – neither of us did – and none of that was her fault. She had said what she thought was for the best at the time and what I should have remembered and been holding on to after everything else had turned so sour.

My fingers reached out for the music box that held her favourite tune and my eyes roved over the very same style of roses that had decorated her bedroom and I finally knew what I had to do. These were the signs. It wasn't magic at all, it was Mum. She was telling me it was time to reclaim Christmas and there was nowhere more comforting, nowhere safer in the world than Wynthorpe Hall, in which to try and do it. If I was going to dig deep and let Christmas back into my life, then there really was no better place to be.

The hall was quiet as I padded back down the stairs and I

was surprised, when I glanced at my watch, to discover that I had been in my room for the best part of the entire day.

'Decided to put in an appearance, have you?' teased Hayley as she bustled through from the pantry and back towards the kitchen. 'I thought you were never going to wake up.'

'What do you mean?'

'Three times I've come up to see if you were planning to do any work today,' she tutted, 'and every time you were out for the count.'

'You should have woken me,' I told her, surprised that I had actually been properly asleep and how much of the day I had lost. 'There's so much to do.'

'I'm only joshing,' she said, playfully punching my arm, 'everything's done and besides, you must have needed it, although looking at you, you don't look much better than you did before you sloped off after breakfast.'

'Thanks, Hayley,' I said, rolling my eyes. 'I'm actually feeling much better.'

'Well that's something, I suppose,' she shrugged.

Together we walked into the kitchen and on catching sight of me Dorothy automatically reached for the radio.

'It's all right,' I told her. 'Don't change it on my account.'

She and Catherine exchanged glances as I bent to fuss Floss, who had done me the honour of leaving her warm bed to come and say hello.

'*Deck the Halls* is actually quite fitting, don't you think?'

I said, standing back up. 'Given the date and the venue,' I added, looking around the vast kitchen that defied all attempts to organise it.

'I suppose it is,' said Catherine, 'although—'

'Although you didn't expect me to say so,' I smiled.

'Quite,' she agreed. 'Are you all right, my dear?'

'I think so,' I sniffed as a traitorous tear escaped and rolled down my cheek. It was quickly followed by another, and the three lovely ladies rushed to my side and ushered me into a chair.

'Whatever's wrong?' frowned Hayley as Dorothy handed me one of her pretty hankies. 'It's not because I teased you about not pulling your weight today, is it?'

'No,' I sniffed, shoving the hanky to my nose and blowing hard. 'Of course not.'

'Are you not well?' tried Dorothy, laying her hand across my forehead to check my temperature.

'I'm fine,' I blubbed, 'better than fine.'

Hayley shrugged her shoulders and looked to Catherine to see what she was going to suggest.

'I'll fill the kettle,' said Dorothy.

Tea, it turned out, was Dorothy's default setting, as was cake.

'Mick and Angus have already left to collect Jamie from the airport,' she continued, 'so I think we're safe to break out these.'

Reverently she placed a battered old Quality Street tin on the table and Hayley eased herself into the seat next to mine.

'Don't let the tin fool you,' she said in hushed tones, 'there's far greater treasure than chocolates inside.'

I looked at her and raised my eyebrows.

'The tin's a decoy,' she informed me, tapping the side of her nose.

I looked at the faces of my new friends and, dare I say it, family, as we drank our tea and indulged in the delicious Lebkuchen biscuits Catherine's German grandmother had been so adept at baking and, thankfully, had passed on the recipe for, and sighed.

Hayley was poised to launch off again and remind us what was left to do before Jamie's plane landed but Catherine stopped her.

'Before we start thinking about all that,' she smiled, 'or start making some serious plans about how we're going to contain my husband's outrageous festive ideas, I think Anna has something she would like to say.'

Dorothy and Hayley looked at me, their mouths slightly open and their eyebrows raised. OK, so perhaps there was a little magic in the Wynthorpe walls, or the ability to read minds, at least.

'Yes,' I began, feeling suddenly shy. 'There is something I would like to say actually.'

I cleared my throat and fiddled with the crumbs on my plate.

'If it's all right with you,' I said, looking at Catherine, 'and only if you haven't already made alternative plans of course, I really would quite like to stay here for Christmas after all.'

'Yes!' said Hayley, punching the air and pulling me into an awkward sideways hug.

'There now,' smiled Dorothy, looking well pleased. 'How about that?'

'I never for one second thought you'd be spending it any-where else,' added Catherine, her smile reassuring me that I couldn't have made a better decision. 'What was it that changed your mind?'

'Was it divine intervention?' giggled Hayley, squeezing harder. 'I love it when that happens.'

'Sort of,' I said, feeling the music box in my pocket dig-ging into my side. 'Something like that.'

Chapter 8

At a little after six that evening Angus phoned to speak to Catherine. Hayley, Dorothy and I were setting the table ready for what was going to be a very late supper. There was a definite buzz of excitement and expectation in the air and although a little nervous about my decision to stay, I was also enjoying the tentative beginnings of really feeling that I was a part of something. It was a long time since I had felt as though I truly belonged or was so welcome anywhere.

'Oh well,' we heard Catherine sigh and say, 'it can't be helped.'

She sounded utterly deflated and we looked at one another, wondering what on earth had happened.

'Will you ring again in the morning?'

We all looked in her direction.

'All right, my darling. Sleep well.'

Catherine replaced the receiver, then turned to us and

shook her head. Hayley snuffed out the candles and Dorothy returned some of the plates and bowls to the warming drawer.

'What's happened?' I asked.

'Jamie's flight has been cancelled,' she said. 'Some industrial action in Europe having a knock-on effect, or something, I couldn't really hear.'

'But they definitely won't be home tonight?'

'No,' she sighed, 'not tonight. This is the last leg of his journey and instead of being the most straightforward it's turning out to be the most complicated of all.' She sounded as fed up and frustrated as Jamie no doubt felt. 'Angus said he'll ring to give us an update in the morning.'

'Oh, love,' said Dorothy, rubbing Catherine's arm. 'I'm so sorry.'

'Oh well,' was her stoic, but unconvincing reply, 'I suppose I've waited this long. One more night won't hurt, will it?'

'They aren't sleeping in the Land Rover, are they?' piped up Hayley. 'Or on those horrid plastic seats in the airport?'

'No, they've managed to get a room at the hotel just next door,' Catherine explained. 'They only had a twin though,' she added, biting her lip.

'Better than nothing, I guess,' I shrugged.

'Mick might not think so by the morning,' said Catherine, with a small smile. 'Have you not heard Angus snore?'

It was down to me to ferry Hayley back to Wynbridge later that evening.

'I hadn't planned to go back tonight,' she explained, after calling home to tell whoever was there that she wasn't staying for the reunion dinner or overnight now after all, 'but it seems a bit pointless to mess up one of the rooms for no reason.'

'But I wouldn't mind helping you prepare it again,' I insisted. 'If you would rather stay I don't mind helping out and besides, how much mess could you make in such a short amount of time?'

Hayley looked at me and grinned and I guessed that on her own time and in her own place her standards of tidiness weren't quite as strict as those she adopted when she was in professional mode. But I really didn't mind whether I ended up taking her back to town or not. If she stayed I would enjoy her vibrant company, but taking her home would give me the opportunity to give my little car, which had been sitting idle for the last few days, a much needed blast.

'Look, do you want me to stay over?' she asked.

'It's entirely up to you,' I told her.

'Because really, I'd like to go home and revise my outfit,' she mused, chewing her nails at the expense of the polish she had apparently 'borrowed' from me earlier in the day.

'OK,' I said, thinking she couldn't possibly have an even tighter pair of jeans to pour herself into. 'That's fine. I'll go and grab my car keys.'

'So now you're trying to get rid of me?'

I looked at her and sighed. She may have been good fun and fast becoming a great friend, but she could also be infuriating.

'Of course I'm not.'

'Well, that's good,' she said, with a wink. 'Because when I make friends with someone they don't ever get rid of me, it's for life.'

In spite of her attempts to wind me up, I was really rather pleased about that.

In keeping with my Wynthorpe routine, early the next morning I pulled on my trainers and headed out into the crisp, frosty air. It was a solitary pursuit that particular day as Floss simply refused to budge and consequently I decided to go a little further and risk a run through the woods, avoiding the witch's house, of course.

Unfortunately, however, I didn't manage to find either the Wishing Tree or the circle of beech trees where Mick and I had gathered logs, but I did add what felt like a couple of extra kilometres to my distance as I got hopelessly lost for a while and ended up, quite literally, running around in circles.

When I finally found my way back to the hall, and was cursing Dorothy and her extra calories which no doubt accounted for my lack of puff, I was surprised to find the Land Rover parked outside the kitchen with the back doors thrown open. I really didn't think I'd been out *that* long and looked down at my muddied trainers in dismay. Sweating, dishevelled and out of breath was not how I had planned to meet any of the Wynthorpe boys, and I wondered if I could possibly somehow sneak in unnoticed.

Given the sudden eruption of voices from the other side of the door, I guessed not.

'So,' began a man's voice I didn't recognise, but which must have been Jamie's. 'Already it starts. I'm barely back over the threshold and you're telling me we have yet more bloody repairs to fund and a Christmas spectacular to finance.'

'But I thought you'd be pleased about everyone coming,' said Angus. He sounded unusually downcast and a little sulky. 'I thought it would be the perfect opportunity to get us all together and finalise everything.'

'And have you talked to Archie about finalising things?'

He didn't wait for his father to answer.

'Because I can tell you right now, Dad, the last time I spoke to him he wasn't very happy that things were still so up in the air.'

'Archie is never happy these days.'

'You know what I mean.'

Angus didn't say anything.

'He's got it in his head that you and Mum are playing favourites, and over this, of all things.'

'But I've told you a thousand times,' said Angus, beginning to sound angry, 'we have no choice. If we don't do it this way, then the family will be in danger of losing everything. *You* know we're right, Jamie, and you know exactly why.'

'Oh, of course I know,' he said, his voice quieter now. 'But that doesn't mean that I'm happy about it. This wasn't how I expected my life to pan out, you know? I thought there'd be more to my existence than – this.'

Obviously I didn't know what 'this' was because I couldn't see through doors and if I had any kind of conscience I wouldn't be listening at keyholes either. I made to walk away but his next words stopped me in my tracks.

'And now you've given us another mouth to feed,' he struck up.

'I think that's a bit strong,' said Angus defensively.

'Another bloody charity case for you and Mum to nurture and mend.'

'Hey, now,' cut in Angus, sounding properly angry. 'You might be tired and fed up, but you can pack that attitude in right now.'

Charity case! I hoped the arrogant sod wasn't talking about me but I had a sinking feeling that he was.

'Tell me why she's here again,' Jamie said in a bolshy tone. 'What's the pretence this time?'

'There is no pretence,' said Angus firmly.

He sounded more than ready to stand his ground, and mine, and I was grateful for that.

'Anna is here to help us organise Christmas.'

I let out a yelp then clapped my hands over my mouth as Floss began to woof.

'Did you hear something?' said Jamie, his voice suddenly far closer to the other side of the door than I was comfortable with.

'No,' said Angus. 'Be quiet, Floss. As I was saying, Anna has great experience and fabulous references.'

That was true. I was very proud of my professional portfolio. I had taken years putting it together, but I had absolutely no experience when it came to organising a country-house Christmas and I had no idea why Angus was so insistent that I had. Why didn't he just tell his son that I was there to support and take care of his mother? And collect wood. And bake cheese straws. And assist Hayley with the dusting. What exactly was my job title again?

'Look, Dad,' said Jamie, 'I don't care whether she organised the last royal wedding – we can't afford a bloody party planner.'

Party planner!

'But we need someone who can—'

What he was going to say next was lost as I heard Catherine shouting excitedly that her baby was finally home and Dorothy sobbing in the background. I ran a sweaty hand over my bumpy ponytail and let out a breath I didn't realise I'd been holding. I had no idea what was going on, but I was bitterly disappointed that just when I'd decided that now was the time to 'step into Christmas', as Sir Elton John so succinctly put it, I was out in the cold – again.

'What's with the outfit?' asked Hayley, wrinkling her nose as she climbed in the passenger seat of my car and flung her bag in the back.

'Nothing,' I shrugged.

'And the perfume,' she choked. 'It reeks in here.'

I looked over my shoulder, ready to pull back on to the road.

'Are they back?' she squealed, making my foot slip off the clutch. 'Is he home already?'

'Yes,' I sighed. 'He's home.'

'Give me thirty seconds,' she said, leaping out of the car again and across the pavement.

What I actually ended up giving her was seven minutes and thirty-nine seconds. When she had sent me a text with directions as to where to pick her up I hadn't expected her to leave me stranded on double yellows and fretting about getting a parking ticket.

'Where the hell did you go?' I demanded, when she eventually came back wearing an even tighter pair of jeans and an even smaller sweater. 'I was worried I was going to get a ticket.'

'I ran home,' she said, blushing profusely. 'Having taken one look at you, I decided to change yet again and you can keep it buttoned, Miss Woodruff,' she added, pointing a freshly painted violet nail in my face, 'because you haven't looked like that since the day you arrived, so pot and kettle springs to mind.'

She was right of course. When everything had gone quiet back in the kitchen I'd slipped inside, up the stairs, and spent a ridiculously long time over my morning ablutions before heading back to town to collect little Miss Tight Fit 2017.

'But you disappeared,' I said, looking about me and knowing there was no point arguing the point. 'And this isn't anywhere near where I dropped you off last night. Where did you go?'

'Home.'

'I gathered that,' I said crossly. 'But where exactly is home?'

'Oh I don't live on this road,' she said, buckling up. 'I just thought it would be easier for you to park here. I'm on the estate. There's no way I'd let you see my place.'

'At least you have a place,' I muttered.

'Believe me,' she said, 'you really wouldn't want my place.'

'Well, if it's that bad why don't you move into the hall?'

She looked at me and chewed her lip.

'Now's not the time,' she said eventually. 'But I will tell you why one day. Now, come on, what did you think?'

'What did I think about what?'

'Jamie, of course!'

'I haven't seen him,' I admitted.

'So, what's with the heels and eyeliner then?' she pounced, clearly not believing a word. 'That's a ridiculously precise line for someone who's pretending they haven't made any effort.'

'I didn't say I hadn't made any effort.'

I had made an effort. I'd made a huge effort, but not because I was out to impress my boss's son. I had gone to so much trouble because I suddenly felt I needed to put my emotional armour back in place and that a professional demeanour, outfit and attitude would supply me with just what I needed to get me through my first, and quite possibly last, encounter with the prodigal son. I didn't know why Angus had lied about what I was really doing at the hall, but if I was going to be challenged, then I was determined to be as prepared as I could be to face whatever Mr Connelly Jr decided to throw at me.

'Let's just say I've heard him then,' I said to Hayley, 'and if his face matches his attitude, then you're welcome to him.'

'Fair enough,' said Hayley, with a sly grin. 'I'll hold you to that.'

Back at the hall there was no sign of Jamie, Catherine or Mick, but Dorothy was fussing over the preparations for brunch and Angus was fiddling about with the Advent calendar.

'Morning, Angus,' I said, ready to cover my tracks. 'What

time did you all get back? I saw the Land Rover parked up when I went to pick Hayley up from town.'

I didn't want him to have any inkling that I had overheard the heated exchange when I came back from my run until I was ready to let him know.

'Good morning,' he smiled, 'good morning. Jamie managed to get an overnight flight in the end, but we didn't ring to say we were on our way because it was ridiculously early.'

'You'll all be ready for an early night tonight then?'

'Indeed we will,' he agreed, stifling a yawn. 'Mick especially as he did all the driving. My goodness, don't you look smart? Now where's Hayley?'

'She's no doubt checking her make-up,' said Dorothy, while trying to juggle two pans and a pile of plates.

'I would offer to help,' I said in passing, 'but I'm only here to plan Christmas.'

Angus looked up so sharply I was afraid he was going to pull a muscle.

'What was that, Anna dear?' he asked.

'I was just saying, did Catherine tell you that I've decided to stay on for Christmas?'

'Yes,' he said, looking to my mind relieved. 'Yes, she did and I'm so pleased. We all are.'

I raised an eyebrow in his direction, but he didn't say anything else. Even if he had really caught the gist of what

I had said he obviously wasn't prepared to give me a heads-up as to what was going on before we were all gathered together.

'There,' said Dorothy, taking a step back and looking well pleased, 'all done. Now, would you go and rally the troops please, Anna? I think Catherine and Jamie are in the morning room.'

Chapter 9

I'd never been an advocate of eavesdropping, but it seemed I had suddenly developed something of a talent for it. I was just about to knock on the door of the morning room to say that brunch was ready when Jamie's voice struck up again and his tone suggested that he was in no better temper than when I had heard him arguing with his father earlier.

'Are you absolutely mad?' I heard him say. 'Do you really expect me to do this without any further discussion?'

'No,' said Catherine calmly, 'I'm not mad. Although I have every right to be, given the sleepless nights and heartache I've endured since you upped and left.'

'I didn't just up and leave,' was Jamie's defensive response. 'I had to get away to think things through and I had things I had to do.'

'But if you'd stayed,' retaliated Catherine, 'we could have

117

talked. You could have put a stop to this ridiculous idea and his pig-headed assumption that it was all going to go in his favour far sooner.'

I wondered if they were talking about Angus and one of his schemes. If they were, it certainly sounded like a big deal, far bigger than the toad-like hobbies and obsessions the women at The Cherry Tree Café had hinted at the day I arrived in town.

'And anyway,' Catherine continued, 'I was under the impression that you had come back because you had decided to go ahead. I was planning to ring David Miller next week. I didn't think there was going to be any need for further discussion.'

'I had made up my mind,' said Jamie. He sounded tired now. 'Still have really. I just didn't expect to come back and find another employee had been installed and there would be yet more wages to pay.'

At least he hadn't called me a charity case this time.

'And from what I can make out about this one—'

I didn't want to hear another word. I had had it proved already that morning that no good came from listening at keyholes and decided it wasn't an occupation I would be making a habit of. I knocked sharply on the door.

'In a minute,' Jamie snapped.

'What is it, dear?' asked Catherine, her face appearing around the frame.

'Dorothy asked me to tell you that she's ready to serve brunch.'

Back in the kitchen Dorothy was fussing over the table and Hayley was hoisting up her jeans. I was amazed there was any room for manoeuvre inside them at all and couldn't imagine she could get a great deal of work done while wearing them. Surely all her efforts for the day would have to be concentrated on just breathing? I was going to be interested to see how much she managed to eat without splitting her seams.

'Anna, my love,' said Dorothy, as we all stood around waiting for Catherine and Jamie. 'Would you go and fetch the extra side plates from next to the dishwasher, please? I seem to have cooked rather a lot and I don't think we'll be able to manage without them.'

I was more than happy to escape the tense expectation oozing from Hayley, if only for a few seconds, and strained my ears to hear if Jamie was going to be more enthusiastic in front of the adoring staff about his return home than he was whilst moaning to his parents.

It was immediately obvious when he had walked into the room because Hayley began to giggle like a besotted fangirl and insisted on delivering what sounded like a well-placed kiss. Her silly simpering was ridiculously unprofessional but it was also typical Hayley: honest, open and spontaneous. Truth be told, I felt a little jealous of her ability to wear her heart so unashamedly on her sleeve.

'You,' she gushed, and I could imagine her standing with her hands on her shapely hips, 'look amazing.'

'And you,' Jamie laughed back, sounding nothing like the borderline aggressive specimen I had been covertly listening to all morning, 'have to stop stealing my lines.'

'Huh,' said Hayley, sounding a muddled mix of blasé and flattered. 'If only I could get a tan like that from two weeks sunning myself in Skegness. Tell me, where is it that you've been again?'

'Never mind that now,' said Dorothy, clearly put out that she had to wait in line, even though she had already seen him once that morning. 'What about another kiss for me then?'

Once the gushing and mutually beneficial appraisals had died down, everyone took their seats at the table and I realised I had been loitering in the shadows far longer than I had intended. It had been my plan to slip in under the radar, but now it was too late and I would have to make a far more noticeable entrance.

'Anna dear,' called Dorothy, when she noticed I still wasn't there, 'have you found those plates?'

I took a deep breath, pinched some colour into my cheeks (an action I almost immediately regretted), picked up the required crockery and walked into the kitchen. Flanked by Catherine on one side and Hayley, who I was sure was trying to squeeze her way onto his lap, on the other, Jamie's eyes flicked up to meet mine and that was when it happened.

Do you remember that moment in *Four Weddings* when ever-so-posh Tom spots very-distant-cousin Deirdre, and declares the fluttering in his heart and head are the result of Thunderbolt City? Yes? Well, multiply that by ten, add a sack full of butterflies and a steam train at full stretch churning around your stomach, and you'll have some idea as to why I hadn't needed to pinch my cheeks at all.

Clumsily I banged the plates on the table, making everyone else look up, and Jamie jumped to his feet, his intense green eyes never leaving my face. He wasn't all that much taller than me and not at all like the man I had imagined courtesy of the monochrome photograph Catherine had shown me in the morning room or from the querulous voice I had heard.

'Thank you, dear,' Dorothy tutted, snatching the plates back up and inspecting them for cracks. 'No harm done.'

Out of the corner of my eye I could see Hayley tapping her hand on her heart and fluttering her eyelashes, but I didn't take any notice. I didn't do anything. I just stood there like a fool, my gaze locked on most definitely the loveliest-looking man I had ever seen. It wasn't just the intense eyes, the abundant freckles and the foppish hair that was in need of a trim, or the tan, although that was all more than enough to be going on with. No, there was a whole lot more happening than that.

I had never held much truck with the idea of love at first

121

sight – surely when people championed that, what they really meant was 'lust at first sight', wasn't it? But suddenly I wasn't so convinced. What I was sure of, however, was that I'd never before just glanced at someone and felt like this in my entire life which, considering how much he despised my presence, how defensive I felt about being labelled a 'charity case' and how determined I was to set the record straight, was a huge inconvenience. It was a gargantuan pain in the backside, actually.

'Jamie,' said Angus, finally realising that introductions were going to be necessary, 'this is Anna. Anna, this is Jamie.'

'Anna,' said Jamie softly, 'I'm pleased to meet you.'

Ever since I'd heard him arguing with Angus earlier I'd been poised to bite back with something pithy and professional when we were finally in each other's company, but hearing him say my name had turned my knees to jelly and my insides to mush. It was pathetic and improper and completely beyond my control.

'Likewise,' I smiled.

Forcibly I dragged my recently abandoned go-to alter ego back out to play her part and let the real me collapse on the sidelines to take a breather.

'I know you have been missed here very much,' I went on in a more clipped and formal tone. 'How was the final part of your journey home in the end?'

I sat down carefully in my seat and waited for an answer.

'Jamie,' Catherine hissed when he didn't say anything, but kept staring, 'do sit down. We're waiting to start.'

'Sorry,' he mumbled, looking confused as he bumped back down on his chair and blinked a few times before clearing his throat. 'It was OK, Anna, thanks. A bit around the houses, but I'm here now.'

'Excellent,' I nodded, while trying to ignore more of Hayley's wild gesturing in the background. 'Great.'

I have absolutely no recollection of what we ate for that meal, but given Dorothy's usually delicious fare I can only imagine that it was wonderful and that there would have been plenty of it. Angus had uncorked a couple of bottles of champagne and we all enjoyed a glass, except for Mick, who stuck to mineral water and gave me a conspiratorial wink when no one was looking.

'So,' said Jamie, as Dorothy stacked plates and handed out the coffee cups. He didn't sound anywhere near as confrontational now as he had when talking about me earlier, 'Dad tells me you're here for Christmas, Anna.'

Technically that was true. I was staying for Christmas, I just wasn't organising it. I was sure I saw a quick glance pass from one end of the table to the other and imagined Angus holding his breath.

'Yes,' I said, 'that's right. I'm here for Christmas.'

Was that a slight exhalation I heard?

'I daresay you'll find the festive set-up here a little different to what you're used to,' Jamie continued.

Also true, given that I always went to such lengths to avoid all things Christmas-related.

'And talking of Christmas,' said Catherine, just as Hayley was about to pipe up and no doubt put her size fives firmly in it, 'your father has had a wonderful idea.'

'Another one?' said Jamie, still looking at me. 'Well I hope this one's cheaper but no less cheerful than the last.'

'He thinks it's about time we reinstated the Solstice celebration,' Catherine continued.

'Really?' Jamie said, looking at his father, his beautiful emerald eyes wide in surprise.

I wasn't at all surprised by his response. I had already assumed that he would hate the idea of more people descending when he had only just arrived back from his travels.

'Actually I always thought it was a shame you gave in and put a stop to it,' he shocked me by saying, before more predictably adding, 'but I'm not sure, what with everything else we still have to sort, that this is the right year to start it up again. I know how things snowball here and if we're not careful you'll be telling me next that you're planning to host the local panto.'

'The panto,' said Hayley excitedly, 'now that's an even better idea than the Solstice celebration. I've never really

124

been a fan of traipsing about the woods on the darkest day of the year.'

Clearly she was yet to reconnect with her Pagan side, but I had started to look forward to searching for the Yule log and listening to tales around the fire.

'I don't know about the pantomime,' said Catherine. 'I think organising the Solstice will be enough for us to be going on with for now and we really are very keen.'

I was further surprised that Jamie was prepared to give in without more of an argument.

'Well in that case, I shouldn't worry too much about it, Mum,' he smiled, reaching for her hand and squeezing it. 'If we really are going to host it, I think Mother Nature has the nuts and bolts of the occasion pretty much covered.'

Hayley snorted inelegantly and turned puce.

'And we're also thinking of asking the ramblers back,' said Angus, keen to share all of his ideas at once now he knew Jamie was in a more agreeable mood, 'and the library group.'

'And the WI,' added Dorothy.

This was surprising news, and as well as wondering why it had all stopped in the first place, I was also curious as to what had prompted the change of heart.

'Well I never,' said Jamie, looking and sounding even more shocked. 'And there was me thinking Archie was going to have his own way for ever. What does he have to say about all this?'

Clearly the recent goings-on, or not, at the hall had been under the influence of one brother more than any other and it certainly wasn't the one sitting opposite me.

'He doesn't know,' said Mick meaningfully.

Jamie nodded and drained his glass of champagne.

'Well, that'll be something to look forward to discussing over the turkey then,' he said, with something like relish. 'I hope you've warned Anna just what's in store now the clan have been called together.'

Neither Catherine nor Angus said anything and I wondered again what was *really* going on behind the scenes at Wynthorpe Hall. Everything had been jogging along smoothly enough when I arrived, but throwing the three brothers into the mix was obviously going to stir things up a bit.

'Be prepared for pistols at dawn,' Jamie said, looking deep into my eyes again, 'recriminations and accusations.'

'You make Christmas with the Connellys sound like a dodgy fly-on-the-wall docu-soap,' I replied.

'Christmas with the Connellys,' he said, biting his lip. 'I like the sound of that. How do you fancy being in charge of the filming, Hayley?'

'I'd rather be in front of the camera, thanks,' she huffed.

'Of course you would,' he said, throwing his arm around her shoulders and giving her a consolation squeeze.

She went an even brighter shade of red and was straight back to her bouncy self.

'But all joking aside,' he said, turning his attention back to his parents, 'I might have disagreed with Archie on practically every single point he's made recently, but he was right about the public liability situation.'

Angus began to shuffle in his seat.

'Please,' said Jamie, appealing to his father. 'Please tell me that you now have a policy in place and that we aren't still in the vulnerable state we were before my dear brother took it upon himself to shut this place down.'

'Shut this place down?' I questioned. 'Was it actually open to the public then?'

The thought of the hall being officially open with no insurance made my heart skip a beat and it had nothing to do with Jamie's fabulous freckles.

'Not formally,' said Jamie. 'There were no guided tours or coach parties or anything.'

'It was all much simpler than that,' explained Catherine. 'And much the same as we'd like it to be again now that Jamie—' she stopped herself from saying whatever was coming next. 'A space for the WI and other local groups to meet and hold events that can't be accommodated in town,' she said instead, repeating what had already been suggested. 'That sort of thing.'

'So did Archie make you shut things down before because he thought the hall, and the family, was vulnerable with no insurance?' I asked, curious to hear the whole story.

'It looked that way for a while,' said Jamie evasively, 'but his real motives for enforcing the changes have come to light now. But they don't really matter,' he quickly added.

I wished they did because I was itching to find out the back story of what was sounding more and more like an intriguing family feud.

'But as you've decided to go against what he wants, Mum and Dad, please tell me you have something sorted and aren't going to give him the satisfaction of seeing us sued for the final few pennies we have in the bank?'

It was obvious to me, even though I didn't know the details, that Jamie had left home to travel the world with more of a justification than wanderlust and that he had come back now for a very specific reason. I hoped I wouldn't have to wait too long before I found out what it was.

I fiddled with my napkin and sat quietly wondering if this intimate conversation would have been happening were it not for the tongue-loosening effects of the fizz, then I remembered we were at Wynthorpe Hall and realised yes, it probably would. Jamie, not unlike his parents, clearly viewed those around the table as his extended family, even the new-girl party planner sitting opposite him.

'No,' said Angus. 'We don't need it.'

'Yes,' shot back Catherine. 'We do.'

Angus shook his head.

'No one who's going to be coming here would sue us,'

he said firmly. 'Everyone will be local and grateful that we're opening our doors again. This place has always been inclusive and generous; you know that better than anyone, my dear. Look at the parties your grandparents used to give.'

'But the world is a different place now,' said Catherine.

'Where there's blame, there's a claim,' Hayley added helpfully.

'And besides,' said Catherine, 'we do have a policy.'

'Since when?' frowned Angus.

'Since I insisted that you should have one,' I chipped in. 'The day you suggested inviting people back to celebrate the Solstice I set one up.'

'And at my behest,' said Catherine firmly.

Jamie looked from his parents to me and smiled.

'Not bad,' he said, 'not bad at all, Miss Woodruff.'

'Not bad for a party planner,' I shot back.

Fortunately Angus didn't appear to have heard.

'So much for trying to save money!' he grunted. 'What a waste.'

'You should talk to Mr Brooke, Angus,' said Mick sternly. 'You'd soon change your mind on that score then.'

'What's Mr Brooke got to do with our dwindling bank balance?' asked Angus.

Mick then went on to explain how Mr Brooke, who sounded like a local nuisance by all accounts, had been awarded over five thousand pounds for injuries incurred while he was trespassing on a neighbouring farmer's land. Angus went very quiet after that.

'Come on,' said Dorothy, trying to lighten the mood. 'Let's see who gets to open the Advent calendar today.'

'I'm guessing this is one of your finds, Dad?' said Jamie, looking over at the wall. 'Who kicked things off yesterday?'

'I had that particular honour,' I said.

'Because we didn't know if she was staying or not,' Hayley unhelpfully butted in. 'So your dad made sure she got in early.'

The girl really was a liability.

'But why would you employ someone to organise Christmas if they weren't going to be here for Christmas?' frowned Jamie.

'She's not here to organise Christmas,' Hayley's dulcet tones rang out again.

'What?'

'Looks like you're up today,' I quickly cut in before disaster struck. 'Your dad has gone to so much trouble. I can't wait to see what he's found for you.'

Jamie looked at his mother for a moment and his stern expression suggested that he was going to get to the bottom of whatever it was that Hayley was talking about just as soon as he could.

'I had a music box,' I babbled on. 'It plays the tune my mum always used to sing when she was baking at Christmas. *Silver Bells* was her absolute favourite.'

'Used to sing,' said Dorothy, picking up on what I had said in my panic to bail Catherine out. 'Was her favourite, my dear – isn't it any more?'

'She died,' I said quietly, amazed that I could share something so private, so monumental in such an informal moment.

'Come on then, lad,' said Mick quickly before anyone had a chance to comment or sympathise. 'Let's see what you've got.'

Personally, the vintage black and mother of pearl Conway Stewart pen Jamie unwrapped didn't mean anything to me, but he nodded, with something akin to resignation, when he saw it and Catherine looked extremely bright-eyed.

'I thought it would be just the thing,' said Angus. 'It's not all that dissimilar to the one your mother used, is it, dear?'

'No,' she sniffed, 'it isn't.'

'Well, in that case, Mum,' Jamie sighed, 'you better make that call.'

Chapter 10

As soon as the kitchen was set to rights – well, as right as the kitchen at Wynthorpe Hall ever was – I asked to have a moment with Catherine on the pretence of looking through the Christmas planning schedule.

'I know what you're going to say,' she said, the second I closed the morning room door. 'I know exactly what you're going to say.'

'Well,' I said, smoothing down my skirt and feeling determined to stop my professional persona from slipping again. 'Let me say it anyway, just to make sure we really are on the same wavelength.'

Catherine nodded.

'Why does Jamie think I'm here to organise Christmas?' I demanded of her. 'Especially now you know full well that my real reason, my sole motive in fact, for coming here was to avoid anything to do with tinsel and turkey.'

Catherine sat down heavily on the sofa.

'Jamie doesn't know I've had an operation,' she said quietly, with a surreptitious glance towards the closed door. 'He knows nothing about the fact that I've been in hospital at all.'

'But why ever not?' I frowned, bumping down next to her. Her surprising admission had knocked the air right out of my annoyance. 'Surely he would want to know about something like that, even if he was on the other side of the world when it was happening?'

'Of course he would,' she continued, 'which is the very reason why we decided not to tell him.'

'I don't understand.'

'If he knew,' she said in a furtive whisper, 'that either Angus or I was unwell he would have been home on the first available flight.'

'And that would have been a problem because?'

'Because,' she sighed, 'it was important that he stayed away until he was ready to come back.'

'Even though you were sick?'

'I wasn't exactly sick.'

I looked at her and raised my eyebrows.

'When Jamie left,' she went on, having guessed that I was in no way satisfied with the unfathomable explanation she had made so far, 'he left in a rush, under something of a cloud and with a huge decision to make. I can't talk about what that decision was just yet, but it was paramount that he was left to his own devices to make it, and the last thing Angus or I wanted was to put our boy under any pressure or obligation to come back until he was absolutely ready to do so.'

'I hardly think he would have felt an obligation,' I interrupted. 'If he had come back, it would have been out of concern. Surely, he had a right to know? What if something had gone wrong and he wasn't here?'

What I felt about the situation hardly mattered, but the fact that I had been drawn into the deception did. There was no way I was going to be able to play the part of the festive party planner Jamie was expecting. I wouldn't do it, I actually couldn't do it, and as fond as I already was of Catherine and Angus, the hall and everyone else, I was not prepared to put myself through the stresses and strains of trying to bluff my way through the next few weeks playing a part I hadn't even auditioned for.

I had only just come to terms with the idea that Mum was trying to let me know that it was all right to let Christmas back into my life. I had only just come round to the idea of staying on at the hall and trying to dig up my festive feelings and lay my ghosts to rest. I certainly didn't need to try and fit someone else's notion of what I was supposed to be.

'But nothing did go wrong,' shrugged Catherine. 'And besides, he's home now. His decision has been made and we can share the news when everyone arrives and hopefully enjoy spending the holidays together.'

I couldn't fail to notice the edge of uncertainty that seemed to slip into her voice whenever 'getting everyone together' cropped up in conversation or the fact that she had included the word 'hopefully' in her sentence. Whatever this decision was that Jamie had made it sounded gargantuan – life-changing possibly – and not only for him.

'And anyway,' she asked, 'how did you find out that that's what Jamie thinks you're here to do?'

'I overheard him and Angus arguing early this morning,' I said truthfully, 'and I saw the two of you panic when you thought either Hayley or I were going to let the cat out of the bag just now.'

'I see,' she said. 'Well, I'm sorry.'

'It's all right,' I said, 'I sort of understand why you didn't want to tell him the truth at first, but if you would like me to stay here for the next few weeks I really do need you to set the record straight.'

Catherine looked aghast.

'I don't want to go anywhere else now,' I told her. 'And I really do want to be here to help out with Christmas and I know I have absolutely no right to make demands, but I can't have Jamie thinking organising everything is down to me. The pressure would be too much. I'm sorry. I just can't do it.'

'No,' said Catherine, shaking her head. 'I'm sorry. We should never have put you in this position. I'll talk to him. I promise.'

'Good,' I said, breathing a sigh of relief.

'But not yet.'

'What?'

'I'm sorry, Anna,' she said. 'I really am, but if you could just give us a couple of days. Give Jamie time to get over his journey and then I'm sure he would take the news better. I promise we'll talk to him in a day or so.'

Personally I couldn't see how waiting was going to make the situation any better, but what choice did I have? Having only just decided I was going to stay I had nowhere else to go, nowhere to hide.

'And what am I supposed to do in the meantime?' I asked.

'Just play along,' she begged. 'He probably won't be out of his room much and he certainly won't be scrutinising what you're doing.'

Had either of us known just how wrong her prediction was we would have come up with a very different plan. One that would most probably have involved me running for the hills.

That afternoon Dorothy went back to baking, Mick and Angus to stacking the log pile and Hayley the vacuuming, although how in those jeans of hers, I have absolutely no idea. Jamie had disappeared in the direction of the stable block for a while, but came back muttering darkly about needing to talk to his mother and that he wasn't sure it was all going to work out after all.

Sitting at the kitchen table, ostensibly working with Dorothy (who along with Hayley and Mick was now very much in the know about my party planner facade) on the endless to-do lists that would make life easier and the whole Christmas extravaganza a success, our eyes followed Jamie's broad back as he headed through the kitchen in search of Catherine.

'So,' said Dorothy, with a nod to where he had disappeared. 'What do you think?'

'I think,' I thought about saying, 'that he's the most delicious hunk of manhood I have ever clapped eyes on. That I wish I had Hayley's ability to flirt, the guts to ask him out and a peephole between our rooms so I could watch him sleeping.'

What I actually said was, 'About what?'

'Jamie, of course,' Dorothy winked. 'Isn't he a sight for sore eyes?'

'Dorothy!' I laughed. 'My goodness me.'

'Well, I'm sorry, dear, but any woman, or man for that matter, with eyes in their head, whatever their age, would be lying if they said otherwise.'

She wasn't wrong, but I had no intention of encouraging her.

'I've known the boys since they were little,' she continued, 'and they're all handsome lads, but young James is definitely the pick of the bunch.'

I could hardly believe my ears. She was no doubt completely right of course, but it was a shock to hear straight-laced, apron-toting, grey-haired Dorothy say as much.

'And I daresay beautiful women everywhere just fall at his feet, don't they?' I sighed.

'Of course,' she said wistfully, 'but he isn't much interested in them and the kind of women he does like always seem to find him a bit intimidating. They fully expect him to know how handsome he is and therefore assume he'll be an arrogant bugger as a result.'

From what I'd seen and heard so far, I didn't think he was particularly arrogant but I did think his attitude would be improved by a night or two in his own bed.

'And of course, when they find out how down to earth he really is and then about this place ...'

Her voice trailed off as footsteps approached along the corridor.

'I'm going to run Hayley home in a bit,' Jamie said, his face suddenly appearing around the door.

'All right, dear,' smiled Dorothy, completely unfazed by the fact that we had almost been caught red-handed. 'She's still Hoovering somewhere, I think.'

'OK,' he nodded. 'In that case this is probably the perfect opportunity for you and me to have a chat, Anna,' he surprised me by saying. 'I think we need to get a few things sorted.'

'All right,' I squeaked as Dorothy winked. 'Absolutely.'

'And you might want to bring your paperwork with you,' he said with a nod to the scrappy lists on the table. 'The sooner we get organising this mad Christmas Dad's so keen on, the better.'

Had I realised just how wrong Catherine was going to be about how much interest Jamie was going take in my clumsy efforts to organise Christmas I would have repacked my bags and resigned with immediate effect. However, my loyalty towards both her and Angus meant that I struggled on as best as I could but by the end of the second day I was ready to throttle their youngest son.

'You know,' he said, shaking his head and throwing my hastily cobbled-together Christmas folder on the table, 'I can't make you out.'

'Oh,' I said, trying my best to smile as I gathered up the papers and magazine clippings yet again.

'Mm,' he mused. 'For a so-called party planner who specialises in Christmas you are woefully lacking in contacts and ideas.'

I bit my lip and threw Catherine another exasperated look. My expression had been nothing other than pleading when turned in her direction all day, but she still hadn't taken the bait.

'You aren't what I thought you'd be at all.'

'And what did you think I was going to be?' I asked through gritted teeth.

'Well to be honest, when I first clapped eyes on you, what

with your designer outfit and professional image, I thought you'd be as much substance as you were style, but from what I've seen so far you seem to be bluffing it.'

If only he knew!

'My initial assumption was that you'd have this family Christmas competently sewn up within hours – although thinking about it,' he went on, fixing me with his hypnotic emerald gaze, 'I don't know why Mum thought Dorothy wouldn't be able to handle things.'

'Perhaps you should ask her?' I suggested, wanting to put an end to his soliloquy and get back to some sort of normality.

I'd seen enough boxes of posh Christmas crackers and personalised cards to last me a lifetime and for someone who for so long had hated the season with such a passion I was fast reaching my limit. I twisted around in my chair but Catherine had made a hasty exit.

'But why trouble her,' Jamie said, following my gaze, 'when I can just ask you? How have you really wheedled your way in here?'

I turned my attention back to my notepad.

'What are your real intentions, Anna Woodruff?' he pushed on, his face thrust closer to mine. 'Are you here for the family jewels or have you somehow secured yourself a too-good-to-be-true salary in return for blowing up a few balloons?'

I licked my lips but kept them buttoned. Not a bad effort for someone under such provocation.

'You're no party planner, are you?' he demanded, louder this time. 'You don't know one end of a Merry Christmas from another.'

He'd certainly got that right. I blinked away my tears as his words hit their mark. Deep down I knew he was only trying to protect his family but his way of going about it had a very keen sting. It was ironic that we were both running along the same rails and both had the Connelly family interests at heart. I hoped it wouldn't be too much longer before he was made aware of that.

'Jamie,' Catherine suddenly called from the hallway, 'I think you'd better come with me. And Anna dear, take the rest of the day off.'

Her words were music to my assaulted ears.

Later that day Jamie insisted that I join him when it was time to drive Hayley back to town. She didn't say much during the journey. Relegated to the back of the Land Rover while I sat in the passenger seat, I daresay she was feeling rather put out that I had hijacked her spot and her one opportunity to have Jamie to herself in such a confined space.

'Mick said he'll come and get you in the morning,' said Jamie as he jumped out to open her door on the stretch of road where I had picked her up before.

'OK,' she said, 'thanks for the lift. I'll see you tomorrow – and Anna,' she called out to me, 'watch your step.'

For a mad moment I thought she was threatening me, warning me off her hunky turf.

'It's icy out here,' she grinned, pointing down to the pavement. 'I'd hate to see you turn your ankle in those heels.'

Laughing, she stuck out her tongue, spun round and swaggered off in the direction of what I guessed was home.

Jamie managed to find a parking space in the market square quite close to The Mermaid pub, but surprised me by insisting on taking my arm until we were safely over the threshold. I could feel the pressure of his taut muscles and the heat from his body melding into mine and silently congratulated myself for not falling at his feet in a dead faint. He might have spent the last two days taunting and offending me but he still had one hot bod.

I knew it was ridiculous to be feeling like this at my age and my cheeks glowed with embarrassment. I was allegedly of sound mind and not known for taking off on romantic, or lustful, flights of fancy. I reminded myself that I was still wearing my work clothes and as such should be capable of playing the role of the professional I had taken so much time and trouble to perfect.

'Why don't you find us a table,' Jamie suggested, his voice raised above the noise of the other customers, who were enjoying the beginnings of a night in the pub, 'and I'll get the drinks?'

'OK,' I nodded. 'Thanks. I'll have a Coke please.'

'Diet?'

'No thanks,' I shrugged. 'There's not much point when Dorothy's in charge of what I eat.'

Jamie laughed and pushed his way through to the bar. It was impossible not to notice the heads that turned in his direction or the number of people who stopped to slap him on the back and welcome him home. The most vocal was the landlord.

'In case you didn't hear, first drinks are on the house,' Jamie grinned, when he eventually found me. 'Courtesy of Jim and Evelyn.'

'That's very kind,' I acknowledged, raising my glass in thanks towards the bar and the eager faces watching our every move. 'So,' I said, turning my attention back to the green eyes and freckles, 'what is it you wanted to talk about? Isn't it about time you accused me of rifling through the family silver cabinet?'

Jamie readjusted his jacket and inched his chair closer to the fire.

'I'd forgotten how cold winter in Wynbridge can be,' he said, ignoring my snarky comment and blowing on his fingers. 'And I've only missed one.'

'It certainly does seem to be a few degrees colder here than everywhere else,' I admitted, already regretting what I'd said.

'I think it's the flatness of the landscape. It lets the wind do its worst without having anything to check it. Most days I've resorted to piling on the layers.'

'But not today,' he said with a nod to my stockings, heels and slim-fitting skirt.

'No,' I blushed, crossing my legs, 'not today.'

'For the last couple of days you've thought you should dress for the role my parents had led me to believe you had come to the hall to take up.'

'Yes,' I said, as I realised that Catherine had finally taken my pleading looks to heart and come clean about her surgery. 'Something like that, although sometimes the work I do does require me to dress up, rather than down.'

I felt the colour deepen in my cheeks. That hadn't come out quite how I planned it to and Jamie raised his eyebrows.

'If I'm employed as a PA, for example,' I explained.

'But not, I suspect, when you're working as a carer or companion.'

'No,' I agreed, 'in my capacity as carer and companion I can usually get away with no heels.'

'So why did you agree to play along?' he asked. 'Were you trying to impress me?'

'Not at all,' I said defensively. He raised his eyebrows again and I went on, determined he shouldn't get the wrong idea. 'I heard you and your dad arguing in the kitchen the morning you arrived home. I heard him telling you that I was at the hall to organise Christmas and I thought it would be in everyone's best interests not to contradict him.'

'So you weren't aware that no one had mentioned Mum's surgery to me?'

'Not then,' I said. 'I had no idea.'

'Well it was very loyal of you to play along for Dad's sake, and Mum's.'

'I know I've hardly been at the hall any time at all,' I told him, 'but I already feel very attached to the place and the people in it. Your parents have been very kind to me and I appreciate that.'

'They're always kind to everyone,' he smiled.

'So I understand.'

His smile faltered as it dawned on him what else I might have heard.

'I'm sorry I called you a charity case,' he said, the colour rising in his cheeks. 'I'm guessing you did hear that part of the conversation as well.'

Now it was his turn to squirm, because from what I'd heard it had hardly been a 'conversation'.

'It's all right,' I said, taking another sip of my drink and thinking there was nothing to be gained from gloating. 'Let's just put that one down to jetlag, shall we?'

'That's very generous of you,' he nodded. 'I appreciate your understanding, Anna, and the fact that you've let me off the hook so easily, especially as I'd already been stuck in Europe for a couple of days and got my head around the change in time zones. I can't justify my behaviour or any of the mean things I said to you at all.'

'Well, let's just leave it then,' I laughed. 'Crossed wires can be a devil to untangle so let's just forget about them, shall we? You know now that I'm here to help your mum convalesce.'

'And you know that I'm back home after spending some time in the far-flung corners of the globe.'

'And have made a massive decision whilst being there,' I added for good measure.

A shadow fell across his face.

'Has anyone told you what that decision was?' he asked.

'No,' I said, my voice catching in my throat. 'Has your mum told you why I was adamant I didn't want to play the role of party planner?'

'No,' he said, eyeing me over the top of his glass. 'Do you think we should share?'

I didn't particularly want to spell out why I had struggled to make the decision as to whether I should stay or go once I had discovered what Angus had really got planned for the end of the year at Wynthorpe Hall, but Jamie had only been home a few days and already there had been a muddle. I didn't much like muddles and thought it would probably be best all round if we wiped the slate clean.

'I think,' I therefore reluctantly agreed, 'that might be a very good idea.'

Chapter 11

'I got the drinks,' I said, 'so you go first.'

'That's a bit sneaky,' Jamie frowned, taking the glass I held out. 'If I'd known that's how it was going to be, I would have got the drinks this time too.'

'Too late now,' I shrugged with a sly grin. 'So come on, tell me, why exactly did you leave home and what is this gargantuan decision you had to make?'

Jamie sat back and shook his head. Whatever it was, he still didn't look very happy about it.

'OK,' he began. 'You know I have two brothers, right?'

'Yes,' I said, surreptitiously easing my feet out of my shoes and tucking them under my chair. 'Christopher is the eldest, then there's Archie, then you.'

'Exactly,' he said.

He stared into the fire, the flames eating up his thoughts.

'And,' I encouraged, 'you do know the landlord is going to be calling time in a bit, don't you?'

'All right, Miss Bossy Boots,' he smiled, his eyes slowly moving from the flames to look back at me. 'I'm getting there.'

'Well get there faster,' I nudged.

'OK,' he said, sitting up straighter. 'A while ago Mum decided, quite out of the blue we all felt, that she wanted to sort out, officially, the future of the hall. You do know it belongs to her, don't you?'

'Yes,' I said, 'she did mention it the day I took her for a check-up at the hospital in Norwich.'

I didn't add that she had sounded worried and weighed down by the responsibilities surrounding it or that she had been concerned Angus had been pestering Jamie to make the decision I was now poised to discover.

'Well, we all kind of assumed that it would be going to Christopher,' Jamie continued.

I myself had assumed the very same thing.

'Because he's the eldest, isn't he?' I asked, just to make sure I really did have it all clear in my head.

'Yes, and that's how it's worked in our family for generations. Irrespective of whether the eldest is a girl or a boy, they are always first in line to inherit the hall and the estate.'

'So what happened?' I asked. 'I'm guessing it wasn't all as straightforward as it should have been.'

'Nowhere near,' Jamie sighed, 'because Christopher didn't want it.'

'He didn't want it!' I wanted to laugh out loud. 'Who on earth wouldn't want to inherit Wynthorpe Hall?'

Jamie looked at me as if I was mad and I have to admit I had for a moment forgotten the look of concern Catherine had worn when she told me that she was the current owner of the hall.

Jamie ignored my outburst and carried on with his explanation.

'Chris, his wife Cass and the boys have a wonderful life in Shropshire, close to Cass's family. They love it there and even though Cass said she would move if Christopher really wanted to, he simply refused.'

'Whatever did your parents say?'

'They were shocked. Nothing had ever been mentioned before because it was just sort of assumed that he would step up and take it all on.'

I took a moment to digest the implications of Christopher's unanticipated refusal.

'So then,' I said, 'I'm guessing it fell to Archie to step into the breach.'

Jamie nodded.

'Didn't he want it either?'

'Oh, he wanted it all right,' spat Jamie, his tone loaded with a loathing I found unnerving. 'He couldn't wait to get his hands on the place.'

I had assumed the motive behind Angus's desire to gather the family to the hall at Christmas was because they were all fond of one another but didn't have the opportunity to get together very often. Jamie's mention of Archie, however, didn't sound friendly at all.

'So what was so wrong about that?'

'Let's just say he seemed a little too eager to get the ball rolling,' Jamie went on. 'And after some digging I finally discovered exactly why he was so keen.'

'Go on.'

'Well, as you know he convinced Mum and Dad to stop the public coming and using the hall. He said it was because of public liability issues and goodness knows what else, but it wasn't that at all.'

'What was it then?'

'To put it bluntly,' he said, shaking his head, 'he wanted the place shut down so that, when he'd taken charge, he and his other half could rock up and play lord and lady of the manor with the least possible inconvenience.'

I tried to imagine the middle brother in the photograph arriving and barking out orders to the staff. Based on what he looked like I couldn't imagine him doing it, but if he had it wouldn't have gone down very well, especially with Hayley. I was pretty certain she would have found somewhere interesting to stick her Hoover pipe if anyone attempted to lord it over her.

'Not that that little piece of theatre would have lasted long given the dwindling money, but from what I can make out he had plans to play the role until . . .'

'Until what?' I quizzed when he stopped talking again.

'Until,' he said, sounding even more appalled than before, 'he gave the nod to the person he'd lined up to buy it.'

'No way,' I gasped. 'He wouldn't do that, surely? Your mum told me the hall has been in her family for ever. Why on earth would he want to sell it?'

'For the money, of course,' seethed Jamie. 'Archie has no idea that I know any of this but I've discovered he has one of those health spa chains lined up to step in as soon as he's had enough of the place and has bled the coffers dry.'

'Well, if that doesn't make Christopher change his mind, I don't know what will.'

I couldn't imagine for one second that he would let his family home fall into the hands of the sauna-and-swim, yummy mummy brigade.

'He knows what I've found out,' said Jamie dully. 'And it hasn't made him change his mind at all. He's still adamant he doesn't want the responsibility.'

'Oh,' I said.

I felt as if the wind had been knocked out of my sails.

'I told him everything as soon as I'd had it all confirmed by the person I'd employed to look into Archie's affairs and when he said it made no difference I had to go and tell Mum.'

'She must have been devastated.'

'She was. And that was when she turned to me.'

'You?'

'Yes,' he said, putting his glass on the table and running his hands through his hair. 'Me. She asked me to step up and take the place on.'

'And what do your brothers have to say about that? Are you going to do it?'

My mind was buzzing with even more questions now.

'The others don't know yet,' he said. 'Archie still thinks he's next in line but I daresay Christopher has worked it out. I asked Mum not to say anything until I'd properly made up my mind and I think Dad's got it in his head that if an announcement is made at Christmas everyone, and by everyone I mean Archie, will just accept it because they won't want to upset the applecart.'

'I see.'

'And yes,' he said, reaching into the inside pocket of his jacket and pulling out the pen his father had hidden in the Advent calendar. 'Apparently I am going to do it, even though I don't want to.'

'Your dad gave you the pen to sign the paperwork,' I nodded, the penny dropping.

'Exactly.'

'But why are you so reluctant to take it on?' I asked. 'Listening to you talking about the importance of the insurance policy, it sounded to me as if you want to protect the place just as much as everyone else.'

'Oh I do,' he said. 'I really do, but believe me, Anna, there's a vast difference between feeling protective towards somewhere like Wynthorpe Hall and then finding yourself completely responsible for it. When I was growing up it was my home, a huge part of my life, but I had absolutely no reason to dream up a future for myself that included it and now all that has changed. If I want to keep the hall in the Connelly family I have to let go of the future I crave.'

I hadn't really had a chance yet to think it through from his point of view. To my mind he was just a lucky rich sod who had been handed something absolutely incredible on a plate.

'Don't get me wrong,' he said, 'I love Wynthorpe Hall, but I'm just not sure I'm ready to stagnate in a tiny corner of the East Anglian Fens.'

'So what are you going to do?' I asked. 'Have you really made up your mind that you're going to do it?'

'I have no choice,' he shrugged. 'We can't lose it and if Archie gets his hands on it then that's exactly what will happen.'

His eyes roamed back to the fire and I sat back in my chair and wondered, not for the first time since I arrived in Wynbridge, where the quiet few weeks I had been longing for had disappeared to.

'So what about you?' he said eventually. 'I've told you my side of the saga, now it's your turn. What are you really doing here and why does planning the Connelly family Christmas turn your stomach?'

I shifted uncomfortably in my seat and focused on my glass.

'Hey, come on,' he said. 'Spill, because you're not getting out of here until you do.'

I opened my mouth to say something, I don't know what, but was saved by the bell. Literally.

'Time, folks, please,' bellowed the landlady as she pulled lustily on the big brass bell behind the bar. 'Don't you all have homes to go to?'

'My goodness,' I laughed. 'Exactly how long have we been sitting here?'

Outside, in the market square, it was bitterly cold. The clear, inky sky was studded with thousands of jewel-like stars and the pavements were glistening with frost. As we set off back to the hall I felt my shoulders relax a little as the Land Rover cab gradually began to thaw and relief that I hadn't had to keep my side of the bargain washed over me. However, the snug and slightly smug feeling was short-lived.

'Why are we stopping?' I asked. 'Is there something wrong?'

A few miles out of town Jamie swung off the road, into a field and up onto a concrete pad put there by a farmer.

'No,' he said, pulling on the handbrake and taking the vehicle out of gear. 'Nothing's wrong. I just thought everyone would already be in bed at home and I didn't want to give you the opportunity to wriggle out of sharing on the pretence that you were worried about waking them up.'

Evidently I hadn't wriggled anywhere close to off the hook at all. I bit my lip, knowing I was really in no position to argue as he had already come clean and kept his side of the bargain, and I wondered just how little I could get away with sharing.

'So, Miss Woodruff,' Jamie smiled, unfastening his seat belt and twisting round to face me, 'tell me exactly the reason behind your desire to work your way through Christmas and why you're the world's most reluctant party planner.'

I took a deep breath and cracked open my window a little. The air was fresh and sharp and I drank it in, feeling its keen sting in my nostrils.

'I accepted the job at the hall, working as a companion to your mum,' I quickly began, 'on the understanding that Christmas wasn't going to be a big deal for your family this year.'

I stole a quick glance as he shrugged his shoulders and raised his eyebrows. I guessed he already knew that much from Catherine and he was beginning to look a little impatient now; as well he might in the rapidly freezing temperature.

155

'Obviously I had no idea that within just days of my arrival your father was going to turn that understanding on its head.'

'Good old Dad,' Jamie smiled. 'You can always rely on him to throw a spanner or two in the works, but what I want to know is why it matters, Anna. What difference does his new plan make to you?'

'All the difference in the world actually,' I sighed. 'Every year I go out of my way to find a position where Christmas, for whatever reason, won't be celebrated in any great way, or if it is, I'll be kept too busy to notice it.'

'Yes,' he confirmed, 'I'd kind of begun to figure that out for myself, but why? What do you have against jolly old Santa? Has he wronged you so badly? Did he deny you the perfect present? Give you the wrong Barbie?'

I turned to face him properly before he said anything else and ended up feeling guilty when he heard the true reason for my loathing of the season.

'My mum died on Christmas Day when I was eight years old.' I said it bluntly because it was the only way I knew I could get the words out. 'I haven't celebrated Christmas since.'

There was a whole lot more to my childhood than that, but losing Mum was the biggest horror, even though the trauma of what followed wasn't lagging all that far behind.

'Oh, Anna,' Jamie croaked, the colour draining from his handsome, tanned face.

I looked back out of the window and up at the stars and blinked a few times.

'I'm so sorry.'

'It's all right,' I shrugged.

'Of course it isn't all right,' he said straight back as he reached across and held my hand. 'How could it possibly be all right?'

Enjoying the comfortable feeling, ignoring the increasing thump of my heart and without really thinking about what I was doing, I laced my fingers through his, absorbed his soothing warmth and willed myself not to cry.

'I never would have made a joke if I'd known,' he said, sounding mortified. 'But what about the rest of your family? Did your father not reclaim Christmas as you got older?'

I thought of the Decembers that followed and the never-ending catalogue of pain that accompanied them.

'Oh yes,' I sniffed, 'he reclaimed it all right.'

I stopped myself again before it all came tumbling out. For years Dad had celebrated not just Christmas but practically every holiday from the bottom of a very big bottle or three.

'But he's not particularly the loving kind,' I said dismissively, trying not to remember how he had driven away the one woman who could have helped him clean up his act and not necessarily replace my mum, but make a mighty fine substitute, 'not towards me anyway, and I don't have any brothers or sisters.'

I had no desire to say anything further. In the last few days I'd shared more about myself than I had in the last twenty years and I had no intention of tearing the gaping fissure open any wider.

'So you see,' I said, taking back my hand and reaching up my sleeve for a tissue, 'we're both as reluctant as each other to meet this Christmas head on, but for very different reasons.'

'You're right,' Jamie nodded.

'You,' I said, after I had blown my nose, 'have everything I've always craved deep down but never dared hope to have: a home to come back to, a loving family and security.'

'And you,' said Jamie, 'have the freedom, independence and opportunity to completely live your own life. The kind of life that I want to hang on to, but am now going to have to give up.'

'Ironic, isn't it?' I smiled.

'Just a bit,' he smiled back, twisting round to reach between the seats for a fleecy blanket. 'Come on,' he said, dumping it on my lap. 'Wrap this around your shoulders.'

'Why? What are we doing?'

'Stargazing,' he said with a nod towards the great outdoors. 'This is as little light pollution as you're likely to get around here.'

'Are you mad?' I gaped. 'It's freezing.'

'Well, hurry up then,' he said, turning off the engine and jumping out of the door. 'I've got an idea.'

The last thing I wanted was to be standing outside, wearing inappropriate footwear in sub-zero temperatures with nothing more than a fleecy blanket between myself and frostbite, but Jamie was having none of it.

'Come on, Woodruff,' he said gruffly, rushing round to open my door. 'Those doe eyes don't fool me. You're tougher than you look.'

Rolling my eyes and gathering the blanket tight around me I gingerly joined him on the slippery concrete.

'If you end up having to give me sick pay because I've caught pneumonia,' I warned him, 'then you've no one to blame but yourself.'

'In that case,' he said, taking a step closer and slipping his arm around my shoulders, 'let's get this over with as quickly as possible.'

'Get what over with?'

'Well,' he said, 'as you just pointed out, each of us seems to have exactly what the other wants. I have the family and the stability,'

'And the crumbling but cosy colossal pile,' I added cheekily. 'And I have the freedom and independence.'

'And the crippling fear of Christmas.'

'Where exactly are you going with this?' I frowned, not liking that he was so relaxed when it came to highlighting my problems, even though I had been so blasé about his.

We both had problems, that was true enough, and we both

now knew what those problems were, so I could see little point in turning into an icicle just to trawl through them again under the stars.

'Well,' he said, looking down at me and pinning me with his emerald gaze, 'I think I've just come up with a way to potentially solve our problems and help give each other what we want in the process.'

'Oh, you have, have you?' I frowned, feeling deeply suspicious but more than a little seduced by his close proximity.

'I have.'

'And you couldn't have explained this in there?' I asked, nodding towards the rapidly cooling interior of the Land Rover.

'Absolutely not,' Jamie insisted, 'because sitting in there, we couldn't see this.'

He pointed to the heavens, his finger stopping when it reached what looked like the brightest star in the sky.

'That's the Christmas Star,' he said, his voice tantalisingly close to my ear.

'No it isn't,' I tutted, stamping my feet to ward off frostbite and following his gaze. 'Is it?'

'Well, it is in my head,' he said a little impatiently. 'And if you wish on that star, then whatever you want most will come true, providing you're prepared to put in the effort to help make it happen, of course.'

I looked from the star to him and quickly back again.

At least he hadn't dragged me through the woods in my Manolos to find the Wishing Tree.

'What do you wish for, Anna?' he whispered.

'I wish I could find a way to fall in love with Christmas again,' I said wistfully.

'And I wish I could fall in love with the hall again,' said Jamie.

We stood in silence for a few seconds, just staring up at the star.

'Is that it then?' I asked when the cold had reached further than I thought possible.

'Not quite,' he sniffed, 'you're forgetting about the effort I said that had to be put in to make it happen.'

'Of course,' I shivered, 'feel free to enlighten me any time before my toes drop off, won't you?'

I loved my shoes with a passion, but they were hardly ideal footwear for standing out in the frosty Fens. Tomorrow I would go back to wearing layers.

'Well, this is how I see it,' he said, rocking back on his heels. 'I happen to love Christmas and I reckon I'm more than capable of making you love it too.'

'OK,' I said warily.

'And you obviously love Wynthorpe, even though you've only been there five minutes.'

'Right.'

'And with your fresh outlook and enthusiasm I'm kind of

hoping that you can help me rekindle my spark for the place and make my future running it more bearable.'

'So in short,' I cut in, 'you think we can each solve the other's problems.'

'That's the gist of it.'

'I see,' I said thoughtfully.

It didn't actually sound like a bad idea at all.

'I think we should make a deal,' said Jamie.

'A deal?'

'Yes,' he nodded. 'You have to do whatever I tell you to.'

I looked at him and raised my eyebrows.

'Only with regards to Christmas planning and activities,' he hastily added, looking a little rosy in the cheek department. 'Whether that's decorating the tree or wrapping presents, you just have to go along with it and I have to—'

'And you,' I interrupted, 'have to work with your parents to reopen the hall, tackle your brothers and follow my instructions for creating a life for yourself that will mean you can have the hall *and* the freedom you crave.'

'Exactly,' said Jamie, holding out his hand. 'That isn't too much of an ask, is it?'

'Absolutely not,' I laughed. 'I mean, we have almost a month to do this, but to be honest,' I added, my smile suddenly faltering, 'I don't reckon much for your chances with me.'

I might have acknowledged that Mum had been sending

me signs to tell me now was the time to embrace the season but there was a long road to travel between finally accepting Christmas still existed and actually enjoying it.

'Now, don't be so defeatist, Woodruff,' Jamie insisted as I placed my hand in his and we shook on the deal. 'There's nothing I like more than a challenge.'

Chapter 12

With the deal sealed under the stars Jamie and I wasted no time in coming up with some ideas that would be instrumental in making the other's dream come true. Clearly we were both ambitious, fiercely competitive and each desperate to see the other cross the finish line to dream-fulfilment first, and I might not have showed it, but I secretly had everything crossed that Jamie would succeed, even if I was going to struggle to complete some of the things he no doubt had lined up for me.

Operation 'Wish upon the Christmas Star' countdown was officially set to launch at six thirty the following morning with a sedate, although admittedly glacial, jog around the grounds, but the whole thing got off to a rocky start because Jamie 'accidentally' slept through his alarm.

'You can't make me do this,' he yawned, his sleepy eyes, mussed-up hair and washboard stomach putting in a brief appearance after I'd been hammering on his door for what felt like forever. 'In fact, I can't see how stumbling about in the frost is going to make me love the place at all. If anything,' he whined, 'it will put me off.'

I was having none of it. I pushed my way into the room, ignoring the desire to wrap my arms around his bare upper half, and began rifling through his piles of clothes for something that would stop the biting wind cutting through to his ribs.

'You know, you can't just barge in here,' he said, attempting to crawl back under the duvet.

'So,' I said, throwing him a fleecy zip-up top and feeling triumphant, 'you're admitting defeat already.'

'Might be.'

'And if this was a game,' I added cunningly, 'you'd have to say that I was already the outright winner.'

'Hey,' he yelped as I sent a pair of trainers flying towards his groin and tried not to notice just how sexy his bare feet and shoulders really were. 'You haven't won anything.'

'So I'll see you downstairs in two minutes?'

'Oh all right,' he groaned. 'All right, but if this isn't worth getting up for—'

'Yes?'

'I'm going to have you making paper chains from now until next Christmas.'

*

Fortunately for me, the early start was worth it, although it took a few laps around the garden before I could make Jamie admit it. By the time we had weaved our way through the neglected walled garden and back to the summerhouse, where I had sat with Catherine just a few days before, the sky had barely lightened and, if anything, looked full of snow.

'Your mum's very fond of the gardens, isn't she?' I said when I had finally caught my breath and my lungs weren't burning quite so much.

'She loves them,' nodded Jamie as he stretched out, using the side of the summerhouse to bear his weight.

He hadn't let on, of course, but having watched his running style and post-workout cooldown, I could tell this wasn't the first time he had donned his trainers to raise his heartrate.

'In fact,' he added, 'I wouldn't be at all surprised if trying to keep on top of all this, and helping Mick out at every opportunity, wasn't in part responsible for her knee problems.'

He looked at me and raised his eyebrows. 'So, if you were hoping to make me admit how lovely the grounds are in your quest to make the place feel like less of a burden, then I'm afraid you've failed.'

I ignored his smug tone, knowing I had a winning idea up my sleeve.

'The upkeep of everything outside is down to Mick, is it?'

'More or less,' he said, looking about him, 'and as you

can see from the state of the walled garden, it's too much for one pair of hands. Dad helps out if something needs hacking down, but he's too easily distracted for the regular, fiddly jobs to hold his interest all year round.'

'So, what you really need out here are a few more hands on deck.'

'Of course,' Jamie agreed, 'but we can't afford a team of gardeners any more. When Mum was growing up there were three or four, and that was before you included the estate staff. They all used to live in cottages we owned between here and town, but they were sold off years ago.'

'Has anyone ever thought about the possibility of getting a team of volunteers together to help out?'

'We occasionally have groups to help with jobs in the woods – hedging, clearing ground and so on.'

'That's not really what I'm getting at,' I said. 'I'm talking about an established group of volunteers who could come to help out on a regular basis, students even.'

'I'm not sure about that,' Jamie frowned.

'There's a small horticultural college in town, isn't there?' I quizzed, knowing full well from the Internet search I'd made the evening before that there was, and that they were always looking for places to take on students to give them practical experience.

'Yes,' said Jamie, rubbing his chin, 'there is, actually. It's affiliated to a couple of the larger colleges in Norfolk.'

'I bet they would jump at the chance to come and work somewhere like this and,' I quickly added, 'I daresay they'd send staff with them, so beyond Mick showing them where everything is, they could be left to their own devices.'

'Maybe,' he said thoughtfully.

'It would be nice to see the place restored to its former glory, wouldn't it, especially the walled garden? You could even hold open days for charity and maybe open to the public a couple of days a week to bring in a little revenue.'

'You'll be telling me next we should convert the stables into tearooms,' Jamie laughed.

'That might not be a bad idea actually,' I shrugged. 'It's something to think about anyway.'

Jamie looked at me and narrowed his eyes again.

'This garden idea would be more work for me though,' he frowned.

'No it wouldn't,' I said, 'not after the initial set-up. I bet Mick and the college, if they wanted to take it on, could run it between them. These things are only as complicated as you make them,' I told him.

'Is that a quote you live by?' he asked.

'No,' I admitted, 'but I probably should.'

'Well, loath as I am to admit it, Woodruff,' he said, looking about him, 'I think you might actually have stumbled upon something here.'

'Excellent,' I grinned.

'Not necessarily the tearoom idea,' he said quickly, 'but getting some students in to help restore the gardens might prove to be a win-win situation all round.'

'You'll need to have a look at those public liability insurance documents though,' I reminded him.

'Of course,' he said thoughtfully. 'Let's go and run it all by Mum and Dad.'

'And Mick.'

'Yes, and Mick, and we'll take it from there if they think it's a good idea. Henry is the chap who organises some bits and pieces for the estate, so I'll give him a bell as well.'

We headed back to the hall and I have to admit I was feeling really rather chuffed to have struck gold on my first attempt.

Catherine and Angus were absolutely thrilled with the idea and even Mick, once he had been reassured that no one would be taking away his pleasure in striping the lawns, was happy to come on board.

'I think it sounds like an absolutely wonderful idea,' enthused Catherine. 'It would be such a joy to see the gardens looking beautiful again. Not that there's anything wrong with your work, Mick,' she quickly added, 'but there's only so much one man can do.'

'I know what you mean,' he said, fortunately sounding not at all put out. 'With a place this size things soon get out of hand, especially during the summer. No sooner are the lawns finished than it's time to start cutting them again.'

Clearly his passion was for turf culture rather than weeding.

'Well, you know I'm always happy to jump on the ride-on,' said Angus helpfully.

'Yes,' tutted Dorothy. 'But the last time you did that you reversed it over the ha-ha and almost broke your neck.'

'Well, the gears can be fiddly,' huffed Angus.

'So we'd be having students coming to work here all year round then, would we?' asked Hayley, who Mick had already collected from town.

'If the college really like the idea,' said Jamie, 'then yes.'

'All those hot, sweaty bodies hoeing the borders . . .' she said dreamily.

Dorothy and Catherine looked at one another and rolled their eyes.

'I was rather hoping to improve the gardens, rather than your view, Hayley! We can't have you upstairs with your nose pressed to the window when you are supposed to be working,' I told her firmly. 'And it won't be just boys.'

'Well, whatever,' she giggled, without even the grace to blush. 'I'm sure we all appreciate the idea, Anna.'

'Some more than others,' said Catherine with a meaningful stare.

'Nothing wrong with enhancing the view and working conditions, is there?' she asked innocently.

I felt my own colour rise as I remembered I had thought

exactly the same thing when I had first seen the photograph of Jamie.

'I seem to remember you telling me that my homecoming had done that?' Jamie pouted theatrically.

'Yes, well,' said Hayley, stealing a quick glance in my direction. 'I have no doubt you're going to be spoken for before long. Now, whose turn is it to open the Advent calendar today, Angus?'

Keen to make contact before the college broke up for the Christmas holidays, Jamie called his estate man Henry, and arranged to meet in town the next day.

'You'll come with me, won't you, Anna?' he asked as he passed me a bowl of Dorothy's delectable chicken soup that lunchtime.

'Me?' I frowned. 'What on earth do you want me to come for?'

Jamie raised his eyebrows and I got the distinct impression that he had my first task lined up. I swallowed and reminded myself that I could hardly expect him to keep toeing the line if I wasn't going to get involved in return.

'Don't look so worried,' he laughed. 'I'm not going to make you go carolling. I just thought that as it was your idea, you'd be better at explaining it than I would.'

'OK,' I said, my shoulders sinking back down to somewhere near where they should be. 'Great. In that case count me in, as long as your mum can spare me, of course,' I quickly added.

'Excellent,' he said. 'Mum's more than happy about it. I've run the idea by her already.'

A slight smile was still playing about his lips and I wondered if he had told me everything he planned for our trip to town after all, but I didn't have time to quiz him further.

'By the way,' Dorothy said, 'I spoke to Angela earlier and she was over the moon. She's going to talk to the others tonight and see what they say, but we're certain they'll be thrilled.'

'What's this?' asked Mick.

'Jamie has already invited the WI back to the hall for their special talks,' Dorothy explained as she refilled his bowl yet again. 'With his parents' blessing of course.'

'You've been quick off the mark, lad,' winked Mick. 'I'll give you that.'

'Like we said yesterday,' said Jamie, 'now Anna and Mum have got the insurance in place there's really no reason why people can't start coming back.'

'I wonder what Archie will have to say when he finds out?' I asked. 'I hope he won't take me to task because I set up the policy.'

'It's nothing to do with him now,' Jamie said sternly. 'If he so much as opens his mouth when he turns up, Anna, you come and tell me.'

Hayley caught my eye and winked.

'And if you have any more bright ideas floating about, let's hear them before the family descend.'

'Well,' I said.

'Here we go,' Dorothy and Mick said together.

'I'm thinking,' I continued, 'as you've already asked the WI, and we're heading to town tomorrow, you could pop to the library and ask the reading group to come back as well.'

'Great,' said Jamie, without a moment's hesitation. 'I'll do it.'

'And I happen to know the head librarian is one of those ramblers,' put in Hayley. 'So you might be able to kill two birds with one stone there.'

Chapter 13

By the time we set off the next morning, having checked that Catherine really didn't mind that I was disappearing, there were a few flakes of snow in the air and the weather report on the local radio station was suggesting we could be in for quite a bit more. Jamie warmed up the Land Rover while I fetched my wellingtons from the boot of my car, along with my thicker Barbour.

'An outfit for every occasion,' he teased, when I jumped into the passenger seat.

'Naturally,' I said, refusing to take the bait or tease him about the size of the holes in the cuffs of his jumper.

The better I got to know Jamie, the more he surprised me. In some ways he seemed to be just a more attractive version of his father, and I hoped he didn't have anything too extreme lined up for my reintroduction to Christmas.

'The library doesn't open until eleven today, so I thought

we'd have a look around the town first,' he announced as he pulled out of the stable yard. 'Check out the trees in the market square and a couple of the festive stalls that Mum said have popped up.'

I swallowed hard and looked out of the window. His suggestion sounded a lot like Christmas shopping to me.

'As long as that's OK with you,' he added, a crease wrinkling his otherwise beautiful brow.

'Of course,' I nodded. 'It'll be fun.'

The snow began to fall a little thicker as we crossed the bridge into town, but it was still bordering on the right side of romantic and it did make the market look very festive – not that a couple of the stallholders looked as if they were particularly enthralled by its arrival.

'So,' said Jamie, pointing up at one of the ginormous trees that I had tried to blank out on the night of the switch-on. 'What do you think?'

'They're actually rather lovely,' I said, because they really were. 'And so big for such a small town.'

The primary-coloured bulbs were twinkling prettily, their impact made all the more effective by the dark skies and dusting of snow. In fact, looking around, the whole town looked pretty. I was amazed that I had allowed myself to think so and vowed there and then to keep my eyes off the pavement from now on and just try to enjoy myself.

I knew my acquiescence was making Jamie's task even

easier, but then he hadn't exactly been reluctant to take my suggestions to heart or given me too much of a tough time. I mean, it wasn't exactly a hardship that I'd had to barge my way into his bedroom when he was half dressed to cajole him into going for a run, was it?

'Better than any you saw last year?' Jamie asked.

'What?' I snapped, panicking that my illicit thoughts had been written across my face.

'Earth to Anna,' he tutted. 'I was talking about the trees. Are they better than any you saw last year?'

'Better than any I've seen in a lot of years,' I told him, feeling relieved that nothing worse than me zoning out for a second or two had occurred. 'To tell you the truth, I do my utmost to avoid shopping between early November and late January. If I need anything, I order online. I certainly don't head to the city or town centre.'

'Seriously?'

'Seriously,' I said. 'It isn't just the big day I've been avoiding, but everything that goes with it as well.'

'Crikey,' he said, thrusting his hands in his jeans pockets. 'Then this might be more of a challenge than I realised.'

I had no intention of letting him know that it might actually turn out to be far easier than he was expecting because I was so determined to make an effort.

'If you want to concede defeat already—' I began.

'Not on your life,' he cut in. 'I haven't even started yet.'

'Jamie!'

I didn't have time to mull over what he might have lined up.

'Ruby!' he called back, waving, before grabbing my hand and pulling me towards one of the stalls.

He let go to embrace his friend and I told my keenly thumping heart that the unexpected action had been instinctive, nothing more.

'And Anna,' Ruby gushed, bestowing a hug upon me as well. 'How lovely to see you again.'

'You two know each other?' Jamie frowned, looking confused.

'Your mum introduced us the night of the switch-on,' I explained, trying not to remember that she had also witnessed my little meltdown. 'And Steve was there too,' I added, just to remind Ruby, who was gazing admiringly at my companion, that she had already found the love of her life.

'So,' she said, not really taking the hint, 'you're finally back.'

'Looks like it,' Jamie shrugged.

'And just in time for Christmas,' she said, stepping aside to show off the attractive stall she was manning.

'Is this all yours?' asked Jamie.

'No,' she said, straightening some bags of gingerbread families and iced buns. 'This is all the hard work of Jemma and Lizzie.'

'The Cherry Tree ladies,' I nodded.

'That's right,' she confirmed. 'I'm just running it for them again until I begin looking for a job in the New Year. I need to replenish the travel fund pot.'

'And what about Steve?' asked Jamie, with a nod towards the neighbouring fruit and veg stall. 'Is he back working with his dad?'

'Of course,' Ruby laughed, 'and happily so. We're already planning our next trip, but we're happy to be home for now and you know Steve loves working with his dad.'

Jamie looked thoughtful and I knew he was wondering if working and living in such close proximity to his own parents was going to be something he could happily settle for.

'So,' said Ruby, with a nod to the stall. 'What can I tempt you with? Have you started your Christmas shopping yet, Jamie?'

'God no,' he said, rolling his eyes. 'You know me, typical bloke. It'll be the usual mad rush before the shops shut on Christmas Eve.'

'You need to take a leaf out of Anna's book,' she shocked me by saying.

'Oh?' questioned Jamie.

'You're all done, aren't you?' she praised. 'And wrapped up as well I'll bet.'

'Absolutely,' I played along, remembering how Catherine

had come to my rescue and it had been assumed that I'd finished my present-buying already.

'Well in that case,' Jamie said, looking quizzically from me to the stall, 'perhaps it wouldn't hurt to make a start.'

I looked along with him and had to admit that everything was beautiful. Practically all of it, Ruby explained, had been handmade or baked by either Jemma or Lizzie. There were more strings of the bunting Dorothy had found and stockings and biscuits and one little trinket in particular that caught my eye. I was almost tempted to pick it up but Jamie reached for it first.

'You have a fondness for silver bells, don't you, Anna?' he said, holding up the slim sliver of dark red leather with tiny bells, which tinkled gently, attached along its length.

'Yes,' I croaked, before clearing my throat. I was pleased he had remembered that I had mentioned Mum's love of the song. 'Yes, I do,' I said again, a little louder.

'In that case,' he said, picking up a bag of gingerbread men to go with it, 'we'll take it, and these.'

Ruby looked at me and smiled and I could feel myself blushing.

'Don't worry about wrapping it,' he said, taking my hand again and this time pushing my sleeve back far enough to reveal my wrist.

'I thought it was a Christmas present,' said Ruby.

'No,' said Jamie, carefully fastening it. 'This is a sweetener.'

'A sweetener?'

'Yes,' he said, 'a sweetener. I need to keep Anna sweet if she's going to see out Christmas with my mad lot, so it's my intention to keep her plied with gifts up until the big day.'

'Lucky Anna,' smiled Ruby, taking the note Jamie gave her and rifling through her apron pockets for change.

'You didn't have to do that,' I said when we were out of earshot, 'but thank you. It really is very lovely.'

I could hear the bells gently tinkling as we walked.

'It really is my intention to ply you with little tokens,' he said playfully, 'and break down your resistance to all things festive. It's part of my plan.'

'Well, in that case,' I said, feeling even happier to play along, 'I really am in for a fun few weeks, aren't I?'

'And of course,' he added, 'you have to wear it at all times.'

'Of course.'

'Because that way,' he grinned, 'I'll be able to keep tabs on exactly where you are!'

I wasn't quite sure how I felt about that but I was grateful that he had been distracted enough not to start quizzing me about my fantasy festive shopping.

It was cosy, warm and soothingly quiet inside the library.

'Perhaps we should find you a couple of Christmas novels to read while we're here,' Jamie suggested, pointing to a large display of books with glossy, sparkling covers. 'I still have my library card in here somewhere,' he said, rifling through his wallet.

'I'm not sure I'm going to have much time to read,' I said doubtfully.

'Of course you are,' he said, reaching for the latest from Trisha Ashley. 'I'm sure you can manage just a few minutes before you go to sleep. There's no better way to end the day.'

I looked at him and raised my eyebrows. I didn't have him down as a reader.

'Miss Woodruff,' he said primly, no doubt misinterpreting my surprise on purpose, 'are you being rude?'

'No, I am not,' I hissed back, blushing profusely. 'And please, keep your voice down.'

Grinning, he thrust the book into my hands and strode off towards the counter, leaving me to mouth apologies to those trying to enjoy a little peace and quiet.

'Well now, that's wonderful news,' the rosy-cheeked librarian was already saying by the time I had fiddled about with the digital card reader and reached them. 'The book group will be delighted.'

'And the ramblers are welcome to walk through the gardens again as well, of course,' Jamie added. 'And you never know, Dorothy might even put on some refreshments like she used to.'

The woman's smile faltered at this suggestion.

'But only if the group would like to come back, of course,' Jamie added, sounding a little uncertain.

'I'll have to ask them,' she said, looking about her. 'Are you sure your mother was in agreement to that?'

Jamie looked at me, his expression suggesting he was just as surprised by her reaction as I was.

'After the letter, I mean . . .' she began, then stopped.

'What letter?'

'The letter from your brother, Archie,' she swallowed, turning puce, but no longer from pleasure.

'I had no idea he'd written to you,' Jamie frowned. 'What did he say?'

The librarian swallowed and fiddled with the pendant on her necklace.

'Well, I don't want to cause any trouble.'

I felt Jamie begin to bristle and placed my hand on his arm.

'There's no trouble,' I smiled, looking down at her name badge. 'We just want to know if there were any problems, Rosemary, so we can sort them out.'

'He said,' she began, her eyes darting nervously between Jamie and me, 'that we had upset Mrs Connelly by littering. That she wasn't well and didn't want to be contacted under any circumstances. That she felt the mess we left was a slur on her hospitality and that if we wished to communicate with the hall again it had to be through him.'

Jamie let out a long, slow breath.

'And we did write back to him, via the address on the letter, because we were certain we hadn't left any rubbish.'

'Of course you hadn't,' Jamie rumbled.

'And we even sent a card,' Rosemary continued in a rush, 'but we never heard anything back. Not a word.'

'Bloody Archie,' said Jamie, loud enough to make those closest turn and stare.

'Jamie,' I said quietly, shaking my head.

He took a moment before speaking again.

'I can only apologise,' he said sincerely to Rosemary. 'Clearly there has been some misunderstanding. I know that you and the group would never litter and Mum knows that too. Please ask the group organiser to call the hall, or even better pop in, and we'll have this whole situation sorted in a heartbeat.'

Rosemary looked as if she was about to burst into tears and Jamie into flames. What a meddlesome man Archie was. I daresay banning the ramblers was all a part of his mad scheme to smooth his selfish way when he took over but to draw Catherine into it was beyond contempt.

'We'll just take this for today,' said Jamie, taking the Trisha Ashley book and his library card from me.

'It's all right,' I said, keen to get him out of the building. 'I've already scanned it out.'

Once outside I suggested we go to the Cherry Tree

straightaway on the pretext of having coffee, but really because I wanted him to cool off a bit before his meeting with Henry.

'Good idea,' he said, taking me by the elbow and steering me in the right direction. 'I could do with some caffeine.'

I couldn't help thinking that chamomile tea would have been a better choice.

Thankfully it didn't take many minutes for him to calm down, outwardly at least, especially as he was flavour of the month as far as Angela, one of the waitresses, was concerned.

'When Dorothy phoned to say the WI could come back to the hall,' she gushed, 'I thought Christmas had come early. I can't tell you how much it means to us to be welcomed back. The hall is such a wonderful venue and we can always attract really interesting speakers when they know the audience is going to be bigger than those we can squeeze into the town hall.'

'Well, I'm pleased it's going to make such a difference,' said Jamie graciously.

'It will, my dear,' Angela smiled. 'It really will. Now, what can I get the pair of you?'

She took our order and Jamie turned his attention back to me.

'Fucking Archie,' he hissed, his eyes blazing again. 'Can you believe it?'

'Given what you told me about him that night in the pub,

I'm afraid I can,' I said honestly. 'Although I have to admit, I'm rather taken aback by your reaction.'

'What do you mean?' he scowled. 'Surely you didn't expect me to be pleased about what he'd done?'

'Not pleased exactly,' I said, having thought it through. 'But I thought you might be able to see the benefit of his outrageous actions.'

He looked at me as if I was going mad.

'Sorry,' he said, shaking his head. 'You're going to have to explain.'

I waited while Angela filled the table with cups, pots and plates.

'The teacakes are on the house,' she whispered. 'Just a little thank-you.'

'Thank you, Angela,' Jamie smiled back.

I was amazed by how he could turn the charm on and off when he needed to.

'Come on,' he said, the second Angela had moved on to the next table. 'Tell me exactly which part of Archie's ludicrous actions are going to be of any benefit to us?'

I couldn't believe he was still being so dense. He was completely blinded by his bad mood.

'All of them,' I said simply as I buttered my teacake. 'His letter, cutting off communication between Catherine and the ramblers, just goes to prove that he has hidden motives about the hall and is a sneaky rat to boot. If you can get a copy of that letter you've got even more proof that he isn't the right brother to take over the running of the hall.'

'But we already know that.'

'Yes,' I said exasperatedly. 'I know that you all know, but he doesn't know that you know what he's been planning, does he?'

Jamie looked thoughtful.

'And he sounds to me like the sort of bloke who'll deny he's done anything wrong unless you've got the physical proof to show he's lying. Archie is still harbouring the illusion that he's going to get his hands on the hall, isn't he?'

'Yes, I think he is.'

'Then start gathering the evidence to prove to him that you know exactly what he's been up to and that he isn't the man for the job.'

Jamie nodded and took a bite of his teacake.

'But the thing is,' he said sadly, 'I can't help thinking that none of this sounds like something my brother would do at all.'

'What do you mean?' I frowned. 'You've described him to me as devious, money-obsessed and desperate to get his hands on the place. Surely this letter backs all that up?'

'Oh it does,' Jamie agreed, 'but absolutely none of this is relatable to the Archie I grew up with. The three of us were always so close, best friends really. I guess I'm just finding it hard to believe that he could have changed this much.

There's nothing about any of this that sits right with me. Mum and Dad always kept us so grounded.'

'Well, what about his girlfriend, Elise?' I asked. 'Could she perhaps be the reason he's changed?'

'I dunno,' said Jamie, shaking his head. 'Maybe. He's certainly more materialistic now than he used to be, that's for sure. His lifestyle is completely different to the one he grew up with and apparently so are his priorities.'

'Look,' I went on, 'whatever the real reason behind all this, I can't help thinking that it won't do Archie any harm at all to see his devious behaviour laid out in front of him. It might be just the wake-up call he needs.'

'Hardly going to make for a happy Christmas though, is it?'

I didn't have a chance to answer before Jamie was on his feet welcoming a thickset man in a checked shirt.

'Henry,' he said, shaking the man warmly by the hand. 'How are you? How's Jess?'

'I'm very well,' he said, taking the seat Jamie offered. 'And Jess is great. She's got everything running like a well-oiled machine already.'

'Of course she has,' said Jamie, patting his friend on the back. 'Anna, this is Henry, our estate man. Henry, this is Anna. She's recently joined the ranks to help Mum convalesce.'

'Pleased to meet you, Henry.'

'Likewise,' he replied. 'Another Christmas recruit, eh?'

he winked at Jamie. 'What is it with the Connelly clan and the festive season?'

Jamie ignored his question.

'Henry's wife had twins just a few weeks ago,' he said instead.

'How exciting!' I said. 'Congratulations.'

'Thanks,' said Henry, quickly pulling out his phone and proceeding to show us a collection of photos of his beautiful wife and tiny boys.

'Anyway,' he said, when he had eventually scrolled through what must have been his iPhone's entire memory, 'what's the news at the hall? I got the impression when we spoke yesterday that some changes are afoot.'

Jamie told Henry about inviting the community back and then asked me to explain what I had suggested to get the gardens back under control. Henry thought it sounded like a wonderful idea and, as luck would have it, he happened to know one of the lecturers at the college who he thought might be interested in setting it all up.

'I knew you were the right person to ask,' said Jamie, leaning back in his chair so Jemma could refill our cups for what must have been the third time.

'Leave it all with me,' said Henry as he made some notes on his screen, 'and I'll see what I can do before the college finishes for Christmas. Your timing couldn't have been better, what with spring just around the corner.'

I looked doubtfully out of the window at the falling snow. Spring still felt like a long way off to me.

'Well, I'd better be off,' he said. 'I've got some shopping to collect before heading home.'

'I would imagine it's difficult for your wife to get to town with the twins,' I sympathised.

'Oh it's not that,' said Henry with a smile. 'She's taken the twins to the riding stables she runs today. Just an admin day, but she won't have time to go shopping as well.'

'She sounds like quite a woman,' I laughed, thinking that if I had recently given birth to just one baby, never mind two, I'd still be struggling to be dressed by bedtime.

'She is,' said Henry proudly, 'she really is.'

'Right,' said Jamie, when his friend had gone, 'I guess we'd better head back to the hall. I don't think we're in any danger of being snowed in, but I've got lots lined up for you to be getting on with, just in case you thought you were nosing ahead.'

'Not at all,' I said, reaching for my coat. 'In fact, I'm looking forward to getting on with things now.'

Jamie didn't look as if he completely believed me.

'I am,' I told him again.

'Can I add your name to the list for the auction next Saturday?' asked Jemma, when she came over with the card machine so we could settle our bill. 'Only many hands make light work and we're a bit down on numbers this year.'

'Crikey,' said Jamie, 'is it that time already?'

'Sure is,' said Jemma. 'Tom spoke to Mick last week and he said there's a fine crop of holly and mistletoe to harvest from your woods this year.'

'Well that's good,' said Jamie, 'and yes, put me down by all means. I'm more than happy to help out.'

'Excellent,' she smiled. 'And what about you, Anna? I don't suppose you fancy giving up a Saturday to help out, do you?'

'With what?' I asked.

'Sorry,' Jamie tutted, 'I keep forgetting you're such a newbie.'

'Does it feel as if she's been around forever already?' asked Jemma.

'Just a bit,' said Jamie, making me blush, but I knew what he meant.

I'd barely been at the hall any time at all, but it was feeling more like home than anywhere else I'd lived in a very long time. If I was feeling like this already, I dreaded to think how I'd be feeling when it was time to pack up and move on in January. My body gave a little shudder at the thought.

'Every December there's a Christmas tree auction in Wynbridge,' Jamie explained. 'Trees are sold along with all sorts of greenery from local places, like the hall.'

'We always have a good supply of holly, ivy and mistletoe to sell off,' Jemma added, 'and since Ruby got involved with rejuvenating the market, the tree sale is now accompanied by a community bake which takes place in the town hall.'

'Some cakes are contributed to go into an auction,' Jamie went on. 'Dorothy always sends three or four.'

Why was I not surprised?

'But in the morning people come to bake cookies and gingerbread families in the kitchens,' Jemma butted in, 'and that's what we really need help with.'

I didn't know what to say. It sounded pretty full-on on the festive front to me, but Jamie didn't give me time to wriggle out of it.

'She'd love to help,' he said meaningfully. 'Wouldn't you?'

'Absolutely,' I said, taking his raised eyebrows to mean that this was just the sort of thing he was planning to immerse me in if I was ever going to find a way to reclaim Christmas. It was his idea of throwing me in at the deep end, I supposed, and I couldn't deny that he had been willing to go along with what I had suggested so far for him.

'You can come in with me in the morning,' said Jamie, 'to help set up and drop off Dorothy's cakes and then stay to help out while I'm lugging trees about in the market.'

'Excellent,' said Jemma, hastily adding my name to the list. 'Two for the price of one, courtesy of Wynthorpe Hall!'

Chapter 14

During the time leading up to the bake sale and tree auction back in town, I didn't really have the opportunity to fret over what I was going to have to face because Jamie proved more than capable of keeping me occupied. I might have kicked things off with an early-morning run and suggestions as to how he could see the gardens and grounds regenerated without so much as having to pick up a hoe himself, but he wasn't so preoccupied with my instructions that he forgot to dole out plenty of his own.

The next few days saw me baking with Dorothy, tidying with Hayley and signing for endless parcels which Angus slyly squirrelled back outside the second they touched the kitchen table. My list of assignments weren't full-on Christmas chores, but they were the closest I'd come in years, and clearing out one of the walk-in cupboards in the hallway with Hayley had given me cause to realise that I wasn't the only person in the world who struggled through the holidays.

'Is there any particular reason why we have to do this now?' I asked my new friend as I pulled out various dusty boxes and bags that didn't look like they'd seen the light of day for years. 'Surely this sort of cleaning can wait until the spring, can't it?'

Hayley looked at me and shook her head in despair.

'Look, just think about it,' she said, stepping forward to relieve me of a particularly grubby-looking box. 'In no time at all this hall is going to be filled to the rafters with family and friends—'

'I know that,' I cut in.

'And they'll all need somewhere to put their coats, scarves and boots, won't they?'

'I guess so,' I shrugged.

'So that's why we need to do this now,' Hayley continued, 'so the entire ground floor doesn't fall into chaos ...'

Her voice carried on, but it didn't reach me. I'd caught sight of something that squeezed the very air out of my lungs and made my heart pound hard in my chest. I'd just opened the lid of the box I had pulled out. They were only toys, a motley collection of children's things, but the teddy bear on top was so unnervingly similar to my own that I felt completely pole-axed. I'd foolishly left him behind on my bed when I left home and had regretted it ever since. I stuffed

193

it back in the box and went to push it towards Hayley, who was now nagging me to hurry up.

'Not that one,' she suddenly snapped.

'But don't you want to go through it?'

'Put it back!' she said again, her voice ragged in her chest and tears quickly coursing down her cheeks in two thick kohl lines.

'Hayley,' I began, but she pushed past me and shoved the box back into the corner of the cupboard then slammed the door shut, banishing it from sight. 'That's not for sorting. No one goes near that box.'

I didn't know what to say. I had no idea Hayley even knew how to cry. She was always so sassy and upbeat. My own upset at seeing the bear was completely diminished by the sight of my friend sitting at the bottom of the stairs and sobbing her heart out. I sat next to her and handed her a tissue.

'I'd completely forgotten we'd put them in there,' she said, her voice juddering as she tried to catch her breath. 'They should have gone away upstairs.'

'Were they yours?'

'They were for my baby.'

'Oh,' I said, 'I see.' But of course I didn't.

Hayley looked at me for a second before carrying on.

'I fell pregnant just before Christmas during my last year at school,' she explained. 'My mum and dad threw me out the second I told them.' She stopped to sniff. 'My nan did a bit of cleaning here at the time and told Catherine and Angus what had happened and they offered to take me in.'

I handed her another tissue.

'They said I could stay as long as I liked, even when the baby came.'

I wasn't at all surprised.

'And what about the baby's father?' I asked. 'Did he come here with you?'

I jumped as Hayley let out a bitter laugh.

'No,' she said, her voice sounding harsh and hurt, 'sir had no intention of leaving his wife but he did leave school pretty sharpish when he found out I was carrying a Christmas miracle. I never heard from him again.'

I wanted to ask about the baby, but she had never mentioned having a child so I couldn't imagine there had been a happy outcome.

'Then my nan died,' she went on, starting to sob again, 'and I lost the baby.'

'Oh, Hayley,' I gasped, wrapping my arms around her. 'I'm so sorry.'

'The hospital said it was probably the shock, but I think it was because I didn't deserve to have a baby.'

'Don't say that,' I said, squeezing her tight and kissing her hair. 'Don't ever say that.'

Hayley shook her head and sniffed again before spitting on the tissue and wiping the make-up from her cheeks.

'Anyway,' she said, sounding more composed, 'I took on Nan's job and Mum and Dad let me go home so that was that.'

I wanted to hear more about it, but she had shut the conversation down. I understood why. I'd done it often enough myself but at least now I knew why Catherine kept a room ready should Hayley want it. Personally I don't think I would have wanted to go back to a home and parents like that, but I wasn't Hayley, was I?

'We'll leave that box then,' I said, standing back up and holding out my hand so I could pull her to her feet.

'One less to worry about,' she smiled, her bottom lip still wobbling a bit. 'Christmas, eh?' she said, trying to sound strong.

'Christmas indeed,' I agreed.

We didn't mention the conversation again and I got on with the job of forcing myself to get involved with every little thing Jamie went out of his way to put his own festive spin on. He was clearly determined to keep topping up my steadily growing seasonal spirit.

My evenings were the first thing he set about transforming. Ordinarily I would head up to my room early, as keen to give the family some space as I was to take a swim in the Jo Malone-scented tub, but Hayley's arrival one morning with a bulging supermarket carrier bag put paid to all that.

'What have you got there?' snapped Dorothy, jabbing at the bag with the handle of the spoon she had been using to stir the breakfast porridge. 'You've not brought your lunch with you today, have you?'

She sounded affronted even before she'd heard what was inside and I hoped for Hayley's sake there wasn't contraband shop-bought food inside.

'What would I want to bring my own grub for?' she bit back, sounding every bit as riled as her friend. 'Best food in the entire county served up at this table and you're accusing me of bringing my own. You should know me better than that, Dorothy Dawson,' she added with a disgruntled sniff.

'Well, I'm sorry,' said Dorothy, the heat evaporating from her tone and her expression sheepish. 'It's just that when I see supermarket shopping bags turn up on my table I can't help feeling put out. It's a natural reflex for me.'

'Well, you needn't worry,' said Hayley. 'Everything in here is for Jamie and none of what's inside has been anywhere near a supermarket.'

I wondered what the bag was concealing and my ears pricked up the next second when she mentioned my name.

'He's got a little surprise lined up for anxious Annie over there.'

OK, so it wasn't *exactly* my name, but it was close enough and I knew she had coined the nickname after she had told me that I needed to 'chill out' when we'd found some leftover

Christmas paper that reminded me of home and I'd had a minor meltdown.

Everyone at the hall knew my mum had died when I was little, but none of them knew that she had actually passed away on Christmas Day. I had only shared that with Jamie and I wanted to keep it that way. I hadn't even mentioned to him what happened during the years that followed and I had no intention of digging it all up. There was no point. Everyone else knew that I had no one to spend the holidays with and as far as I was concerned that was all they needed to know with regard to my aversion to December the twenty-fifth. I didn't need to try and rekindle my Christmas spirit with an eager audience assessing my every move, no matter how well intentioned their interest.

I was just about to ask Hayley what it was that Jamie had asked her to bring in the offending bag, when the man himself charged into the kitchen and plucked it from the table.

'Well done, Hayley,' he said with a wink. 'I knew I could rely on you not to forget.'

'I've even remembered the popcorn,' she beamed, tapping the side of her nose and soaking up her idol's praise. 'And before you pipe up again,' she added, planting a kiss on Dorothy's cheek, 'this stuff came from the healthfood shop, not the supermarket. It's strictly make-your-own.'

'Well that's something, I suppose,' Dorothy sniffed.

'Excellent,' laughed Jamie. 'Has the post been?'

'It's on the side,' said Dorothy, brandishing her wooden spoon in the general direction.

'This one's for you, Anna,' he said, sorting through the pile.

'Me?' I questioned. 'But no one knows I'm here.' And more to the point, I had no one to send me anything.

'It's for you via me,' Jamie explained. 'It's your second festive present.'

'Second?' said Hayley, her eyebrows shooting up and a teasing smile playing around her lips. 'My, my, and it isn't even Christmas yet!'

I looked at her and shook my head. On more than one occasion she had tried to trip me up and make me confess my true feelings for Jamie but I was having none of it. She was also convinced that he harboured not entirely professional feelings for me, but I wasn't getting drawn into discussing that theory either. The lid was staying firmly shut on that particular box. I ripped open the packaging and pulled out a journal and a pack of Christmas-themed stickers.

'It's for you to write in,' Jamie grinned. 'I thought it would be a good idea for you to write down all the things you've loved about Christmas this year so that if you waver about celebrating again in the future you'll have something to remind you that it isn't really all bad.'

'Thank you,' I swallowed. 'What a lovely idea.'

'It's inspired,' Hayley winked. 'You must have really given that some thought, Jamie.'

That night, just as I was about to excuse myself and head off to the sanctuary of my room and another chapter of the Trisha Ashley novel we had borrowed from the library in town, and which was proving irresistible, Jamie spoke up before I had a chance.

'Now tonight,' he said, pulling Hayley's laden carrier bag out from under his chair and plonking it on the table, 'I'm offering a slight alteration to the evening's usual entertainment.'

'Oh yes?' said Dorothy, her eyes fixed firmly on the bag. 'And just what exactly is it that you're proposing?'

'Film night,' he announced, carefully tipping out what looked like at least twenty DVDs. 'Christmas film night, to be precise,' he added, looking purposefully at me. 'I thought it might get us all in the spirit a bit. Gee us all up for the big day and give Anna here something to write about in her new journal.'

'It's a lovely idea,' said Catherine, stifling a yawn, 'but if you don't mind, dear, your father and I will pass on this occasion.'

'But—' began Angus.

'But nothing,' said Catherine.

She had a tone of voice, I had discovered, which although soft brooked no refusal. Not even from her husband.

'I think we can all of us agree that the one person sitting at this table who doesn't require further "geeing up" as you put it, Jamie, is your father.'

'You do have a point, my dear,' Angus grinned. 'In fact, if I don't dial the excitement down a bit I think I might be in very real danger of peaking even before the rest of the family get here!'

'Fair enough,' said Jamie, smiling at his mum. 'I'll let you off this time, Dad, for Mum's sake if nothing else.'

'Thank you,' said Catherine, sounding a little relieved.

'And what about you, Anna?' Jamie asked. 'You're up for it, aren't you?'

It was amusing that he was even asking because given the deal we'd struck up I knew I had absolutely no option but to join in with what he was suggesting.

'Absolutely,' I said. 'I think it's a great idea. I can't remember the last time I watched a festive film.'

That wasn't true at all, I suddenly realised, because I could pinpoint exactly the last such film I'd watched and when. Snuggled up in Mum's bed we'd watched Bob Hope in *The Lemon Drop Kid* for the millionth time. It was the last time I had heard her sing *Silver Bells* and I hoped to goodness that wasn't one of the DVDs Jamie had lined up, but if the bag had come from Hayley's collection then I reckoned I'd be safe. *Home Alone* was much more her line, I was sure.

'And you can count me in,' said Dorothy eagerly. 'It'll make a change from listening to the radio.'

'And me,' said Mick, stretching in his chair. 'Although I can't promise I'll still be awake by the time it's finished.'

'So, what have you got lined up for us then?' I asked with a nervous nod towards the teetering tower of cases.

'I thought we'd ease in gently,' said Jamie, clearly more for my benefit than anyone else's. 'It isn't strictly a Christmas film, but it's a classic, and in my experience everyone loves it.'

'*Bridget Jones*,' I laughed as he brandished the case, 'perfect.'

'You boys go and get the fire stoked up then,' said Dorothy, with a fine disregard for sexual equality, 'and Anna and I will make the popcorn.'

The evening was such a success, apart from Mick snoring his way through the opening credits and beyond, that I agreed we could repeat the experience every other night from then until the family arrived, and possibly beyond if they were interested.

Snuggled on the sofa next to Jamie, sharing a blanket and a ginormous bowl of maple-syrup-flavoured popcorn, with Dorothy quietly crocheting in another chair until she started to drop off and took herself to bed, was, in my opinion, a wonderful way to while away a December evening. I was touched to discover that Jamie had numbered the DVD cases to keep me feeling that way. *Bridget Jones* was number one, while *National Lampoon's Christmas Vacation* came in at number nineteen. Apparently, the more intense the festive family fun, the higher the number.

'And we'll be watching them in order,' Jamie said seriously. 'There'll be no skipping numbers. Over-exposure would be a major setback to your progress.'

'Is that right?' I smiled.

'It is,' he insisted. 'We have to take things nice and slow.'

My stomach gave a flip as I thought of all the things I would like to take 'nice and slow' with my employers' son, along with a few that would be better going as fast as a steam engine. This whole love/lust thing I was feeling was a huge inconvenience, but I was just about managing to keep a lid on it, most of the time.

I felt the heat rise in my cheeks and decided to let myself off just this once. Given our close proximity and the fact that I had just watched Bridget secure her happy-ever-after, my own feelings were bound to come to the fore, even if they were misplaced.

'Well,' I said, 'I'm very touched that you care so much about my progress and that you're taking my wellbeing so seriously.'

'Oh I don't care a jot about that,' he joked, pulling my half of the blanket over to him. 'I just want to win.'

'Win?' I said, trying to pull the blanket back.

'Yes,' he said, tugging harder. 'It's imperative that I make you fall in love with Christmas far harder than you make me fall in love with the hall, remember?'

'Oh right,' I said. 'I see. It's like that, is it?'

'Absolutely,' he said, ripping the blanket right out of my hands. 'I will be victorious.'

Well, we'd see about that, wouldn't we?

As it turned out, 'falling in love with Christmas' wasn't the tricky part of the deal and I soon came to realise that Jamie's endeavours to get me to join in the Connelly Christmas were actually the easy bit. When it came down to it, I could manage to cope with the 'trimmings', the festive films and leftover rolls of wrapping paper. My problems surrounding the season ran far deeper and were flagged up to me in horrid and exacting detail the afternoon Angus asked me to look in the lofts with him for the boxes of decorations.

To be honest, I hadn't really been up for the expedition at all, but Mick had taken himself off to the woods and Catherine was keen to ensure her husband had a chaperone.

'You don't mind, do you, Anna dear?' she whispered. 'Only it would be such a comfort to know where he is for the afternoon and exactly what he's up to.'

She had a point. We hadn't been able to keep proper track of him for days and still had no idea where all the parcels he had been taking away had disappeared to.

'All right,' I reluctantly agreed. 'But only if you promise not to do anything too strenuous while I'm gone.'

I had barely spent any time at all acting as either Catherine's carer or companion, but no one seemed to mind, least of all the lady herself, who found more comfort knowing what her husband was about than having me hanging on to her coattails at every turn.

'I promise,' she said. 'I have about a thousand Christmas cards to write so that should keep me out of mischief for a while.'

I don't know what I had been expecting, but the space referred to as 'the lofts' at Wynthorpe Hall bore absolutely no resemblance to those I had encountered before, accessed via a metal ladder and a hole in a ceiling that was always slightly too small. The lofts at the hall were in fact a series of rooms at the back of the property which had once been servants' quarters and were reached by a full-size staircase and a proper door.

'Oh my goodness,' I gasped as Angus flicked a switch, lighting up a long corridor which had doors leading off left and right.

'Don't worry,' he chuckled. 'She won't bite.'

Slowly I took in the grand space assigned to storage and then the shocking spectacle Angus was fondly patting.

'What on earth?' I spluttered, my hand flying up to my chest.

'I know,' said Angus, still laughing. 'I should have warned you. I keep meaning to get Mick to help me move her, but she's such a weight. Perhaps if Jamie helps as well . . .'

Standing erect at what must have been well over seven foot was a real, but thankfully stuffed, brown bear, complete with bonnet, shawl and shopping basket.

'This is Dolores,' said Angus fondly by way of introduction. 'She's been in the family for ever.'

Given her age she looked incredibly well preserved.

'And she's dressed for the shops because?' I asked, my eyes drawn to her sharp teeth and claws.

'That's Catherine's fault, I'm afraid,' Angus explained. 'When my good lady wife was a little girl she was terrified of this poor old bear, who had pride of place in the dining room.'

I didn't blame her. I was a full-grown woman and I was pretty frightened myself.

'So,' Angus continued, 'her mother thought it might help if she dressed her up and gave her a name.'

'And did it work? Was Catherine any less terrified?'

'No,' said Angus, sounding surprised. 'Apparently not, and as soon as she took over the running of the hall she had dear old Dolores banished from sight.'

He sounded rather regretful about that and I imagined he would be all in favour of having her reinstated if he got the chance. I didn't ask for fear of setting off a chain of thought that would see the old bear dressed up as Santa to amuse the grandchildren. And probably give them and me nightmares for a month.

'She's quite a weight,' he went on, 'and an awkward shape. It isn't easy manoeuvring her while avoiding her claws and teeth, so this is as far as she's got.'

'Well,' I said, 'I'm sure Catherine is happier to have her out of sight. Do you think we should get on? Dorothy will want to serve tea soon.'

It hadn't taken many nights under the Connellys' roof for my calorie-counting routine to slip and a new one, which revolved around the delights of the kitchen table, to step up and take its place. I made a mental note to extend mine and Jamie's early-morning running route by an extra few hundred metres, lest the extra padding really did decide to stick.

'That's a very good point,' said Angus, fondly patting Dolores on the arm one last time before wombling off down the corridor, muttering under his breath.

I followed on behind, taking in the laminated alphabetical signs that were attached to each of the doors. Someone had instated quite a storage system up in these 'lofts'.

'This was all Catherine's idea,' said Angus when we reached the room marked 'C'. 'We haven't got enough rooms for every letter, of course, but oddly enough there isn't much point in designating an entire space to each of them.'

'What, like "X" and "Z"?' I guessed.

'Exactly,' he nodded. 'Although the zebra does take up a fair bit of space.'

I really hoped he was talking about a cuddly toy.

Along with a couple of dozen boxes marked 'Christmas', the 'C' room also contained cots, curtains, cushions and curios and, not surprisingly, it wasn't many minutes before Angus was diving into all the boxes and the purpose of our visit was completely forgotten.

'Well, well, well,' he chuckled. 'What are these doing here?'

Neatly stacked next to a box marked 'cameras' were packets and packets of photographs.

'Looks like Catherine's system has had a slight malfunction.'

He sounded almost delighted and made the announcement with a wink. I felt sure he would have favoured a far more random approach to storage, had he been able to get away with it.

'This lot should be in the "P" room, surely?'

I didn't answer him. I couldn't. All the time I had spent avoiding the cinnamon and crackers and it was something as simple and innocuous as a selection of silly family snaps that was to prove to be my undoing.

Two fat tears coursed unbidden down my cheeks as I flicked through one set after another. In some the three boys were young, all under ten, while in others they were surly-looking teens, uncomfortable in the bodies that had grown a little too quickly for their age, but one thing shone through in each and every set.

Love.

Pure and simple.

The Christmases and birthdays captured were such happy occasions, filled with family, security and an overwhelming outpouring of love. I looked at Catherine, younger in some shots, older in others, but showing adoration for her family at every age. However, it was the pictures of Angus that were most striking. In many the boys were climbing all over him, wrestling and rolling about, but in all of them they were laughing.

Here was a father who understood the value of family and was immersed in it at every stage of his sons' lives. Had anything, God forbid, ever happened to Catherine when the boys were young, Angus wouldn't have shunned and abandoned his responsibilities. The thought would never have entered his head. He would have accepted the challenge and continued the work of shaping them into the men they were today. He wouldn't have reached for the nearest bottle and forgotten the promises he had made.

'Dear girl,' he cried out now, suddenly noticing my distress. 'What on earth?'

Without another word he dropped the pile he had been flicking through and rushed to my side, and I, without a care for whether it was appropriate employee etiquette, threw my arms around him and sobbed.

'My darling girl,' he said, making no attempt to pull away. 'You're all right. You're home with us now. You're safe.'

When my tears eventually began to subside he sat me down on a packing box and set about tidying the photographs we had dropped. There was no drama, no demand to be told what all the fuss was about, and I felt an even stronger rush of affection for him because of it.

'You know,' he said, smiling kindly at me as he packed the pictures away, 'family doesn't always mean blood, Anna. Sometimes a person will just find themselves somewhere and they will realise that the folk around them can love and be loved every bit as much as a mother or father, sister or aunt, and sometimes,' he added meaningfully, 'even more.'

I was just about to answer him and explain that I was beginning to understand that, when I heard the sound of heavy footfall along the corridor.

'Is everything all right?' came Jamie's voice even before he appeared. 'I thought I heard someone crying.'

'Crying?' questioned Angus, his tone suggesting the idea was absurd. 'Poor Anna here had the fright of her life when she spotted Dolores out there, but no, no tears.'

'That's all right then,' said Jamie, sounding relieved.

I was touched by his reaction. He had no doubt panicked that I had found the trip to look for Christmas decorations a stretch too far and rushed to make sure I was all right. Not for the first time that day I thought how very lucky I had been to be offered the position working here, at this time of year. For once my cup really was running over.

'No mad women or men in the attic here,' Angus muttered as he carried on plundering boxes and sent a conspiratorial wink in my direction.

'Well, I'm very glad to hear it,' Jamie said, 'but Mum says can you leave this for now and come down to the kitchen? Molly's on her way and she wants to talk to you about the Solstice celebration.'

Chapter 15

I took a moment to compose myself and Angus gave my hand a comforting squeeze as we walked back down the stairs.

'All right?' he asked, taking care not to look directly at me and set me off again.

'Yes,' I nodded. 'Yes, I'm all right. Thank you for not saying anything to Jamie.'

'I didn't think you'd want a fuss.'

'You were right,' I told him. 'The less fuss the better, as far as I'm concerned.'

'I have a feeling,' Angus tutted, 'that you've been chanting that mantra for far too many years, my dear girl.'

He was right of course, but I wasn't about to acknowledge the fact and risk opening the floodgates again.

'One day,' he said, when I didn't answer, 'you'll hear how most people have ended up here and how they never liked to make a fuss, even though their lives were in real turmoil.'

I didn't tell him that Mick and Hayley had already told me how they came to be at the hall but said instead, 'Well, you better make it sooner rather than later. You haven't forgotten I'm on an eight-week contract, have you?'

Without warning he let out his best Father Christmas belly laugh, which set Floss woofing in the kitchen.

'Now come on, Anna,' he said. 'I don't think you'll really be going anywhere in the New Year, do you?'

We'd already reached the kitchen door so I didn't have time to answer his question or ask if he was being serious, but deep inside I think I already knew what I hoped the answer would be.

Sitting at the table drinking tea with Catherine and Dorothy was a young woman with a cascading mass of auburn curls and incredibly large, pale blue eyes. There was no sign of the witch Molly anywhere. I hoped she wasn't going to suddenly appear out of thin air because I really wasn't in the mood for shocks or surprises.

'Molly Trotter!' cried Jamie, himself appearing from somewhere behind Angus and me and bowling between us to get into the kitchen. 'It's so good to see you!'

The girl jumped up to return his hug and I felt the heat rise in my cheeks as I realised I'd made a whole heap of assumptions based purely on the looks of the stunning pre-Raphaelite vision before me.

'And you,' she said, warmly returning Jamie's embrace and

making me feel even hotter in the process. 'Gosh, you look well,' she added, 'your aura's positively pulsing.'

'Steady on,' said Jamie, taking a step back, but still hanging on to her hand. 'I think you'll find I'm just pleased to see you.'

'Jamie!' scolded Dorothy, before Catherine had a chance.

'Same old Jamie,' laughed Molly.

'Don't mind them, Anna,' said Angus, nudging me further into the room. 'They're always like this.'

'Anna,' said Jamie, only just remembering that I was there. 'Come and meet Molly.'

'Hi,' I said, stepping forward and for some reason feeling unusually shy as I held out my not quite steady hand.

'Anna,' Molly smiled, her pale eyes taking me in and her hand resting in mine. 'It's lovely to meet you at last.'

'At last?'

'Yes, I've seen you around and about of course, but it's good to finally meet.'

I felt my temperature spike again and hoped she wasn't aware of the scaredy-cat reaction I had displayed when I had spotted her walking through the woods.

'Molly's our token girl,' said Jamie, pulling out the chair next to her and offering it to me.

Gratefully I took it but I wouldn't have minded sitting a little further away. For some reason Molly made me feel uncomfortable, possibly even vulnerable, but I wouldn't have been able to really explain why. However, I did know I couldn't shake off the feeling that in the two seconds she had held my hand, and her limpid eyes had swept over me, she had deduced a damn sight more about me than I had about her.

'What do you mean "token girl"?' I asked Jamie.

'I grew up on the estate,' Molly herself explained. 'I was the only girl around when the boys were growing up. My grandmother and mother both lived in the woodsman's cottage at the edge of the wood and now I live there on my own. I'm hoping that I'm going to be able to carry on living there for the foreseeable future at least.'

'You have no worries on that score,' Catherine piped up. 'You won't be going anywhere in my lifetime.'

'Or mine,' Jamie added.

I don't think anyone else heard him, or if they did, they didn't comment, but I took his two brief words as further indication that he had no plans to shy away from his post as the next custodian of Wynthorpe Hall.

'So you see, Anna,' Catherine continued, 'Molly grew up playing in the gardens and around this table with our three boys. In many ways she's the daughter we never had.'

'And consequently, the token girl,' Jamie cut in. 'Although you were never much of a girly girl, were you, Mol?'

'No,' she agreed. 'I suppose not.'

'She was always dragging us off into the woods,' Jamie

continued. 'Trying to teach us about plants and birds, her pockets weighed down full of stones with holes in.'

'They're witches' stones actually,' said Molly, reaching into her coat pocket and pulling out a smooth pebble which had a hole right through one end. 'I found this one for you, Anna.'

'For me?' I gulped.

'Yes,' she smiled, handing it over.

It felt warm and soft as I turned it over in my hands, my index finger tracing the outline of the hole. I held it up to the light and looked through it.

'Well, would you look at that?' said Jamie, reaching into his pocket and pulling out his own holey stone, which could have passed for the twin of mine. 'They're the same.'

They really were almost identical.

'Anna's is just like the one you gave me before I went off on my travels, Molly. What a coincidence.'

'I'm pleased to see you've still got it,' said Molly, 'but it isn't a coincidence at all. Now, tell me about the Solstice. There's a rumour flying about the estate that you're all set to reinstate the celebration. Is it true?'

From what I could gather the Solstice celebration was going to happen much the same as it always had, and by the time we had emptied the teapot not once but twice, it was decided that Molly and some of her friends (or should that have been coven) would get the ball rolling by spreading the word, organising the ceremony and preparing the woods.

'I'll get Shelley to draw up a flyer,' she said enthusiastically.

'And we'll get them printed,' chipped in Jamie.

It sounded like the event was going to involve quite a few people and I was relieved it would all be happening under the protection of the public liability insurance policy. The practicalities of the policy might not have been particularly spiritual in origin but they did make me feel a little more relaxed about it all, and judging by Catherine's benevolent expression I was sure she was feeling the same way.

'And what about gathering the Yule logs?' asked Molly. 'Are you still happy for folk to do that? As long as they go about it in the right and respectful way, of course.'

'Absolutely,' said Angus, 'and actually, it's going to be down to Anna to pick ours this year, isn't it, my dear?'

'Apparently,' I swallowed.

I hadn't realised there was a 'right and respectful way' to go about it and hoped I was going to be guided as to what to do.

'It's her birthday, you see,' Angus added.

'What, on the Solstice?' Molly smiled.

'Yes,' he nodded. 'So it's only fitting that she should choose.'

'How exciting,' Molly laughed, her pale eyes seeking me out again. 'Have you always celebrated the shortest day as well as your birthday, Anna?'

Had she seen me dressed up in my work outfit and Manolos she wouldn't have dreamt of even asking.

'No,' I admitted, feeling a bit of a fraud, 'I've rarely even bothered with my birthday to be honest, and I didn't know all that much about the Solstice until this afternoon.'

The sharp intake of breath around the table made my palms heat up and my heart thump and I knew those gathered were more concerned about my lack of birthday parties than my ignorance about the Solstice. Yet again I had unwittingly almost said more than I should and I quickly closed my mouth, lest I should give any more away. Jamie had no doubt guessed why I hadn't celebrated the passing of another year, but no one else knew the significance of the timing.

'I'm always too busy working, you see,' I eventually added, as if that was a justifiable reason for not treating myself to some candles and a balloon.

'Well, in that case,' Molly insisted, 'we'll make it even more of an occasion. The timing couldn't be more perfect, especially as you're so determined to make a fresh start.'

'Is she?' said Jamie, his ears no doubt pricking up when he thought there was an opportunity to nudge ahead in the Christmas countdown stakes.

'You know full well that she is,' said Molly, her light eyes now honed in on him. 'You both are, and the turning of Nature's wheel will give you both the extra impetus you're going to need.'

I had no idea what she was talking about, but no one else at the table looked as if they thought her way of talking was strange, and I certainly wasn't going to turn down the 'extra impetus' she spoke of. In fact, I was ready to embrace it with open arms and give myself the chance of a life that was happily lived for twelve months of the year rather than ten and a very little bit.

'Well in that case,' I surprised myself by saying out loud, 'I'm looking forward to the celebration even more now.'

'That's excellent,' said Molly, 'and I can promise you, we will make this year one that you certainly won't forget.'

'Unless of course Dorothy makes the mulled cider as potent as last time,' piped up Angus. 'As I recall no one remembered a thing that year!'

Before Molly left I thanked her for the holey stone and she promised to show me the Wishing Tree the next day, when we would all meet in the woods to gather the greenery in readiness for the auction at the weekend.

'You aren't out of the woods, so to speak, just yet, Anna,' she told me, 'but I can promise you, you're well on your way.'

By Friday morning the snow had all but gone and the day dawned dull and grey. Jamie and I didn't bother with our early-morning run because as Mick was so keen to point out—

'You'll need all your strength to shift this year's crop.'

And he wasn't wrong.

Obviously I had no idea how much glossy, bright-berried holly and mysterious mistletoe was normally gathered, but the packed trailer and Land Rover suggested that this was a bumper winter harvest.

'It's all about balance,' explained Molly, who had pitched up early to help. 'There has to be enough left for the birds and wildlife, otherwise it's just humans pillaging for their own ends and to my mind there's already enough of that going on in the world.'

She had a point.

'But I do love the thought of people still wanting to dress their homes and hearths with Nature's bounty in the traditional way,' she went on.

'Even if it is just over the threshold?' asked Jamie, who had wandered over brandishing a bunch of slightly battered mistletoe.

'Even then,' confirmed Molly as she skilfully ducked out of the way before Jamie had a chance to plant a kiss on her rosy cheek.

'And what about you, Anna?' he said, turning his playful attention squarely in my direction.

'I don't think so,' I laughed, quickly jumping up and rubbing my hands over my jeans to brush away any moss and leaves that had got stuck during our earlier exertions. 'I don't mix business with pleasure,' I added primly.

'But you do admit it would be a pleasure?' he teased.

'Oh be quiet,' I batted back. 'All this fresh Fen air and exercise has gone to your head.'

'All right,' he said, sneakily changing course, 'but what if I were to suggest that a kiss under the mistletoe would enhance your holiday spirit?'

I knew exactly the game he was trying to play, but I wasn't falling for it. Just one touch of those sensuous lips would mean disaster for me and he would just have to accept that this was one festive suggestion that I was not prepared to tick off my list.

'I'll give it a go,' said Hayley, dropping the tiny bundle of holly she was carrying and marching between the few locals who had turned up throughout the morning to help. 'Anything that'll relieve the boredom and warm me up a bit is most welcome!'

She'd done nothing but moan about the cold and the state of her nails all morning and I'd been wondering why she'd bothered to put in an appearance at all, but now it was obvious. Jamie, holding a bunch of mistletoe and offering free kisses, was one Christmas bonus she wasn't prepared to miss out on.

Without so much as a hint of hesitation, or a care that she had gathered quite an audience, she flung her arms around Jamie's neck and pulled his lips down onto hers. Everyone, except Molly, Mick and me, began to laugh, clap and stamp, and I had to look away. There might not have been anything remotely romantic about it but it was too much of a spectacle for me.

'So?' asked Jamie expectantly when Hayley eventually released him.

Hayley delicately wiped her mouth and let out a contented sigh.

'About a seven, I reckon,' she said seriously.

Anyone would have thought she was rating an Olympic event.

'Seven!' spluttered Jamie, sounding outraged. 'Objection! I demand a recount.'

'Well, you better give me another kiss then,' said Hayley eagerly.

The sly young thing.

'See if you can convince me to up my score.'

'I think that's enough to be going on with, thank you,' said Mick, stepping between the flirtatious pair. 'You're incorrigible, Hayley. If only you'd put as much effort into gathering this greenery as you have into winding him up we'd have been done hours ago.'

Hayley snatched up the previously abandoned holly and flounced over to stand next to me.

'I can't say I'm all that sure what that word you just said means, Mick, but it didn't sound particularly pleasant. I'm off to find someone who will appreciate my sense of fun. If that's all right with you.'

Mick rolled his eyes and Jamie began to laugh.

'And you're no better,' Mick tutted in Jamie's direction. 'You shouldn't encourage her. Come and give me a hand shifting this trailer. That'll soon dampen your ardour.'

'I thought you said you didn't like him,' Hayley said quietly to me as she began to walk away.

'I don't,' I said.

'You do,' she said. 'You should have seen your face.'

'Is that why you did it?' I called after her, but she wouldn't answer. 'Were you trying to prove a point? Because it hasn't worked, you know.' She really was an infuriating friend.

The show finally over, everyone turned back to the job in hand and Molly remembered her promise to introduce me to the Wishing Tree. I wasn't going to pass up the opportunity to put some distance between myself, Jamie and the sprig of mistletoe he had now tucked into his top pocket. I had thought I'd got my inconvenient feelings firmly under control but if the thump in my head during his clinch with Hayley was any indication I definitely hadn't.

'Where are you two skulking off to?' he called after us as we slipped away.

'Never you mind,' Molly called back. 'You just get on with your work, Jamie Connelly.'

I couldn't hear his response and when I turned back to look at him, he and all the others were already out of sight. I gave a little shudder and turned up the collar on my jacket.

'It can be a nuisance sometimes, can't it?' said Molly wistfully.

'Sorry,' I said, 'what can?'

'Falling in love.'

I stopped and stared at her.

'You're really very fond of him, aren't you?'

I didn't know what to say.

'Isn't that what made you shudder?' she asked. 'Those inconvenient feelings akin to love that you can't control?'

'No,' I said, shaking my head. 'No, you couldn't be more wrong.'

Molly didn't say anything. She and Hayley were poles apart in some ways but peas in a pod in others.

'It's the woods,' I said, looking around and trying to make her understand. 'They scare me a little. That's why I shuddered. They remind me of the staircases at Hogwarts.'

'What do you mean?'

'Well, every time I think I've got the layout clear in my head, something changes and I'm lost again.'

'A bit like in life really.'

This was all getting too weird for me.

'No,' I said, 'just here, amongst these trees. I think I've got life all figured out now.'

'Do you?' said Molly, spinning round to face me.

I didn't answer and we walked on a little further in silence until a tinkling noise stopped me in my tracks.

'It's all right,' Molly said, 'it's just the tree.'

In a clearing on our right we came suddenly upon the Wishing Tree, bedecked in ribbons, fabric, letters, flags and even keys, all fluttering in the breeze, brushing one another and dancing to their own strange yet melodic tune.

'Oh wow,' I gasped. 'It's beautiful.'

It was stunning yet strange. There was no birdsong, just the sound of gentle movement amongst the bejewelled branches.

'Where has this breeze come from?' I whispered.

'From the tree perhaps,' said Molly mysteriously. 'How else would the wishes get carried away if there was no wind to take them?'

Rooted to the spot, I looked up among the tokens that had been left, wondering what the stories behind them all were.

'Are you going to make a wish?' asked Molly.

'I don't think there's anything I want now,' I said.

Had she shown me the tree even just a few days before, her question might have elicited a different response, but surprisingly I felt like a different person now. Living and working at Wynthorpe Hall had unlocked my heart as well as my head and, for the time being at least, I felt certain that my life couldn't possibly get any better.

'My life has changed so much in such a short space of time,' I explained, more to the tree than to Molly, 'that I don't think there's a single thing I need to ask for.'

Perhaps I should have been thinking about saying thank you instead.

'You aren't the first to feel that way,' Molly smiled. 'Problems here seem to have a way of unravelling until they simply don't exist any more.'

I knew she wasn't just talking about my situation. She was talking about the things Hayley, Dorothy and Mick had been through, and perhaps even experiences of her own.

'It's a truly magical place, isn't it?' I said, stepping forward to place my gloved hand on the gnarled trunk.

'Well, I've always thought so,' Molly agreed. 'Although you have to be prepared to tap into your own magic if you really want things to happen. You have to take some responsibility.'

'Do you think so?'

I had begun to think the recent unexpected twist in my path was more to do with fate than anything I had decided to do or not to do, but Molly thought differently.

'Absolutely,' she said firmly. 'So, do you still not want to make a wish?'

'Not today,' I said, taking a step away from the tree. 'Perhaps on my birthday.'

I still hadn't really had the opportunity to assimilate the sudden changes being at the hall had brought about, and although happy in my work and enjoying playing my part in the deal I had made with Jamie, I couldn't dismiss the niggling twinge of doubt that was trying to muscle its way in and snatch back my good fortune.

Opportunities and Christmases like this just didn't happen to people like me, and without really thinking about what I was doing I turned back to the mysterious tree and wished with all my heart that it wasn't all going to turn out to be too good to be true.

Chapter 16

I had no real opportunity to mull over the concerns that my life was suddenly 'too good to be true', because there was too much happening at both the hall and in town. Thinking about anything other than Christmas cakes, puddings and trees for next twenty-four hours at least was going to be impossible, so I decided to just give myself up to the situation and go with the flow.

Dorothy had been delighted with the new jam thermometer she had produced from the Advent calendar early that Saturday morning, but unfortunately it hadn't held her attention long enough to stop her fussing.

'Now you won't forget to take these extra cakes with you, Anna, will you?' she nagged as Jamie and I got ready to leave for the tree auction and bake sale. 'And tell Jemma there are three more puddings to come. I'll bring those myself later.'

The entire expedition had been planned in minute detail

right down to the last second, but she was still in a flap. Jamie looked at me from the other side of the table and tapped his watch. He was as keen to get the day kicked off as I was, but thanks to Dorothy's insistence that we should check the details just once more, we knew we wouldn't be going anywhere fast.

'I'm driving in with your father,' she told Jamie, who already knew. 'And we'll be there around eleven.'

Angus had received a phone call the evening before as we sat enjoying supper after a hard day's work collecting the greenery, and he had graciously (and greedily) accepted the role as chief taste tester of the Christmas cupcakes some of the local schoolchildren were entering into the bake sale competition.

'Oh yes,' we heard him say, 'I would be absolutely honoured. Will there be many entrants, do you think?'

The answer had proved such a shock that he had decided to forgo his breakfast to ensure he had enough of an appetite to take a bite of each one. Angus going without his porridge was an unheard of situation, Mick told me, and everyone was mightily shocked. Especially Dorothy, who had then gone out of her way to tempt him with all manner of treats should he pass out from hunger before the first sugar-loaded hit found its mark.

Angus wandered into the kitchen now, still in his pyjamas and dressing gown with his hair standing up in its usual early-morning lumps and tufts. Catherine was hot on his heels and looking understandably exasperated.

'Which of these,' said Angus, holding up two pairs of apparently identical trousers for our scrutiny, 'would you say has the most give? Ideally I could do with an elasticated waist, but in the absence of jogging bottoms, these will have to do.'

'Come on, Anna,' huffed Jamie.

Clearly he had had enough.

'Let's leave the madhouse and head up to town.'

With the cakes and the packed Land Rover and trailer we wove our way to town and across the bridge that spanned the River Wyn. The market square was already heaving and the scent of pine and fresh-cut greenery filled my nostrils even before I'd seen any of the trees that were to be auctioned. One glance at the gathering crowds warned me that the switch-on had merely been a warm-up for what I was going to have to cope with now.

'You all right?' asked Jamie as he reversed deftly into the space Chris was directing him towards.

Evidently the groan that had escaped my lips unbidden hadn't gone unheard.

'Is this going to be too much, do you think?'

'Of course it is,' I told him with a wry smile so he would know I was only partly joking. 'But given how you've jumped feet first into everything I've suggested you should do to fall in love with the hall again, I can hardly wimp out now, can I?'

'Well, I suppose not,' he said, sounding concerned, 'but I promise I won't hold it against you if you change your mind.'

'Really?'

'Really,' he said, jumping out to unhook the trailer, 'because I reckon this is going to be a little out of your league,' he carried on. 'We're not even halfway through the DVD collection yet.'

'Oh never mind,' I said, rushing around to help him. 'I'll risk it. I mean, how bad can it be?'

By the time we had helped Chris unload the trailer, remembered the cakes and I had been ushered up the town hall steps, through the double doors and into the cinnamon-scented chaos within, I already knew the answer was 'pretty bad'. The place was a full-on seasonal assault on the senses, but there was no time to have an attack of the vapours. The event looked as if it needed help and plenty of it.

'You're here!' squealed Lizzie from the Cherry Tree when she caught sight of me and the cake tins loitering in the doorway. 'And not a moment too soon. Come with me and I'll show you where you can wash your hands and we'll find you an apron.'

She took charge of Dorothy's contribution and steered me towards the kitchens.

'Good luck,' mouthed Jamie as I watched him backing towards the doors.

He gave me a thumbs-up which I returned before being swallowed up by the excited, chattering throng. For some reason I felt a lump forming in my throat and hastily swallowed it away. Watching Jamie walk out felt as though someone had taken my security blanket away and I suddenly realised that I had become perhaps a little too reliant on his solicitous cosseting during my mission to reclaim Christmas.

It was merely days ago that I had been so proud of my independent and professional status and now here I was, relying on a man (albeit a very kind one), to tell me what to do in order to achieve my goal. I needed to pull myself together before I slipped any further down the co-dependent route. Not that Jamie was relying on me for anything, I was sure.

'You all right?' asked Lizzie, when I didn't take the apron she was offering.

'Yes,' I said, two spots of colour lighting up my cheeks. 'Sorry. I'm just trying to take it all in.'

'Amazing, isn't it?' said Jemma, as she rushed over and popped the lids off the cake tins to have a look at what Dorothy had sent. 'Wow. These are gorgeous.'

Three beautifully iced Christmas cakes sat nestled in their wrappings of protective parchment. They had all been decorated differently. One was clearly made with a family in mind and was topped with a group of individually made snowmen, women and children, while the other two were simple but elegant and ornamented with edible holly, berries and festive ribbons.

'Dorothy said she'll bring the puddings with her later. She's driving in with Angus.'

'From what I heard he was rather excited to be asked to judge the cupcakes,' laughed Lizzie.

'Yes,' I told them, 'you could say that.'

'He's going all out this Christmas, so I understand,' gossiped Jemma. 'Rumour has it that he's offered to house the sleigh in the stables at the hall, and the ponies that go with it, in return for free use of it during the rest of December when the family comes to visit.'

'Well, I don't know about that,' I said, wishing I'd had more of a chance to keep an eye on his shenanigans.

Catherine would be furious if this rumour turned out to be true. She had had an inkling that Angus had more than a healthy interest in the sleigh when he played the part of Santa at the switch-on, but as nothing further had been mentioned, I had naïvely assumed he had become preoccupied with something else. Unfortunately, given what Jemma had just let slip, it seemed that I was wrong.

'But you can never tell with Angus, can you?' I said, shaking my head and trying not to give the rumour too much credence.

'Absolutely not,' said Lizzie as she rushed off. 'But he certainly keeps us locals amused, that's for sure.'

That was one way of looking at the situation, I supposed.

'And what have you got planned for Christmas, Jemma?' I asked, keen to change the subject.

'Well, we were supposed to be home alone,' she told me, 'just the four of us, but Tom's sister is having a few problems so she's coming to us now. That's not an issue though. The kids love her and many hands make light work where children are concerned.'

That much I knew from experience. There had been more than one occasion in the past when I had wished I had the capability to clone myself.

'Anyway,' said Jemma, 'that's enough chitchat. We better crack on. Let's get you some coffee and then I'll set you to work.'

'Excellent,' I said, trying to sound not quite as nervous as I felt.

The town hall was a lovely building, but the acoustics left a lot to be desired and it wasn't long before the sound of voices was drowning out the carols and cheesy Christmas tunes that were being pumped out through the sound system. Within minutes everyone who had signed up to 'bake on the day' in the kitchens, along with me, was up to their necks in flour, eggs, garish-coloured frosting and tiny silver balls. I was assigned to help distribute the ingredients, keep the Brownies on their toes washing and drying dishes and make sure the trays that came out of the ovens had the correct family label when they were transferred to the cooling racks for collection later in the day.

It was hot, noisy work but it was also good fun. Everyone was having a wonderful time and I forcibly pushed down my sadness that I hadn't had the chance to come to an event like this with my mum and just focused on how lucky I was to be there, helping out and making the day fun for everyone else. The morning was so busy I didn't have time to so much as glance at the clock and was consequently shocked when Angus and Dorothy arrived with the rest of the puddings.

'It can't be eleven already,' I gasped, readjusting my head-scarf with floury hands and smudging my nose in the process.

'It isn't,' muttered Dorothy, 'it's half past. We're rather behind, thanks to the tree auction.'

'How's it going out there?' I asked.

Immersed in my own busy morning I'd completely forgotten about the trees and greenery being sold outside.

'Marvellous,' chuckled Angus. 'We have all the trees for the hall.'

'Inside and out,' said Dorothy, rolling her eyes.

Just how many had Angus bid on, I wondered.

'And now I'm ready to judge,' he announced, rubbing his hands together with relish.

He looked as though he was thoroughly enjoying his day out in town.

'Before you begin,' I said, expertly tearing off another set of labels for the next batch of cakes that were due to come out of the oven, 'what's all this I've heard about you taking ownership of Santa's sleigh for the next few weeks?'

Dorothy had already bustled off to help the WI ladies with the teas and coffees and Angus looked to where she was standing and back to me with eyes wide with surprise and more than a hint of guilt.

'Oh look,' he said, pointing over my shoulder. 'There's Amber from Skylark Farm. You must come and say hello.'

There was no point pushing the issue, especially not in this noisy hall where he would find it so easy to feign deafness, so, after checking there was someone else available to take up my post, I went with him to meet Amber, the lady partly responsible for the delectable sausage rolls Dorothy and I had been churning out to stock the freezer.

She told me all about how she had moved to the farm on the outskirts of Wynbridge with her partner Jake and set about turning around the fortunes of the place with the help of the orchards and a piggy diversification project. It turned out she was also partly responsible for my cider-induced wobbles the night after the switch-on as well.

'I'm not helping out much at the moment though,' she said, affectionately rubbing her heavily pregnant belly, 'but as soon as this one's born I'll be back at it.'

I sat with her and her daughter, and her friend Lottie,

chatting about what it was that they thought made the town so special.

'There's such a strong sense of community,' explained Lottie, who ran a vintage caravanning holiday experience deep in the Fenland countryside. 'And don't get me wrong, I did have some opposition when I first announced my business idea, but it wasn't long before I was welcomed to the fold and feeling like a local. I'd been a bit of a loner before I moved here,' she admitted, 'but by and large I was greeted with open arms and I wouldn't want to live anywhere else in the world now.'

'She's also in love with the local vet who happens to be sex on legs,' whispered Amber, 'which may have something to do with her preoccupation with the place.'

Lottie stuck her tongue out at her friend and Honey, Amber's daughter, gasped to see such bad manners from a grown-up.

'And what about you, Anna?'

It was on the tip of my tongue to say that I was a bit of a loner too, but I didn't. However, Lottie's admission had got me thinking. The morning had been great fun, even for an outsider like me, and I realised how much better it could have been if Wynbridge had been my hometown and I really knew the people I had been helping.

I felt slightly nauseous as I realised that because I moved around so often I never gave myself the opportunity to put down roots anywhere. Three months was about my maximum timescale for staying anywhere and then I was off.

I let out a long sad breath, knowing that if I didn't stop chopping and changing soon I was destined to always be the girl who was peering in through the window and trying to join in, but not truly belonging anywhere. Before I came to the Fens I didn't care about my indifference to community or my solitary existence. I actually thrived on it, I liked the freedom because it stopped me having to face up to things, but now I wasn't so sure.

Perhaps there was more to life than the contents of my suitcase suggested. Perhaps everyone's assumption that I wouldn't leave Wynthorpe Hall when my contract was up really was a possibility. Ever since I had decided not to run away and made my pact with Jamie to reclaim Christmas I had been 'feeling things' and really that wasn't so bad, was it? I felt my face flush at the thought of really staying put.

'Anna?' said Amber, her voice cutting through my unsettling thoughts. 'Lottie asked how long you're going to be working at the hall.'

'Sorry,' I mumbled.

I opened my mouth to try and offer an answer, but what it would have been I never discovered, as I felt two hands come to rest on my shoulders and turned to see who Lottie and Amber were now smiling up at.

'I've just come to see how you're getting on.'

It was Jamie of course.

'Good,' I said, feeling flattered that he had found the time to come and find out. 'It's been fun.'

'Really?'

I saw a quick glance pass between the two friends at the table. No doubt they were wondering why he'd questioned my response. After all, why wouldn't I have been having fun?

'Really,' I said meaningfully. 'Gosh, you're hands are freezing.'

I could feel the cold reaching through to my skin, even though I was warm and wearing layers. Jamie grabbed a vacant chair, plonked himself in it and held out his hands, clearly expecting me to rub them and get his circulation going again.

'I still have some gloves in my jacket from yesterday,' I said, ignoring the temptation. 'I'll get them if you like.'

By the time I got back to the table Amber had introduced Lottie to Jamie and he was ready to head back out and help with the clearing up.

'I only came in to see how you were faring,' he said, when I passed him the gloves.

I wasn't sure if it was my imagination or not, but he sounded disappointed that I had disappeared for so long.

'And I have a surprise for you later,' he added.

'Lucky Anna,' laughed Amber and Lottie in perfect unison.

Now it was my turn to stick out my tongue.

'What is it?' I asked, turning my attention back to my security blanket.

'You'll see,' he said mysteriously. 'Nice to see you, ladies. And Anna?'

'Yes?'

'Please try and stop Dad from eating all the cakes. I thought he was supposed to be sampling them, not devouring them whole.'

'I'll see what I can do,' I told him, 'but I'm not making any promises.'

'Well, well, well,' teased Amber, even before he was out of earshot. 'Aren't you the lucky one?'

'Lucky one?' I frowned, my eyes now tracking the slow progress Angus was making along the table he was supposed to be judging. The plates he had left behind were looking appallingly depleted.

'Yes,' said Lottie, backing up her friend's words. 'Jamie's quite a sight for sore eyes, isn't he?'

'Says the woman who's dating sex on legs,' I smiled back.

'Is he single? Do I detect a little romance?' she went on.

'Mm,' sighed Amber, blissfully. 'He is single, although I daresay he's had his fair share of romance while he's been off on his travels.'

She was right, of course. Jamie had probably had women falling at his feet in every country he had visited on his way around the world, so why either of them would think he was even remotely interested in me was something of a mystery.

'As tempting as a Christmas romance would be,' I said, trying not to sound like a complete killjoy, 'I'm afraid I don't mix business with pleasure.'

'You mean you aren't interested?' asked Lottie, sounding shocked.

'Now come on, Lottie,' laughed Amber. 'I didn't hear her say that.'

Chapter 17

The afternoon was every bit as busy as the morning and by the time the last crumb had been sold, and Angus had left looking a little green around the gills, my feet and back were aching in equal measure. It was only the thought of a deep, hot bubble bath that helped me power through the last hour, and I hoped that the surprise Jamie had planned involved an early night snuggled under the duvet – but not together, of course.

'Thank you so much for your help today,' said Jemma, when we had finally finished sweeping and stacking the chairs.

'It's been a pleasure,' I told her and I really meant it.

This whole Christmas malarkey wasn't turning out to be anywhere near as tough as I'd thought it would, but then, I reminded myself, I'd never tried it on for size while working somewhere as special and supportive as Wynthorpe Hall.

'You will come back to town before you move on, won't you?' she asked. 'We have lots of Christmas events still to come.'

'If she moves on, you mean,' chipped in Lizzie.

'Of course,' said Jemma. 'I do hope you decide to stay. We all do. Wynbridge has so much to offer.'

'As does Wynthorpe,' grinned Lizzie as Jamie appeared in the doorway, windswept, ruddy-cheeked and looking every inch the romantic hero.

'You all set?' he asked, after congratulating everyone on another successful sale.

'Yes,' I said, 'I'll just grab my jacket.'

'And you might want to brush your hair,' he suggested, biting his lip and trying not to laugh.

I ducked off to the loos and rolled my eyes at my reflection. At least half a bag of flour had found its way into my hair and the blob of red frosting on the end of my nose really completed the Rudolph look.

'Better?' I asked when I came back out, feeling considerably less dishevelled but still shattered.

'You'll do,' he shrugged.

'What a charmer,' teased Lizzie.

'Isn't he just?' I tutted. 'Still,' I said, 'I'm only heading for a bubble bath and bed so I don't suppose a little flour will hurt.'

'You're not going to bed yet,' said Jamie, holding the door open and letting in a blast of biting Wynbridge wind. 'I have plans for you.'

'Woo!' came the collective response of every woman left in the hall.

'He doesn't mean like that,' I called back.

'Do I not?' questioned Jamie, his mouth close to my ear.

I didn't answer, but I did make a point of reminding myself that he flirted with practically every woman he came across and that I was probably no more special to him than anyone else.

Fortunately we didn't have to walk too far before I discovered what his real plans were. Just through the bar of the packed Mermaid pub and into the quietest corner of the restaurant.

'I hope this is all right?' he asked, pulling out my chair and helping me out of the jacket it had hardly been worth putting on.

'It's perfect,' I said, sinking into my seat and feeling the warmth from the log fire reaching my toes. 'Although I can't promise I'll be the most charismatic company this evening. I'm absolutely whacked.'

'I know you just wanted to get home,' he said, 'but we'd get drawn into eating with the others back at the hall and I wanted to talk to you on your own.'

'Oh?' I said, picking up the menu and idly wondering if it was time to start seriously thinking about reining in the calories again.

Our early-morning exercise seemed to be having little impact when it came to staving off the ounces, which were rapidly turning into pounds. Jamie didn't say anything else and I looked over the top of my menu to find him running a finger around the inside of his collar and looking unusually flushed.

'So, what did you want to talk about?' I ventured. 'I hope you aren't going to tell me I'm not keeping my part of our deal because I have plenty more things lined up for you to think about during the next few weeks.'

The time was ticking by and I wouldn't be able to say 'a few weeks' soon. My allotted contract at the hall was going to dwindle to 'a couple of weeks' and then just 'days' before I knew it.

'No,' he said, 'it's nothing like that.'

I tried not to look too deeply into his seductive green gaze. I was still smarting over his kiss with Hayley in the woods, although I was sure, given what she had said afterwards, that that had been her intention. I had tried to hide it, of course, but my reaction to witnessing their brief bout of tonsil hockey was a timely and very real reminder that my feelings for this lovely man had been nudged a long way into the wrong side of appropriate. Whatever I decided to do when my contract was up, I didn't need any more emotional baggage while I was trying to make up my mind.

'You really had a good time today,' he said eventually, 'didn't you?'

'Yes,' I said, 'I did. When I first got there I thought it was going to be tough watching all those families enjoying themselves together, but it wasn't. In fact, if anything, I felt lucky to be a part of it.'

Obviously Jamie didn't know all of the reasons why it had been so hard, but he knew enough, for now. It was astonishing to think that, in spite of the fact that so many years had slipped by, coupled with what I had managed to face up to in the last few days, there was still a massive slab of heartache that I couldn't bring myself to share with anyone. I hoped that if I ever did feel capable of telling the whole sorry tale to Jamie then he would be able to forgive me for holding some things back. Given that he had managed to lay all his cards on the table so soon after we had met I hoped he wouldn't feel cheated because I hadn't been able to reciprocate.

'That's great,' he said, but his smile didn't quite reach his eyes and I wondered if he in fact had an idea that there was still more to add to my horrible history.

'Hey,' said a voice behind my chair. 'Mind if I interrupt?'

It was Ruby.

'Not at all,' said Jamie.

He sounded almost relieved.

'How did the sale in the hall go?' she asked me.

It was only then that I remembered that Ruby was the one

responsible for originally setting up the bake sale and cooking sessions and getting them going.

'It was wonderful,' I told her. 'Every last crumb was sold and the cake-baking activities went down a storm.'

'Excellent,' she said. 'I only managed to pop in for five minutes. I couldn't get anyone else to man the stall so I've been out in the cold all day.'

'Poor you,' I sympathised.

I really had had the better deal as far as location was concerned.

'Well, I'll leave you to it,' she said. 'Thanks for taking part, Anna. Jemma said you were a great help and fitted in a treat.'

I couldn't help but grin. The thought of 'fitting in' was as welcome as the warm fire, but the look on Jamie's face when she went back through to the bar soon extinguished my smile.

'Are you all right?' I asked. 'Have I done something wrong?'

'No,' he said, picking up his menu. 'Of course not. It's nothing. Forget it.'

'But you said you wanted to talk,' I reminded him.

'It doesn't matter. Shall we just order? Otherwise we'll be here all night.'

We ate most of the meal in silence and it wasn't until the chocolate pudding with cream and two spoons was at the table that we struck up a conversation again.

'Mum's instructed our solicitor to draw up the paperwork for me to take over responsibility for the hall,' he said, sounding less than enthusiastic. 'So everything could be signed and sealed, potentially, even before Christmas.'

'So soon,' I said. I had thought things would be officially settled in the New Year and that just the announcement to the rest of the family would be made over Christmas. 'And is that all right with you?'

I was relieved to know the reason behind his change in mood, but incredibly sorry that he hadn't had enough time to really fall in love with the hall and feel completely convinced that he was doing the right thing.

'I guess,' he shrugged.

'You sound resigned to it,' I said.

'I suppose I am,' he shrugged.

'So you still aren't completely sure it's the right thing to do?'

'Oh, it's the right thing to do,' he said. 'I'm just not sure that it's the right thing for me.'

I could understand why he felt that way. I had been banking on having the time to give him so many ideas and potential projects to mull over that when the day dawned to sign on the dotted line he would have been all fired up and raring to go – much like he had miraculously managed to start making me feel about Christmas – but apparently it was all going to be over and done with before I had a chance to hit my stride.

So far all I'd come up with was an insurance policy that opened the hall back up to the public and a gardening scheme that reduced some of the responsibility for maintaining the grounds. There was nothing to keep Jamie hooked, nothing that he could get his teeth into. I would just have to work faster if I was going to make those green eyes really sparkle again.

'You said when we spoke about it before,' I ventured, 'that you wanted travel to be part of your future, didn't you?'

'Yes,' he said. 'Yes, I did.'

I sat back and waited, hoping he was going to open up and add something else.

'But I didn't explain why,' he finally said.

Perhaps I wasn't the only one holding back after all.

'I thought the reason was obvious,' I commented. 'I assumed you wanted to see more of our wonderful world.'

I always treated myself to two long-haul holidays a year, so I could appreciate his desire to explore far-flung places.

'Well, that's always a great reason for boarding a plane,' he said, 'but there was far more to my expeditions than sightseeing.'

It was rather sad that he was already using the past tense when talking about something that had so recently been such a big part of his future.

'What do you mean?'

'My travels were more about working to make a difference than bronzing myself in the sun,' he said slowly.

I could tell he was choosing his words with care, just as I did when I was trying to explain something that was close to my heart and that I didn't want to leave open to misinterpretation.

'What sort of work?' I asked. 'Make a difference to what?'

'The lives of the kids I've been working with for the last nine years for a start,' he said.

'Working with?' I frowned. 'I don't understand.'

I had thought his recent trip abroad was all about getting his head straight while he tried to fathom whether or not he was going to take over ownership of the hall, but clearly he had been coming and going for far longer than that.

'It all started when I was on holiday the summer after I graduated from university.'

'Go on,' I encouraged, eager to hear more.

'A group of us flew out to Africa – Kenya, to be precise. It was supposed to be a bit of a "beach and bar" break while we made up our minds what we were going to do with our lives, but we were booked to stay for well over a month and I soon got bored with the set-up of propping up the bar all night and sleeping all day.'

I was relieved to hear it. I didn't have him pegged as the type who would enjoy a brash lads' holiday in the sun. I hadn't even realised people flew out to Kenya to do that sort of thing. It seemed like one hell of a wasted opportunity to me.

'So, what did you do?' I asked.

'I took myself off exploring some of the spots that weren't on the tourist trail.'

'That could have been dangerous.'

'It could,' he agreed, 'but what it actually turned out to be, was brilliant. I discovered a charity that was working with orphaned children and I started to help out. I cooked meals, scrubbed floors, even taught for a while, and by the time we were due to come home, I was hooked.'

'I see.'

'I couldn't wait to go back and I've been dividing my time between there and a couple of other places, as a volunteer, ever since.'

'It all sounds rather more productive than some extended gap year,' I said.

Jamie laughed, but he didn't sound amused.

'Anna,' he said seriously, 'I'm thirty years old – why would I still be on a bloody gap year?'

I shrugged and took a long sip of wine.

'Oh don't tell me,' he said, sitting back. 'You assumed I was the rich kid who hadn't anything better to do than spend Mummy and Daddy's money while I waited for my inheritance.'

I looked at him and raised my eyebrows. We hadn't known each other long, but I had hoped he thought better of me than that.

'Sorry,' he said, leaning forward again. 'I didn't mean to snap. It's just, that's the kind of assumption everyone makes.'

'Since when have I been everyone?' I asked.

'Sorry,' he said again. 'I guess because I don't talk about it much, people just think I'm off on holiday all the time and as a result I get defensive.'

'Well there you are then,' I said. Now it was my turn to sound defensive. 'How was I supposed to know you'd been coming and going because of work? As far as I knew the only reason you had for travelling, this time around at least, was to try to make a decision about the future of the hall. I thought you were fretting over your lost freedom, not your lost job, and if what people assume about you rankles so much, then why don't you set them straight?'

He shrugged.

'I find it hard to talk about,' he said quietly. 'And to be honest I've had more than enough ribbing about it from my brothers, especially Archie.'

'What do you mean?'

'He's always the first these days to say I should get a proper job. That because I donate back the tiny allowance the charity I volunteer for gives me, I'm sponging off Mum and Dad.'

'But that's ridiculous.'

Jamie looked at me.

'I know that deep down,' he said, 'and I'm sure Archie does really. He never used to have this kind of attitude but it has made me think about what a very privileged position I've been in to have been able to do this for so long.'

'Just because you have a bit of money behind you doesn't invalidate the work you do,' I said seriously. 'I'm sure your contribution to the charity is just as effective as everyone else's. Besides, if you'd wanted to, you really could still be drifting about on an extended gap year but you chose to make a difference to the world instead!'

Jamie burst out laughing and so did I when I realised how angry I was on his behalf.

'Perhaps you could say all that to Archie when he turns up for Christmas.'

'Oh believe me,' I said, polishing off my wine, 'there is plenty I would like to say to him. Most of which would probably get me the sack.'

'I doubt that very much,' Jamie smiled, reaching across the table for my hand and making my heart stop for a moment. 'I don't think any of us are in a rush to let you go, Anna.'

I swallowed hard, squeezed his hand and then let go. The butterfly feelings simply had to be ignored. We may have been enjoying a wonderful evening together but I was still at work, I reminded myself, with the boss's son. A certain element of professional behaviour was still required.

'So,' I said, 'what are you going to do then?'

'I have no idea,'

'Can you not split your time between volunteering abroad and running the hall?'

'I don't think so,' he said sadly. 'Not realistically. Neither place would be getting my full attention and both deserve it.'

'I'm sorry,' I said.

'So am I,' he sighed, 'but as far as I can see, there's no way around it.'

'I suppose not,' I said, the tiniest seed of an idea just beginning to take root in my brain, 'and I can appreciate how hard it must have been for you to walk away from those kids.'

'I'm going to keep in touch as much as I can,' he said sadly. 'But leaving that last time was one of the hardest things I've ever had to do.'

The fact that he cared so much made me care for him all the more.

'Of course,' I nodded, 'but—' I stopped myself for fear of sounding insensitive.

'But what?'

'Well,' I said hesitantly, 'you know, there are plenty of kids here in the UK who are also in need of help.'

It hadn't felt like all that long ago that I had been one of them.

'I do know that,' he said, thankfully not taking my words the wrong way.

It wasn't my intention to suggest that one set of kids could be swapped for another, but I hated the thought of the love and attention he had to offer going to waste now life had turned a corner he hadn't seen coming.

'But more volunteering would mean more time away from the hall,' he said. 'Whether I've had to take a plane or a train to help out somewhere, it would still take my focus away from home.'

'But not if the work was on your doorstep,' I said, the idea slowly growing and taking shape.

'What are you talking about?' he said, pouring me some more wine.

'Look,' I said, 'why not set up your own charity at the hall?'

Jamie looked understandably confused, but I pushed on nonetheless.

'Set something up that will benefit kids in the UK. There are plenty of under-eighteens who are in real need of a break from their lives, whether because they're stuck in the care system, going off the rails or even carers themselves who don't often get the chance to be just kids.'

'But what sort of thing could I offer?'

'I don't know,' I laughed, 'I'm making it up as I go along. What about converting the stable block?'

'Into what? And anyway, I thought you'd earmarked that for teas and coffees for the garden visitors.'

'No,' I said, thinking about the space and realising it could be so much more than a glorified teashop. 'Turn it into accommodation. There's enough space there to make a residential centre. You could offer bushcraft courses in the woods, fishing in the river, flora and fauna walks in the garden. Give those lonely, abandoned and overworked kids a break from their hard lives and the opportunity to get out into the great outdoors. You could even provide a counselling service.'

Jamie looked at me and blinked, then called the waitress over and asked if she could find him some scrap paper and a pen. We spent the rest of the evening with our heads together writing down ideas, some completely impractical, some perfectly manageable, and eventually coming up with the very real beginnings of a plan which would transform running Wynthorpe Hall from an unwanted obligation in Jamie's eyes into a gorgeous gem.

By the time the landlord called time the sparkle was definitely back in his beautiful emerald eyes and I was feeling exhilarated rather than exhausted.

'Come on,' he said, gathering together our collection of notes. 'Let's carry this on outside.'

When we had parked up on the concrete pad from which we had been stargazing just a few nights before, my head was full of even more ideas and we jotted them down, Jamie adding his own, until the scraps of paper were completely full.

'I have to ask,' he said, flicking through the sheets and then turning to face me.

'About what?' I smiled.

My heart felt fit to burst and I knew I was every bit as excited about the potential venture as he was.

'What you said back in the pub about children being lonely, abandoned and overworked.'

'What about it?'

'Well,' he said, 'it seemed to me that you were including yourself in that category.'

I had hoped that in all the excitement he hadn't picked up on that. Suddenly my heart felt as if he'd taken a pin and popped all the air right out of it.

'I know you lost your mum,' he said gently, 'but what about your dad? You do have a dad, don't you, Anna?'

'Yes,' I said, blinking away the image of the man who had put me through more highs and lows than I cared to recall, 'I do, but if it's all right with you, I'd really rather not talk about him. Let's just say my childhood wasn't a happy one and leave it at that, shall we?'

'All right,' said Jamie, 'but what about a home?'

'What do you mean?'

'Do you have a home, Anna? A home of your own, to live in when you aren't working?'

'I'm always working,' I shrugged dismissively, 'or on holiday. I like to treat myself ...'

'So no permanent address,' he probed again.

'No,' I said primly. 'I have a PO Box and storage. It's all I need.'

Jamie nodded, but didn't push further, and I turned my attention to the darkness beyond the window.

'You do realise you've probably beaten me hands down with this idea, don't you?' he said a few moments later. 'There's absolutely no way I can trump this and make you fall in love with Christmas any harder than I've fallen in love this evening.'

It wasn't until I was topping up the hot water in my bath a little later that I realised he hadn't specified what it was exactly that he had fallen in love with.

Chapter 18

Thanks to our brainstorming session in the pub, the following week was set to be even busier than any of us could have predicted. It was kicked off with the usual – but this time extended – Sunday meeting over lunch in the Wynthorpe kitchen.

The rest of the family was due to arrive the following weekend and it was decided that putting up the decorations would happen the week after that when everyone was all together, rather than 'this instant', as suggested by a still very excited Angus. I have to admit to being rather relieved by this decision as I still wasn't sure how I was going to cope when faced with a hall full of twinkling lights and baubles.

Once the rest of the plans for the week had been discussed, everyone's attention turned to Jamie, who was looking every bit as bright-eyed and bushy-tailed as his father and was clearly eager to literally bring something else to the already laden table.

'So,' he began, looking around and shuffling together the papers I recognised from the night before into a slightly more organised heap, 'as you all know, I've come back in time for Christmas to sign on the dotted line and take over responsibility for running the hall.'

Everyone nodded.

'And we couldn't be happier about it,' said Catherine, her expression a cocktail of pride and relief. 'And,' she added, 'we really do appreciate the sacrifices you have had to make in order to do it.'

Jamie got up from his seat and went round the table to give her a hug.

'I know you do, Mum,' he said quietly, 'and I'm sorry it took me so long to make up my mind and I'm also sorry for what you've had to worry about in case I decided not to take the place on.'

It didn't take a genius to work out that he was referring to the underhand and horrid scheme Archie had been cooking up, should he have managed to get his grubby paws on the place. I was rather looking forward to seeing how he would react when he realised that because of his greed and lack of family allegiance, ownership of the place had been lost to him for ever.

'However, the decision has been made and my pen is

poised,' Jamie continued, pulling the beautiful fountain pen Angus had given him out of his shirt pocket. 'But I feel it's only fair to tell you that there are fresh plans afoot for the place now I'm taking up the reins, and I hope that after Anna and I have explained them, you'll all be as excited about this new venture for the hall as we are.'

I couldn't believe he had included me in making the announcement and was now looking at me intently, expecting me to kick things off.

'Right,' I said, clearing my throat and wishing I'd had enough time to prepare something or at least swap my trainers for my Manolos. 'Well . . .'

'Oh and don't be put off by Anna's delivery,' Jamie cut in with a wide grin. 'I gave her absolutely no warning that she was going to have to do this.'

'Yeah,' I said, feeling a smidgen more relaxed, 'thanks for that, Jamie.'

'Does this mean that you've decided to stay?' asked Dorothy eagerly. 'Will you be moving here on a permanent basis now?'

Her question came way out of left field and I had no idea how to answer, so I simply said, quite truthfully, 'That isn't something that's been discussed yet.'

Catherine instantly opened her mouth, no doubt to reaffirm her conviction that she wasn't expecting me to move on, so I launched into the gist of what Jamie and I had cooked up between us before I was sidetracked into making a decision there and then.

'When I heard that Jamie was coming home in time for Christmas,' I began, 'I had no idea that he had been working abroad or that he was going to have to give that work up in order to take over here. I had assumed that he was merely a tourist, broadening his horizons, but when he explained that he was actually leaving behind almost a decade of volunteering and how hard he had found it to walk away from the projects he was involved with, I suggested—'

'After a glass or two of red wine,' Jamie embellished with a wink.

I had no idea how he thought that was relevant. Unless of course he was now thinking the idea was so bonkers that only someone under the influence could have come up with it.

'I suggested,' I said again, 'that he should consider setting up some sort of charity here at the hall, with a view to helping children in this country.'

'But what have we got here that we could possibly give?' said Dorothy, looking about her as if the answer was spelled out in the chaotic jumble that was the kitchen.

'Well, there are the grounds, for a start,' said Jamie, thankfully taking over where I had broken off. 'Anna reckons we could use pretty much all of the outside space. Run courses in the woods.'

'Den-building and things,' I put in.

'Fishing in the river,' Jamie continued. 'And,' he said, taking a deep breath, 'if you think it's a good idea, we could even apply for funding to convert the stable block into a proper residential centre so people could stay for a few days, rather than just the one.'

'From what I've seen of the stables, you have more than enough space to accommodate possibly half a dozen children at a time,' I said. 'And they could visit during the school holidays to enjoy the hall and the grounds all year round.'

I could feel a lump forming in my throat as I thought how wonderful it would be for them to be able to talk to other kids who had been through similar things, kids their own age who really knew what it felt like to be them. I wished I'd had that sort of opportunity available to me.

'What sort of children do you have in mind?' asked Angus. 'How on earth will you be able to choose who to help?'

Here I looked to Jamie to carry on. This was going to be 'his party', so to speak, and his answer was a complete surprise.

'Well,' he said softly, 'having talked to Anna a little about her own experiences and having spent half the night trawling the Internet, I think we should set up a charity to specifically look after the needs of children who have suffered the death of a parent.'

I could hardly believe what I was hearing. It was as if he'd accessed my thoughts and was offering exactly what I had wished for, for my younger self.

'What do you think?' he asked, turning to Angus and Catherine. 'Does that sound like a good idea to you? It felt like a logical step to me; having worked with so many orphaned children in Africa, it kind of ties in with some of my experience and knowledge. Of course I'm not an expert and the Fens are a far cry from the shanties, but it just feels right. Does that make sense?'

'It makes perfect sense,' Catherine and I said together.

'Were you very young when your mother passed, my dear?' asked Dorothy.

'Yes,' I said, 'I had just turned eight.'

I didn't explain just how close to my eighth birthday the tragic day had been.

Angus looked at me as Dorothy sympathetically shook her head and Mick muttered 'poor little bugger', or something that sounded very much like it. I knew Angus was thinking about the tears I had shed in the loft and the photographs that had instigated them. He had just slid one of my puzzle pieces up against the other and discovered it was a perfect fit.

He nodded his head and turned back to Jamie.

'I think it sounds like an absolutely wonderful idea,' he said kindly. 'I would imagine there's many a child, and teenager come to that, who would benefit from such a charity.

They could come here and forget their troubles, for a while at least.'

'And we've always been known to lend a helping hand to those in need,' smiled Catherine, adding her support to the idea.

'That you have,' said Dorothy as she began to gather plates. 'That you have.'

The general consensus was that this idea was the perfect opportunity for Jamie to combine taking over the running of the hall with carrying on the kind of work he was so passionate about, and I was thrilled for him.

'Of course, this isn't the sort of project you can just rush headlong into,' he said, his face flushed with excitement. 'There are all manner of rules and regulations to contend with, staff to find, hoops to jump through and red tape to decipher, but it will all be worth it. I'm sure of that. I can already see it in my mind's eye.'

'So can I,' agreed Mick. 'That stable block will make a perfect residential centre. The bedrooms could be up in the haylofts and the offices and communal areas could be underneath, in the actual stables themselves.'

'Along with a dining room,' added Dorothy. 'Although we'll have to think carefully about how I can cater for so many extra mouths. It'll be batch-baking, and plenty of it.'

'We won't be expecting you to cook for everyone, Dorothy!' laughed Jamie.

She looked most put out, and my heart skipped a little as I pondered who exactly the 'we' was that Jamie was referring to.

'Unless you'd like to, of course,' Catherine quickly stepped in. 'What we really need,' she added, 'is someone to help you project-manage everything, Jamie. Someone who has the vision to imagine how the place could run on a day-to-day basis as well as what the children will really need.'

'And who do we know who could possibly fill those boots?' mused Jamie as all eyes turned to me.

Chapter 19

'Have you thought any more about Mum's suggestion that you should stay on?' Jamie asked me a couple of days later while we were checking out the stable block on the pretence of planning out the conversion. In reality we were searching for Angus's hiding place for the mysterious packages that were still turning up, and getting alarmingly bigger.

'She didn't specifically identify me,' I reminded him as we looked behind and under things in vain. 'Where on earth is he putting them all?'

'No,' he agreed, ignoring my attempt to change the subject. 'But it was obvious that she meant you, Anna. She can't possibly have meant anyone else.'

I knew he was right, of course, but I was trying not to think about it all just now, not when I had the rigours of my first Christmas back in the real world to contend with first.

'Anna!' said Jamie, much louder this time.

'What?' I gasped, spinning round to face him. 'Have you found something?'

'No,' he said, shoving aside a straw bale. 'I thought I had, but suddenly I'm not so sure.'

'What are you talking about?'

'You,' he said accusingly. 'What's with you at the moment?'

He sounded almost cross, certainly impatient, and I wasn't really sure that I had done anything to justify his obvious annoyance.

'Nothing,' I shrugged, pulling my ponytail over my shoulder. 'I thought you'd be happy that I'd helped you find a solution to your doubts about taking this place on.'

'I am.'

'Then why are you snapping my head off? I'm just trying to do my job. Your mum's really worried Angus is up to something, and in case you – and everyone else for that matter – have forgotten, the whole point of me actually being here is to help her, in whatever way I can.'

'But what about you?'

'What about me?'

I still couldn't get my head around the fact that he hadn't worked out that my life was all about worrying more about other people than myself. Helping and supporting other people was the thing that paid my wages, so I couldn't just nudge myself to the top of my priorities list whenever I felt like it.

'You're being offered a future here,' Jamie said, his tone softer. 'Some real security and the chance to be a part of a family. A family who thinks a hell of a lot of you.'

I fiddled with my hair again and looked out of the high window at the bare branches of the trees beyond. I couldn't shake off the feeling of déjà vu. After Mum had gone I had had this 'family' carrot dangled under my nose on a previous occasion and couldn't deny that what had happened then was having an impact on my ability to make a decision this time around.

'And not just for Christmas,' he continued. 'This could be for ever, Anna. I thought that was something you were beginning to accept you might actually want, as opposed to this nomadic life you are currently living.'

'It is,' I said quietly, my shoulders sagging and ridiculous, unwanted tears springing to my eyes. I realised if I couldn't pluck up the courage to try and trust again, I was in danger of losing far more than just my Christmas bonus. 'I am.'

How could I explain to him that I was absolutely terrified of getting it wrong? Terrified that if I turned them down and left, as I had originally planned to, that by the end of January I would regret what I had done, but not know how to make my way back? And also terrified that if I said yes, I would perhaps find the Connelly family too claustrophobic or, more honestly, my feelings towards Jamie would get in the way and stop me doing my job properly.

The kids he was planning to help didn't deserve that. They were entitled to the very best support they could get, and if I messed up I certainly wouldn't be the person capable of giving them that.

I couldn't believe that what was supposed to be the usual Christmas contract had turned into something so potentially life-changing – or, more in line with what I was feeling in that very moment, life-destroying. When had it all started to fall apart? Was it the moment Hayley showed me to my room and my head was filled with thoughts of Mum, the second I turned the handle on the music box or the instant my eyes met those of the man standing in front of me?

'Look,' said Jamie, taking a deep breath and a step closer. 'Let's get this sorted right now, shall we?'

'But I still haven't made up my mind,' I faltered. 'I still don't know what to say.'

'I know you don't,' he said, reaching out, his hands finding my waist as he quickly pulled me towards him. 'But I'm kind of hoping this might help you decide.'

I could feel the heat from his hands through my shirt and before I had a chance to protest he had lifted my chin and lowered his lips to mine. The kiss began tenderly enough but the second our tongues touched Jamie let out a low moan and the fireworks started. As one we fell back onto the straw bales. His body felt hard on top of mine and our hands were as urgent as our mouths. Blazing kisses made a trail from my jaw to my breasts and I wrapped my legs around him, pulling him even closer as I arched my back to meet him.

'I knew,' he gasped, struggling to pull my shirt out of my jeans, 'that first moment I saw you in the kitchen.'

The image came back to me with alarming clarity. I had been wearing my work uniform, my go-to professional outfit. Work, I reminded myself.

'Don't,' I said, the bubble suddenly bursting and my legs loosening their grip as common sense kicked in. 'Don't say it.'

'Why not?' he groaned, kissing me again, as his hands worked their way beneath my clothes. 'I mean it, Anna. I've fallen—'

'No!' I said, louder this time and forcefully pushing him away.

He rocked back and straightened up, looking down at me as I scrambled to sit up.

'I know you feel the same,' he said, the heat still in his eyes and his breathing shallow in his chest. 'Don't you?'

'No,' I said, looking everywhere but at him as I readjusted my clothes and checked my hair for tell-tale strands of straw. 'I don't know. I'm not sure.'

Almost every part of me was thrilled and flattered that Jamie Connelly lusted after and possibly even loved me, every bit as much as I lusted after and loved him, but what if starting up with him ended as quickly as it had begun?

Were the feelings I thought I had for him worth risking the future I was being offered by his family? If our relationship turned out to be just a fling then I would have to leave after it was flung, and if by then I'd set my heart on staying I didn't think I would be able to bear it. After all, my heart had been compromised before and look how that had turned out. The outcome might not have been my fault but the heartbreak was still mine to carry around.

'What is it that you want, Anna?' Jamie asked.

He sounded as confused as I felt.

'I'm sorry,' I told him, 'but right now I have absolutely no idea.'

I guess deep down I wanted to have my cake and eat it. I wanted Jamie and the family and the dream job. I wanted the fairy-tale ending, but fairy-tale endings didn't happen to girls like me. A second-time-around family had turned out all wrong, so why would it be third time lucky?

Jamie didn't say anything but went back to searching for the parcels his father was proving so adept at hiding.

'I'm sorry,' I said again, pulling the emotion out of my tone and trying to sound more in control than I felt. 'The last thing I want is for you to think I'm messing you around.'

'I don't,' he said, turning back to me and pulling a strand of straw that I had missed out of my ponytail. 'It's fine. I should never have kissed you – it was completely inappropriate.'

He was right, it was. It was the most unprofessional few seconds I had ever encountered in my entire career, but it was also the most thrilling. Just the thought of his weight on top of me sent shivers up and down my spine and made me want to risk doing it all over again. And more.

'But if you knew,' he continued, looking at me just a little too intently, 'if you really knew how hard it is for me to keep my hands off you. How hard it's been for me ever since that moment you walked into the kitchen the first day I was back.'

I wished he'd stop saying 'hard'. The word was doing nothing to strengthen my resolve to keep the tiny distance there was between us. I opened my mouth to admit that I really did feel the same way but changed my mind at the last moment.

'Look,' I said instead. 'It isn't that I'm not flattered.'

Jamie narrowed his eyes.

'But?'

'But I have to look at the bigger picture,' I swallowed. 'My professionalism is on the line here. I've worked for years to build up my reputation and I can't afford to jeopardise it, just on a . . .'

'On a what?' he frowned.

I opened my mouth to answer but was distracted by a sound from below. Jamie took the opportunity to cut in.

'I do get that you're scared,' he said, taking a step back as someone began to climb the ladder to the hayloft, 'but I just wanted you to know how I really feel about you. I thought it might help you make up your mind. That it might make all the difference, you know?'

'I'm sorry Jamie,' I said huskily. 'But I just can't take the risk.'

I didn't have time to think about what he might have said to that because Angus's head popped up comically through the hatch. Jamie might have kissed me with the intention of showing his true feelings but I was relieved to have nipped the steamy moment in the bud, even if it was belatedly.

'I thought I heard voices,' smiled my employer. 'Is everything all right?'

'Yes, Dad,' Jamie sighed as he surreptitiously checked his own hair for stray straw. 'Everything's fine. We were just checking out the space up here, trying to get a feel for how it would work when it's converted into bedrooms.'

Angus nodded and we all looked around. There was certainly enough room for four or five small bedrooms, assuming permission was granted for the conversion and research proved there was a demand for such a charity. Personally I had no doubts at all that it was a fantastic idea, but I also knew it would take a lot of logistical untangling, planning and managing. It didn't take much for me to imagine myself standing next to Jamie and helping to run the place.

'It's perfect really, isn't it?' said Angus as he struggled to his feet and strode about, pacing out the space. 'Especially with the stables down below. That double stall at the far end would make a cracking games room if it was cleared out.'

'And there you've hit the nail on the head, Dad,' said Jamie sternly. It sounded very much as if his frustration with me was now being directed at his father.

'What do you mean?'

'All that junk you've accumulated from car boot sales—'

'Junk!' Angus shot back, sounding outraged.

'Yes, Dad,' Jamie frowned, shaking his head. 'Junk. It will all have to go.'

Angus puffed out his cheeks and his shoulders slumped.

'I suppose it's about time I had a good clear-out,' he relented a little sulkily as he looked out of the window at the set of stocks I had spotted the very first day I arrived. 'Perhaps we could have a sale?' he suggested, sounding much more like his old self. 'And any money raised could form the beginnings of the charity fund.'

'I think it's going to take more than a few quid raised from passing on a load of old tat, Dad,' said Jamie without thinking.

'But it's a great suggestion,' I quickly cut in before Angus felt mortally offended or was put off the idea and jumped to working out how he could squeeze everything into the already packed loft rooms in the hall.

'Yes I suppose it is,' said Jamie a little begrudgingly as he finally caught my meaningful stare. 'It would be one way to kick-start the project and generate some publicity.'

'Perhaps the radio would feature us,' said Angus wistfully, looking into the middle distance, 'or even the local TV!'

'Well,' said Jamie uncertainly, 'I'm not sure about that.'

'And I bet there's some real gems hidden here and about,' said Angus, his eyes lighting up even brighter. 'I bet the guy who does those quirky features for the BBC would love to come and have a look.'

Personally I wasn't quite so convinced, but it sounded like Angus had found a new pet project, and if it took his focus away from the town sleigh, even if just for a while, then I was more than happy for him to let his imagination run away with him.

The air between Jamie and me was a little frosty after our intimate encounter, but with Angus none too keen on the idea of the pair of us sorting through the junk/gems in some of the stables, and us having made a calculated guess that that was most likely where the parcels were hidden, we had agreed to stick together and muddle on, even if we were back to working on a more formal footing.

That evening, after watching the hilarious US festive film *Deck the Halls*, we decided that we would leave Angus to his own devices for now. We also decided that, with Christmas creeping closer every day, we would have to put the charity plans on the back burner until the New Year, along with my decision about whether I should stay or go.

'I'm sorry about earlier,' Jamie mumbled as we walked back to our neighbouring bedrooms that night. 'I don't know why I got it into my head that telling you how I feel and kissing you like that would help.'

'Well, no harm done,' I shrugged, trying to make light of what had happened, even though I hadn't been able to think of anything else.

'But for a minute there,' he reminded me, making me turn as crimson as Santa's trousers, 'you weren't exactly fighting me off.'

'Well of course I wasn't,' I laughed, rolling my eyes and shaking my head with the intention of convincing him that it was no big deal. 'You're a handsome guy, James Connelly, and a girl knows a good thing when it's pressed up against her.'

The connotation made me flush even redder, but it seemed to do the trick. Jamie laughed along with me and I carried on, keen to hammer home the point.

'And having seen you kiss Hayley under the mistletoe I was kind of expecting you'd work your way to me, to be honest.'

'But that wasn't how it was at all,' he interrupted as the laughter died on his lips. 'I meant every word of what I said, or what I was trying to say.'

'Well, whatever,' I smiled. 'A single girl has to make the most of every mistletoe moment that comes her way at this time of year.'

I was trying to diffuse the tension, but Jamie's embarrassed expression suggested I had failed miserably.

'Do you really mean that, Anna?'

'Of course,' I lied.

'Well in that case,' he shrugged, turning as red as I had been just seconds before, 'we really won't say another word about it.'

His abrupt ending to the conversation left me in no doubt that he really had got the message, and been hurt in the process, and although I regretted having to deceive him, and myself, I knew deep down that it was all for the best.

Chapter 20

Jamie and I did our best to stay out of each other's way during the next couple of days and the slight chill that had developed between us didn't go unnoticed.

'So, what's all this about you guys setting up some charity together?' gushed Hayley when she returned to work after some unusual time off at home in bed nursing a nasty head cold.

The hall had been quiet without her and I had thought I had been missing her bubbly, brash presence until she marched in and made the awkwardness between Jamie and me one hundred times worse.

Jamie shrugged in response to her questioning as he stacked his breakfast dishes next to the sink, but he didn't answer her.

'Well,' she huffed. 'I'm pleased to see it's got you all fired up because for a while there we thought you might not have anything to keep you occupied once you'd decided to leave all that charitable work behind and take over here.'

'Anna will tell you,' he said, sounding peevish. 'And we are all fired up. We're just a bit too busy with Christmas and everything to give it much thought right now.'

'What's got into him?' she sniffed, even before he was out of earshot. 'Has something happened between you two?'

She turned her slightly puffy but still kohl-outlined eyes in my direction.

'I bloody knew you fancied him!' she said, sounding smug. 'The look on your face after I kissed him in the woods proved it and I knew it would only be a matter of time.'

'Nothing has happened,' I hissed back.

'You're lying,' she carried on in a sing-song voice.

'And no,' I went on, trying my best to look her in the eye, 'I don't fancy him.'

She sauntered over to a cupboard and pulled out her plastic crate full of cleaning products, along with an extendable feather duster which she then wafted in my direction.

'Carry on like that,' she said mockingly, 'and you'll end up with a nose long enough to rival Pinocchio!'

I didn't have long to worry about Hayley making the awkward situation worse, or to wallow in my nerves about meeting the rest of the family, who were due to arrive that weekend, because within the next few minutes Angus managed to put himself squarely back at the top of my list of priorities.

'What's he done now?' I asked, as Catherine rushed into the kitchen clutching a note and wearing a worried expression.

I had soon learned to recognise her furrowed brow that heralded an 'Angus problem'.

'I'm not sure,' she said, briefly scanning the paper again before passing it to me. 'What do you make of it?'

I didn't have a chance to make anything of it because Jamie walked in and plucked the note from my grasp. He shook his head as he read it, then screwed it into a tight ball and tossed it in the bin.

Catherine looked from Jamie to me, then back again.

'Well,' she said, sounding as cross as it was possible for her to sound. 'I can't see how that is going to help us.'

'He says he's gone out,' Jamie shrugged. 'So he's gone out. I'm certainly not going to go chasing around after him, Mum, and you shouldn't either,' he said, nodding at me.

'But he hasn't taken the car,' Catherine tried to explain.

'Don't you have friends visiting later today?' Jamie reminded her. 'Friends you haven't seen for months and who you've been looking forward to catching up with?'

'Well, yes.'

'Then in that case you should be grateful for the peace and quiet.'

Catherine didn't look so sure.

'He'll turn up, Mum,' Jamie said, his tone more forgiving

as he planted a token kiss on her cheek and grabbed his jacket before calling to Mick. 'He always does.'

He and Mick headed outside and Dorothy looked at me and raised her eyebrows.

'Do you want me to have a scout about outside and see if I can find him?' I offered.

After all, it was more my responsibility to put her mind at rest than anyone else's.

'I don't mind,' I told her.

'No, it's fine,' she said, looking over at the bin and the crumpled note. 'I daresay Jamie's right. Angus is a big boy now. He really should be capable of looking after himself.'

'As long as you're sure.'

'I am,' she said firmly. 'Why don't you run Dorothy into Wynbridge? You said there were a few things you needed to collect ahead of the weekend, didn't you, dear?'

'I did,' said Dorothy, waving a couple of lists in my direction.

'I'm not sure I'll be able to get all that in my little Fiat,' I said, trying to focus on the reams of writing.

'Take the Land Rover then,' said Catherine, nodding at the keys in the fruit bowl. 'At least with it gone I'll know Angus is somewhere on site.'

The journey into Wynbridge was a real treat. The elevated position of the Land Rover gave a far better view of the landscape and I kept pulling over to take in the far-off horizon and frosty fields. Dorothy, who had seen it all before of course, wasn't quite so thrilled with the slow progress.

'Am I not right in thinking,' she tutted when I pulled over for the third time, 'that you've been out and about in this thing with Jamie? And that you had a lift in it the night of the switch-on before he was even back?'

'You are right,' I told her, as I pointed out a hare that had darted out from a ditch and was streaking across the furrow, 'but you hit the nail on the head.'

'What do you mean?'

'I've only been out at night, when it's dark.'

'Shame you weren't about in July then,' she sniffed. 'We'd be getting on far quicker.'

I drove straight into town after that, lest I really got in Dorothy's bad books and she thought about skimping on my portion sizes.

The little town was as busy as ever and I had barely parked before she was snatching up her shopping bags and opening the door.

'Market first,' she announced, playing fast and loose with the rules of road safety as she set her sights on Chris Dempster's fruit and veg stall.

The man himself was off delivering around the county, but Steve was there, as was his mum, Marie.

'Why ever didn't you ring the house?' she asked Dorothy,

who wasted no time in manhandling the produce. 'You know Chris will always fit a stop at Wynthorpe Hall into his rounds.'

'Especially if a slice of your fruitcake is on offer,' Steve chipped in with a wink.

Dorothy began selecting what she wanted and passing it to Marie to bag up.

'This is just a few extra bits and bobs I wanted to pick for myself,' she explained, before hastily adding, 'not that there's ever anything wrong with what you send.'

'I'm relieved to hear it,' said Steve, pretending to be offended.

'Ignore him,' said Marie, sensing Dorothy's discomfiture. 'And introduce me to this lovely young lady.'

'This is Anna,' said Dorothy.

'Of course,' Marie smiled. 'I've heard all about you, my dear. How are you settling into life at the hall? Not always for the fainthearted, is it? What with that exasperating Mr Toad to contend with!'

I didn't say anything. I don't think she was expecting an answer. Her questions were more statements of fact, from what I could make out.

'Are you all set for Christmas then?' she asked, turning her attention back to Dorothy.

'I think so,' said Dorothy thoughtfully as together she and Marie loaded up the bags she held out before passing them to me to carry.

'Here,' said Steve, rushing forward. 'I'll give you a hand.'

'Thanks.'

'Organised enough to come to the wreath-making tomorrow anyway,' Dorothy added. 'I'm looking forward to it, and Mick has picked some more lovely greenery for me to bring along.'

'What's this?' I asked, transferring a heavy bag from one hand to the other.

'You should come along,' said Marie, with a kind smile. 'The more the merrier, eh, Dorothy?'

'What a good idea,' said Dorothy. 'How are your floristry skills, Anna?'

'Non-existent,' I said truthfully.

'Well never mind,' said Marie. 'We'll soon have you up to speed.'

Steve and I carried the bags over to the Land Rover and he explained that the wreath-making was another seasonal event at the town hall, only on this occasion wreaths and table decorations were the order of the day rather than cakes and biscuits. It sounded like another hugely popular event.

'Mum organises and runs most of it,' he said. 'She's a trained florist. She used to have her own shop, but now she runs things from her side of the stall and uses the warehouse to make up any orders that come in.'

'What happened to the shop?' I asked.

Looking around the market square I could see there were

lots of interesting little shops and I couldn't help thinking that a proper florist shop would have fitted in a treat. I looked back at Steve, who had gone quiet.

'My brother was killed in a motorbike accident,' he said quietly as we were almost back at the stall. 'Lots of things changed for all of us after that.'

'I see,' I nodded, his admission striking a chord.

'I'd love to come tomorrow,' I told Marie enthusiastically. It felt good taking charge of lining up a festive event for myself, but I hoped Jamie wouldn't take it the wrong way and think that I was prepared to manage without him. I still hadn't forgotten the deal we had made under the stars and wanted to see it through, even if denying my feelings for him was making it awkward. 'But you'll have to tell me what to do,' I added.

Steve rolled his eyes.

'Don't give her permission to order you about,' he laughed. 'She's bad enough without it.'

Laughing, we parted company and Dorothy went to join the queue at the butcher's while I was dispatched to the bakery.

'I'm pleased you've decided to come with me tomorrow,' she said later, as we sat sharing a chicken baguette in the Land Rover cab, waiting for our toes to defrost. 'It will take your mind off meeting the rest of the family.'

'I am a bit nervous about that,' I admitted.

I had been wondering what they would all make of me and my undefined role.

'That's only natural,' said Dorothy. 'Especially when you might end up like the rest of us.'

'What do you mean?'

'A permanent fixture,' she smiled. 'You can't possibly really be thinking of moving on in January, can you?'

I didn't say anything.

'I know you haven't been with us all that long,' she said kindly, 'but you're part of the furniture already and I know Jamie would be mortified if you went.'

'Would he?'

Had everybody noticed the chemistry between us, I wondered?

'Of course,' she laughed.

'Well,' I admitted, 'I have been thinking about staying; especially now everyone thinks setting up the charity is a good idea.'

'I'm relieved to hear it,' she said. 'For Jamie's sake, if no one else's.'

'I think you're reading too much into Jamie's feelings, Dorothy.'

She shook her head.

'Because I'm sure he has women the world over ready to fall at his feet.'

'Doesn't matter,' she shrugged.

'Why not?'

'Because,' she said, affecting a southern American accent and shocking me to my core, 'unless you are completely stupid, that boy is head over heels in love with you!'

I choked on my baguette and twisted round in my seat to look at her. It wasn't only what she had said that was a huge shock, but also the way she'd chosen to say it.

'*Top Gun*?' I swallowed.

It wasn't word for word but it wasn't far off.

'God I love that film,' she giggled with an impish grin.

Unfortunately we didn't make it back to the hall as early as planned because we got lost on the journey from Wynbridge to Skylark Farm to collect the leg of pork Dorothy was planning to cook for Sunday dinner.

'If anyone asks, we'll blame Jerry Lee Lewis,' she laughed, as we finally swung onto the drive.

She had insisted on a rather raucous chorus or three of *Great Balls of Fire* and consequently her internal satnav had gone a little awry. I couldn't remember the last time I'd laughed so much and knew exactly what I was going to be buying my passenger for Christmas now.

'Finally,' huffed Jamie, as I pulled up outside the stable yard to offload the bags of shopping.

He didn't look at all happy and Dorothy and I exchanged glances as I pulled on the handbrake and cut the engine.

'Where the hell have you been?'

'To town,' I said, jumping out. 'We had things to collect.'

'Your mum said it would be fine,' said Dorothy, waving him away so she could open the back door.

'Well, poor Hayley's waiting to get home,' he said. 'She should have gone hours ago.'

'So why didn't you just take my car?' I snapped back, annoyed that he seemed so determined to stamp all over my good mood. 'The keys are in the kitchen.'

'Come to that,' said Dorothy, 'why couldn't you take your dad's car?'

'Flat battery,' he muttered, 'and I didn't want to jump it from yours,' he said before I had a chance to suggest it, 'because there's enough happening already without throwing something else going wrong into the mix.'

'What is it?' I demanded, my hand reaching for his arm. 'What's happened?'

'Oh, I daresay it will turn out to be nothing,' he said, running his hands through his hair before my hand came to rest.

The gesture didn't go unnoticed and I guessed he didn't want me touching him. Since I had given him the brush-off I shouldn't have been surprised, but it did hurt a little.

'Go on,' I encouraged.

'It's Dad,' he sighed. 'He still isn't back.'

'You mean he's been gone all day?' questioned Dorothy

as she handed Mick, who had come out to help, a couple of the bags.

'Looks that way,' he said. 'We're starting a proper search. I thought I'd found him when his phone rang but he'd left it in the playroom.'

The playroom, I had discovered, was the one room in the hall assigned exclusively to Angus. No one went in there and nothing was ever tidied. He was king of the castle within those four walls, and having somewhere specific to fiddle and invent did seem to stop him spreading his mess too far and wide.

'Is your mum worried?' I asked.

'What do you think?' said Jamie witheringly. 'Just like the rest of us she hadn't even noticed he wasn't back until her friends commented on the time and left, and now she feels terrible.'

'And I don't suppose it helped that we were so late,' I said, biting my lip.

Had Dorothy been home to serve tea on time, as she usually did every day, then we all would have realised he hadn't been seen and would have initiated a search when there was at least a little light left.

'I told you Jerry would get us in trouble,' Dorothy said to me.

'Who?' asked Jamie.

'Never mind,' I said quickly.

Mick looked at his colleague and I guessed he knew of her fondness for young Mr Cruise and his fast-flying friends.

'So what are we going to do?'

'Well, I'm going to get Hayley home,' said Jamie, jumping into the Land Rover as Hayley finally appeared. 'She still isn't feeling too great and needs to get to bed.'

I took a look at her and saw he was right. She looked decidedly less than chipper, but I still didn't appreciate the way he seemed to be directing his annoyance about everything that had happened towards me.

'I'm all right,' Hayley sniffed, sounding anything but. 'I'll see you in the morning and don't worry about misery guts,' she said of Jamie. 'He's been in a foul mood all afternoon.'

'Don't do anything until I get back!' Jamie called from his post behind the steering wheel.

'I'm sure he will have turned up by then!' Dorothy called back, but she didn't get a response. 'Come on,' she said to me. 'Let's have a bite to eat and decide where to start looking for the silly old fool.'

Chapter 21

I didn't even make it halfway through the warming mug of marshmallow-topped hot chocolate Dorothy had quickly whipped up while Jamie was driving Hayley back to town.

'I can't just sit here and do nothing,' I said, dumping my mug back on the table and looking at the concerned faces around me. 'Are you absolutely sure he isn't anywhere here in the hall?'

'We've checked the playroom and the lofts,' said Mick, 'twice.'

'And every other room we can think of,' added Catherine with a shake of her head.

'He's been nosing about in the stables quite a bit during the last few days,' I said, my brain ticking over as I tried to think about all of the other places he could possibly be.

I didn't even want to entertain the idea that he might be hurt somewhere outside and unable to alert us as to his whereabouts.

'I've looked in there,' said Mick. 'In the stables and up in the hayloft.'

I glanced up at the clock on the wall.

'And the woods,' I asked. 'What about there?'

'Jamie and I have been working out there today,' Mick confirmed. 'We would have seen him. We've even had Molly on the case. If Angus was somewhere in the woods, she'd know about it.'

'Well, I can't just sit here,' I said again.

'But didn't Jamie say to wait?' Dorothy reminded me.

'He did,' I said, standing up and pulling on my coat again, 'but I have to do something. It's getting really cold out there now and if he isn't in here somewhere then he must be outside.'

Dorothy nodded and Catherine didn't try to stop me.

'I'll take a torch,' I said, 'and Mick, will you check the playroom just once more, just to be sure?'

'Will do,' he said, also abandoning his drink.

'I'll probably be back before Jamie, hopefully with Angus in tow, but I've got my phone in case you find him before I do.'

It was freezing outside and the sky was clear, the stars bright. I didn't know where I was going to look that hadn't already been investigated, but I headed towards the stable yard looking for clues. It didn't take many seconds to find one.

The yard itself was decidedly empty and I couldn't believe that no one had taken on board the fact that the little tractor and cherry picker had been moved. Penny to a pound, if I found them, I'd find Angus. Pulling my coat tighter around me I set off into the garden. I'd give it ten minutes and if I hadn't found him by then I'd just go back to the hall and call 999.

Stumbling along, I'd soon visited every spot in the garden that was accessible to such cumbersome equipment and I jogged back towards the hall to see if there was any sign of either Angus or the machinery around the actual building. Scanning up and down, my torch missed the muddle of cables on the path and as I stepped into them, they snagged around my ankle and sent me sprawling.

'Shit,' I muttered as I pulled myself to my feet and felt a warm trickle running from my knees down the inside of my jeans. 'Shit.'

Two grazed knees for Christmas, how lovely, but at least I'd found my quarry.

'Angus!' I shouted, as the beam of my torch sought out the silhouette of the cherry picker at full stretch leaning up the side of the hall. 'Angus!'

Mick had been telling him not to use the wretched thing because it kept getting stuck, but the daft old bugger had obviously ignored him and was now doubtless trapped in the bucket, which was almost as high as the eaves. But what was he doing up there? I looked again at the muddle of cables and the 'eureka' moment struck. Of course! That would account for the plethora of parcels. He was putting up Christmas lights, no doubt trying to surprise everyone by doing a Clark Griswold.

'Angus!' I called again.

He had to be up there, but why wasn't he answering? I tried pressing the button to lower the blasted bucket and pulled at the levers but nothing happened. I hesitated just for a second, then sent Jamie a text explaining where I was and what I thought had happened and then I began to climb.

It hadn't looked so far from the ground, but when I heard the gravel crunching below, far below, as footsteps came running and I dared to look down I soon realised I wouldn't survive the fall without a fair few broken bones.

'What the actual fuck are you doing?' shouted Jamie.

'What, in life?' I called back. 'Or right at this moment?'

My attempt to make light of my foolish decision didn't go down well at all.

'Are you completely mad?'

He sounded absolutely furious and I hoped my hunch about his father was right because it was the only thing that was going to help me survive his wrath. Now was certainly not the time to remind him that the hall did at least have a comprehensive public liability insurance policy should I slip and break my neck.

'I'm sure he's up here!' I called down.

I tried to shake my hair out of my eyes and my hands slipped a little against the icy drainpipe I was attempting to climb up. Had it not been for the ivy clinging to the walls and the gnarled trunk of the ancient wisteria which was giving me a reasonable foothold, I don't think I would have made it far at all.

'Jesus, Anna!' Jamie bawled. 'You're going to kill yourself!'

My arms were aching by the time I was level with the bottom of the bucket, but there was no way I was going back down.

'He's definitely in there,' came a voice from somewhere high above my head. 'I can see him.'

It was Mick. He was at the very top of the house, leaning out of a window and looking down.

'But he's not moving.'

I wondered for a moment if it would have been better, safer even, if I had climbed out of the window and down, but thinking about the wide ledges up there I knew I couldn't have summoned the courage to go over the edge, and anyway it didn't matter now. The only way was up, and quickly before my arms gave up completely.

Using the last of my energy and throwing out what had to be the most unusual wish to the Wishing Tree, I let go of the drainpipe, momentarily trusting the strength of the ivy, and made a sideways grab for the edge of the bucket before hauling myself inside.

'Yes, he's here!' I shouted down to Jamie. The whole machine swayed as I leant over the side. 'But he isn't conscious.'

Mick's head disappeared from view and, in the torchlight, as best I could, I put into practice the first-aid skills everyone hopes they'll never have to use when they turn up to take the course. In the tiny space I manhandled Angus into the best recovery position I could manage and stripped off as many warm layers to cover him in as I dared without risking hypothermia myself. It was a huge relief to hear him groan as I shuffled about in the cramped conditions.

'I'm going to throw some blankets down,' said Mick.

A coat would have been better, but I was grateful for anything he could quickly lay his hands on.

'And the ambulance is here,' Jamie called up, rushing away in the dark to give them directions.

Unfortunately the fire crew took longer to arrive, no doubt because of the hazardous travelling conditions, and while I waited all I could think about was trying to get Angus warm and keep him breathing.

By the time I had shouted various details down to the paramedics I could see the blue beams of the fire engine lights flashing through the trees and into the wider landscape and knew that no matter how wonderful the display Angus had been planning, nothing would have been able to lift my spirits more than those lights telling me that help was on its way.

It took what felt like hours for Mick and the guys on the ground to try and work around the machine's dodgy wiring, but eventually they freed the stuck mechanics and the contraption made its jerky descent, with me shaking like a leaf and hanging on for dear life inside. The glacial conditions finally began to have an impact as I gradually ran out of adrenalin, and my ankle and knees began to throb.

'Jesus, Anna,' scolded Jamie, once his father was safely transferred to the back of the ambulance and was being checked over. 'Of all the dumb-arse things I've ever seen, that has to take first place.'

I knew he was only having a go at me because he was scared, but a quick thank you wouldn't have gone amiss. Perhaps it would come later, when he'd had time to calm down.

'I thought she was actually rather brave,' winked the fireman who had lifted me out of the bucket and set me back on terra firma. 'Her quick thinking has probably made all the difference to your dad.'

He tossed me another blanket to wrap around my shoulders, as I still hadn't got back the clothes I had stripped off to try and raise Angus's temperature.

'Have you ever thought about joining the fire service?' the guy carried on. 'We could use a nimble little thing like you to help us out in tight spots.'

I felt myself blush and Jamie muttered under his breath before stalking around the side of the hall to where the ambulance was parked. I hobbled on behind as best I could and listened in on the conversation.

'Looks like hypothermia,' the paramedic explained, 'and possible concussion. We think he might have had a bump on the head.'

No doubt it was hard for them to tell with Angus.

'He's a bit out of it,' carried on the younger attendant, 'but don't worry, we've seen worse.'

'This one might need a quick check-over,' said Jamie, who had spotted my bloody knees.

'No,' I said, shaking my head. 'You get off. I'm fine. It's just a scratch from when I tripped over.'

Jamie shrugged and the crew slammed the ambulance doors shut before heading off.

'I'll go and tell Mum what's happened,' said Jamie as he watched the blue lights disappear from sight.

Fortunately, Dorothy had been able to keep Catherine inside the hall while the drama was playing out. Seeing her husband being loaded into the back of an ambulance was the last thing she needed. I looked up at the hall to see if I could spot any tell-tale cabling that would give Angus's antics away, but as far as I could tell, there was nothing. Either he'd crashed out before he got started or he'd hidden the cables very well.

'What are you looking at?' asked Jamie, following my line of sight. 'You haven't had a bump on the head as well, have you?'

I ignored his churlish tone.

'This was in the bucket,' announced the fire chief, who came striding over with what looked like a rather large lump of masonry.

'If that's what hit him on the head,' I tutted, 'then no wonder he was out for the count. I wonder how long he'd been up there?'

'And more to the point, why was he up there at all?'

Obviously Jamie hadn't spotted the cables that were lying about, and I wasn't about to fill him in.

'Anyway,' he said, taking the lump of brick, 'I just need to go and talk to Mum. I'll be back out in a bit.'

After telling Catherine what had happened, Jamie set off with his mother and Mick for the hospital and Dorothy made hot drinks for everyone who was left behind. In true Wynthorpe style she had even warmed a batch of sausage rolls in the Aga and, with no new emergency to attend, the crews gratefully piled into the kitchen and tucked in.

I had added as many layers as I could to my top half and was gingerly cleaning my knees when I looked up and spotted my rescuer standing over me and watching my progress with interest.

'Could have been worse,' he smiled when he realised I had caught him staring.

'Could have been fatal,' I said, shaking my head.

'I was talking about what happened to you, not Angus.'

'So was I,' I said and we both laughed. 'It was scary up there for a while.'

'I can imagine.'

Given that he tackled raging infernos and untangled mangled metal for a living, my little drama must have looked like a walk in the park. My mind flitted back to Angus and his crazy one-man illumination project.

'He's a law unto himself, my boss,' I tutted.

'Oh we know that all right,' sighed the calendar-worthy fireman. 'It isn't the first time we've been out here on a rescue mission.'

'Really?'

'Really,' he nodded. 'Have you heard about the time—?'

Whatever anecdote he was about to reveal was cut short by the radio the crew chief was carrying.

'Right, lads,' he said, abandoning his sausage roll, 'time to go.'

'Let me take you for a drink,' said the cheeky guy next to me, 'then I'll tell you all about it without any interruptions.'

'I don't know,' I said doubtfully. 'That probably wouldn't be a good idea.'

'No time to argue,' he said, making for the door. 'Meet me in The Mermaid at six tomorrow night. I'm Charlie, by the way.'

And with that he was gone.

Chapter 22

I found Catherine surprisingly calm the next morning.

'I haven't got time to fuss,' she told me. 'And besides, Angus is absolutely fine, thanks to your speedy actions.'

I stole a glance at Jamie, but he still wasn't having it that my actions had been anything other than stupid and sat mulishly in the corner, brooding over a mug of coffee.

'And I'm hopeful this bump on the head will have taught him a lesson.'

My eyes swivelled back in Catherine's direction.

'Oh, who am I kidding?' she sighed. 'He'll never learn, will he?'

'Probably not,' I sympathised. 'When will he be coming home?'

'Tomorrow,' she said, 'hopefully, as long as he promises to take things easy, of course. So in reality I would imagine it will be Monday.'

'So he isn't going to be here to see everyone arrive tonight?' I groaned. 'He must be devastated.'

I knew that he would be more disappointed that he was going to miss out on the chance to be at the door to welcome everyone home than he was about having failed to get the lights up.

'Had he not been such a fool about these bloody decorations he could have been here,' said Jamie. 'He should have asked for help.'

'And what would you have said?' asked Catherine.

'I would have told him it was a ridiculous idea and that this is a listed building, not a sprawling American suburb in a cheesy Christmas film.'

'Exactly,' said Catherine, 'and then he would have gone off and done it on his own anyway.'

I hadn't mentioned my suspicions about the lights to anyone, but Mick had spotted the cabling when he was tidying up early that morning and thought it best to spill the beans.

'And how are you bearing up?' Jamie asked me. 'You're supposed to be going with Dorothy to the wreath-making in town today, aren't you? Will you need me to drive you in?'

This was the first time he had said anything even remotely caring since The Incident (as it had been named), and I was grateful that the ice in his tone was beginning to thaw, even if it was only a little. I already had enough on my plate trying to keep my nerves about meeting the rest of the family in check. I didn't need to be worrying about winning back the friends I thought I had already made.

'What's all this about a hot date?'

I looked from Jamie to the kitchen door as Hayley bustled in, rosy-cheeked and full of mischief. She didn't usually work on Saturdays but was making up for being ill and had insisted she would pop in for the morning, just to check the bedrooms were ready so that no one would be able to find fault with her hard work. That was hardly likely. From what I'd seen she'd managed to primp and polish every last corner of the ginormous hall and, although an incorrigible gossip, her work ethic really was second to none. Not that I would have told her that as she marched in and stamped all over the tiny glimmer of goodwill Jamie had just shown me. Considering she went home sick the evening before she was looking remarkably recovered.

'Aren't you more concerned about Angus?' I asked, pointedly trying to shame her into changing the subject.

'Angus is fine,' she said, shrugging off her coat. 'I've just been to see him.'

'At this time?' frowned Catherine, looking up at the clock. 'How on earth did you get in?'

'My neighbour is a nurse,' she said in a matter-of-fact tone. 'This week she's working the graveyard shift.'

What an unfortunate turn of phrase she so often adopted.

'She sneaked me in.'

'Well I never,' tutted Dorothy.

'And he seemed fine to me,' Hayley went on. 'Although a bit surprised to see me of course. I'll wind him up about that when he comes home. Tell him he must have been hallucinating or something.'

'But he was all right?' Catherine questioned, choosing to ignore Hayley's wicked sense of humour.

'Right as rain,' she shrugged. 'Although I did give him a bit of an ear-bashing about what a silly selfish sod he was.'

I bet he, and the rest of the patients, loved that.

'But how did you know?' I asked.

'We all know he's a silly sod,' she said, shaking her head.

'No, not that,' I said. 'How did you know he was in the hospital?'

'Your hot date,' she grinned. 'My dad saw him in the pub last night. Dad loves a bit of gossip about this place.' Her smile faltered for a moment and I wondered if her dad gave her a hard time about working at the hall, given everything that had happened. 'Apparently,' she went on, 'he was telling everyone what had gone on here.'

I could have slapped myself for asking. My curiosity about her ability to winkle out gossip had put her right back on to me and Charlie the fireman.

'I was at school the same time as your Charlie,' she said, making me cringe.

'He isn't my Charlie,' I said, looking across at Jamie. 'He just happened to be one of the chaps who turned up to help last night.'

'Well, whatever he is,' she went on, 'by all accounts, he's quite taken with you.'

'Oh Anna,' smiled Dorothy, 'you've got yourself another admirer.'

Another admirer! I couldn't believe she'd said that or that Hayley hadn't picked up on her faux pas. If Dorothy was hoping to push Jamie into making a speedy declaration in front of them all, just one look at his face would have told her that she was going the wrong way about it.

'And she's going out with him tonight,' Hayley rattled on with a knowing nudge and a wink oozing innuendo.

'Is she now?' said Jamie, as he thumped his mug down on the table. 'In that case you better get a move on, Anna. I don't mind waiting if you want to pick out a nice dress to wear.'

'I'm fine thanks,' I said, feeling a little hurt that he had reacted so childishly.

I had had absolutely no intention of meeting Charlie in the pub later that evening. In fact I had been all set to ring the station and leave him a message explaining that I wouldn't be able to make it, but now, looking at Jamie's thunderous expression, I was actually going to consider turning up. And I'd make a point of enjoying myself, to boot. I had tried to let Jamie down as gently as I could, and with good reason, but if he couldn't accept the situation then I wasn't going to miss out on a bit of fun.

'And don't worry about running me about today,' I said. 'I'll be fine to drive.'

It felt good being back in the busy town hall, even if driving in had been a somewhat painful experience, owing to my injuries of the night before. This time the air was filled with the scent of fresh-cut greenery, cinnamon sticks and clove-studded apples and oranges, rather than freshly baked cakes.

'You made it,' beamed Chris's wife Marie, when Dorothy and I arrived. 'I wondered if you'd be able to get away. How's the patient?'

Clearly she was in the know as to what had happened, and I reminded myself that this was the reality of life in a small town. News always spread like wildfire, especially if there was an element of risk and drama involved.

'And look at you,' she said as she watched me hobble towards an empty chair. 'Let's get that ankle elevated.'

Driving into town really had been a stupid idea and I knew I was going to suffer for it, but after Jamie's snarky comments, there was no way I was going to let him chauffeur me about.

'You should have taken Jamie up on his offer of a lift,' said Dorothy as she filled out some forms and set about gathering various bits and pieces together for us to work with.

'I didn't want to put him out,' I shrugged. 'And I'm sure

he has enough to contend with today, especially with having to visit his father in hospital on top of everything else.'

Dorothy looked at me for a long moment.

'I know I tried to make a joke about him falling for you,' she said, 'but I really meant it.'

I didn't say anything.

'Is there already something going on between you two?' she asked.

'Me and Angus?' I joked, avoiding her eye.

She tutted and settled herself on the chair next to mine, but thankfully didn't probe any further. I honestly wouldn't have known what to tell her if she had.

'Are you ladies warm enough?' asked Lizzie from the Cherry Tree as she leant between us. 'We're having some problems with the heating today.'

She was wearing an ivy and mistletoe crown and a pair of feathery wings. I wondered if she was meant to be an angel or a fairy.

'It is a bit chilly,' said Dorothy who, I only just noticed, was still wearing her coat. 'You'll need to report it if it doesn't sort itself out.'

'I know,' tutted Lizzie. 'It's the Fair tomorrow. I can't imagine the dealers will be very happy if they end up selling their wares in an icebox.'

She wandered off to help Marie, who was fiddling about with the thermostat on the wall next to the kitchen.

'What's the Fair?' I asked Dorothy.

'It's an antique sale,' she explained. 'Well, not just antiques – all sorts of things really. This new vintage trend plays quite a part now as well. Lots of dealers come here a couple of Sundays before Christmas and it's a hugely popular event with the locals and a great opportunity to buy some presents that are a little out of the ordinary.'

'Sounds far more exciting than the usual bath-bombs,' I agreed.

Dorothy looked confused and I guessed she had no idea what a bath-bomb was.

'It's a bit like bubble bath,' I explained.

'Oh,' she said uncertainly, 'right.'

'Although I'm sure,' I laughed, 'if left to his own devices, Angus would put a very different spin on it.'

'You're not wrong,' she said, passing me a small terracotta pot which was, hopefully, going to form the basis of my table decoration. 'He'd no doubt blow the bath to kingdom come.'

An hour later, thanks to the dodgy heating, which had now gone into overdrive, the hall was sweltering.

'I've tried to turn it down,' said Marie, as she peeled off another layer, 'but nothing's happening. The engineer is on his way.'

'Perhaps you'd better open the door for a bit,' suggested Dorothy as she fanned herself with one of her many shopping lists.

'What do you think?' I asked, carefully turning my pot around and trying not to dislodge the candle in the centre, which wouldn't stand straight no matter how hard I tried to cajole it into behaving.

'I think you've done very well,' she congratulated me, before adding, 'for a first attempt.'

'Perhaps this one can stand on a windowsill out of the way somewhere,' I said. 'We won't light the candle; just draw the curtains in front of it.'

'It isn't that bad,' Marie chuckled. 'Here, try wedging another bit of holly in at the back.'

Her suggestion helped and by the time I had finished titivating, my pot was just about passable. Predictably, however, Dorothy had made half a dozen to my one, but it didn't matter. I'd had a lovely morning.

'These always sit down the middle of the dining table,' she proudly explained as she began to pack her completed pots into a sturdy cardboard box. 'Catherine is very fond of them and I'm going to make some orange pomanders for the fruit bowl. They always smell lovely. Do you want to help with those?'

I looked at her doubtfully.

'They're really easy,' she said encouragingly. 'Impossible to get wrong.'

The pomanders were easier to make than the table decoration and I was almost able to keep up with her output. By the time we were halfway through I smelt like a Christmas pudding and my mind, left to its own devices, had wandered back to the hall and the family.

'Exactly how long have you been living at the hall?' I asked Dorothy, when she came back with two more cups of tea and some mince pies courtesy of the WI ladies who were manning the kitchen.

I had offered to go but Dorothy was insistent that I kept the weight off my ankle for as long as possible. She sat down with a groan and scrutinised the quality of the pies before passing a couple to me.

'Decades now,' she said. 'And Mick's been around almost as long, although he still has a couple of years to serve before he catches up with me.'

She sounded very proud to be the longest-serving member of the Wynthorpe Hall staff.

'I came one Christmas,' she went on wistfully, 'when the boys were small, and I just never left.'

Suddenly I remembered something someone had said not that long after I had arrived.

'That seems to be a bit of a theme at the hall, doesn't it?'

'What's that?'

'Turning up at Christmas,' I said. 'And then not moving on.'

'Um,' she said, 'Mick was a festive arrival as well. He came to us fresh from the Army.'

From what he'd told me, he wasn't quite as 'fresh' as he would have liked to be, but I wasn't going to let on to Dorothy that he had already told me about his drinking and his wife's betrayal. Both he and Hayley had talked to me in confidence and until they each mentioned it in front of one another, I was keeping quiet. I had been the victim of gossip myself in the past and would never repeat anything unless I had been expressly told I could do so.

'And what about you?' Dorothy asked. 'Are you really going to be packing up and leaving us in the New Year?'

Part of me thought it would be a shame to break the tradition, but if I did decide to stay there was still an awful lot to think about and sort out first. Not least, what exactly my relationship with Jamie was going to be.

'I don't know,' I sighed. 'Before the charity idea, I thought it would be easy to go because Catherine would be better – not that there's anything really wrong with her now – and I didn't think there would be a job for me to stay and do.'

'And now?' Dorothy asked gently.

'Now I really don't know,' I said, trying to focus on the charity rather than Jamie and the hayloft. 'Have you always been the cook?' I asked, switching the emphasis of the conversation back to her.

'No,' she said, 'I was a jack of all trades once upon a time. I always helped out in the kitchen, but I was nanny to the boys first.'

'Do you have any children of your own?'

'No,' she said shortly. 'No kids.'

'Were you ever married?'

'Yes,' she said, 'a long time ago. He wasn't a nice man. I thought he was in the beginning but he wasn't. He liked a drink and he liked to throw his weight around when he'd had a few. Sometimes I wonder where I found the strength to leave him.'

Unfortunately I understood exactly what she meant.

'My dad turned to drink after we lost Mum,' I said quietly, thinking that the lure of alcohol had a lot to answer for when it found its way into susceptible hands. 'It made everything we were going through so much worse.'

I'd never told anyone that. Dorothy nodded and I knew she understood.

'He never married again then?'

'He almost did,' I told her. 'But it didn't work out.'

I wished with all my heart that it had. She hadn't arrived until I was in my teens but Sarah Goodall was the one person in my life I came to trust after Mum had gone. She was the only woman Dad took up with who could keep him off the bottle and she had guided me through my final two years at high school. She wasn't my mum but she didn't try to be, and I loved her all the more for that. She was a good woman but there was only so much she could take and the Christmas I turned seventeen, Dad's return to the bottom of a bottle proved too much and she left. She wanted to take me with her but had no claim on me. I should have just gone, or at least kept in touch.

I sipped my tea in silence and spotted Dorothy looking at me.

'If it's safety and security you're looking for, Anna,' she said, her eyes surprisingly bright with tears, 'then you won't find anywhere better on the planet than our Wynthorpe Hall.'

I nodded and squeezed her hand as a little voice in the back of my mind piped up, '*But what about love?*'

By the end of the day the town hall was awash with all manner of seasonal sprigs and it seemed to take as long to clear away as it had to make the decorations everyone was so proud to show off. Dorothy had gone on to arrange gargantuan wreaths for both the back and front doors of the hall, and eyeing them on the table I hoped my little Fiat would be able to fit them in along with all the other bits and pieces.

'Don't worry about not having enough room in your car to get this lot home,' said Dorothy when she came back from her stint of washing dishes, 'and don't be cross.'

'Why would I be?'

She nodded over my shoulder and I turned to see Jamie standing in the doorway talking to Lizzie, who was still wearing her wings and crown.

'Did you ring him?' I asked Dorothy.

'She did,' said Jamie, walking over. 'And as I had just left Dad at the hospital we thought it would be easier for me to take all this,' he said, pointing to the boxes and wreaths, 'as well as Dorothy, back in the Land Rover and leave you and your date in peace.'

'How is your dad?' I asked, choosing to ignore the comment about my meeting in the pub and knowing I should have been more grateful that I was being spared the extra journey.

'He's fine,' he said, shaking his head. 'Bloody grateful to you, of course.'

At least someone was.

'And keen to see you.'

'Perhaps I should pop in this evening?' I suggested, trying to meet him halfway.

'What,' he teased, 'and miss out on the opportunity to hear tall tales from your handsome hero?'

'That's a good point,' I said, turning my back on him and feeling annoyed that I had let my guard down. 'I suppose your dad can wait.'

'Oh for goodness' sake,' Dorothy scolded, 'you two are worse than a pair of kids. If you're so bothered about her seeing this chap, Jamie, then why don't you ask her not to?'

I held my breath, waiting to see how he would react to

such a blatant suggestion, but he was still determined to stamp his feet and have his toddler moment.

'I'm not bothered what she does,' he pouted. 'And anyway, why is it so hot in here? Have you been fiddling with the radiators, Anna? Trying to set the alarms off and make your young man come running with his hose?'

He was obviously enjoying behaving like a spoilt brat, but I had no desire to take the bait and give him the argument he so clearly desired, especially in such a public arena. It hadn't even crossed my mind at that point that he was probably feeling jittery about seeing his brothers and explaining to them that he would be the one taking over at the hall, not Archie.

All I could think about was that he was still aiming his annoyance at me and I hadn't worked out why. However, had I stopped to think about him heading to the pub with a hot lady firefighter then I would have understood part of the reason for his foul mood far sooner. Just hours ago he had told me how he felt about me and now here I was, having shrugged him off, getting ready for a date with another guy. I really needed to find a way to convince him that I wasn't bothered whether I saw Charlie again or not.

I turned back to try and explain but he had already picked up one of the boxes and made his way to the door, almost colliding with the heating engineer, who had finally decided to put in an appearance, but not in time to save the day.

'You all right?' asked Dorothy.

'I'm fine,' I told her. 'I'm not planning on being long. I'll be back in plenty of time to help get supper ready for when everyone arrives.'

'You don't have to rush,' she said. 'If you're having a nice time, then stay.'

'I'm only going because I haven't had a chance to let him know I can't make it,' I explained to her instead. 'I'm really looking forward to meeting the family and I don't want anything to get in the way of that.'

'All right,' she said.

I couldn't help thinking she sounded relieved.

'We'll see you later.'

Fortunately my ankle felt far better than it had earlier in the day and the short distance between the town hall and the pub was easy to manage. En route I tried to think of what I could say that wouldn't make my super-speedy desertion look quite so obvious, or make Charlie feel abandoned, and decided that the arrival of the family, and my need to help at the hall, was the ideal – and actually genuine excuse. However, as it turned out, I needn't have worried about coming up with one.

'So,' said Charlie, after we had awkwardly exchanged smiles and greetings. 'What can I get you to drink?'

'Just a Coke, please. I'm driving.'

'Lemon?'

'Yes please,' I said, 'and plenty of ice.'

'So,' said Charlie again. He looked and sounded far less confident out of uniform, although the pale blue shirt and dark jeans did nothing to diminish his broad chest and blue eyes. 'What have you been up to today?'

I didn't get a chance to explain about the wonky candle creation, or the exotic temperature of the town hall, as his pager burst into life along with another guy's further along the bar.

'Shit,' they both groaned simultaneously.

'Sorry,' said Charlie. 'I'm on call and the other engine is already out. I have to go.'

'Don't worry,' I said.

'We'll do it another time.'

'Sure,' I said, knowing it would never happen and feeling lucky to have been let off the hook so easily. 'Another time.'

Chapter 23

I had mixed feelings as I headed back to the hall. On the one hand I was pleased to have been able to leave the pub so soon so I could get ready to meet the rest of the Connelly family, but on the other, I was riddled with nerves. To my mind, the family arrival heralded the *real* start of Christmas and that was a big deal for me in lots of ways.

At least, I thought, as I turned off the road and onto the drive, thanks to the extra hour or two my abandoned 'date' had afforded me, I would now have the chance to gather my thoughts in a nice relaxing bubble bath and pick out the outfit that would make me feel most confident when trying to explain my unusual role in the Connelly brothers' family home.

Or not.

A large four-by-four I hadn't seen before was parked in the stable yard and, judging by the kiddies' travelling paraphernalia in the back, Christopher and his wife and boys had already beaten me to it. I locked my Fiat and tried to fight off the unwelcome feeling of déjà vu. This was exactly how my first encounter with Jamie had come about and look how that had worked out. I hoped I wasn't about to hear something else about myself I'd rather not.

'Anna?'

I let out a small scream and a string of expletives as Jamie appeared out of the darkness, carrying a loaded log basket.

'Oh my God,' I gasped. 'Don't you think I've had enough heart-rate-raising experiences in the last twenty-four hours?'

'Sorry,' he said, biting his lip.

I could tell he was smirking. I must have looked a right idiot, but he shouldn't have crept up on me like that.

'What are you doing out here?' I demanded, clasping my chest as I tried to cover my embarrassment.

'Log duty,' he said, putting down a basket that was full to the brim. 'What are you doing back from town so soon? Was Charlie-boy too hot to handle?'

'Oh shut up,' I snapped, turning back towards the hall.

Jamie stepped forward, caught me by the elbow and turned me back to face him.

'I'm sorry,' he said, shaking his head.

He did at least sound as though he meant it. In fact, he sounded totally miserable.

'It's all right,' I shrugged.

'No, it isn't,' he said. 'I've been acting like a total prat.'

'That's true,' I said, a small smile tugging at the corners of my mouth.

'But you know why, don't you?' he said urgently. 'I really did mean everything I said the other day, Anna.'

I took a moment to let that sink in. We were supposed to be putting our potential feelings for one another to one side, along with my decision about whether I should stay on at the hall or go, but it was proving hard. Trying to keep the lid on Pandora's Box, especially as it had sprung open once already, was proving tricky.

'And the thought of you with another guy,' he continued with a little shudder.

'Yes?' I asked, knowing my desire to hear him say it was putting me in very real danger of lighting the touch paper all over again.

'I hate it.'

'You were jealous,' I whispered.

'Of course I was jealous.' He frowned. 'How would you have felt if I'd asked out the cute paramedic?'

I didn't want to answer that. I already knew how I would have felt, courtesy of how my stomach had clenched when I had watched him kissing Hayley in the woods.

'But I didn't have a chance to say no before he had to go,' I said instead.

Jamie hadn't been there when Charlie had asked me out

and I wanted him to know how it all *really* happened, not how he was probably imagining it had happened.

'And there was no time to cancel, and besides it was only supposed to be a drink in the pub.'

'That's what Dorothy said.'

'When?'

'On the way back from town,' he sighed. 'She said you didn't really seem keen on the idea and were only going to The Mermaid so you could tell the guy you had to come back to work.'

'Well, there you are then,' I said.

'So am I forgiven?' he asked.

'There's nothing to forgive.'

'But did you want to go out with him?'

'No,' I said truthfully, 'I really didn't, and I know you were hurt when I stopped our kiss and when I stopped you saying those things to me, but I didn't stop you because I didn't want us to kiss or hear you say . . .'

'That I'd fallen for you.'

'Exactly,' I swallowed.

I had relished and relived every second of him saying those words and pressing his body down onto mine. I had saved them up and savoured them in the long, dark nights that had followed.

'But,' I said quickly, to remind myself as much as him, 'I stopped you with the best of intentions. You said yourself that I'm being offered everything I could ever dream of here, didn't you?'

'Yes.'

'So then you have to understand how afraid I am that I'll mess it all up.'

'But you won't. We won't.'

'But I might,' I said softly. 'We might.'

Jamie nodded and scuffed at the frosty ground with the toe of his boot. I hoped he understood what I was trying to convey.

'I just don't want to see you with anyone else,' he said.

'I don't want to be with anyone else,' I told him. 'I just want to see if I can get through this family-filled Christmas your father has lined up and then think about the rest of my life – and the possibility of whether there can be an "us" – after that.'

'Of course,' he said with a sigh. 'And I know I shouldn't be pressurising you like this. It's just that I really need an ally right now, someone I can rely on. It's going to be tough telling the others that I'm taking over and about the charity idea. It would be good to know that you really are with me on this, Anna.'

'Of course I'm with you,' I said, thinking back to the night we made our deal under the stars. 'I told you I'd find a way to help you fall in love with this place again,' I reminded him. 'And I'm sticking by that promise.'

'And I told you I'd find a way to help you enjoy Christmas again, didn't I?'

'Yes,' I said, 'you did, and since then you've given me so much more besides.'

His fingers reached out for mine and I was tempted to give in as he closed the gap between us.

'Jamie!'

'Yeah?' he answered, rolling his eyes.

'Have you got those logs?'

'Yes. I'm coming.'

'Well, hurry up, will you?'

'Christopher,' Jamie explained to me, with a nod back towards the hall. 'We better go in.'

'OK.'

'But we're friends again, yes?'

'Absolutely,' I said, taking a deep breath. 'We always were.'

'With benefits, perhaps?' he smiled cheekily, his eyes glistening as he picked up the log basket.

'Don't push it,' I laughed, following on behind. 'Let's just take this one step at a time, shall we?'

If the hall kitchen had seemed packed before, it was positively bursting at the seams now, and that was without Hayley and Angus and their larger-than-life personalities bouncing off the walls.

'Here he is,' smiled Catherine, when she spotted Jamie

with the basket. 'And Anna,' she added, 'we weren't expecting you back so soon. Come and say hello to everyone. Everyone!' she called, raising her voice above the chattering din. 'This is Anna.'

The room fell silent and four extra sets of eyes turned curiously to me. I felt myself blushing in spite of my efforts to look cool and not at all fazed. My ankle was still uncomfortable and I couldn't wait to take the weight off it, but by the looks of it I wouldn't be escaping up to my room anytime soon.

'Well, now,' said Christopher, his eyes crinkling at the corners as he smiled. 'Hello, Anna. It's nice to see Dad's taken on some young blood to liven things up around here.'

'Cheeky boy,' tutted Dorothy.

'You have met Hayley, haven't you?' I asked, knowing he was teasing and that I needed to give him an adequate response. 'No livening up necessary around here when she's in full flight.'

Christopher nodded in appreciation and formally held out his hand, which I leant across the table to shake.

'I'm Christopher,' he said, 'the eldest one.'

He was taller than Jamie and more solidly built. His eyes were green too, but nowhere near as striking.

'Pleased to meet you, Christopher, the eldest one,' I smiled.

'And this is Cassandra,' he said, pulling his wife to his side.

'But everyone calls me Cass,' she said, dazzling me with her beautiful smile.

'Hello, Cass,' I nodded.

She was quite possibly one of the most striking women I had ever seen. Tall and slender with a curtain of sleek blonde hair and the sort of figure that could wear absolutely anything with sophistication and finesse. She was just the sort of woman I aspired to be when I grew up. Assuming I ever did, of course.

'And this pair are our pride and joy,' said Christopher teasingly, pointing at the two boys, who had already got bored of looking at me and gone back to making a fuss of Floss.

'I'm Hugo,' said the taller of the two, assuming a grown-up demeanour and standing up to shake hands just as he had seen his father do. 'I'm like Dad. I'm also the oldest.'

He said it as if it made him king of the world, and when he looked witheringly back at his younger sibling, who was clinging fast to the teddy under his arm, I guessed he thought he was.

'I'm Oscar and I don't always have my teddy,' said Oscar defensively, when he spotted his brother looking at him with disdain. 'I just fell asleep holding him in the car and forgot to put him down when I came in.'

Hugo shook his head and went back to stroking Floss.

'Of course you did, darling,' said Cass, gathering her younger son into her arms.

'And besides,' I said to make him feel better, 'it wouldn't have been nice for poor old Ted to be stuck out there in the dark and cold when we're all in here saying hello to one another, would it?'

'Exactly,' said Oscar, who I could tell was just desperate to suck his thumb but didn't want anyone to see.

Cass looked at me over the top of her son's head and smiled and I felt my shoulders relax a little, relieved to have said the right thing.

'So what's all this about Dad then?' Christopher asked his mother as Jamie went to offload the log basket and I helped Dorothy lay the table for supper.

'How did you get on?' she asked in a low voice while everyone else was occupied with conversations and jobs of their own.

'He was called to an emergency,' I said. 'So that kind of let me off the hook.'

Dorothy nodded and passed me the cutlery basket.

'Not that I'm pleased someone was in trouble, of course,' I quickly added, 'but it did mean I didn't have to come up with an excuse to leave.'

'Mm,' she said with a wink. 'It might have sounded a bit odd if you just turned up and admitted to being in love with the boss's son.'

The oven timer began blaring out before I had time to get over the shock or attempt to correct her, and as I watched her rearranging pots and pans I realised that she might be much older than Hayley, but she was every bit as much of a minx.

Getting on for an hour later, we could all see that little Oscar was going to be asleep on his feet if we didn't eat soon and Dorothy's carefully cooked supper was going to spoil.

'I thought it was too good to be true, Mum,' said Christopher, pointing at his younger son and rolling his eyes. 'When you said Archie had managed to blag some extra time off and we'd all be arriving together, I said to Cass that he'd mess it up. Didn't I say that, Cass?'

'You did,' Cass confirmed.

'He has to make an entrance,' Christopher went on, sounding annoyed.

'Perhaps we shouldn't wait any longer,' said Cass. She was clearly keen to smooth the way.

Catherine had just given us the nod to take our seats around the kitchen table when the house phone on the sideboard rang and Mick rushed to pass it to her so she didn't have to get up again. I hoped her knee wasn't giving her any trouble and made a mental note to have a quiet word with her about it as soon as I got the opportunity.

'Well now, my goodness,' we listened to her say, 'that's terrible. I hope there hasn't been too much damage.'

'Well done handling Christopher, by the way,' Jamie, who had set himself next to me, leant across to whisper in my ear.

'What do you mean?' I asked, keeping one ear on what Catherine was saying.

'I watched you,' he said.

'What?'

'You had him sized up as soon as he opened his mouth, didn't you?'

My eyes flicked momentarily to Christopher, who was looking at his mother.

'You knew he was testing you to see what sort of response you'd come up with,' Jamie went on. 'A lesser girl would have crumbled. I'm proud of you, Anna.'

He squeezed my knee, making me jump and in the process bang my legs on the underside of the table, which drew everyone's attention.

Cass smiled down at her plate and Dorothy raised an eyebrow.

'Well,' I whispered back, 'I'm delighted I passed his little test. And gained your approval,' I added with an eye roll. 'But don't push it.'

Jamie smiled and withdrew his hand.

'So that's two down,' I said. 'Just one more brother to go for the treble.'

'Just don't go making Archie fall in love with you,' he said seductively.

'I'll try not to,' I said, feeling somewhat nettled that he was making my determination to keep things professional between us so difficult.

'What's up?' he asked, turning his attention back to Catherine as she hung up the phone.

He was certainly a smooth one. It was as if our conversation and his clandestine caress hadn't just happened.

'It's not Dad, is it?'

'No, no,' said Catherine thoughtfully. 'Not your father. It's the town hall. Apparently there's been a fire.'

'A fire?' gasped Dorothy.

'Yes,' said Catherine. 'It's out now, but from what I can gather, the damage has been quite extensive.'

'I'd bet my Christmas bonus on it being that wretched heating system,' Dorothy declared.

'The heating?' Catherine repeated.

'Since when do you get a Christmas bonus?' chipped in Christopher.

'Yes,' Dorothy carried on, ignoring him. 'It was completely out of control earlier today and they had to call an engineer out to try and fix the thermostat.'

'It was like a sauna in the hall,' I said, adding my own contribution to the drama and realising that this was doubtless the emergency that Charlie had had to rush off to.

I hadn't noticed any flames or fumes when I left The Mermaid so it must have really taken hold after I had driven away.

'It was far too hot,' nodded Dorothy. 'We had to have the

doors open at one point. I wonder if that's where Charlie was headed, Anna?' she said to me.

'Probably,' I mumbled, not wanting to talk about my terminated date. 'So what will happen to the Fair tomorrow?' I asked, only just remembering what Dorothy had said about it earlier in the day. 'It won't be able to go ahead now, will it?'

'Oh bugger,' groaned Cass, eliciting a giggle from the boys. 'I was counting on the Fair for some last-minute present-shopping.'

I had to admit I had been thinking about popping along myself. In fact, for the first time in years the idea of Christmas shopping was making me feel more bouncy than bilious.

'So was I,' said Catherine and Dorothy together.

'Everyone will be so disappointed,' Catherine continued. 'During the last couple of years the town has really pulled out all the stops to bring everyone together at Christmas and the Fair is always a highlight.'

'And it won't be just the customers who are missing out,' said Christopher sagely. 'The traders are going to be out of pocket as well, aren't they?'

'Oh yes,' said Catherine. 'I hadn't thought of that. This would have been the last time quite a lot of them set up before Christmas.'

'What a shame,' said Dorothy.

'Well, why don't we have it here then?' Jamie suddenly

piped up. 'Why don't you ring the organiser, Mum, and offer the hall as an alternative venue for this year?'

His eyes flicked to me, looking for some support.

'But it's too short notice,' said Catherine. 'We can't possibly be ready in time. How would we let everyone know?'

'You could always have it in the week instead?' I suggested. 'That way there'd be time to spread the word, print off some posters and make an announcement in the pub. From what I've experienced, it doesn't take long for word to get around in this neck of the woods.'

'You've certainly got that right, Anna,' said Cass. 'And if you ran it for a little longer, perhaps people could come in the evening.'

'I could make some mulled wine,' said Dorothy thoughtfully.

'But what about insurance?' frowned Christopher.

'Don't worry about that,' said Jamie, winking at me.

'But we have the Solstice celebration on Thursday, don't forget,' said Mick, pointing at the calendar.

'Oh I'd forgotten about that,' I said, surprised that my birthday had crept up on me without the usual nausea and dread.

'So, we'll have it on the Tuesday then,' said Catherine determinedly.

'That would give us a couple of days to decorate the hall and set up,' I joined in.

'And we'd still have a day or so after to prepare for the Solstice,' Jamie added.

We all looked at one another and smiled.

'As soon as we've eaten,' said Catherine, 'I'll go and make a few calls.'

'My goodness,' laughed Christopher, nudging Cass. 'And there was me worrying that the place was going to be in turmoil with Dad running amok, when actually—'

'When actually,' Cass cut in, 'it's all running like a well-oiled machine.'

'A new and improved well-oiled machine,' Christopher embellished.

'Apart from Granddad's head,' said Hugo solemnly.

Everyone laughed.

'But I take it you have got some PLI now, Mum? You must have if you're having the Solstice celebration again,' Christopher went on, suddenly sounding far more serious. 'Please tell me you have.'

'Of course,' said Catherine. 'Anna sorted it all out, didn't you, dear? In fact it was one of the very first things she helped to organise when she arrived.'

'I thought you were supposed to be looking after Grandma's leg,' said Oscar.

'She's been looking after all of us,' said Jamie wistfully. 'And a grand job she's been making of it.'

I could feel myself beginning to blush under everyone's

scrutiny and hoped no one was searching for a hidden meaning in Jamie's words, because it wouldn't take a genius to find one.

'Is there something you might want to tell us, little brother?' asked Christopher.

For a moment I panicked, thinking he was talking about how I had, in one mad moment in the hayloft, crossed the line between professional and passionate, but fortunately he was barking up a completely different tree.

'Why do I get the feeling,' he continued, 'that our being here is only partly to do with Christmas?'

'Well,' said Jamie, taking a big breath and looking at Catherine for approval, 'I hadn't planned to say anything until we were all together.'

'But what with your father still in hospital,' Catherine tutted.

'And Archie being so late,' Jamie added.

'I think you should say something now,' Catherine confirmed.

'OK,' he said, smiling at his mum before turning to Christopher.

'Well, come on,' his brother goaded, sounding how I imagined Hugo did when he got tired of playing with Oscar. 'Out with it.'

'Yes,' said Cass, stifling a yawn, 'do put us out of our misery, for goodness' sake. I've just endured being cooped up in a car for hours with three Connelly men, so I could do with cheering up.'

There was an edge to her tone that suggested more than she was actually saying, and I couldn't help wondering how she had been feeling all the while the future of the hall had been in such a state of flux. Looking at her harried expression, I got the impression that she had been half expecting her husband to cave and agree to taking on the running of the place, just to have it settled once and for all.

'Yes, do tell us, Uncle James,' frowned Oscar from his seat next to Catherine.

His words told us all that the future of the hall had indeed been the hot topic on the journey and that the four little ears in the back had taken in every word.

'All right,' Jamie began, the tips of his own ears turning quite pink as he awkwardly pushed back his chair. 'As you all know, Mum has been trying to make arrangements as to who will take over the hall in the future.'

'Yes, yes,' said Christopher in a sing-song voice as he rolled his eyes. 'And we all know what a disappointment I turned out to be because I didn't want it.'

'Oh shut up, Chris,' Cass scolded, nudging him sharply in the ribs. 'Go on, Jamie.'

'And we all know about the catastrophic project Archie has been planning to put in place,' Christopher added, sounding suitably chastened.

'Indeed we do,' said Catherine sadly.

Jamie stood up and fiddled with his napkin to avoid having to look his brother in the eye. It was the first time I had ever seen him looking truly nervous, and the fact that he cared so much endeared him to me all the more. This was clearly a huge moment for him. A declaration in front of Christopher that would seal his future and possibly mine if I did decide to stay and help with the charity.

'And,' he finally went on, 'with all of that in mind, it hasn't actually been quite as straightforward as it might have been.'

'You can say that again,' said Catherine, smiling again.

'However,' said Jamie, with a slowly spreading smile which soon filled his whole face, leaving no one in any doubt that he had made the right decision, 'everything has now been resolved and, as soon as the ink is dry on the paperwork next week, I shall be the one taking over and looking after Wynthorpe Hall.'

'Well I never,' said Christopher, slumping in his chair as a cheer went up. 'You've gone and saved the day.'

Having now met Christopher and started to get the measure of him, I had an idea as to just how difficult it must have been for him to stick to his decision once Jamie had told him what Archie really had planned for the place. He looked as relieved as Cassandra.

'Yes,' said Jamie, 'I suppose I have.'

'Champagne, I think,' beamed Catherine. 'Would you collect a few bottles from the cellar please, Mick?'

'With pleasure,' he nodded.

'I'll give you a hand,' I said, hopping up as Dorothy began sorting dishes.

I thought it only fitting that the family should have a few minutes to themselves. Not that any of them would have minded if I hadn't moved, of course.

'And can we expect a little announcement from you, anytime soon?' asked Mick as he took my hand to guide me down the deep spiral steps to the cellar. 'Have you decided whether you're staying or going?'

'I haven't known whether I'm coming or going since that first afternoon when I parked up in the yard,' I answered, trying to make light of the question.

'There's nothing unusual in that!' quipped Mick. 'That's just how life is here. Never a dull moment and thanks to your charity idea it's only set to get brighter.'

'Yes,' I agreed as he handed me a couple of dusty bottles from a well-stocked shelf and pointed out a few more boxes of lights Angus had been sneakily hiding. 'I suppose you're right. I wonder how the others are going to feel about it all.'

'I bet they'll be delighted,' said Mick, looking back at the parcels. 'More thrilled than I am to find this little lot anyway.'

Now the rest of the family were gathering I couldn't help worrying that I might have overstepped the mark. Jamie might have spent the last couple of weeks cooking up ways to make me enjoy Christmas again, and to me that was a really big deal of course, but compared to what I had been a part of and done it was just a drop in the ocean.

My suggestion that Jamie should set up a brand-new charity at the hall and open it up to the wider world beyond the reaches of Wynbridge potentially meant that the place was entering an entirely new phase in its history. Without really realising it, I had become instrumental in changing the course of the Connelly family home for ever.

'I'm certain that Christopher and Cass will be over the moon, at least,' said Mick. 'The other one might take some talking around, but it isn't really anything to do with him now, is it?'

I didn't much like the sound of how he put that. The last thing I wanted was to be the one responsible for further rancour between Archie and the rest of the family. But then, I reminded myself, had he not been such a money-grabbing arse, the situation would never have arisen. Had he not set his sights on selling up and out I would have just been looking at the six weeks of winter in the sticks I had originally signed up for. Suddenly that particular prospect didn't look or sound quite so appealing.

'I suppose not,' I mumbled as Mick fiddled about turning off the light and closing the heavy wooden cellar door.

'Come on,' he said. 'Let's not keep the boss waiting.'

Back in the kitchen the level of chatter had risen to quite a din and it soon became obvious that Jamie had let his excitement get the better of him and had already told Christopher and Cass all about our plans to set up a charity.

'I gather you were the one responsible for this idea,' said Christopher to me after he had popped one cork and Jamie another.

'In part,' I said, keen to play down my role in the possible venture until I knew how he felt about it. 'I just thought that if Jamie had a project here that reflected his passion for the work he had been doing abroad, then it would make his decision to take over even more alluring.'

'You clever thing,' said Cass, clinking her flute against mine before taking a long sip of champagne. 'That's some deep and ingenious psychology.'

'Well,' I shrugged as the fizzy bubbles tickled my nose, 'I don't know about that. I just thought it made sense.'

'It makes perfect sense,' said Christopher, who was already visibly more relaxed.

He draped an affectionate arm around my shoulder, courtesy of the two flutes of champagne he had downed in quick succession, coupled no doubt with the immense relief that no one was going to try and talk him into changing his mind. Clearly he was now looking forward to a straightforward festive celebration with his family.

'And what about you, Anna,' asked Cass as she eyed me over the rim of her glass. 'Are you going to stay on and help set everything up?'

'I'm only under contract until the beginning of January,' I swallowed.

'Contract!' laughed Christopher with an earth-shattering hiccup.

'So?' said Cass.

'I think,' said Catherine with perfect timing and loud enough for everyone to hear, 'we need to have a toast before we've drunk all of this.'

'Hear, hear!' everyone agreed as Mick and Dorothy rushed around refilling and topping up glasses.

'To Jamie,' said Catherine, beaming at her youngest boy as Floss leapt out of her basket and began yapping madly at the back door. 'And Anna,' she added, smiling warmly at me, 'and the exciting future of Wynthorpe Hall.'

Jamie came to stand by my side and took my hand in his. It was a gesture that didn't go unnoticed by anyone and I was too surprised to pull away.

'To Jamie, Anna and the hall,' the gathered group chorused as Floss continued to make a fuss.

'So,' said an unfamiliar voice. 'What exactly are we all celebrating then?'

Chapter 24

I don't quite know who or what I was expecting to see when I turned around, but the sight that met my eyes was quite a surprise. One sharply dressed Connelly brother and an extremely groomed Glamazon were framed in the doorway. The Glamazon had a designer bag clasped to her side and it was wriggling and writhing as Floss continued to make a fuss around her feet.

'Floss!' Mick called sharply and the scolded dog slunk slowly back to her bed where she then flopped down and watched us all with reproachful eyes.

'Archie,' said Catherine.

She stepped forward and kissed her son on the cheek.

'And Elise,' she added.

I noticed there was no kiss for the girl on his arm.

'Why are you so late?' Catherine asked. 'You should have called. I've been worrying about you. We all have.'

'Really?' said Archie.

He sounded disbelieving as he stared pointedly at the almost empty bottles of champagne.

'You've disguised it well.'

I felt Jamie tense up next to me and squeezed his hand, trying to telepathically tell him not to rise to his brother's ill-tempered words. He squeezed back then let go.

I was sad to see that there was no hug or handshake between any of the brothers, especially as it had been so long since they had all been together, and I was also disappointed that the fully charged celebratory atmosphere had disappeared without trace. The air suddenly felt heavy and oppressive, whereas before it had been light and filled with laughter. Now you could have heard a pin drop.

'It was my fault really,' said Elise, just as the silence became embarrassing.

She didn't sound particularly upset about being the cause of their late arrival.

'Well, Suki's really.'

'Suki?' frowned Catherine.

'My new baby,' Elise said fondly as she teetered over to the table in what looked to me very much like counterfeit Jimmy Choos.

Having taken Elise in from top to toe, I couldn't see her as the kind of girl who settled for second best and I wondered what the story was behind her fake footwear.

It was hardly my place to think it, but to my mind both she and Archie looked ridiculously out of place in the relaxed Wynthorpe kitchen and I hoped that wasn't what everyone had thought about me the day I rocked up in my Manolos and tailored skirt. I was almost relieved that Jamie hadn't been there to witness my arrival, although he had seen me in an only marginally less uptight get-up the day he came back.

Perhaps I was just being overly critical because I hadn't warmed to the pair and their late appearance. I was sure Angus had mentioned something about their change of arrival meaning they would be driving up straight after work, so that doubtless accounted for their designer attire and lack of time to change.

We all watched on as Elise carefully placed her bag on the scrubbed table, checking she had everyone's attention before she undid the zip a little. Floss stealthily slid out of her basket and crept on her belly across the floor as a tiny white head and two incredibly pointed ears popped out.

'Oh my,' said Catherine as Hugo and Oscar pushed through for a better view and the little doggy face looked around with huge, tentative eyes. 'You've got a puppy.'

'Whatever is it?' demanded Cass.

She didn't sound at all impressed and I could see from the slightly sour expression Elise was now wearing that this was not the gushing and cooing reaction she had been expecting her new bundle to receive.

'She's a teacup Chihuahua,' she pouted peevishly as she scooped the trembling scrap out of the bag and up to her chest. 'And she isn't a puppy any more. This is as big as she'll get.'

'Sweet,' said Oscar, giving his teddy a squeeze.

He was the only one, apart from Elise of course, who seemed even remotely keen on the little thing. Even Archie looked a long way from being labelled the proud father. His next words explained why.

'And she doesn't travel well,' he snapped. 'So we had to keep stopping. She threw up twice on the way here, once all over my freshly valeted interior.'

'Are you talking about Elise or the dog?' teased Cass, raising an amused eyebrow in my direction.

'It's not her fault,' said Elise, her bottom lip quivering. 'She's a very delicate little thing.'

Christopher had a wicked smile on his lips and I felt sure he was going to say something even more inflammatory than his wife just had, while Floss looked as if she was sizing Suki up for a suppertime snack.

'You do know there's no such thing as a teacup Chihuahua, don't you?' I quickly interjected in an attempt to diffuse the situation. 'It's just a term breeders use to describe the size of the pups.'

'Is that right?' said Archie, his eyebrows raised in surprise as it finally dawned on him that there was a new girl amongst the crowd.

'No it isn't,' said Elise, eyeing me with something like loathing. 'They're a new breed. Anyway, who are you?'

She clearly didn't appreciate my Chihuahua knowledge, even though I had shared it with the best of intentions.

'You must be Anna,' said Archie smoothly.

'That's right,' I said, wondering how much he knew about me already.

'Oh yes,' said Elise scathingly. 'You're the new help.'

'Crikey, you don't change,' said Christopher before anyone else had a chance. 'There's really no need to be a bitch – or does it just come naturally, Elise?'

'Time for bed,' said Cass, quickly gathering her own brood together and shepherding them towards the door before an argument broke out.

Evidently this was not going to be the kind of happy-ever-after Christmas family reunion that was written about in romance novels, and I knew the fact that Archie had caught us all in the post-toast excitement of Jamie's announcement would make the news even harder for him to take. Now it was going to look to him like we had celebrated ahead of his arrival because we all knew how pissed he was going to be when he was told he wasn't in line to inherit after all.

'I'll give you a hand,' I said to Cass, keen to leave the boys to it. 'Show you which room Hayley thought the boys would like.'

'You don't have to do that,' said Cass.

'It's fine,' I told her, with a backwards glance at Elise. 'I'm the help. It's what I'm paid to do.'

Once the boys were in their pyjamas and settled I read them a story while Cass unpacked their bags and arranged the many teddies Oscar had insisted he needed to see him through Christmas.

'You're a natural,' she whispered as we quietly closed the door and headed back along the landing.

'Years of practice,' I told her. 'And of course, kids are always easier to handle when they aren't your own.'

That was one nugget of wisdom I had accumulated very early on in my career.

'What exactly is it that you do?' Cass asked. 'I thought you were here to look after Catherine.'

She sounded more curious than anything, and not at all patronising like her potential sister-in-law.

'I am,' I said, 'sort of. At least, that's what I was originally employed to do. But I soon discovered the job descriptions are pretty blurred here.'

'You can say that again,' Cass laughed.

'So I've been doing all sorts of things since I arrived,' I explained. 'But in real life I occasionally work as a nanny.'

'Rather you than me.'

'Or a personal assistant, companion or carer.'

'Sounds varied.'

'It is,' I said, 'and it suits me.'

I ignored the little voice in my head that was keen to turn that statement into 'it used to suit me'.

'Do you move around a lot?'

'Yes,' I said. 'I travel all over. You'd be amazed how many people need "help".'

Cass nudged me and smiled.

'Don't worry about old bitchy-britches down there,' she said with a nod towards the stairs.

'I'm not,' I said. 'I don't hold any truck with folk who wear fake designer footwear.'

'No way!' Cass squealed.

I knew instantly that I had made a mistake telling her that but it was too late to take it back.

'Really?' she said, her eyes alight as she plucked at my sleeve. 'Aren't they the real deal?'

'No,' I said in a whisper 'They're not, but you didn't hear it from me.'

'Mum's the word,' she giggled, tapping the side of her nose. 'Crikey. I wouldn't know the difference between one high-end heel and another, but I would have thought Elise would. Are you sure they're phoney?'

'I'd bet my very real Manolos on it,' I told her with a wink.

We hadn't taken many more steps along the landing before the sound of raised voices flew up the stairs to meet us.

'Oh dear,' I said, peering over the banister. 'That can only mean one thing.'

'Yep,' agreed Cass. 'Catherine has just told Archie he's not getting his grubby mitts on this place after all. I take it Jamie has told you what his dear brother had planned for the hall should he have been the one to take it on?'

'Yes,' I said, 'and at the time I struggled to believe anyone could be capable of something like that. But now ...' I hesitated.

'Yes?'

'Now I've met him,' I said in a low voice, 'and her, I'm beginning to understand.'

Cass nodded sadly.

'He's certainly not the same guy he used to be,' she confided, her words confirming what Jamie had said the day we had found out about the letter to the rambling group. 'When I first met him he wouldn't have even considered suggesting doing something like this, let alone seeing it through. I mean, can you imagine what it would have done to Catherine and Angus to see Wynthorpe turned into a health spa, of all things?'

I shuddered at the thought.

'I bet madam would have loved it though,' she added. 'She would have swanned about all day having her pores perfected and her legs waxed.'

I didn't doubt for a second that she was right, and

wondered again if perhaps Elise might have been the real driving force behind the project.

'Have Archie and Elise been together very long?' I asked.

'A while,' said Cass. 'Archie works for her father. He was a good guy until he hooked up with him and then started dating the boss's daughter, but my guess is she won't stick around now.'

'No?'

'No,' she said. 'There's no golden ticket now, is there?'

'I suppose not.'

I didn't want to say too much more, even though I agreed with everything Cass had just said. Elise didn't look to me to be the type to hitch her wagon to anything other than a lucrative thoroughbred, but I quickly stopped myself from saying as much. That level of bitchiness wasn't my style at all, and I had already flagged up her fake footwear – but really, she only had herself to blame for that. The silly woman had gone out of her way to upset me, even though I had tried to rescue her when the conversation had turned against her precious pet.

'I think I'll slip off to bed,' I said to Cass. 'Give you all some time alone to talk things through. You don't need me hanging around, and besides, we've got a busy few days ahead.'

'Oh no you don't,' said Cass, catching my hand and linking her arm through mine. 'You aren't going anywhere. I've seen the way Jamie looks at you, so you're coming back down with me.'

'What?' I squeaked. 'I don't know what you mean.'

'Yes you do,' she said, brooking no denial. 'It's obvious you're a Wynthorpe resident now, Anna, and the person who came up with this charity idea to boot, so it's only right that you should stick out the wrath of Archie with the rest of us.'

I couldn't imagine for one second that the evening was how Catherine had envisaged it would be when Angus had announced that he was gathering everyone together to celebrate Christmas and Jamie's homecoming.

For a start, Angus wasn't there to smooth things over. Had he been, and in spite of his mischievous character, I felt certain that he would have nipped the sniping and snarling in the bud, especially as quite a lot of it seemed to be coming from Elise's direction rather than Archie's. However, in Angus's absence, the few hours before bed that first night were filled with recriminations and accusations, and I sat on the sofa listening to the angry words and wondering if it was ever going to be possible to pull everyone back together in time for the twenty-fifth.

Thankfully, those already in the know had seen fit not to mention the charity idea Jamie and I had cooked up and I hoped that little secret would stay under wraps until Archie had had the opportunity to digest the fact that he wasn't now facing a future handed to him on a silver salver.

Both Christopher and Jamie had wasted no time in telling

him that missing out was all his own fault, and Archie sat with his head in his hands, shell-shocked that they had known what he had had in mind all along. He didn't even dare look at his mother.

No one wanted to stay up late that night and personally I wouldn't have been at all surprised to come down to breakfast the following morning and find everyone had left again. Thankfully, however, that was not the case.

Chapter 25

Next morning the skies were crisp and clear and, without having planned to, Jamie and I found ourselves in the kitchen, pulling on our trainers to go for an early run, at exactly the same time. I had no intention of pushing my luck because my ankle was still a bit on the tender side, but I wanted to get outside and clear my head before the day began.

'I didn't knock on your door,' Jamie said under his breath as he struggled with his laces, 'because I thought you might still be asleep.'

'Huh,' I huffed, 'I wish. I've been tossing and turning all night.'

'Snap,' he tutted, smiling faintly. 'Fucking Archie,' he spat, his sudden change of tone making me jump. 'And fucking Elise, come to that. I'm so sorry about what happened last night, Anna.'

There had been an awkward few minutes when we had

gone up to bed and Elise had realised that she hadn't been assigned the lovely Rose Room. The tension had escalated tenfold, of course, when she twigged that I had it.

'But it's my absolute favourite,' she had pouted at Archie, no doubt assuming that her theatrics would get her her own way. 'And it's one of the family rooms,' she added. 'I don't see why it should be given to—'

'If you say "the help" once more,' said Jamie, who happened to be right behind her, 'I'll—'

'You'll what?' Archie scowled back, stepping around Elise, who looked smug, and Suki, who was trembling and terrified.

Catherine had quickly stepped between her boys.

'Elise,' she said, 'you and Archie are in the Ivy Room at the far end of the corridor this Christmas, unless you'd prefer to be in Archie's old bedroom in the attic? That can quickly be arranged.'

Elise didn't say anything else, but I could tell she was just bursting to.

'Now stop making such a silly fuss,' Catherine continued, sounding uncharacteristically cross as she addressed the troublesome trio, 'and get to bed, all of you. We've a busy week ahead and I'm expecting everyone to help out.'

That had been the end of it, aside from the odd slamming door and muffled voices, and I had consequently ended up not sleeping and then getting up even earlier than usual for a run to burn off some of my annoyance. Given Jamie's bad language and furrowed brow, I thought it would be a good idea to steer us both around the longest possible route, even if I was going to have to take it slowly.

'Come on,' he said, unlocking the kitchen door and stepping out into the sharp, biting air. 'I need to get out of here.'

I had real trouble keeping pace with him, and not just because of my ankle. My lungs were burning by the time we stopped for a breather at the back of the hall and surveyed his father's abandoned handiwork, the Wynthorpe illuminations.

'I know you're cross about all of this,' I panted, nodding at the lengths of bulbs that had been festooned across the facade and around the windows. 'But I think that really he just wanted to surprise everyone.'

'Yes, I know he did,' Jamie agreed, surprising me with a smile. 'He's an annoying old sod, but his heart is in the right place.'

I was pleased he was able to acknowledge that. Angus might have been one of the most exasperating men I had ever met, but he was also the most thoughtful and generous.

'In that case, you won't give him too much of a hard time about it all, will you?'

'No,' said Jamie, wiping the sweat from his face with the sleeve of his sweatshirt. 'He meant well. He always does, and I'm actually hoping,' he confided, 'that if I can rope Mick and

Christopher into helping, we'll be able to surprise Dad when he comes home from hospital tomorrow by having them all strung up and twinkling. How does that sound for an idea?'

'Perfect,' I nodded, feeling moved by the kind proposal. 'He'll love that. Everyone will.'

'That's what I thought,' Jamie agreed, 'and given Archie's reaction to the news last night I can't help thinking it's more important than ever that we pull together to put on a united front.'

'I dread to think what he and Elise will have to say about our charity idea,' I said, biting my lip as I scrolled through their potential scathing comments in my head.

'I don't care what *she* thinks,' said Jamie, sounding scathing himself. 'Besides, between you and me, I don't reckon she'll stick around for long once she realises that Archie really has blown it and missed out on his chance to take over here. She'll soon be off, latching on to someone else who she thinks will give her the chance to swan around and play Lady Muck.'

I had a feeling he was probably right, but what a blow to Archie's already dented ego that was going to be.

'But, believe it or not, I do care about Archie,' Jamie continued, a deep frown forming. 'I'm going to need all the help I can get to make this place, and the charity, a success, and as far as I'm concerned that has to begin with a strong core, a strong family core.'

Jamie was obviously as generous and forgiving as his father. I wasn't sure that, if I were in his position, I would have cared whether I had Archie, the brother who had been prepared to throw it all away, on my side or not.

'And of course that core includes Dorothy,' he told me, counting the names off on his fingers, 'and Mick and Hayley and you, Anna.'

'I know,' I swallowed. 'I know.'

They were all, it seemed to me, waiting for me to give them an answer, but I still didn't have one to give, and the arrival of such hostility in the form of Archie and Elise had only served to confuse my thoughts even further.

Before the showdown the night before I had been able to visualise a real future for myself here, standing shoulder to shoulder with Jamie, as we developed the charity and served the local community, but now I wasn't so sure. Dramatic, probably, but I couldn't help thinking about Demelza Poldark and how, in the eyes of some, her kind-hearted character never quite made the transition from kitchen-maid to mistress of the house. If a flame-haired beauty couldn't pull it off, what chance did I have?

The lights were on in the kitchen by the time we got back and for the first time ever I felt dubious about crossing the threshold, but I needn't have worried. Catherine was very definitely still in charge, and listening to her at the helm I knew there would be no more drama or falling out on her watch. And neither, for a while, would there be time to worry about my own preoccupations, which was probably no bad thing.

'Excellent,' she said, when Jamie and I walked into the kitchen. 'Two more early birds for the Wynthorpe breakfast table.'

Hugo and Oscar were already happily ensconced and tucking into bowls of steaming porridge. Their parents, however, didn't look quite so bright-eyed and Archie, who arrived at exactly the same time as us, looked exhausted.

'I think I'll just go and freshen up,' I said, keen not to be in his presence for any longer than was absolutely necessary.

'Don't disappear on my account,' he said, eyeing me through tired, bruised eyes and sounding far less boisterous than he had just a few hours ago. He ran his hands through his mussed-up hair and yawned. 'And if it makes any difference, Elise won't be down for ages.'

I wasn't sure if he was actually trying to make amends, but a least his comments acknowledged that he was aware that I had been hurt by how the pair had spoken to me the night before.

'Well, she better not be too long,' Catherine cut in before I had time to respond, 'because I have jobs for you all this morning. And I do mean all of you.'

'I thought everyone around here got a day off on a

Sunday,' Archie grimaced, pulling out a chair and plonking himself heavily down on it.

'Normally they do, but not today,' said his mother sternly, 'and especially not when there's a Christmas Fair to organise in record time.'

As it turned out, Catherine hadn't slept well either and had been on the phone long before it was light, doing what she could to ensure that the annual Fair would still go ahead, albeit at an entirely different venue.

'As Jamie suggested last night,' she explained to us all, 'the Fair really shouldn't be cancelled and therefore I have arranged for it to happen here this year. It will be going ahead on Tuesday as discussed, so it won't interfere with the Solstice celebration, and setting up will commence tomorrow after-noon, which means—'

'Trees and decorating today?' asked Oscar hopefully.

'Sort of trees and decorating today,' she said, fondly stroking his hair. 'I'm going to put you boys,' she added, looking between her three sons and two grandsons, 'in charge of fetching everything down from the lofts and posi-tioning the trees that Mick has been tending to in the stable block since the auction. Then we can all come together to decorate them tomorrow and put everything else up at the same time.'

'OK,' said Jamie and Christopher together, while Archie shrugged and the two boys squealed in excitement.

'And Anna,' said Catherine, turning to me, 'I was won-dering if you could possibly design some posters explaining the change of venue and run them to town while the rest of us carry on with things here?'

'Of course,' I said obligingly.

I was more than happy to have the opportunity to make myself scarce for a while. Archie's exhaustion might have taken the edge off his attitude but I was sure it wouldn't last long, and as far as Elise was concerned, well, being tired wouldn't do her any favours at all.

'And, if you think you'll have time, I have another little errand,' Catherine added, 'but I'll fill you in on that after you've had your shower.'

With everyone occupied – apart from Elise, who Archie still couldn't coax out of bed – the festive feeling at the hall, both inside and out, quickly cranked up a notch, and I took a moment to run a duster over Angus's beloved Advent cal-endar and brace myself for what was to come.

Jamie had been setting the Christmas pace for me up until that point, but with the time slipping by and the arrival of two understandably very excited children, the rollercoaster was off and running and there was no chance of jumping off now. Not that I found I wanted to. If anything it was a relief to have so much to do because it stopped me brooding over my own miserable Christmas memories.

The next few days looked set to form the backdrop for the

perfect country-house Christmas, assuming the adults could be mature enough to put their differences aside, and I was very keen to be a part of it. The only person who seemed hell-bent on spoiling the party was Elise, but if Jamie was right, she wouldn't be around all that much longer, and I looked forward to her potential departure almost as much as I was beginning to look forward to Santa's imminent arrival.

'I hope you don't mind taking these to town, Anna, dear,' said Catherine as she watched over my shoulder in the morning room while I hastily prepared some posters advertising the change of date and venue for the Fair on my laptop.

'Not at all,' I told her truthfully, as I copied and pasted in a lovely photograph of the hall in the snow. 'And what was the other job you needed me to do?'

She crossed the room and quietly closed the door.

'Would you be a love and go and pick Angus up from the hospital?'

I stopped what I was doing and looked up at her in surprise.

'He's really coming home today?' I asked. 'But it's Sunday. I thought they were going to keep him in until at least tomorrow.'

That was what we had all been counting on anyway. It was amazing how much more we had all achieved when we didn't have to stop and keep one eye on our employer and his mad antics. If Catherine really was in earnest then I would have to warn Jamie that he didn't have the extra hours he had been banking on to get the lights up and finished after all.

'He's driving them all potty,' said Catherine, sounding deadly serious. 'That's the staff as well as some of the patients.'

'Oh dear,' I said, biting my lip to stop myself from laughing.

It wasn't funny really, but it was a relief to know that the blow to the head hadn't had too much of a calming impact on my employer's personality.

'The duty sister wants him out,' she continued in a low voice, 'before he has the place in even more turmoil.'

Clearly there was already *some* turmoil, and I thought of the poor overworked, underpaid staff with more than a little sympathy.

'Fair enough,' I said, quickly skimming over the details on the poster once more before I hit the print icon. 'In that case I'll collect him after I've dropped these off at The Mermaid.'

'And I was hoping,' Catherine added, 'that you would explain to him about Archie's reaction to the news that Jamie's taking over here before you get back.'

I stopped what I was doing as the significance of what she was suggesting sank in. Surely it wasn't my place to talk about any of that with Angus?

'But wouldn't that be better coming from either Jamie or Christopher?' I asked, keen to pass on the responsibility.

'Probably,' she sighed, 'but unfortunately they're both still so het up about the situation that I can't trust either of them to just explain the facts without resorting to drama.'

She was right of course.

'And the last thing Angus needs right now,' I said thought-fully, 'is more drama.'

'Exactly,' Catherine smiled, taking my hand and giving it a squeeze. 'I knew you'd understand, and don't worry,' she added with a wink, 'I'll warn Jamie so he can get a head start with the lights.'

Much to my delight, and Floss's disappointment, there was no sign of either Elise or Suki before I set off for Wynbridge and I hoped Catherine would have a chance to properly set her straight about my role at the hall before Angus and I got back.

Archie had gone off willingly enough with his brothers to start on the tree and decoration chores and, as far as I could tell, his spoilt other half was the only real fly in the ointment at the moment. Left to his own devices I was sure Archie would soon see the error of his ways and come to terms with why Jamie was taking over and not him, and with a stroke of luck he might even end up thinking it was actually all for the best. But not if Elise was there to keep winding him up and sticking her perfectly sculpted little nose in, of course.

I knew Jamie was sure she would soon be flouncing off, but I was suddenly concerned that she wasn't the type to give up without a fight. I could all too easily imagine that if she didn't end up getting her own way she wouldn't think twice about spoiling the party, and indeed the whole of Christmas, for everyone else.

The day was glacial but clear and bright as I set off for town and, in spite of the current problems back at the hall, I found myself smiling as I crossed the River Wyn and parked up in the quiet market square. There were no stalls set up because it was Sunday, but a few of the shops were open and, with the ginormous trees and various shop-front lights and seasonal displays, the little town really did look as pretty as anywhere featured on the Hallmark television Christmas channel.

The smile lighting up my face was as much for myself as the jolly spectacle and I could feel a bubbling sense of excitement building in my belly as the Big Day drew ever nearer. I felt so proud of just how far I had come, with Jamie's help of course, in such a short space of time. My unexpected enthusiasm for the season really was nothing short of a Christmas miracle.

Jim was just opening The Mermaid door to begin his day of trading as I gathered together the posters and locked my car. He waved to me across the square and beckoned me over.

'Just the man,' I said, handing over the bundle of posters. 'Catherine said you were happy to put up a few of these and pass on some others to promote the change of plan for the Fair.'

'Absolutely,' he beamed, leading me back inside and out of the chilly air. 'Evelyn and I are happy to help however we can.'

'Even though the loss of trade is a bit of a blow,' said Evelyn from her station behind the pumps. 'We're usually packed out in here when the Fair's on but we won't see a soul if they're all at the hall.'

'Well it can't be helped, my love,' shrugged Jim. 'And at least the Fair isn't cancelled altogether. I think we'll be able to weather one day's loss of takings.'

'I suppose,' she relented with a disgruntled sniff before disappearing through to the back.

'And what about the town hall itself?' I asked as I heard the pub door open and close behind me, the Wynbridge wind dancing momentarily around my ankles. 'Is the damage really bad?'

'Here's the chap you need to ask about that,' said Jim, nodding to someone over my shoulder. 'He was first on the scene.'

'And last to leave,' piped up a voice I recognised.

'Charlie,' I said, turning to face him.

'Hello again, Anna,' he smiled. 'You haven't been here all night waiting for me to come back, have you?'

We all laughed at the thought and I accepted Charlie's offer of a belated drink while he explained what had happened inside the town hall. Just as Dorothy and I had predicted, it had been the out-of-control heating thermostat that had caused the trouble, but thankfully the damage wasn't anywhere near as bad as some were making out and the place would be up and running again in no time at all. From what I could make out, the New Year's Eve party was in no real danger of being cancelled.

'But of course it's a cruel blow for the Christmas Fair,' said Charlie, shaking his head.

'It is,' I agreed, 'but all's not lost.'

'No?'

'Catherine has offered Wynthorpe Hall as an alternative venue,' I explained, handing him one of the posters. 'So it isn't a complete disaster. It's happening on Tuesday now, but running later so people can come after work if they want to, as well as during the day.'

'Well that sounds like a wonderful idea,' smiled Charlie, 'and typically generous of the folk at Wynthorpe Hall.'

'Yes,' I said, 'from what I've seen and experienced since I've been here I couldn't agree more.'

'The hall might not be right in the heart of town,' he mused, 'but it's always been top of the list when it comes to helping out the community.'

I was pleased he had glossed over the recent cancellations and gaps in the social calendar that Archie's sneaky whee-dling and scaremongering about insurance had managed to achieve. If everyone in the town felt as grateful for the Connelly family's generosity as Charlie did, then I had no doubts that everyone would get behind the charity venture when the time came to go public.

'In that case,' I said, draining my glass and hopping off my stool, 'I can't help thinking the townsfolk are very lucky. Especially now Jamie has come home.'

Charlie looked at me for a second and I quickly reached for my coat to avoid having to look back. I hoped a dreamy sigh hadn't escaped my lips when I mentioned Jamie's name, but given the intent way Charlie was looking at me I had a horrible feeling that it might have.

'Indeed they are,' he said, helping me into my coat. 'And the people who end up working there don't do too badly either, with or without the full complement of Connelly sons residing under the roof.'

That much I knew for myself, but I didn't comment. I didn't trust myself not to make more of a hash of the conversation than I already had.

'Are you still planning to move on after Christmas?' Charlie asked when I didn't say anything. 'Or are you staying put?'

It never ceased to amaze me just how much everyone in a small community knew about everyone else's business. I hadn't realised my allotted time as a Wynthorpe employee was such common knowledge.

'My contract will come to an end in January,' I said evasively.

Charlie looked at me and winked.

'That wasn't actually what I asked,' he smiled knowingly.

Chapter 26

'Are you here to collect Mr Connelly?' asked a harassed-looking nurse, the second I set foot through the double doors that led to the few tiny wards in the little hospital in Wynbridge.

'Yes,' I said, 'yes I'm here to take him home.'

'Thank God,' she said, jumping up from her chair in the nurses' station. 'Let me help you find him and then we'll get the discharge procedure underway.'

'Don't you know where he is?' I asked.

'Keeping tabs on Mr Connelly,' she sighed resignedly, 'has not been easy, I'm afraid.'

'Of course,' I said sympathetically.

I could well imagine that Angus hadn't in any way conformed to the usual docile patient who arrived with concussion and mild hypothermia.

'Let's get his things together first,' said the nurse, 'and then we'll track him down.'

Considering he hadn't been at the hospital for more than a day and a half, the area around his bed was cluttered with an awful lot of things. Discarded clothes, newspapers covered in scribbles and drawings, a couple of origami swans and a few too many toffee wrappers littered the little table and locker. As far as I could tell, the blow to the head hadn't changed Angus's personality in the slightest. But perhaps that was a good thing. In truth I think I would have been disappointed to find him anything other than his rascally old self.

'Mr Connelly has been telling everyone that there's a new family member at the hall,' said the nurse as we began sorting and tidying. 'Can I take it that's you then?'

I wasn't quite sure how to answer her question. Obviously I was the newest addition to the fold, but being called 'family' so soon after my arrival was still taking some getting used to. The fact that I liked it so much actually made me feel rather vulnerable, because I didn't know how I was going to feel if I did decide to leave when my official time was up. It had been a long time since I'd had family to lose and I didn't much like the thought of parting company with the Connellys, who had so readily welcomed me as one of their own. And of course the thought of leaving Jamie tugged sharply at my heartstrings.

'I'm currently working there,' I said, not wanting to put too fine a point on my role. 'I'm helping Mrs Connelly recover from her recent surgery. I'm not sure if that makes me count as family though.'

But of course I knew it did. Every one of them had told me so on more than one occasion, and I felt myself go hot as I thought how they would feel should they have been privy to my side of this conversation with the nurse. They would probably be most offended that I hadn't confirmed myself as one of their close-knit clan.

'Are you a nurse then?' she asked.

'No,' I said, 'not really. I'm more of a companion and carer really.'

'Mr Connelly said you'd given them all a bit of a shake-up since you arrived,' she went on, obviously having assumed that I was the new family member he had been talking about. 'He was saying something about how you and the youngest son were the future of the hall.'

'Well, I don't know about that,' I laughed, trying to make a joke out of this life-changing declaration. 'I'm sure you know for yourself that Mr Connelly comes out with a lot of things. Perhaps it was the concussion talking.'

'Perhaps,' she shrugged, thankfully not pursuing the subject further. 'Let's go and find him, shall we?'

I used the time we were searching the wards to gather my thoughts and compose myself. What on earth had made Angus say all of that? Was it actually the blow to the head or had he really picked up on the fact that Jamie and I had feelings for one another, even though I had been determined to keep them under wraps? I was going to have to watch my step around him from now on. I didn't mind Angus and Catherine and the rest of the staff knowing that I was considering staying on to help set up the charity, but I wasn't sure I was too keen on the idea of everyone mulling over the state of my heart as well.

I might have fallen headlong for the boss's son, but I still wasn't sure what I was going to do about it and consequently didn't want it becoming common knowledge. Thanks to her astute observation and womanly intuition it appeared Cass had noticed and guessed more than I was happy for her to know. She had seemed happy enough, but I dreaded to think how the others would feel about it all. The thought of Elise cottoning on that 'the help' had fallen for the boy above stairs was too excruciating to be borne, and that was even before I had considered what she might say.

'This'll be him,' said the nurse as she spotted a bed at the far end of one of the wards with the curtains closed.

She marched past the other empty beds and sent the curtains rattling back along the poles.

'Snap!' shouted out a man who was propped up in the bed at the exact same moment.

He must have been in his nineties but sounded as sprightly as Hugo back at the hall.

'Bugger!' came the collective cry from the rest of the group as they slapped down their cards.

'Gambling!' scolded the nurse when she spotted the pile of toffees and Liquorice Allsorts. 'And on a Sunday. You should all be ashamed of yourselves.'

None of the assembled crew looked particularly ashamed, but then the nurse didn't sound convincingly outraged either.

'Anna,' beamed Angus, when he spotted me. 'How lovely to see you, my dear. Come and meet my new friends.'

The nurse rushed off to attend to a ringing buzzer and Angus introduced me to his geriatric gambling pals as the heroine who had risked life and limb to save him from certain solidification. They were all mightily impressed and I wondered just how much Angus had embellished the tale during its multiple retellings and whether I should set them straight. In the end I decided not to. They all looked far too impressed with Angus's version of events to want to hear mine.

'Come on then, Mr Connelly,' I said, formally trying to round him up when it was obvious that I was going to have to cajole him into changing out of his pyjamas and getting into the car. 'Have you forgotten everyone is waiting to see you?'

'Everyone?' he questioned.

'Yes,' I said, 'Oscar and Hugo are panting for a sight of their granddad.'

For a scary second or two I thought he had completely forgotten all about the hall and his family and the wonderful

Christmas he had been planning, but I needn't have worried. His brief confusion was actually brought about because he had something far more pressing on his mind.

'Has a delivery arrived for me?' he furtively asked me after insisting that his old friend sitting in the bed should keep his packet of snap cards and carry on the game with the others.

'What sort of delivery?' I pounced.

'About ten foot long and six foot high,' he said, throwing his arms out wide in an attempt to demonstrate the worryingly large dimensions of this latest purchase.

'Can't say as I've noticed one.'

'Good,' he sighed, nodding his head. 'That's good. I'm sure if it had been delivered you, and everyone else, would have noticed.'

Given the dimensions, I was sure he was right.

'Come on then,' he said, shaking each of his friends by the hand before heading back to his own ward. 'Let's get going. You can fill me in on the news on the way, Anna. I have a feeling there's going to be plenty of it.'

I didn't feel brave enough to start with the big news so I eased myself in by explaining what had happened at the town hall and how the Christmas Fair was now going to be held at Wynthorpe on Tuesday, instead of at the town hall at that very moment.

'Well, that's wonderful news,' said Angus, clapping his

hands together. 'Not about the town hall, of course, but the fact that we get to play host. It will be the perfect place to unveil—'

'It was Jamie who suggested it,' I said, cutting off the mention of whatever it was he was planning to unveil and knowing I couldn't put off the explanation of events surrounding the change of ownership announcement for much longer.

If I chickened out for many more miles I wouldn't have told him about Archie's reaction at all, and I had promised Catherine I would bring her husband up to speed before we got back.

'I'm not surprised,' said Angus proudly. 'Jamie is one hundred per cent the right person to be taking over the hall, and with you by his side, my dear, I know we are all in safe hands.'

'But I haven't made up my mind yet,' I feebly began. 'I still don't know if I'm going to be staying on or not.'

'But why would you want to go?' he asked. 'Although I daresay you could find another job in a heartbeat,' he added.

I didn't have the heart to tell him I already had one lined up. That it had in fact been lined up for the last six months.

'Why would you want to leave the man who has stolen your heart?' Angus went on softly. 'Why would you leave him alone to set up the charity you have been dreaming of running together?'

So he knew it all then.

'Look, Angus,' I began.

'Anna,' he interrupted, 'please don't say another word. I know in my heart that you aren't going to be leaving us next month. I've known it from the moment you arrived, even before Jamie came home, and the fact that you have fallen in love with my boy and that he loves you back, is quite simply the icing on the cake for me. I know you all think I'm a silly old fool who is always getting into scrapes and making everyone roll their eyes.'

I gripped the steering wheel a little tighter.

'And I am that fool, of course I am, but I do have the sense to see what's happening right before my eyes, even though the sensible young person it's happening to is blind to it. Or at least pretends to be.'

I nodded, but didn't say anything. My mind was a muddle, and I wondered if Jamie had any idea that his father knew there was more between us than a potential business venture.

'Now,' said Angus, settling back in his seat, 'tell me how that middle son of mine has reacted to the news that he's missed out on the money pot he has been pinning his hopes on.'

Angus didn't seem at all surprised by how Archie had responded to the revelation that Jamie was taking up the reins and I didn't need to say a word about the less-than-lovely Elise because he had already drawn his own very accurate conclusions about her.

'She's little style and even less substance, that one,' he grumbled. 'But,' he added, echoing what others had already said about her, 'she won't hang about now. Now she knows Archie isn't going to inherit, she'll drop him like a hot potato. Personally I wouldn't be at all surprised if these mad ideas of Archie's originated with her – her and her money-mad father.'

It would have been so easy, easy and completely inappropriate, for me to get drawn into a bitchy conversation about Elise, but I didn't. Where she was concerned I was determined not to put a foot wrong, especially as I had already indiscreetly mentioned her fake shoes to Cass.

'Anyway,' he mused, 'all this talk is making me hungry. Do you think Dorothy has done us a dinner?'

Dorothy had of course 'done us a dinner', and a vast one at that, and it was a very happy Connelly band who sat down to enjoy it. Hugo and Oscar had enveloped their beloved granddad in hugs when we arrived back and the kiss I witnessed between him and Catherine quite made my heart race. How wonderful to have reached their age and still feel so in love, especially when one half of the partnership was such a perpetual pest. My admiration for Catherine increased beyond measure as I watched her take her place next to her husband, knowing of her never-ending patience with his little foibles and fads.

'So, where is he then?' Angus asked, looking along the table at the two empty seats.

'And more to the point,' snapped Dorothy, 'where is she and that blasted dog?'

'If you're talking about Uncle Archie and Elise,' said Hugo, 'I saw them go out about an hour ago.'

'What, and they didn't say anything?' Dorothy was outraged and didn't care a jot that Catherine and Angus knew it. 'How rude. What am I going to do with all these extra puddings?' she tutted, pointing at the plateful of mile-high crispy Yorkshires.

'Ah now, Dorothy,' said Angus, sounding deadly serious as he tucked his napkin into his shirt collar, 'I might just be able to help you out there.'

As always, Dorothy's lunch was divine and I knew she had piled on the extra puddings in the hope that she would tempt super-svelte Elise into filling her boots, but I wouldn't have reckoned much for her chances, even if the waif in question had been present at the table. There was no way you achieved a figure like Elise's by consuming carbs. My own figure, I had noticed in the bathroom mirror, had become slightly more rounded since my arrival, but I didn't really mind. I rather liked the softer edges, although I wouldn't have won a bet that I could still fit into the pencil skirt I had arrived in.

When everything was finally cleared away we all followed Jamie and Christopher around the hall to check the positioning of the trees that had been bought at the auction in town. They had all been planted up in vast pots and stood erect and obliging, ready to be made even more beautiful when the decorations went on the next day. Goodness knows how the men had managed to manoeuvre them but they were a magnificent sight.

'You really have done us proud this year, Mick,' said Angus, patting his friend on the back. 'Thank you so much.'

'You're welcome,' said Mick gruffly, clearly uncomfortable at being made a fuss of. 'The pots were all just lying around outside so I thought I'd clean them up and we'd use them, rather than the usual plastic ones we have to try and disguise with paper and ribbons.'

'Well, they look beautiful,' said Catherine. 'I wonder what other forgotten treasures we've got lying around out there?'

'You'd be amazed,' said Mick, sounding really rather excited. 'The old orangery and empty glasshouses are actually full of gems like these.'

'One day,' said Catherine wistfully, 'I would love to see the orangery restored.'

'I'll add it to the list,' smiled Jamie, kissing his mother's hand. 'Can you remind me, Anna?'

'Will do,' I smiled back, pretending to write it all down.

'We're going to need one rejuvenated orangery for my wonderful mother,' he continued while I carried on scribbling on an invisible notepad, much to Oscar's delight.

'You're so silly,' he giggled.

Eventually we moved on from admiring the first tree in the sitting room to the gargantuan one in the main hall. This was where the bulk of the Christmas Fair stalls would be set up and I knew the stunning eight-foot specimen standing proudly by the side of the huge but currently unlit stone fireplace would be a crowd-pleaser.

We all gazed upon the scene in awe until Christopher broke the silence.

'Do you know,' he said to his sons, pointing to the other side of the tree, where there was a carved wooden chair so large it could easily have been mistaken for a throne, 'if you're really good and really lucky, Father Christmas himself will come and sit in that chair right there and read you a bedtime story.'

Even Hugo looked suitably impressed as the adults shared secret smiles and little Oscar's mouth fell open.

'Wow,' he breathed, clutching Cass's hand as tightly as his beloved teddy bear.

'And if you think this is a beauty,' said Mick, 'wait till you see the one outside.'

We all piled back into the kitchen to grab our coats and warming glasses of mulled wine which Dorothy had set to heat on the Aga before we had begun the tree tour. The air was scented with cinnamon and orange and she had even remembered to make hot chocolate for Mick and the boys, all topped off with a generous swirl of thick cream and marshmallows.

'Did you manage to get the lights finished?' I whispered to Jamie as everyone began pulling on their coats, boots and scarves.

'You'll have to wait and see,' he said with a wink, which of course could only mean one thing.

It was even colder outside than before, and already dark. The stars were shining brightly in the inky sky as all together, with Catherine carefully supported by Jamie and Christopher in case she tripped, we shuffled around the side of the hall to the front, where Mick and the boys had set up yet another magnificent tree.

'Wow,' gasped Hugo, his head stretched back as far as it would go as he tried to see to the very top. 'This is massive.'

'We reckon it must be ten foot,' said Mick, sounding like a proud fisherman describing his catch at the end of the day. 'At least.'

'Possibly nearer twelve now it's in the pot,' said Jamie, boosting Mick's ego a little further.

'This will certainly guide everyone in the right direction when they come to the Fair,' added Cass. 'I can't wait to see it all lit up.'

'And talking of lights,' Jamie said quickly, before everyone's teeth started chattering, 'if you could all walk towards the drive a little way, there's another surprise that I want to show you.'

'What is he talking about?' Catherine asked me as I walked with her now that Jamie couldn't.

'No idea,' I shrugged.

I didn't like to lie, and to Catherine of all people, but this was one seasonal surprise I had no intention of spoiling.

'Are you all ready?' Jamie shouted from somewhere out of sight, just as our toes were beginning to go numb.

'Yes!' we all bawled.

'Hurry up, for pity's sake!' Christopher added. 'It's freezing out here.'

'OK!' Jamie shouted back. 'Here goes nothing.'

For the briefest moment there really was nothing to see, and then it happened. Hundreds of warm white lights began to twinkle around the doors, the windows and even under the eaves of the hall. It was breathtakingly beautiful, like something out of a real-life fairy tale, and I felt my eyes fill with tears. Listening to the gasps and comments around me I knew everyone else was equally impressed.

'Is this what ended up putting you in hospital, Angus?' Cass called to her father-in-law.

'It is,' he called back. 'I'd say it was all worth a bump on the head, wouldn't you, my dear?' he asked Catherine as he bent to kiss her cheek.

'I'm not sure I would go that far,' she told him, 'but it is beautiful. Is this what you've been disappearing to do every day for the last couple of weeks?'

'It is,' he said.

I could see his fingers were crossed behind his back so I knew this wasn't the whole story, and I was sure Catherine realised it too.

'Well done, my boy,' he beamed, as Jamie jogged over to where we were all standing. 'You've done me proud.'

'There wasn't actually all that much left to do,' Jamie admitted. 'I have no idea how you managed to do this without anyone noticing, Dad, but kudos to you. You've made a great job of it. It looks fantastic.'

'Are there any more around the back?' asked Cass.

'There sure are,' Jamie confirmed. 'It's all set up to look just like this.'

'Amazing,' she sighed, looking back at the warm glow the hall was now bathed in.

Clearly she was as enraptured by the idyllic scene as I was.

'Did you manage that last window?' Angus asked his son with a frown.

'Yep,' said Jamie, 'and I could even see the battered brickwork that knocked you out, Dad, so we'll have that repaired when this lot comes down.'

'How on earth did you manage to reach it?' Angus quizzed.

He was clearly impressed that his son had managed to succeed where he had failed.

'Let's just say it was a bit of a stretch and leave it at that,' said Jamie, clearly unwilling to elaborate on the risk he had taken while his mother was present.

'Is it going to be worth taking them all down again?' I asked.

I couldn't help thinking that as it had been such a gargantuan task getting them up it hardly seemed worth taking them all down, only to have to repeat the exercise again next year.

'We'll talk about it in the New Year,' said Jamie.

'Something else to add to the list,' I suggested.

'Exactly,' he said, cheekily putting his arm around my waist and pulling me close to his side the second everyone was looking back towards the hall. 'I really do hope you're going to be here to work through that list with me, Anna.'

Looking at the beautifully lit hall and listening to the chatter and excitement, I hoped I was going to be there too. I really did still have some pondering to do but I think in my heart, at that point, I pretty much knew, even if my head still had some catching up to do.

'Actually, we'll have to think carefully about that, you know, Anna,' said Angus, tracking back to my point about leaving the lights up. 'Your suggestion might not be quite as practical as you no doubt thought it was.'

'Really?'

'Yes,' he said, sounding deadly serious, 'because we might want to change things next year, mightn't we? Go for a bit of colour perhaps or maybe add some music.'

'Oh good grief,' groaned Dorothy, who was just about in earshot. 'He thinks he's that Buddy fellow from *Deck the Halls*!'

'Well,' I said, keen to dismiss all thoughts of Angus in the role played by Danny de Vito, 'let's just enjoy them as they are for now, shall we?'

Everyone was in agreement that the lights were a most welcome addition to the Connelly Christmas set-up, especially with the Fair coming to the hall.

'This will certainly get the place noticed,' Jamie said to me.

'You're not wrong,' I said thoughtfully. 'And you know, talking of getting noticed, it might not be a bad idea to get the local press to do a write-up about the Fair. Keep the place in the minds of the wider community so when it comes to finding support for the charity, the name of the hall and the kindness of the family who owns it will already be in everyone's thoughts.'

'That sounds like an excellent idea,' he agreed. 'You're just full of them, aren't you?'

'I have been known to come up with the odd one or two,' I responded playfully.

He turned his face towards me and I just knew he was

going to try and kiss me again. I didn't want him to kiss me in front of everyone but the thought of his lips on mine shoved me closer to the edge of giving in than was in any way acceptable or appropriate. However, a beeping car horn stopped us in our tracks, and our little gathering parted to allow the vehicle through.

'What the hell's gone on here?' asked Archie as he came to a halt next to where Jamie was standing.

'What?'

'All this, of course,' said his brother, pointing up at the pretty hall. 'However much has this all cost?'

I hardly thought he was the one who should be worrying about how the hall funds were being spent, especially when he had proved himself so willing to squander them.

'Not much,' shrugged Jamie, who I guessed didn't actually have a clue but wasn't prepared to admit it. 'Dad got the lights online and we put them up together.'

I liked how he was claiming part of the responsibility for the decision. The united front he had told me about was clearly something he was intent on reinforcing.

'Right,' said Archie, looking back at the lights again.

'Don't you like them?' Christopher asked, peering in through Elise's window and making Suki snarl in surprise.

'I do actually,' Archie conceded. He sounded surprised.

'I had a feeling you would,' said Jamie, sounding a little choked as he punched his brother on the arm.

'It looks tacky,' said Elise scathingly, cutting across the moment, 'and cheap.'

'No it doesn't,' Archie bit back.

'It's like an overgrown council estate,' Elise carried on with a haughty sniff before pressing the button to shut her window.

Christopher straightened up. He was sniggering at her predictable reaction but I was wondering just how many other things Elise and Archie didn't agree on. Perhaps Angus's suggestion about her and her father would turn out to be right after all.

'Oh I don't know, Elise. It could have been worse,' Jamie, who was still leaning through Archie's window, relished telling her. 'Dad really wanted multi-coloured chaser lights, inflatables and a mobile disco.'

'Like Buddy in *Deck the Halls*,' Archie burst out laughing.

It was the first time I'd seen him laugh. It suited him and I hoped his trip, wherever they had been, had helped him gain some perspective or at least start to come to terms with his changed future.

'Exactly,' Jamie laughed back.

'Dreadful,' shuddered Elise, clutching Suki a little tighter as her delicate sensibilities took another battering. 'Come on,' she said peevishly to Archie, 'I want a hot bath before I go to bed.'

'The Ivy Room has only got a shower,' Archie dared to remind her.

Elise glared at him and then back at the hall as Archie pulled smoothly away. Had she not been such a bitch I would have offered her a swim in the Rose Room tub, with a drop of Jo Malone bubble bath to sweeten it, but one more look at her sour expression helped me decide to keep my mouth firmly shut.

Chapter 27

Getting Hugo and Oscar to go to sleep that evening took a toll on everyone, except Elise of course, who had disappeared up to her and Archie's room by the time everyone had finished admiring the lights and had come in to have a warm in the sitting room. She didn't reappear all evening, thank goodness, and Archie only stuck with the family for as long as he thought he could get away with before being moaned at by his impatient love interest. I don't know if anyone else noticed, but to me their far-from-united front seemed a telling indication that the cracks in their relationship had widened considerably since the announcement that Jamie was taking over at the hall.

'Did you know the boys were having these?' Cass asked me as we tried to encourage her sons to settle down at bedtime.

'I did,' I told her, 'but so much has happened since the auction that I forgot all about them.'

Two tiny Christmas trees had magically appeared in the boys' room and sent their excitement shooting through the roof.

'If these have been delivered,' said Hugo knowledgeably, 'then Santa must think we've been good enough this year to get a present or two.'

'Are you sure, Hugo?' Oscar urgently questioned his older, and therefore undoubtedly wiser, brother. Clearly he wasn't convinced. 'But what if we wake up in the morning and they've gone again?'

'Then,' I said with a sigh, 'Santa will have seen how naughty you've been about going to sleep tonight and told the elves to take them back.'

It might have been a cruel trick, but given how late it was and what an early start we had to look forward to the next day I thought it was justified.

'I bet if there's one in Uncle Archie's room it'll be gone in the morning,' said Oscar furtively as he finally snuggled down with his ted.

'He's not that bad,' said Cass, tucking him in tightly.

Oscar shrugged, or tried to.

'I do actually like Uncle Archie,' he said, 'but not Elise.'

'No,' said Hugo, 'no one likes Elise.'

I was interested to see that Cass didn't say anything to try to alter their opinions.

'I don't think any of the grown-ups have got trees in their rooms,' I told the boys by way of explanation.

'That just goes to prove that you've all been naughty this year then, doesn't it?' said Oscar with a giggle.

Unusually it was my alarm clock that woke me the next morning, and I still felt so tired I didn't think I could face going for my usual run around the grounds. There was no sound from Jamie's room next door either, so I guessed he was probably feeling about as sprightly as I was.

Shoving my feet in my chilly slippers I crossed the room and peered out of the window at the garden below. It was still dark but the Christmas lights were glowing and I could see it had been snowing for a little while. A light, icing-sugar dusting covered everything, enhancing the fairy-tale setting which I just knew was going to provide the perfect backdrop for the Christmas Fair the next day.

I watched as the Land Rover appeared through the stable-yard gateway, its headlights lighting up the falling flakes, and guessed that it was Mick going to town to collect Hayley. I knew she was going to be full of herself this week and couldn't wait to see how she and Elise got on. God help Suki if she had made any kind of mess on the Ivy Room floor or furniture.

A light knock on my door brought me back to the present and I went to answer it. It could only be Jamie and I quickly tried to come up with a plausible reason for not wanting to go for a run before I lifted the latch. It was a pity my ankle had made such a speedy and complete recovery really.

'Have you seen the weather?' he yawned through the gap in the door.

Thankfully he was still in the T-shirt and shorts he slept in and not his running gear.

'There's no way we can run in this,' he added, sounding far from disappointed. 'We've no idea where the ground's frozen. It's probably treacherous and what with your dodgy ankle and everything—'

'Are you sure?' I asked, forcing myself to sound far brighter than I felt. 'We could at least go and have a look, and my ankle feels much better. I'm up for it if you are.'

It felt good to have the upper hand so early in the day and I enjoyed making out that he was the only one who didn't want to venture out.

'Oh I know that,' he grinned, suddenly wide awake as he tried to force the door open a little wider, 'but I was talking about our outside exercise routine.'

'So was I,' I said, flashing him a smile and keeping a tight hold on the door.

It really was far too early for this kind of flirtatious back and forth.

'Morning, you two,' came a voice from further down the corridor. 'Are we all set then?'

'Morning, Dad,' said Jamie, taking his foot off my door and turning to face his father, who was already up, dressed and ready to face the day.

'Come on then,' he said, ushering Jamie back to his room. 'Chop-chop. There's plenty to do.'

'I know that,' Jamie muttered, 'I was just trying to make inroads into *doing* some of it right now.'

Fortunately his cheeky comment seemed to go straight over his father's head.

'Well, you can't do it in your pyjamas, can you?' Angus tutted.

Fortunately we were saved from hearing his son's potentially bawdy answer as Hugo and Oscar came bouncing along. They grabbed Angus and pulled him off towards the stairs that led to the kitchen.

'I'll deal with you later,' said Jamie with a wink.

'Oh will you now?' I laughed, before quickly closing the door again and turning the key in the lock. I was really going to have to watch my step with Jamie in such a mischievous mood. If I wasn't careful we'd be back to the hayloft scenario and I was trying so hard not to waver.

Listening to the discussion during breakfast I soon worked out that decorating Wynthorpe Hall was going to be nothing like the sort of decorating I had been used to when I was growing up. The place was so ginormous it was impossible to festoon everywhere with tinsel and trimmings, even though I was sure Angus and his grandsons would have been up for that if they'd been given the chance.

'The main focus needs to be on the trees,' Catherine reminded us. 'If we can have the one outside and the one in the main hall finished first, and then add the greenery as soon as Molly has dropped it off, then we should all be out of the way, in there at least, before the traders arrive to set up.'

'That reminds me,' said Dorothy, jumping up. 'Chris Dempster called. He's going to be here before lunch with a load of trestle tables and a few chairs. The traders have their own cloths and so on, but if we could have the tables arranged before they arrive it would make setting up so much quicker for them.'

'And I'm expecting a delivery myself before lunch,' said Angus.

This was no doubt the delivery he had asked after when I picked him up from the hospital.

'And if it's all right with you, my dear,' he continued, trying to sweet-talk his wife, 'it would be a great help if I could commandeer Mick and Jamie to give me a hand.'

Catherine looked at him suspiciously.

'That sounds good to me, Dad,' said Jamie. 'That way I can keep an eye on him, Mum,' he added.

'That's true,' she nodded. 'All right, just please make sure you've put out the ladders and everything before you help your father. Our main priority is getting the public areas finished first,' she reiterated. 'The tree in the sitting room and all the other bits and pieces can be finished later this evening and early tomorrow.'

Hugo and Oscar looked a little disappointed at hearing this. Clearly they had been hoping to get cracking on the brace of trees that were still in situ at the foot of their beds. Santa obviously thought they had been good boys this year.

'I can sort out the ladders and things,' said Archie, who had slipped unnoticed into the back of the kitchen. 'Unless you've got something else you want me to do.'

'That would be a great help,' said Catherine, her cheeks going slightly pink. 'Then you could help decorate the trees with everyone else.'

She sounded thrilled by his offer to help and I was sure she must have been feeling relieved that he wanted to be involved with at least some of what was happening.

'And what about Elise?' Cass asked. 'I could do with a hand keeping an eye on the boys and decorating their trees later on if she can see her way fit to leaving her room.'

I couldn't help but wince at her words and the boys in question looked more than a little alarmed at the thought of decorating their beloved branches with Elise of all people.

'Perhaps later,' said Archie a little sheepishly as he ran his hands through his hair. 'She has a bit of a headache this morning.'

'Must be all the fresh country air,' muttered Jamie, who knew she hadn't breathed in so much as a single lungful of it.

'Helping me in the kitchen would soon sort her out,' chipped in Dorothy. 'Thankfully Anna and I stocked the freezers to capacity for us lot days ago, but I'm going to be hard at it today to make enough to feed the hungry hordes who will be coming to the Fair.'

She hated slackers and time-wasters and I had absolutely no doubt that she had Elise pinned as both. Personally I didn't think a stint helping out in the kitchen would 'sort her out' at all, and the image of her in one of Dorothy's floral aprons was almost enough to make me laugh out loud.

'What are you making?' Christopher asked. 'I happen to be a dab hand at making fairy cakes these days.'

'Don't ask,' said Cass, rolling her eyes when we all looked from him to her for an explanation.

'Thank you, lovely,' Dorothy said to Christopher, sounding suitably impressed. 'But I haven't got to make anything sweet. The lovely ladies from The Cherry Tree Café are bringing their mobile teashop and will be serving sweet treats from there. I'm sticking to the soups and savouries.'

'I can't help you there, I'm afraid,' said Christopher sadly. 'My flaky pastry is anything but.'

'Not to worry,' said Dorothy, who I felt sure was actually going to be happier left to her own devices. She had just flagged up the work she had to do as an opportunity to show Elise up as the lazy madam she was.

Suddenly I felt a little sorry for Archie. I hadn't forgotten what his plans had been for the future of the hall, of course, or the sneaky letter he allegedly had written to the ramblers, but at least now he knew the truth about what was happening he hadn't headed straight for the hills, unlike his high maintenance girlfriend, who had apparently taken almost permanent refuge between the high thread-count cotton sheets. At least he was making an effort.

'I have some really strong painkillers if Elise needs them,' I discreetly offered, trying to smooth the way for him at least a little.

It was only then that it dawned on me that I hadn't had so much as a single headache since I arrived at the hall. Ordinarily at this time of year I was plagued with the damn things and took so many tablets that by Christmas Day I could have rattled out the tune of *Jingle Bells* just by jumping up and down. This place really was turning out to be a cure-all, for me at least, and in so many ways.

'Thanks, Anna,' Archie smiled, sounding relieved to have found at least half an ally.

Hayley's arrival with Mick stopped everyone in their tracks for a few minutes and it was good to see Christopher teasing and winding her up just as he had done with me the evening we met. Somehow the fact that he treated Hayley just the same as he had treated me made me feel even more as if I really had the potential to belong.

'Right,' she announced when she had finally hugged

Hugo and Oscar, kissed Cass and inspected the bump on Angus's head. Archie, I noticed, got nothing more than a frosty nod. 'From what Mick's told me we have tons to do today, so had we not better get on with it?'

'Absolutely,' said Catherine, trying to catch Angus's attention and stop him filling the boys with the sweets they had just discovered in their allotted drawer on the Advent calendar. 'Where would you like to start today, Hayley dear?'

'Um,' she said, winking at me as she shrugged herself out of her coat, 'I think I'll give the bedrooms a quick once-over. I'll start in the Ivy Room.'

It didn't take many minutes of Hayley crashing about upstairs with the Hoover for Elise to drag herself from her 'sickbed' and down to the kitchen, and just one look at her sulky expression proved that she didn't have a headache at all. No one with brain-ache would have been capable of pulling off a frown like that. Mind you, given the amount of Botox fillers I reckoned she had subjected herself to, I was amazed she was capable of showing any emotion at all.

She drifted into the kitchen, making a great show of holding the still trembling Suki high up out of Floss's curious reach, at exactly the same time as Molly called in to say that she had dropped off the greenery from the woods at the garden gate. I was amused to see how the two women reacted to one another.

In a nutshell, Elise looked at Molly, who was wearing her trademark hand-knitted jumper with the ragged sleeves, with thinly disguised disdain. I got the impression that she regarded the hall's witchy friend with as much dislike as something she might have stepped in while wearing her dubious Choos. In complete contrast, Molly didn't take any notice of Elise at all.

'Hey, Anna,' she beamed, her cheeks aglow from the chilly air and her cloud of hair framing her striking face. 'I hear there's an even busier time ahead of Christmas lined up for the hall now?'

'That's right,' I said, confirming what she already knew. 'Not content with just reinstating the Solstice celebration, Catherine has offered to host the Christmas Fair as well.'

'That's fantastic,' she said, her gaze only just falling on Elise, who was standing stock-still and taking in every word. 'Not fantastic for the town hall, of course, but it's great that the Fair can still go ahead.'

'Exactly,' I agreed. 'And have you seen the lights?'

'I couldn't miss them,' she laughed. 'I can even see them from the bedroom in the cottage.'

I hadn't for one second thought they would be visible to anyone within living distance, but I had forgotten all about Molly and her quirky little cottage in the woods and I guessed everyone else had as well.

'They aren't a nuisance, are they?' I frowned.

'Not at all,' she said, her eyes flicking back to Elise again. 'I think they look really pretty actually and I only have to draw the curtains if I want to block them out.'

'That's all right then,' I said, feeling relieved.

'I probably won't though,' she mused. 'I can't remember the last time I drew the curtains in any of the rooms.'

I supposed, living in the depths of the woods, there wasn't really any need, but Elise's sharp intake of breath suggested that she wouldn't have been caught dead with her life on display after dark in her own home. Her reaction drew Molly's attention again.

'Molly,' I said, realising an introduction was in order, 'this is Elise. I'm guessing the two of you haven't met?'

'No,' said Molly with an open smile, while Elise shot me a look that could have curdled cream on the bleakest winter day.

Clearly she had absolutely no desire to be introduced to any woman who didn't pluck her eyebrows into submission on a regular basis.

'She's Archie's other half,' I elaborated to Molly, thinking I could hardly abandon the introduction having only just got the ball rolling.

'Is Archie here?' Molly asked excitedly whilst ignoring Elise's snub with admirable aplomb. 'I haven't seen him for ages.'

'He's outside,' I began.

Without another word she rushed off back through the kitchen door and into the winter wonderland. Her reaction to his presence suggested that she had no idea that Archie was currently in everyone's bad books or that had he been given his own way she would have found herself without a roof over her head in no time at all.

'I wonder what that was all about?' Elise was shocked into saying.

When she realised she had unwittingly spoken to 'the help' she went back to her silent scowling.

'Perhaps,' I said teasingly, enjoying my role as devil's advocate, 'Archie's an old flame.' Elise looked suitably shocked. 'I mean,' I added, 'you wouldn't rush off like that for just anyone, would you?'

I was only winding her up, of course, but the way Molly and Archie reappeared wrapped in each other's arms I couldn't help but wonder whether there was a nugget of truth in my suggestion and a quick look at Elise's face told me she was mulling over the exact same thing.

'Oh come on,' we heard Archie say, 'it's my only vice.'

'Well, it's a disgusting one,' said Molly. 'You've come home to enjoy Christmas with your family and drink in the fresh Fenland air and you pollute it with your foul fags. You stink, Archie Connelly. How can I possibly kiss you under the mistletoe now?'

I felt my own face go red on Archie's behalf as he stumbled

into the light, his arms still flung casually around Molly's shoulders, with clearly no idea his heart's desire had made her way out of bed. I remembered what Jamie and Catherine had said a couple of weeks before about Molly being the token girl, and the daughter they never had at the Wynthorpe table, but this pair looked more cosy and familiar than any siblings I'd ever come across.

Archie spotted Elise and dropped poor Molly like a hot potato.

'Have you been smoking?' asked Elise through clenched teeth.

'It was just the one,' said Archie. 'I was desperate.'

Molly slunk further into the shadows, evidently aware of the argument she had unleashed but probably so concerned for Archie's health she thought it was worth it. However, a sudden furore around the back door let the nicotine addict off the hook as his nephews came trotting through, still wearing their snow-encrusted boots.

'You have to come and see!' they said as one. 'Come and see what Granddad's had delivered.'

The sound of a reversing beeper met my ears and I knew that whatever it was, it was going to be big.

'Here,' I said, passing Elise a jacket from the many hung up next to the back door. 'Slip this on and we'll go and see.'

For a moment I thought she was going to refuse, but the jacket in question was my own, relatively new and still very smart Barbour and clearly its status and style wasn't lost on Elise, who allowed me to help her into it while she continued to clutch Suki to her chest. I was beginning to wonder if the little dog actually had legs of her own. I'd certainly never seen her use them.

'Come on!' called Archie, who had already rushed back outside with Molly. 'Come and look.'

Given that it had been mentioned before, I shouldn't have been surprised to see the beautiful glossy red sleigh being eased off the back of a low loader, but the fact that it was accompanied by four ponies that had arrived in a massive horse box was something of a shock.

The majority of the Connelly clan stood around with their mouths open, but Angus and Mick were right in the thick of it, shouting commands about positioning the sleigh and guiding the ponies down the ramp, before passing them on to anyone who found themselves near enough to take the reins. Fortunately the stocky little steeds seemed to be docile creatures, well used to the fuss their arrival anywhere caused, and took what was happening around them in their stride.

'I thought this would be just the thing to liven up the Fair,' said Angus, who appeared so giddy with excitement I was amazed he hadn't required smelling salts to keep him on his feet. 'Mick and I are going to offer rides up and down the drive and around the paddock,' he rushed on enthusiastically.

I watched Mick for a moment or two. The way he was

handling the little ponies, a bridle in each hand, suggested this wasn't his first time dealing with all things equine and I guessed that his time serving in the Army had more than likely revolved around horses.

'That's an outright lie, Angus Connelly,' said Catherine with a shake of her head. She didn't sound cross or exasperated and I could see she was almost as excited by the unexpected arrival as her husband. 'You didn't even know the Fair was happening until a few hours ago. None of us did for certain. You've had this planned for weeks, haven't you?'

Angus kicked at the gravel with the toe of his boot as Jamie caught my eye and winked. He was another one who seemed more than happy with the situation and I remembered how he had mentioned the sleigh and his father in the same breath on the day of the tree auction and bake sale back in town.

'Yes,' Angus admitted, with a grin he simply couldn't wipe away. 'I thought it would be a nice surprise and I had planned to ask the locals to come and have rides, but now the Fair is coming it's just all worked out even better. Mick has already helped set the stables up. You aren't annoyed, are you?'

'It's a bit late to ask that, Dad!' shouted Christopher, who was helping position the sleigh next to the tree by the main door to create the perfect photo opportunity.

'No,' said Catherine, 'I'm not annoyed.'

As the sleigh was pulled into its final position I caught the gentle sound of the little silver bells that were studded all the way along the length of each of its reins. I took a moment to think of Mum and thanked her for pulling me in the Connelly family direction this Christmas. I also spared a thought for Sarah Goodall, and hoped that wherever she was celebrating this year she was happy and content.

'We're going to have sleigh rides and silver bells at the Christmas Fair here at Wynthorpe Hall this year,' Catherine laughed. 'What could be more perfect than that?'

By the time the traders began to arrive to set up for the Fair that afternoon the ponies were happily bedded down in the stables and there was an even deeper dusting of snow, which lent itself beautifully to the occasion. Everyone present was falling over themselves to thank both Catherine and Angus for so generously saving the day, and Dorothy, Cass and I wove our way amongst the throng offering top-ups of tea and biscuits, all the while having a sneaky look at the pretty things that were being unwrapped and displayed.

As well as traders selling antiques and vintage finds, there were lots of local artists and crafters, and as I looked around I knew I wasn't going to have to go any further if I really wanted to bite the bullet and do some Christmas shopping of my own this year. I might not have known the people at the hall for all that long, but I knew them well enough to have worked out that the Fair was going to offer something for everyone I wanted to buy for and I hoped I would be able to slip away to town at some point to get some cash.

Fortunately, that evening Angus offered me the perfect opportunity.

'You should have put the angel on first,' tutted Hayley, who had decided that as Elise was such fun to wind up she was going to stay the night, but on the pretext that no one would have to risk a journey in the snow on her behalf and that she would be on hand to help out from first thing the next day. 'We'll never get it up there now.'

We were all spending the evening together in the sitting room, decorating the last of the trees. This one, in the family's private space, was definitely my favourite. The box of decorations reserved for it was full of treasures that spanned decades and included some less than artistic angels which the three Connelly boys had themselves created in their youth.

'Can anyone remember whose turn it is to go on top?' shouted Christopher above the sound of the Christmas CD and the crackle of the fire, next to which Floss had curled herself up.

She was in a bit of a grump having given up worrying at Elise to let Suki use her legs.

'I think Jamie should go on top this year,' said Cass.

The man himself looked at me and waggled his eyebrows suggestively. I ignored the innuendo and carried on helping the boys polish the dozens of baubles that were waiting to be awarded their coveted spot.

'Good idea,' Jamie heartily agreed with his sister-in-law. 'Come on, Anna,' he added, pulling me unceremoniously to my feet. 'You can help me get it up.'

I shook my head and tried to pull away.

'You,' I said in a low voice while trying not to laugh, now that everyone was looking, 'are incorrigible.'

'I'm talking about the angel,' he said innocently as he lifted me up and carried me across the room. 'You can stick her on top of the tree.'

'Oh,' I said, turning puce. 'Right.'

'Why has Anna gone all red?' asked Oscar.

'Because Uncle Jamie is being a little bit rude,' said Angus.

Cass passed me the angel with a knowing smile and I let out a silly squeal as Jamie lifted me a little higher and angled me towards the tree. For a second I thought we weren't going to make it, but one final stretch, which ended with Jamie's face sitting level with my groin, saw the angel in situ and had everyone cheering.

'Is there nothing you can't do?' Jamie whispered in my ear as he lowered me back to the floor.

'Apparently not,' I told him, trying to avoid his emerald eyes as I smoothed down my shirt.

I couldn't help thinking he wasn't being particularly fair. Yes, he'd declared his feelings for me, but we'd agreed not to talk about them, or my decision as to whether to stay or go, until the New Year, and yet here he was flirting at every opportunity. I put his behaviour down to Christmas madness; it clearly ran in the family.

'And now I have something you can do for me,' said Angus, stepping up and thankfully cooling the moment. 'Come along, Anna.'

The task Angus had in mind was most convenient, given that I was hoping to have a run into town, and I gasped in shock and awe when he showed me what it was he needed my help with.

'This,' he explained, as he carefully opened an ancient, velvet-lined crimson box, 'originally belonged to Catherine's great-grandmother.'

'Oh Angus,' I breathed. 'Are they real?'

'They are,' he chuckled. 'Each and every one of them.'

Lovingly nestled inside the exquisite box was a delicate diamond bracelet. There were too many stones to count and I felt my breath catch in my throat as they glistened and sparkled as they caught the light.

'I don't usually bother much with jewellery,' I told him, my fingers itching to touch, 'but this is extraordinary.'

I had once had a treasured piece of jewellery of my own. As far as I knew it hadn't held any great financial value but the sentiment attached to it was beyond measure and I still felt its loss keenly, especially at this time of year. I pushed the thought of it away, along with the memory of yet another catastrophic Christmas, lest my tears betray me.

'It's also broken,' said Angus sadly. 'Catherine has never much mentioned it before, but she saw something similar being set out on one of the stalls earlier and it reminded her of this piece.'

'Was it genuine?' I asked, suddenly concerned that perhaps we should have installed a little more security to look after the stallholders' wares for the evening. 'The piece at the Fair, was it real?'

'No,' he chuckled, 'it was paste, but very pretty, and it set me to thinking about this, so I phoned my jeweller pal in town and he's agreed to mend the clasp in time for Christmas. I thought it might make a nice present. We don't generally buy each other anything, you see, but with all we've been through this year I thought this would be a suitable token.'

'I think it's a wonderful idea,' I said dreamily. Angus really did have a heart of gold.

'I'd like to see Catherine wearing it again,' he said. 'She always used to, on special occasions, before the clasp gave way.'

'And I'm guessing you'd like me to take it to town?' I asked. The trip really couldn't have been better timed.

'If you don't mind,' he said.

'Not at all,' I told him, taking careful possession of the beautiful box. 'I'll run it in first thing in the morning.'

'Thank you, my darling,' Angus beamed. 'And remember, not a word to anyone.'

I took a moment to admire the bracelet again before taking it up to my room and then heading back downstairs. I could hear an argument raging in the sitting room and rushed to investigate what had happened to spoil the evening we had all been enjoying so much.

'But she can't have just disappeared,' Elise was sobbing on the sofa, with Archie looking careworn at her side.

'What on earth's happened?' I said to Catherine.

'It's your father,' she said, rolling her eyes. 'He got fed up with Elise carrying that blasted dog around and when he came back in he insisted she let her have a little run around.'

I didn't pick her up on the fact that I wasn't actually Angus's daughter because I was too intrigued as to what had happened next.

'And did she?'

'Yes,' said Catherine, sounding surprised that Elise had done as she was told for once. 'She put her on the sofa right next to where she was sitting, but Suki was having none of it and jumped straight down and ran over to Floss.'

'And?' I encouraged, hoping that Floss hadn't made a meal of the snack-size pooch.

'They pranced about each other for a bit and then zipped off. Elise was already having an attack of the vapours and now no one has seen hide nor hair of them and she's inconsolable.'

We both started to giggle like a pair of schoolgirls and Elise shot me yet another of her cream-curdling stares.

Chapter 28

I think that at some point during that night practically everyone heard the naughty doggy duo tearing through the hall, but no one would have been quick enough to catch sight of them. Not that I imagined anyone beyond poor, nagged Archie would have leapt out of bed to try and get a look. I knew for a fact Jamie hadn't, because he told me so during our run the next morning.

'There was no way I was going to try and round them up,' he said, as he held open the garden gate and I slipped through.

'Me neither,' I told him as I struggled to keep my footing in the snow. 'I'm sure the exercise will do Suki no end of good and Floss will be loving the extra company.'

'You're probably right,' said Jamie as we set off through the freshest snow, which was harder to run in than I had expected. 'We used to have another dog, a little terrier. Mum was devastated to lose her to a tumour way before her time and none of us could muster the energy to take on another puppy.'

'That's so sad,' I said sympathetically.

'We always meant to get another dog eventually, but with everything else that's happened since, it kind of got pushed down the list of priorities.'

That was understandable. Puppies were hard work.

'Isn't there a greyhound rescue place around here?' I asked. 'I seem to remember something in the local paper about a charity near town that was expecting an influx in the New Year.'

'Yes,' said Jamie, 'I think you're right. Perhaps we could go and pick one out together, Anna.'

I knew he was pushing to see if I had made up my mind about staying but I still wasn't prepared to make a commitment just yet. There were a lot of people milling about the hall now and I was coping with the intense family feeling pretty well, but would I feel the same way if that level of togetherness was something I would have to deal with for ever, rather than just a few weeks? Part of me thought I'd be fine, but until I was singing one hundred per cent from the same hymn sheet as everyone else I was keeping quiet.

Jamie slackened his pace a little.

'And how are you really finding this run-up to Christmas?' he asked.

It was uncanny how he could read my thoughts like that.

'I'm enjoying it,' I told him honestly. 'It hasn't been any-where near as hard as I thought it would be.'

'But you still aren't completely convinced, are you?'

I loved and hated in equal measure the way he could read me. Being able to bluff my way through would have been so much easier.

'I'm getting there,' I told him. 'I had thought the family arriving would make it harder, but actually it hasn't. They're all so nice.'

'Apart from Elise.'

'I'm sure there's some good in her somewhere,' I said charitably, although I didn't really mean it. If there really was something good in her, it was buried pretty deep. 'And Archie seems to be coming round to the idea that you're taking over.'

Thinking about his behaviour and attitude since the night he was told what was happening, I realised he seemed barely bothered by the change in his fortune.

'I wonder what he'll make of the plans for the charity though,' Jamie frowned. 'I reckon he's going to resent it just because it's something else that's connected to me.'

'What do you mean?'

'Well, he's never really understood why I wanted to work for nothing,' Jamie explained. 'And since Elise has been on the scene, he thinks you go abroad just to soak up the sun and spend some of the inflated salary you've allegedly worked for by pushing some paper about and fiddling with a few buttons for your potential father-in-law.'

As far as Jamie was concerned, these days he and Archie were poles apart, but I wasn't so sure.

'He's more interested in designer this and labelled that,' he went on, picking up the pace again and slipping in the snow a little in the process.

'Are you sure that isn't just Elise's influence you're talking about?' I called after him. 'I reckon she's the one pulling his strings and the one responsible for the changes in him. If he was left to work things out for himself, I think your brother might even come on board with the charity idea.'

Jamie looked back at me and shook his head. Clearly he thought I was barking up completely the wrong tree.

'Come on,' he said, 'we've still got loads of stuff to do.'

He wasn't wrong. I still had to make the trip to town.

'Can I take the Land Rover out this morning?' I asked when I caught him up. 'I need to go to town and don't think I fancy making the trip in my little Fiat.'

'I'll run you in if you like,' Jamie offered.

'No,' I said, perhaps a little too quickly as I thought of the promise I'd made to keep the bracelet-mending a secret for Angus. 'Thank you,' I added, 'but I can manage.'

'You aren't planning to meet your hunky fireman again, are you?' Jamie asked, sounding a little sulky. 'I don't think I can give you permission to take a Wynthorpe vehicle if you're planning a romantic liaison with another man.'

He wasn't doing a very good job of trying to make out he didn't care.

'No,' I told him. 'I've no liaison planned, romantic or otherwise.'

'That's all right then,' he said, stopping dead so I ran into him.

He caught me in his arms and lifted my chin so he could look down at me.

'Your nose is as red as Rudolph's,' he smiled as he quickly lowered his mouth to mine.

The fireworks the warmth of his lips set off in my system cancelled out the cold and it was a struggle to pull myself away.

'You shouldn't have done that,' I told him.

'I know,' he said, looking far from ashamed. 'I know. I just can't help myself.'

We walked back to the hall in silence and I found Elise hanging about in the corridor when I went up to get changed.

'Everything all right?' I asked when I caught up with her just a few steps from my bedroom door.

I had no idea what she had been up to, but whatever it was it certainly made her turn a shade pinker when she realised she'd been spotted.

'Not really,' she sniffed, her eyes filling with tears, which I couldn't help wondering if she could summon on command. 'I still can't find Suki and I'm worried she's going to get outside.

She's far too delicate to survive for long out in the snow.'

She was right about that – the tiny little thing wouldn't stand a chance out in the chilly air.

'I shouldn't worry,' I said, trying to rally her and set her mind at rest. 'I'm sure she and Floss will turn up in the kitchen as soon as they're hungry, and everyone's being careful about keeping the doors closed.'

'You're right,' she agreed, drying her eyes and sounding far more soothed than I would have expected. 'Perhaps I should take some of her special food downstairs for Dorothy to put out to tempt her.'

'That's an excellent idea,' I said, stepping neatly around her and wondering why she couldn't put the doggy dish out herself. I didn't mention the fact that Floss would probably wolf the lot before Suki so much as got a look-in. 'Now if you don't mind, I really must get on. I have to drive into Wynbridge this morning and from what I've seen so far, the roads are going to be a bit dicey.'

'Then why don't you take Jamie with you?' she suggested. 'Or Mick? Let one of them drive you in rather than risking it yourself.'

'I can manage well enough,' I told her, feeling more than a little put out that she had assumed I had no faith in my bad-weather driving skills. 'And besides, I need to go on my own.'

I could have kicked myself for letting that slip, especially as I was supposed to be keeping my trip a secret.

'Oh,' said Elise, now sounding a little too intrigued about the purpose of my expedition for my liking, 'you sound like you're on a mission.'

I had no idea where her sudden interest had sprung from, or where her desire to engage me in conversation had come from either for that matter. Part of me wanted to ask outright what she was playing at, but the soft-hearted part was thinking it probably wouldn't be a bad idea to keep her onside, especially if we really were going to end up spending Christmas under the same roof. Most of the family had assumed she would disappear now she knew about the inheritance change of plan, but she still looked pretty settled to me.

'Something like that,' I said evasively, reaching for the door latch, but then my manners got the better of me. 'But I won't be long,' I added. 'If everything's all set for the Fair when I get back, and providing Catherine can spare me, I'll help you look for Suki if you like.'

'Yes, please,' she said. 'I'd really appreciate that, Anna.'

The drive into Wynbridge was as tricky as I had predicted, but I was more preoccupied by thoughts of my room back at the hall than by the state of the roads.

There had definitely been something amiss in the Rose Room when I walked back into it after my shockingly friendly chat with Elise, but I couldn't for the life of me fathom what it was or shake off the feeling that it was in some way connected to her.

Zoning into the final leg of my journey I parked as considerately as I could in the snow-covered car park and, hoping I had managed to squeeze between the designated white lines, went in search of the jeweller's, for which Angus had given me only sketchy directions.

I eventually found the tiny shop tucked away down a dark side street at the furthest end of the market square and out of general sight of the bustling shoppers. The cobbles beneath my feet had been kept mostly free of snow thanks to the overhanging buildings on either side, and the peeling signage put me in mind of Diagon Alley from Harry Potter's wizarding world. I half expected Mr Ollivander himself to come and serve me, and my expectations actually turned out not to be all that wide of the mark.

'You must be Anna,' smiled the octogenarian shopkeeper as he pulled a gold watch out of his waistcoat pocket and scrutinised the time. 'Dear Angus said I should expect you to arrive about now. I'm Howard Dryden, at your service.'

'I'm pleased to meet you, Mr Dryden,' I said, taking in the ancient fixtures and fittings and the slightly fusty smell of the place. 'Yes,' I confirmed, 'I'm Anna.'

'As I understand it,' he went on, his beetle eyes lighting up as he rubbed his hands together, 'you have got something really rather special for me to work on today.'

'Indeed I have,' I said, reaching into my bag and reverently pulling out the classy, crimson case.

Mr Dryden held out his hands and took careful possession of the beautiful box. He gently placed it on a mat on the glass counter and opened it up. The gasp that escaped his lips made me jump and for a horrid moment I thought he had found the case was empty, but of course it wasn't.

'Oh my,' he tutted, running a tender finger over the stones, which to my eyes still looked magnificent. 'These diamonds should be dazzling,' he told me seriously, 'but they've lost practically all of their sparkle.'

'Oh dear,' I said, taking a closer look. They looked fine to me but I bowed to his far greater experience. 'That's terrible.'

'It is,' he sadly agreed, 'but don't you worry. I can mend this clasp in a heartbeat and by the time I've finished cleaning and polishing, Catherine will need to dig out her sunglasses before she can look at these beauties close to again.'

I was sure Angus would be thrilled and, having waited for Mr Dryden to write out an old-fashioned handwritten receipt and established that I would be coming back on Friday to collect the case and its precious contents, I was in need of a quick caffeine fix before I collected some cash and headed back to the hall.

Parked just beyond The Cherry Tree Café gate was a tiny pink caravan bearing the same name and being carefully packed with boxes of mismatched teacups, saucers and side plates, along with dozens of Tupperware tubs.

'Hey, Anna,' said Lizzie as she hopped out of the caravan door and rubbed her hands on her apron.

'Is this your mobile teashop?' I smiled, pointing to the diminutive van and feeling completely besotted.

'Sure is,' she beamed proudly, her smile spreading. 'This is Jemma's third baby really.'

'Fourth if you count Tom,' said the woman herself as she carried out yet more tubs from the café.

'Of course,' guffawed Lizzie. 'I was forgetting about Tom.'

I thought it was a bit mean to lump her husband Tom in with the children, but then I remembered how an elderly lady I had looked after a couple of summers before had told me to always keep in mind that the man in my life, no matter how old, would always be my biggest baby. Recalling how Jamie had sulked earlier when he thought I was coming to town to see Charlie, part of me thought she was probably right. Not that Jamie was necessarily the man in my life, of course.

'And in some ways my most successful offspring,' Jemma added with a wink. 'This little beauty,' she explained with an affectionate pat on the paintwork, 'had practically paid for herself after the fifth time we'd taken her out.'

'And you're bringing her to Wynthorpe for the Fair this afternoon, aren't you?'

'We sure are,' said Lizzie. 'We've even fitted some fairy

lights, although from what I've heard about town, Angus has already trumped us on the decoration front, hasn't he?'

She was obviously talking about the sleigh and I thought of how beautiful the hall was going to look in the fading light with the Fair in full swing and everything set up.

'Well,' said Jemma, with a nudge. 'Has he?'

'You'll just have to wait and see, won't you?' I teased as I manoeuvred past the van and through the gate, 'but I can promise you, you won't be disappointed. No one will.'

After my restorative coffee, and a warm iced and spiced bun (but let's keep that between us), I took out what cash I needed and headed back to the hall. No more snow had fallen but it was bitterly cold and quite simply the most exquisite backdrop imaginable for holding a Christmas Fair.

'Any sign of Suki?' I asked Elise, who was miraculously still out of bed and even more miraculously helping Dorothy set out and prepare the food, ready for when the hungry hordes of festive shoppers descended.

'Yes,' she laughed as Dorothy handed her another pile of plates. 'She's been hilarious, hasn't she, Dorothy?'

The corners of Dorothy's mouth began to twitch as she answered.

'You can say that again,' she agreed, with more gusto than I thought her capable of. 'Although I'm not letting the little rascal get away with pinching any more of my sausage rolls.'

I couldn't believe my ears. If Floss had nabbed so much

as a crumb, not that she would have done because she had impeccable manners, but if she had, Dorothy would have been furious. And yet, here she was laughing off Elise's lap rat's misdemeanour as if it was all some jolly joke. I didn't know how Elise had done it but she had somehow managed to wrap Dorothy around her little finger.

I knew I shouldn't have felt quite so put out about it. Catherine had wanted the family to come together for Christmas and now it looked as though they all had, but there was something about the sudden turnaround in Elise that rankled with me.

'Anna,' said Jamie, his head appearing around the doorframe at the far end of the kitchen. 'I thought I heard your voice. Can I borrow you for a sec?'

He disappeared again, taking his frown and serious tone with him, and I quickly pulled off my boots so I could follow him. Elise shrugged and went back to her chores and I headed off towards the morning room, wondering what was behind both her suddenly chirpy demeanour and Jamie's furrowed brow.

'What's up?' I asked, unravelling my scarf.

He didn't answer immediately, but stood staring into the fire.

'Close the door, would you?' he eventually asked. 'I won't keep you a minute.'

'Whatever's wrong?' I demanded, feeling more than a little unnerved by his unusual formality. 'Have I done something wrong?'

Chapter 29

Jamie took his time before answering, which only served to shift my trepidation up a gear.

'No of course you haven't done anything wrong,' he said when he eventually came back from wherever the mental expedition and unexplained frown had tugged him off to. 'This is nothing serious.'

'Well, out with it then,' I said, keen to hurry things along. 'The Fair will be opening any minute and there are still things to do.'

He shuffled from one foot to the other, even then still reluctant to say whatever it was that was on his mind.

'Jamie,' I began again, but he cut me off.

'It's a bit awkward actually,' he said finally, rubbing a hand around the back of his neck.

'Then you'd better just say it and get it over with, hadn't you?'

It wasn't the way I would usually address someone I was working for but the Connellys and I were beyond formal and polite now. Our relationship had crossed over into something far more personal and significant, or so I thought.

'It's about your application to work here.'

'What about it?'

'Your references, to be precise.'

'My references?' I snapped, growing impatient. 'What about them?'

'You did supply some, didn't you, Anna?'

'Of course I did,' I told him, feeling further nettled.

Who on earth would apply for such a prestigious position – any position, come to that – without supplying references, and more to the point why was he asking, when I'd heard Angus himself, on the morning Jamie had arrived home, stressing that I had furnished him with some very good ones?

'And do you know if Dad pursued them?'

'Of course I don't,' I hit back. 'What business is it of mine whether he went through the usual channels or not?'

Thinking about how quickly Angus had offered me the job after my telephone interview I knew he probably hadn't, but that was really nothing to do with me.

'But knowing now how things happen around here,' I continued, 'I daresay he didn't. You'll have to ask him about it, won't you? But tell me first, what's the problem?'

'There's no problem,' Jamie shrugged. 'It doesn't matter, not really.'

I can't say I believed him and I think he knew it.

'It's just that now I'm taking over,' he added, 'I want to keep everything up to date and accounted for – you know. Start as I mean to go on sort of thing.'

'And that includes interrogating the staff, does it?'

'Oh, Anna,' he sighed. 'You know you're so much more than staff to me.'

'No, I don't,' I said firmly. 'Not right at this moment anyway. What on earth has made you ask me about this now, on such a busy day?'

'Like I said,' he shrugged again, 'I'm just trying to get my house in order.'

'Hall, you mean,' I corrected, making a vague attempt to put us both in a better mood and lighten the atmosphere but failing. 'Anyway,' I said, 'I have my portfolio upstairs and it's bursting with references. I'll bring it down.'

'There's really no need,' he said, trying to reach for my hand but I moved away.

'Clearly,' I said, taking another step towards the door, 'for some reason, there is.'

I had no idea what had prompted Jamie to start asking about applications and references but having quickly photocopied the relevant paperwork and slipped it under his bedroom door in an envelope marked 'Private and Confidential', I turned my attention back to the Fair, which was now in full swing, and tried to forget about any potential trouble that might have been looming on the horizon. Dorothy had kindly dismissed my offer to help in the kitchen.

'You go and enjoy yourself,' she had said. 'There's nothing much left to do here.'

And so I did.

Just as I had known it would, the hall lent itself beautifully to the occasion and as more people started to arrive and the air became filled with spices from the kitchen and voices from the choir, who had set themselves up next to the roaring fire, I gave into the festive feeling and delighted in the kind of shopping and present-buying I had never before indulged in as an adult.

'Having fun?' asked Hayley sometime later when she found me weighed down with a plethora of bags and pretty boxes.

I hadn't purchased anything really extravagant, but there was so much on offer it would have been impossible to resist slipping in a few extra little things for myself.

'Isn't it wonderful?' I beamed, looking around for anything I might have missed and feeling delighted that so many people had come.

Word had certainly got round about the change of venue and there wasn't a wasted inch of space anywhere.

'You really are a changed woman,' Hayley teased, reminding me that on the night of the switch-on in town I hadn't so much as considered buying a single thing and had snapped her head off when she pointed it out.

She was right, of course. I was changed. Jamie had promised to find a way to give me Christmas back and he had, and I hoped he felt as happy with what I had helped to give him in return. Up until our exchange in the morning room I had thought he was more than satisfied, but his words and demeanour had made me feel uncertain of everything.

'Anyway,' said Hayley, 'I better get on. I'm trying to track down something in particular for Dorothy.'

Once again she was swallowed up by the crowds and I looked about me, my eyes falling on a stall I hadn't yet explored. Even though the jewels and trinkets clearly weren't all genuine, the beautiful display, offset by a backdrop of voluptuous and voluminous purple velvet, glistened and sparkled with as much gusto and finesse as those on show in the Tower of London.

This was doubtless the stall that had reminded Catherine of her beloved but broken bracelet. I had almost scanned every piece when my eyes fell upon something which made me gasp out loud and scattered my thoughts to the four winds.

'Unusual, that, isn't it?' commented the stallholder, who had registered my attention but not my surprise.

I nodded dumbly. My voice had died in my throat but thankfully my eyes produced no tears.

'Take it out of the box if you want a closer look,' he encouraged.

I had no desire to touch it but the guy was around the table before I could stop him, unfastening the little cameo from its velvet cushion and holding it up for me to take. I put down my bags and took it in my hands, which were less than steady.

It was certainly the same and I could hardly believe my eyes. I had wanted to see it again for so long that for a moment I thought my eyes were playing tricks on me and that my brain had conjured up some sort of hologram.

'You all right, love?' the man asked, finally tuning into my reaction. 'You look as though you've seen a ghost.'

'I'm all right,' I nodded, my voice dragging itself up from the depths. 'I'm just rather surprised to see this, that's all.'

Lightly I ran my fingers over the once familiar chalky blue background and then over the pair of lovebirds and flowers that made up the simple but exquisite decoration.

'It's genuine,' the stallholder continued now I had unfrozen a little. 'Victorian. The setting is silver and the birds—'

'And flowers,' I finished for him, 'are made from coral and pearl.'

'That's right,' he grinned. 'You've never seen one before, have you?'

'Years ago,' I said, unwilling to go into details. 'Where did you find this?'

'House clearance up the road a couple of weeks back.'

I nodded, relief flooding through my body. It wasn't mine then.

The last time I had seen this brooch, or its twin, it hadn't been sitting on my mother's little dressing table in its usual allotted spot, but somewhere quite different. My most beloved possession had been the very last thing I looked at before I packed my bags and left home. I felt a lump forming in my throat as I wondered what my mum, and indeed Sarah, would have made of me leaving without it tucked away in my bag for safekeeping.

'Hello, Anna,' said Angus, who had been politely working his way around all the stalls during the course of the afternoon. 'What have you got there?'

'Just a brooch,' I said, quickly putting it down and turning my back on it lest my emotional tug to spend the last of my cash, and a lot more besides according to the price tag, got the better of me.

'It's very beautiful,' Angus said, peering over my shoulder.

'And very expensive,' I added, before remembering my manners and addressing the stallholder. 'Thank you for showing it to me.'

'Let me know if you change your mind about it,' he said as he carefully reattached it to its display cushion. 'And I'll put it to one side for you.'

'Thank you,' I smiled, risking one last look, 'but I won't change my mind.'

'You've been busy,' said Angus, taking in my purchases as I gathered them up and moved away from the stall.

'I have,' I told him, 'and I've thoroughly enjoyed myself.' I didn't explain about the shock of seeing the brooch again after so long. 'I've got everything I need now, so I'm going to put this lot in my room and get back to Dorothy in the kitchen. She hasn't let me do anything all afternoon.'

'Well,' said Angus, biting his lip, 'by all means go and offload your shopping, but if Dorothy can still spare you I've got another favour to ask.'

'All right,' I reluctantly agreed, wondering what I was letting myself in for this time.

'And bring a coat,' Angus added as I headed for the kitchen, 'and some gloves.'

When I opened my bedroom door I discovered the envelope containing my photocopied references had been pushed back underneath. I picked them up and dropped them on the bed. It didn't look to me as if they had even been opened. However, I refused to let my mind backtrack over the awkward conversation Jamie and I had had earlier and went off in search of Angus once again.

'So,' I said when I finally found him tucking into one of the warm mince pies Jemma from the Cherry Tree was selling, 'what exactly is it you want me to do?'

'Oh, now,' he grinned, wolfing down the last mouthful and brushing his hands together. 'Come outside and I'll show you.'

The last favour I had undertaken for my much loved employer had been both simple and safe, but looking at the ponies, which appeared far more frisky now they were attached to the sleigh, I wasn't quite so convinced that I could say the same this time around.

'They're quite placid,' he said, taking my hand and leading me towards the sleigh seat. 'They're just keen to get on.'

'You mean you want me to climb in?' I asked, pulling away slightly as a crowd began to gather.

'Yes,' he said. 'I want to take people around the grounds but no one will give it a go until they've seen someone else take the first trip.'

I could hardly blame them. The contraption had built up quite a speed on the night of the switch-on and that was without acres of open ground to tempt the ponies into a canter.

'Oh Angus,' I said, 'I'm not sure.'

'I'll come with you, if you like,' said Jamie, who had wandered up with a blanket tucked under his arm. 'I daresay it will be very romantic once the thing gets into its stride.'

It was the getting into 'its stride' that I was worried about, but I was relieved to hear he sounded far more like his usual self now than compared to when he had been giving me a grilling about my references, even if romance wasn't supposed to be on the cards.

'How did you find my credentials?' I couldn't resist asking.

'Can we not talk about that now?' he pleaded.

I shrugged off his seductive gaze and turned my attention back to the red sleigh and tinkling bells. Was it my imagination or had the sound of them just got louder? If this was Mum's way of telling me to climb inside I wasn't sure I was keen to acquiesce with this particular suggestion.

'Oh, Angus, are you giving sleigh rides?'

In pristine cashmere and with her hair cascading over her shoulders Elise appeared in the doorway.

'I am.'

'Then count me in,' she shocked me by saying. 'What fun. Do you fancy it, Jamie?'

He looked from her to me as if unsure what to do.

'Sorry, Elise,' I said, climbing aboard and pulling Jamie in with me. 'We're going first.'

Before I had a chance to change my mind and jump out, Angus had hopped into the driving seat and we were off.

'Here,' said Jamie, unfolding the blanket as the group of bystanders clapped and cheered and we lunged forwards, 'wrap this around your legs.'

After a jerky start and some candid advice from Mick, the

sleigh began to move off and Elise marched back into the hall. Jamie looked at me and grinned.

'What?' I snapped.

'Nothing,' he said, pulling me closer.

I let him. As long as he didn't start quizzing me again, or mention the fact that he knew I had been filled with jealousy as I imagined him sleighing through the winter landscape with Elise cosied up to his side, then I was happy to stay where I was and enjoy the ride.

'You two all right back there?' Angus called over his shoulder.

'Yes,' Jamie called back. 'You just watch where you're going.'

The trip around the perimeter of the gardens and woods was over all too soon and Jamie leant forward to ask his father if he could take us around again. There was quite a queue forming outside the hall door and I knew there would be no rest for the ponies now until it was dark.

'I bet,' said Jamie into my ear, 'that the day you turned up here, determined to work your way through yet another Christmas, you never dreamt that you'd be shopping for presents, making mince pies, taking sleigh rides and planning a whole new future, did you?'

'No,' I said, stealing a look up at him. 'I really didn't.'

He kissed the top of my head and I couldn't resist snuggling closer to his side.

'And I bet you didn't think you'd be looking forward to your own future quite so much either, did you?'

'God no,' he laughed, the sound resonating through his chest. 'I really can't thank you enough for all you've taken on here, Anna.'

'I haven't said I'll take anything on yet,' I reminded him, 'and I still want to know what all the fuss was earlier about my references.'

'I'm sorry about that,' he said dismissively. 'I made a mistake.'

'What sort of mistake?' I asked, pulling away a little. 'Did you suddenly think I was some sort of fraudster trying to wheedle my way into a rich family's affections?'

I was only teasing him, but the look on his face suggested there might have been some truth behind my silly suggestion.

'Did you?' I said again, seriously this time.

'Of course not,' he said, tugging the blanket free from my legs. 'Come on, time to get off. Looks like you're going to have a busy couple of hours now, Dad.'

'Thanks to you two,' said Angus with a wink, 'I think we're going to be busier here at the hall for a lot longer than that!'

Chapter 30

As much as I would have liked to, I didn't have a chance to pin Jamie down and demand an explanation as to what the 'mistake' was that he had made because there was so much else going on we didn't end up having another single second on our own.

The entire Christmas Fair had gone down as a roaring success and the organisers had asked if Catherine and Angus would consider holding another one the following year. Not necessarily the Christmas Fair, as that would hopefully be returning to its traditional location at the town hall in Wynbridge, but another, possibly in the summer when people could bring picnics and enjoy the gardens.

Catherine handed the idea over to Jamie, who would be in charge by then, and notes were made in the diary, with the potential addition of some entertainment in the gardens during the evening. Angus was already talking about swapping the sleigh for a little trap so he could carry on giving the trips, which had gone down a storm, and I knew he had been Googling new stable block options for one of the fields so he could indulge Mick and keep a couple of ponies after the original block was converted for the charity.

I couldn't have been more thrilled that life at Wynthorpe was picking up pace and I had almost made a final decision as to whether or not I was going to be moving in to enjoy it when my contract came to an end.

'Happy birthday, darling girl!' chorused Catherine and Angus when I went down to breakfast on the morning of the Solstice celebration.

'We've made you a cake!' clapped Oscar, jumping up and down in excitement while Hugo pulled out a chair for me to sit on.

I hadn't had a chance to get worked up about my looming birthday. What with clearing up from the Fair and preparations for the ceremony in the woods, it had kind of fallen by the wayside on my list of priorities, but there was nothing unusual about that. I never gave it a second thought, as a rule. As far as I had been concerned it was just another day on the calendar, but as with most things in the Connelly household, birthdays were clearly a big deal and something to be cheered about.

'And there are cards,' Oscar gushed.

'And presents,' said Cass as she scooped up her son and gave him a kiss.

'My goodness,' I blushed, looking at the laden table. 'I can't remember the last time I was made such a fuss of!'

'Don't you normally have a cake?' asked Hugo, as he watched his mother and Oscar counting out the candles.

'I don't usually have anything,' I told him truthfully.

The look he gave me suggested he didn't believe a word, but Cass frowned and shook her head.

'I don't like the sound of that at all,' she said. 'From what I've heard, Anna, you work far too hard.'

'But not today,' said Jamie, who had crept up behind me. 'There'll be no work for you today at all, Anna.'

'Is that right?' I laughed.

'It is,' he said, sitting next to me. 'Today I am going to be your personal slave. Whatever you wish will be my command.'

'Lucky Anna,' said Elise coquettishly as she and Archie came in and joined everyone around the table.

Archie looked at me and rolled his eyes. He hadn't said as much but I knew he had taken on board the not particularly subtle shifting of his girlfriend's allegiance. I was in absolutely no doubt that Elise was setting her sights on the only Connelly brother left who could fulfil her lofty ambitions to take up the role of lady of the manor, and the horrible thing was that Jamie appeared to be indulging her. Not encouraging her stupidity exactly, but not nipping it in the bud either. I was fairly certain she was barking up the wrong tree, given the way he said he felt about me, but her behaviour was disconcerting to say the least.

'Yes,' I said, blocking her out and keeping my eyes firmly on Jamie. 'Lucky me indeed.'

Hayley's timely arrival with Mick thankfully broke the simmering tension and she rushed in to plant a sloppy kiss on my cheek and thrust a card and present into my hands.

'We haven't done cards and presents yet,' said Dorothy.

'We haven't even done the cake,' said Oscar, waving the candles about and sounding frustrated at the slow progress we were making.

'Well come on then,' said Hayley, rushing to the pantry. 'Let's crack on.'

Jamie made a great fuss of standing behind me and covering my eyes with his hands while the cake was prepared and the cards and presents were arranged around it. I have to admit it felt rather nice being the centre of attention for once and being made such a fuss of. Ordinarily I was the one in charge of making sure life ran smoothly and events were a success for everyone else.

'Happy birthday to you,' everyone began to sing, and finally I was allowed to peek.

Molly had arrived during my temporary blindfold and she waved and smiled from the spot at Archie's side which she had hastily filled. I couldn't help but wonder if Elise had picked up on the chemistry between the two, but my thoughts were distracted by the gargantuan chocolate cake in front of me. The outside was decorated by a fence of chocolate-covered fingers and the top was full of Maltesers, with at least a dozen pretty red polka dot candles wedged in between. It was quite simply breathtaking and I smiled at Dorothy to show my gratitude for her efforts.

'Everyone helped,' she told me, 'everyone managed to do something.'

That made me feel even more grateful because I knew it wasn't always easy for her to give up her kitchen and let other people get stuck in.

When the moment finally came I didn't have a clue what to wish for. My life seemed suddenly to be filled with practically everything I could ever want, including my own personal manservant for the day, and so I gave the wish away and blew out the candles in one big puff.

'Hip hip hooray!' shouted Christopher as he popped the cork on a champagne bottle and everyone else joined in, 'Hip hip hooray!'

It took some time to kiss everyone and thank them and I don't think anyone noticed how long Jamie tried to keep me in the shadows making sure he received his own lingering thank you while Dorothy distributed cake and bubbles for breakfast.

'What did you wish for?' asked Oscar, who surreptitiously made his way onto my lap and helped me open the cards when I sat back down. I was saving the presents for later.

'I can't tell you that,' I said, jiggling him on my knee and making him giggle. 'It's a secret.'

'I bet I know,' he laughed, through another sticky mouthful of the delectable chocolate and cherry cream-filled sponge cake which had been hidden by the decorations.

'Oh, do you now?' I said, just about resisting the urge to tickle him.

'Uh-huh,' he gurgled. 'I bet you want what I heard Elise saying you'd got your heart set on.'

'And what was that?' I asked, stopping the jiggling as I looked around to check no one else was listening.

'I heard her on the phone,' he said, lowering his voice an octave or two because he knew he shouldn't have been eavesdropping.

'And what did she say?'

'She said you wanted to stay here and play Princesses.'

'Did she now?' I frowned, not quite sure Oscar had heard correctly.

'Well, something like that anyway,' he said, before taking another large bite. 'At least she said you thought you already were a princess or something like that.'

I let him slip from my knee and looked across the kitchen to where the wicked witch of the fairy tale herself had managed to corner my potential handsome prince yet again.

Fingers crossed she was going to take a bite of her own poisoned apple before long, but just in case, I was going to be on hand myself if it became necessary to stop her forcing it down Jamie's throat instead.

The morning passed quickly, and shortly after lunch more guests arrived to take part in the Solstice celebration. This crowd was very different from the one at the Fair and I was introduced to so many people I knew I wouldn't have a chance of remembering all their names, even though I was usually pretty skilled at that sort of thing.

There was one old lady called Annie, with periwinkle eyes, who stood out from the crowd however, and she was accompanied by a curly-haired lad called Ed, who carried what I thought looked like a tame jackdaw on his arm. They were an unusual bunch of people to say the least, preparing to walk through the woods in search of Yule logs while carrying lanterns to light the way back later that evening. Molly, wearing a shimmering cloak, reminded me of my first impression of her the day Mick and I had been collecting wood.

Catherine had elected not to come and was staying at the hall with Dorothy and Elise, who was giving Suki a much-needed bath. The little dog had been running amok with Floss since the night she made a bid for freedom and was certainly nothing like the pampered pooch who had arrived in her own Louis Vuitton carrying bag. I could tell that Elise was secretly seething, but credit to her, she had managed to keep a lid on it, so far at least.

'For those of you who haven't taken part in the celebration before,' said Molly when we reached the circle of beech trees in the wood, 'I'll explain what is going to happen and then we can search for our Yule logs before coming back to the Wishing Tree for the ceremony itself.'

As I listened to her explain how, once we had found the log we wanted, we had to ask for permission from the tree, the woods and the universe to take it, I felt a mixture of excitement and trepidation. This was like nothing I had ever experienced before and I hoped I didn't get it wrong. How on earth was I supposed to know which log to select? The ground was littered with them and they all looked pretty much the same to me.

As had become my habit during moments of stress I ran my hands over the smooth surface of the holey stone which I always carried in my pocket now. The repetitive action made me feel a little soothed, as did the kind words of the lady who had gifted it to me.

'Anna, don't look so worried,' Molly smiled as everyone began to fan out. 'You'll know it when you see it.'

And she was right.

Jamie, Angus, Floss and I had been wandering around for about half an hour when I realised I was walking with purpose, as if I was being drawn to a certain spot. It was hard to explain, but as I reached a magnificent oak and began to circle its trunk, sifting through the leaf litter and logs, I knew I was going to find what I was looking for and when I did I was rather pleased I had the boys to help me because it was pretty immense.

Far too large for a regular fireplace – but of course the Wynthorpe grates were anything but regular – the log was gnarled and had pieces splintering off in all directions. It looked as if it had been torn from the tree, rather than just fallen of its own accord, and I would have staked my life on it being in that spot at that moment with me in mind.

'Is this it then?' said Angus. He sounded very serious and there was no hint of amusement in Jamie's expression either.

This was clearly an incredibly important tradition to the Connellys and indeed everyone who had shown up, and the burning of the Yule log was highly significant to their Christmas celebrations – or perhaps that should have been Yule celebrations as we were standing amongst the local pagans and wiccans.

'It is,' I said, putting down my lantern and laying one hand on the log and the other on the trunk.

I closed my eyes and thought about what Molly had said about asking for permission. I had thought I'd feel silly and prone to giggle, but I didn't. She had been right – when the time came, I had known exactly what to do, and I hoped that when push came to shove it would be just the same when I had to rubber-stamp my decision about my future.

Once everyone had found their logs and gathered at the beech trees again, we moved on to the Wishing Tree, where Molly and Annie created a circle, which felt like proper witchcraft to me. Then, with everyone sitting inside the circle, we watched a fascinating reenactment of the battle between the Holly King and the Oak King and the passing on of the crown, which was all a part of the turning of Nature's wheel and the changing of the seasons. After that, the circle was opened again and everyone lugged their Yule logs back to the house, where more guests had arrived and Dorothy and Catherine were waiting with mulled cider and a plentiful buffet.

'So what did you make of it then?' asked Catherine as she admired the massive piece of oak Jamie and Christopher had struggled to carry and set down next to the fireplace in the hall.

'It was wonderful,' I told both her and Annie, who had wandered up to join us and was appraising me with her periwinkle gaze. 'I know I didn't really understand all of it,' I admitted, 'but it was very special. It would have been nice to actually see the sun set,' I added, 'but unfortunately we can't control the weather.'

'My dear,' said Annie, lightly laying her hand on my arm, 'there are many things in life that we can't control.'

'That's true enough,' I sighed.

'But you must remember,' she said, increasing the pressure of her hand a little and ensuring I looked at her, 'that just because we can't see something, just because we can't hear it or feel it, it doesn't mean that it isn't still there. The sun was still shining away up there today, even if we couldn't lay our eyes on it. We always carry its power and the belief that it is above us in our hearts.'

She might have been referring to the sun but I knew she wanted me to interpret a deeper meaning. She was talking about Mum. She was confirming what I had been feeling almost since the first moment I arrived at the hall. Just because my mum was no longer physically present, it didn't mean she wasn't actually around. The roses, the music box, and the sleigh bells themselves were all signs that she was still with me, and as long as I carried her around in my heart and looked out for her, she always would be. Unable to find the words, I simply nodded and placed one of my hands over Annie's.

'What on earth?' laughed Cass, who had now joined us but was distracted by a commotion that was happening on the other side of the room.

I followed her gaze and my eyes fell upon Elise, who had arrived wearing her finest designer outfit and with a squirming, decidedly fluffy-looking Suki wedged under her arm. In other circumstances she would have looked elegant but in the hall at Wynthorpe among the local cloak-clad pagans she looked rather ridiculous, and the fact that she was swaying a little did nothing to help her blend in.

'I thought you said your parents were having a party?' she hiccuped to Archie in a voice that carried far further than she probably realised. 'This isn't a party,' she snorted, 'this is a gathering of Middle Earth wannabes.'

I looked at Annie, who started to chuckle. I was relieved she had a sense of humour.

'Oh dear,' said Catherine, sounding embarrassed.

'I'll deal with her,' said Cass, marching over and steering Elise by the elbow back towards the kitchen.

I allowed myself a tiny smile. The wickedest witch at the party looked like she'd taken her apple and turned it into very strong cider.

'I'm so sorry,' said Catherine.

'You've nothing to apologise for,' said Annie sharply. 'I'm sure you didn't pour the drink down the poor creature's throat.'

I didn't have time to enjoy Elise being referred to as a 'creature' as the sound of raised voices filled the air again and this time Hayley was joining in.

'Anyway,' I heard her yell in response to whatever Elise had said first, 'you're nothing but a blood phoney with your fake Jimmy Choos and your surgically enhanced tits!'

'How dare you!' Elise retaliated. 'These were a present from Archie.'

I wasn't sure if she was talking about her shoes or her breasts.

'They're fake,' came Hayley's voice again. 'Anna said so and she knows what she's talking about. She's got a wardrobe full of designer footwear.'

Out of the corner of my eye I saw the Connelly brothers making a dash towards the argument, but not before Elise had left her parting shot.

'Yes, well,' she shouted, her voice reaching as far as the rafters, 'she's also got a bag full of Catherine's jewellery which no doubt went some way to buying them. I bet you aren't thinking she's the princess you all had her pinned as now, are you?'

I stood open-mouthed as everyone's eyes turned to me.

With all the poise and elegance I would have expected of her, Catherine quietened her guests, apologised profusely for the interruption and insisted everyone carried on enjoying their evening. Then she told Archie to get his girlfriend upstairs and that she would deal with her in the morning, but I wasn't going to be satisfied with that.

Elise had accused me of stealing just hours after Jamie had questioned me about my references, and it didn't take a genius to work out that the two things were connected. I was going to clear up this allegation and the sooner the better.

'Forget it,' Cass hissed in my ear. 'She's pissed and she's

poison. No one believes a word she said. We all know you better than that, Anna. She's a scheming madam and she's also drunk. Just let it go.'

'But I can't,' I said, shaking with anger and fear.

'You have to.'

'You don't understand,' I told her, smiling for the benefit of the curious guests who were still looking in my direction and no doubt wondering what on earth was going on. 'I did have some jewellery in my bag and it was Catherine's.'

'Well I'm certain you had good reason,' she said straightaway, and right there and then I could have kissed her. Not a shadow of doubt or suspicion had crossed her face and I truly appreciated that, especially as Jamie hadn't come anywhere near me to back me up since Elise had disappeared upstairs with Archie.

'Of course she did,' said Angus, rushing to my side. 'I'd given it to her. It's Catherine's diamond bracelet.'

'The one with the broken clasp?' Cass questioned.

'Yes,' I said. 'Angus asked me to take it to town to get it fixed as a surprise for Catherine on Christmas Day, but what I want to know—' I said, feeling even more furious.

'Is how Elise knew,' said Angus and Cass together.

'Exactly.'

It seemed to take forever for the last few guests to leave. With all the in-house entertainment they had witnessed earlier in the evening I was certain the hard core were hanging on to see if anything else was going to happen, but they were out of luck. Neither Archie nor Elise reappeared all evening, which was just as well because I would have been hard pushed not to wrap my hands round her throat. As soon as the last plate and glass was stacked the rest of us rushed to the sitting room to confront Elise's nasty allegations.

Adamant that she was right and I was the one who was going to end up with egg on my face, she had been polishing her story and waiting for everyone to assemble.

'How did you know about the shoes?' was the first thing Archie hissed to me when I walked into the room.

I had been hoping for an apology, but clearly that was going to have to wait, assuming it was going to come at all.

'Believe me,' I told him, 'I've worn enough designer footwear to know when a bogus pair crosses my path.'

'The guy who sold me those Choos said she'd never know the difference.'

'Well,' I said, feeling rather amused, 'in his defence, *she* didn't, did *she*?'

'I hope,' Hayley cut in, 'you stumped up for the real things when it came to her—'

Fortunately her second breast reference of the evening was cut off by the arrival of Angus. He looked absolutely furious and the room fell silent as he marched across to the fireplace and cleared his throat. Elise, not sensing the atmosphere was stacked against her, stood up and began to deliver her well-rehearsed sermon.

'I'm so sorry to have shattered your illusions about your latest recruit this evening, Angus,' she began, sounding only marginally more sober than she had earlier. 'But I've said to Archie on more than one occasion that you and Catherine are literally putting your lives and your property at risk by taking in these waifs and strays who turn up on your doorstep with their sob stories.'

Angus began to chew his lip and I wondered if I were going to witness him really losing his temper.

'I know you are both very fond of Mick, Hayley and Dorothy and I'll concede that so far so good when it comes to keeping them out of the silver drawer, but the same cannot be said for this one.'

At this point she actually pointed across the room at me, and Cass, knowing the full story, began to look well and truly amused. I had no idea how Mick, Hayley and Dorothy were managing to keep quiet but I admired their restraint.

'So what has this one done?' asked Christopher.

I could tell from his tone that he knew I was innocent and that he was happy to help Elise secure her own noose. She didn't however, have a clue.

'Yes, Elise,' I asked, 'what exactly have I done?'

'You've been stealing,' she said with relish. 'In your bag right now, you have Catherine's beautiful diamond bracelet.

Of course, I'm sure someone like you would have no idea how much it's really worth.'

'I bet she knows it's worth a darn sight more than your nasty shoes,' spat Hayley.

Clearly the silence from the Wynthorpe employees wasn't going to last much longer.

'And if you'd got as far as a pawn shop,' Elise continued without missing a beat, 'you would have had a very pleasant surprise, but fortunately you aren't going to get that far.'

'All right,' said Cass sternly, with a wink for me. 'I think Anna should go and get her bag and I'll go with her to make sure she doesn't offload the loot on the way back.'

'Good idea,' agreed Elise.

I knew Cass was having fun gearing up to humiliate Elise, but I was more concerned by Jamie's reaction – or should I say, lack of reaction. Rather than springing to my defence he hadn't said a word, and I would have bet a winning Euromillions ticket on it being Elise who had planted the idea about chasing up my references in his head. Was he really thinking that I could have done this terrible thing?

'Come on,' said Cass, guiding me out of the door and along the corridor. 'This is going to be brilliant,' she gushed. 'We're finally going to be rid of her.'

I didn't say anything.

Back in the sitting room I walked across to the coffee table and tipped my bag upside down and shook it out. My purse and car keys, along with some tissues, tampons and a Dior lipstick cascaded out, but there was no sign of the Crown Jewels.

'I can't believe this is actually happening,' said Catherine, her voice catching in her throat. 'I'm so sorry, Anna.'

'Why are you apologising?' Elise snapped, reaching over and snatching the bag from my grasp.

'Be careful with that,' I warned her as she yanked open zips and checked the lining for secret compartments. 'Unlike your shoes, it's genuine and vintage.'

'She must have offloaded it already,' she seethed, ignoring what I had said.

'Perhaps she took it to town,' said Angus. It was the first time he had spoken and had I not seen his mouth move I wouldn't have believed the thunderous tone was actually coming from him.

'Yes,' said Elise, throwing my bag back down and latching on to the idea. 'Of course, she's sold it already.'

'I can't stand this,' said Catherine, beginning to sob.

'Me neither,' said Angus. 'Elise?'

'Yes?'

'You are quite right, Anna did have the bracelet in her possession and she has got rid of it already.'

'I knew it!'

'Because I gave it to her.'

'What?'

'I gave it to her and asked her to take it into Wynbridge to the jeweller's to have the clasp mended as a surprise for Catherine on Christmas Day.'

'But—'

'No but,' said Angus. 'Anna had the bracelet at my bidding.'

Elise's bottom lip began to tremble but I found no satisfaction in seeing it. I threw my scattered possessions back into my bag and zipped it up.

'But—' she said again, before I cut her off.

'What I would really like to know,' I said, struggling to stop my voice trembling, 'is how you knew I had the bracelet in my bag.'

'That's a very good point,' said Christopher. 'How did you know, Elise?'

'Well, I . . .'

I had no intention of sticking around and listening to how she had slipped into my room and rifled through my things. She had obviously been in there the morning I caught her looking sheepish in the corridor after my run. She had no doubt looked through everything, all my private things, and I hated her for the intrusion almost as much as I hated how she had suddenly changed her attitude towards me because she thought she had an ace up her sleeve and could unmask me as a thief at any given moment. What a truly wicked woman.

I didn't know what it was that I had done to become the focus of her horrid attention and I didn't much care.

'If you will excuse me,' I said, trying not to notice the pile of still unopened birthday presents which were stacked next to the fire or the fact that Catherine and Cass were holding out their hands to me, 'I think I'll go to bed. Thank you for making yet another of my birthdays so memorable, Elise.'

Chapter 31

When I fell into bed that night I had no intention of leaving my room for at least the next day or so, Christmas or no Christmas, but the thought of enduring the no doubt endless knocking as Dorothy, Cass and Hayley, and possibly even the boys, tried to coax me out was too much to cope with. So, even before there was so much as a hint of light on the horizon, I slipped out of bed, hastily dressed, grabbed my jewellery-free bag and left.

I had briefly toyed with the idea of leaving for good, but that wasn't my style, and neither was it something I could have done to Catherine and Angus. They had shown me nothing but kindness and consideration from the moment I arrived at the hall and I couldn't bear the thought of disappearing without saying goodbye to them and everyone else.

I didn't know how I was feeling about Jamie. Of course he hadn't joined in with Elise's accusations, but he hadn't gone out of his way to spring to my defence either. For someone who claimed to be in love with me and who wanted me to be his partner in both work and life, he hadn't put up much of a fight to keep me, and there was still the unfinished business of the sudden interest in my references to clear up.

Just when I had been poised to tell everyone at the hall that I was really staying for good, this horrid thing had happened and now the pendulum had swung back the other way, a long way back the other way. Truth be told, I was beginning to feel that I had reached the end of my time there now, even before I had reached the end of my contract. What a difference a day really did make.

Celebrating Christmas with their families and loved ones might suit some, and yes, I had almost made it there myself, but what my father had done after we lost Mum had left its mark deep in my heart. There had been the years marred by his drunkenness, along with those spent in the company of his string of less than suitable girlfriends, and of course there were the happy few with Sarah. She was the only woman who had been prepared to give her all to make a difference to our lives and the one he ended up hurting more than the rest put together.

I could see now that the scars he had left meant that I wasn't really cut out to be part of a family and I guessed I never would be. That claustrophobic feeling of family togetherness was bound to smother me in the end and I would end up leaving anyway. Perhaps, in time, I would be thanking Elise for saving me a whole heap of extra heartache – heartache that I would have ended up associating with the season and in consequence, struggling with it even more.

Without really thinking about where I was headed I drove into town and pulled up in the car park at the end of the market square. There was a light on in The Cherry Tree Café kitchen but it wasn't open. The only place showing any sign of life was the newsagent's and as I craved coffee rather than a cigarette and a red top, I decided to stay put and wait until Jemma appeared and twitched the 'closed' sign round to 'open'.

I must have dozed off for a while and when I woke my neck was stiff, my feet were frozen and my mobile was vibrating away in my bag. I pulled it out and switched it off without looking at the screen. I had no desire to talk to or message anyone from Wynthorpe Hall and, even though it was Friday, the day Mr Dryden, the jeweller, and I had agreed on, I wouldn't be collecting Catherine's bracelet now either.

I eased myself out of my little car, locked it and went off in search of some much-needed caffeine.

'Crikey,' said Jemma, when she caught sight of her first customer of the day, 'you're keen, aren't you?'

'What did you do,' said Lizzie, 'wet the bed?'

'Lizzie!' admonished her friend. 'You know I hate that expression.'

'It's one of my mother's finest,' said Lizzie with a grin.

Fortunately their banter saved me from having to explain my early a.m. presence and I ordered my coffee and two slices of toast before retreating to a tucked-away table to mull over my still muddled thoughts.

I had barely pulled off my jacket before the café bell rang out again.

'Another early bird,' said Lizzie as she greeted a man in his sixties who was wearing a smart suit and coat and had a bundle of papers tucked under his arm. 'Your good lady isn't here yet,' Lizzie went on.

'That's all right,' he said, 'I'm only here for coffee. I've a busy morning planned away from my desk, but I'll be back just after lunchtime. Will you save me some quiche please, Jemma?'

'Will do,' she called through from the kitchen.

'So where are you off to?' wheedled Lizzie. 'Anywhere nice?'

'I'm popping to Wynthorpe Hall actually,' he said.

My ears pricked up at the mention of the hall.

'Then you probably won't need quiche,' said Jemma as she appeared with my order stacked neatly on a tray. 'Dorothy will fill you up, won't she, Anna?'

'Absolutely,' I said, smiling at the thought. 'You'll probably still be stuffed at dinner time if she has anything to do with it.'

'Are you Anna by any chance?' asked the man, coming over.

'That's right,' I told him.

'How lovely to meet you,' he said, pulling off his gloves and holding out his hand. 'I'm David Miller, the Connellys' solicitor.'

'How do you do,' I said, reaching across the table as Jemma tried to deposit my breakfast, so I could shake his hand.

'I know all about you, of course,' he said, dumping down the paperwork and sitting on the chair opposite.

'Oh?'

'Yes,' he said, 'Jamie came to see me last week,'

He looked around and spotted that Jemma and Lizzie were being kept busy at the counter by a sudden influx of trades-men in high-vis waistcoats and hardhats and carried on in a much quieter voice.

'He said that if it wasn't for you and all your wonderful ideas he'd be heading back to Africa in a couple of weeks.'

'Did he?' I swallowed, adding sugar to my coffee without thinking.

'Yes,' he said, 'he did.'

'Did he say anything else?'

'Well,' said Mr Miller, shifting in his seat and looking a little uncomfortable.

'Sorry,' I said, 'I shouldn't have asked.'

'No, it's all right,' he said. 'I'm sure you already know, my dear, that he's fallen head over heels for you.'

I nodded but didn't answer, wondering if that still really was the case.

'And he was quite put out the last time we spoke because I had insisted that he should make sure your references and whatnot were all up to scratch, even though you were clearly already far more to the family than just an employee.'

'That was your idea?' I said, feeling a flicker of hope in my chest.

'It's my job to protect the family's interests,' he said importantly. 'It was nothing personal, Anna, but the Connellys have always had a knack for attracting members of staff with, how can I put it, unusual backgrounds, and you can't be too careful.'

He was right, of course.

'There was one very unfortunate, but isolated occasion,' he went on, 'when a rather special piece of jewellery disappeared along with a young man who was supposed to be restoring some woodwork and so—'

'And so you see it as your job, as their solicitor,' I finished for him, 'to ensure that no one else who rocks up at their door is going to take them for a ride, or their fortune away in a suitcase.'

'Exactly,' he said, looking relieved that I understood. 'The fact that Jamie is totally and utterly in love with you made that particular conversation really rather awkward,' he said, gathering his papers again, 'but I had his best interests at heart.'

'Of course you did,' I said.

No wonder Jamie had gone a little quiet during the last couple of days. He was no doubt feeling torn between what his heart was telling him and the difficult instructions his head was full of, courtesy of his friendly family solicitor. I have to admit my own heart did go out to him a bit. I might have had problems of my own to contend with, but then, so did he. I can't deny I was saddened that it seemed he had entertained the idea that I might have taken the bracelet, but in his position, and having already had such an experience, might I not have had doubts myself?

'Are you going to the hall this morning to complete the paperwork which will mean Jamie's in charge from now on?' I asked.

'Yes,' Mr Miller said, patting the pile of papers. 'It's all here. You are going to be there to witness the momentous event, aren't you, Anna? I can't imagine he would want to proceed if you weren't there to watch him.'

Mr Dryden was surprised to find me pacing up and down the pavement, waiting for him to open up the shop, but now I had finally made up my mind I just wanted to pay for the repairs to Catherine's bracelet and get back to the hall. I knew

I had to take my place next to Jamie and watch as he signed on the dotted line – lots of dotted lines actually. David Miller had agreed to delay slightly so I would have time to get back before it all happened, but time was short and Mr Dryden was painfully slow when it came to opening up.

'Right on the dot,' he smiled as he let me in. 'I didn't expect to see you quite so early.'

'Is the bracelet not ready?' I frowned. 'Do you want me to come back later?'

I was none too keen on the idea of having to drive back again, but if it was the only way then I would have to do it.

'No, no,' he laughed. 'Don't you worry. It's all ready.'

He slipped back behind the counter and then into another room.

'It's in the safe,' he said, tapping the side of his nose. 'For safekeeping. I won't be a minute.'

Elise would have no doubt been delighted the family jewels had been kept under lock and key, but I just wanted to grab them and go.

'Here we are,' he said eventually. 'Now, what do you make of it?'

The beautiful box opened with a creak and for a second I thought he had replaced the bracelet with another. The diamonds I had dropped off were nothing compared to these sparkling jewels.

'My goodness,' I said, my voice catching in my throat.

'I told you I'd give them a clean and polish, didn't I?' he chuckled, obviously flattered by my reaction. 'A bit of elbow grease makes all the difference.'

'You're not wrong,' I agreed, looking around the shop as the light bounced off every available surface. 'And the clasp?'

'As good as new,' he said proudly. 'Catherine will be able to wear this again in perfect safety now.'

Personally I didn't think that if I had owned something so valuable I would have been brave enough to wear it at all, but then, what was the point of having it tucked away out of sight? If I had still been fortunate enough to have Mum's precious cameo I knew I would have pinned it to every outfit I ever wore. I guessed that something being worth a fortune didn't actually make any difference to its sentimental value. And as far as saving things 'for best', well, one day there would be no more best occasions, would there?

'I'm sure she'll be delighted,' I said, thinking what a shame it was that Elise's spiteful accusation meant that the gift was no longer going to be a surprise.

Angus had been so proud of his idea and now that awful woman had taken the shine right off the lovely gesture. I hoped she would be long gone by the time I got back to the hall.

'What do I owe you?' I asked, suddenly mindful of the time ticking away.

'Nothing, my dear,' said Mr Dryden with a dismissive wave of his hand. 'Angus has long since had an account with me. He can settle up next time he's in town.'

I thanked Mr Dryden heartily, accepted his seasonal salutation as graciously as I could and headed to my car for the journey back. Hopefully, if I was in time, I would have the chance to watch Jamie take over the running and responsibility of the hall.

I was more than a little disappointed to see Archie's car still parked in the stable yard, but the situation wasn't as bad as it could have been.

'Where the heck have you been?' asked the man himself, jumping out of the driving seat.

I didn't think it was really any business of his, but my manners prevented me from telling him where to stick his questions.

'Jamie has been frantic,' he went on. 'We were beginning to think you'd left for good.'

'If you must know,' I said haughtily, 'I've been to town to collect your mother's bracelet.' I bit back the desire to tell him that I hadn't switched it for a paste copy during the trip back. 'And anyway, if you were that worried, why didn't you just send your girlfriend into the Rose Room? I'm sure she would have worked out that I hadn't packed my cases and done a bunk. She doesn't miss much else.'

'I'm so sorry about her,' said Archie, his gaze dropping to the frosty ground. 'I really had no idea she'd been snooping in your room.'

'It's all right,' I shrugged, knowing there was no point holding a grudge against him, especially if I was going to be staying put.

'Actually,' he sighed, looking back towards the hall, 'I'm sorry about a lot of things now.'

'Like what?'

'Oh it doesn't matter,' he told me, 'just some ridiculous ideas I had in my head about this place. Ideas that Elise and her ambitious father had actually come up with and that I was stupid enough to go along with.'

His admission didn't surprise me at all.

'Ideas I was stupid enough to adopt as my own before I'd even thought through the potential harm I was doing,' he mumbled. 'I'm ashamed to admit I was flattered by the attention from the pair of them and got so caught up in their ambition that I mistook it for my own – not that that's an excuse of course.'

He was talking about his idea to sell off the hall and turn it into a health spa, but I wasn't going to let him know that I was aware of any of that. What with Elise to contend with and her wrath over the fake shoes, I felt he already had enough on his plate this Christmas. Right on cue, Suki and Floss appeared around the side of the stable-yard wall. Suki was already looking grubby again. Archie bent to stroke her head.

'Elise will be furious when she sees the state of her,' I said, stifling a smile.

'Oh, I shouldn't worry about that,' said Archie, straightening back up and linking his arm through mine. 'I packed her off in a taxi about an hour ago. We won't be seeing her again.'

'But what about Suki?' I frowned. 'How come she's still here?'

'I'm afraid she hasn't turned out to be the little lapdog Elise thought she was, so she's left her behind.'

I was sure Suki was delighted about that.

'But what about your job?' I gasped, only just remembering the wider implications of Elise's disappearance.

'Oh I think I can live without it,' Archie laughed. 'There's more to life than an inflated pay cheque.'

Everyone was gathered around the table in the kitchen drinking tea when we walked in and as foolish as I felt for rushing off, my heart leapt at the sight of them all. They might not have been my family, they might not have even all been related to one another, but I felt a genuine affection for them all and was very much looking forward to becoming a part of their clan, assuming Jamie still wanted me to join, of course.

'Where the hell have you been?' he demanded, jumping

up and rushing round the table to take me in his arms. 'I was beginning to think you'd gone for good.'

'She'd only popped to town,' said Archie, rolling his eyes. 'I told you that you were stressing for no reason. You've always been the dramatic one.'

Jamie didn't appear to be taking much notice of his brother, or of anyone else for that matter.

'I'm so sorry I doubted you,' he whispered. 'I'm so very sorry.'

He looked deep into my eyes.

'It's OK,' I said, my voice little more than a strangled sob. 'It's OK.'

Without another word he began to kiss me, oblivious of the whoops, claps and cheers going on around us. It was some minutes before we came up for air and realised that Mr Miller had arrived and was setting out his pile of papers.

'Right,' said Jamie, pulling his special pen out of his shirt pocket, 'tell me where I have to sign.'

Chapter 32

Personally I wasn't familiar with the German tradition of exchanging gifts on Christmas Eve, but as everyone gathered around the cosy fire with the sound of Carols from King's in the background I was all in favour of adding another new ritual to my recently rediscovered fondness for the festive season.

'We have Mum to thank for this,' said Jamie, who nuzzled up to my side on the sofa and sent butterfly kisses up and down my neck. 'Her mother's side of the family were from Germany and this was something they always used to do.'

'Hey you two,' said Hugo, having spotted what was going on as Oscar blushed behind his teddy, 'get a room.'

'Oh leave them alone,' smiled Archie. 'True love is hard to find.'

'As you have so eloquently proved,' teased Christopher, earning himself a sharp dig in the ribs from his wife.

'Never mind about true love,' said Hayley, rubbing her hands together. 'Let's just get to the presents.'

Just like with the Advent calendar it was Angus who was in charge of present distribution and everyone was well pleased with the gifts they unwrapped. So preoccupied was I with enjoying watching everyone else opening their treats I hadn't realised that I had been left until last and that all eyes were on me until Angus handed Jamie a small box.

'We can't even begin to tell you, Anna,' Jamie began, sounding genuinely choked, 'how pleased we are that you made your way to us this Christmas.'

'Thank you,' I whispered, blinking back tears of my own.

'I know,' he continued, 'we all know,' he added, looking around, 'that Christmas isn't an occasion that you have particularly enjoyed in the past, for one reason or another.'

He squeezed my hand as I nodded in agreement.

'But things have changed now,' said my beloved, 'and we know that from now on things for you, and for all of us, are going to be very different.'

He handed me the gift and tenderly kissed my cheek. My hands were shaking as I tore at the paper and opened the box.

'Oh Angus,' I sobbed, looking over at him. 'You did this, didn't you?'

'I might have mentioned to Jamie how taken you were with it,' he shrugged. 'That was all.'

*

That night in the Rose Room, after Jamie and I had made love, I reached across and picked up the exquisite cameo and ran my fingers over it, delighting in the once familiar feel of it against my skin.

'My mum had a brooch exactly like this,' I finally felt able to explain. 'It was supposed to be mine.'

'What happened to it?' Jamie asked, tucking my hair behind my ear so he could see my face.

'My father gave it away,' I sniffed. 'But not to the right person.'

'I don't understand,' Jamie frowned.

'I gave it to him,' I explained. 'To pass on to the wonderful woman I had hoped would become my stepmother. She had lived with us for a while and had a quiet way of making everything better. In the end my father thought she was too quiet for him.'

'Oh, Anna,'

'On the day I thought he was going to propose to her,' I sniffed, 'I gave him the brooch in lieu of an engagement ring, but he turned back to the bottle instead and, blind drunk, ended up giving it to this dreadful woman he used to drink with in the pub after we first lost mum.'

'That's terrible,' said Jamie, propping himself up on one elbow.

'I know,' I said, 'and the worst of it was, I couldn't do anything about it. He broke my heart all over again that day. He threw Sarah out and took up with his old drinking partner who he then moved into the house. She had always hated me because I reminded her of my mum. She couldn't wait to see the back of me. She made my life hell.'

'What a terrible situation,' said Jamie, 'and what an awful father for not seeing what was going on under his nose.'

'To tell you the truth,' I told him, 'I think he did know, but it was his fondness for a drink that blurred the edges and stopped him seeing my life for what it really was.'

Jamie was quiet for a moment before asking, 'So what happened to the brooch?'

'I left it behind when I ran away just after my eighteenth birthday. It was Christmas Day,' I said, shaking my head. 'At the time I didn't think I would ever want to see it again after what he'd done but it wasn't long before I regretted leaving it.'

'Yet another ruined Christmas.'

'It was just another in a long line,' I sighed.

'And you've been moving ever since, haven't you?'

'Yes,' I said, 'I suppose I have.'

'Well not any more,' he said, putting the brooch to one side and pinning me to the bed. 'From now on you're staying right here, in my hall and with my family.'

I couldn't help thinking how ironic it was that ever since the moment I arrived at the hall, and in the town for that matter, everyone had been telling me I wouldn't be moving on when my contract came to an end, and here I was, all set to start a whole new life.

The charity plans were ready to be put into action and even Archie, now purged of Elise and her father's awful ideas and poison pen letters, had been talking about getting involved and helping out. And it hadn't gone unnoticed that as soon as everyone had started talking about going to bed he had offered to take Floss and Suki out because it gave him an excuse to pop and see Molly. I wouldn't have been at all surprised if a romance was beginning to blossom there, and I was sure he was going to announce he was moving home soon. I was thrilled that the future of Wynthorpe Hall, which was thankfully now also my future, was looking very bright indeed.

'I think you'll find they're my family as well now,' I told Jamie, trying to suppress a giggle as I felt a huge weight lift from my shoulders.

'And I don't care what you say,' he said, ignoring me and kissing me firmly as he pressed his hot body down on top of mine. 'You're staying put whether you like it or not.'

'Oh I like it,' I laughed, 'I like it very much indeed.'

Acknowledgements

What a phenomenal year this has been! Not one, not two, but three paperbacks have found their way out into the world and hopefully into your hearts and I absolutely have to begin by saying a huge and heartfelt thank you to the fabulous team at Books and the City for making it all happen. An incredible amount of work goes into turning pages of prose into a beautiful book and I am so grateful to now have five such beauties gracing my shelves. You guys really are a dream team and I love you all!

Sleigh Rides and Sliver Bells is especially dear to me as I have carried the Wynthorpe Hall setting in my heart for years, just hoping to give it the opportunity to take centre stage. Needless to say, when the call came asking if I would consider writing another Christmas tale I absolutely jumped at the chance to let it shine, so thank you Emma Capron for making that call and for letting me write the book of my dreams.

As always, massive thanks, hugs and kisses are needed for

my hugely supportive family. Now that I have made the leap to writing full-time I don't have to split myself into quite so many pieces and can actually manage a coherent conversation or two during daylight hours. However, the jury is still out as to whether or not they think this is a good thing.

And last, but never ever least, I have to thank my author pals, the many, many bloggers and the generous readers who make the endless hours at the keyboard so worthwhile. Your support, encouragement, tweets, messages and reviews really make a massive difference. Earlier this year I was told, by someone who wishes to remain anonymous, that reading one of my books had made her forget about all the horrible things that were happening in the world and I really can't ask for more flattering praise and encouragement to keep writing than that. I hope my books will continue to offer an escape for many years to come.

I wish you all a very merry Christmas and thank you for travelling back to wonderful Wynbridge with me once again. May your bookshelves, be they virtual or real, always be filled with fabulous fiction!

H x

Christmas has arrived in the town of Wynbridge and it promises mince pies, mistletoe and a whole host of seasonal joy.

Ruby has finished with university and is heading home for the holidays. She takes on a stall at the local market, and sets about making it the best Christmas market stall ever. There'll be bunting and mistletoe and maybe even a bit of mulled wine.

But with a new retail park just opened, the market is under threat. So together with all the other stallholders, Ruby devises a plan to make sure the market is the first port of call for everyone's Christmas shopping needs.

The only thing standing in her way is her ex, Steve. It's pretty hard to concentrate when he works on the stall opposite, especially when she realises that her feelings are still there . . .

This Christmas make time for some winter sparkle – and see who might be under the mistletoe this year . . .

OUT NOW IN PAPERBACK AND EBOOK